Eye Killers

AMERICAN INDIAN LITERATURE
AND
CRITICAL STUDIES SERIES

Gerald Vizenor and Louis Owens,
General Editors

Eye Killers

A Novel

by

A. A. Carr

University of
Oklahoma Press
Norman and London

This is a work of fiction. Names, characters, places, and incidents are either the product of the author's imagination or are used fictitiously, and any resemblance to actual events, locales, or persons, living or dead, is entirely coincidental.

Carr, A. A. (Aaron Albert), 1963–
    Eye killers / by A.A. Carr.
       p.   cm. — (American Indian literature and critical studies series ; v. 13)
    ISBN 0–8061–2707–4 (acid-free paper)
       1. Indians of North America — Fiction.   I. Title.   II. Series.
    PS3553.A7626E95   1995
    813'.54 — dc20   94-36175
                                                                              CIP

Eye Killers is Volume 13 in the AMERICAN INDIAN LITERATURE AND CRITICAL STUDIES SERIES.

The paper in this book meets the guidelines for permanence and durability of the Committee on Production Guidelines for Book Longevity of the Council on Library Resources, Inc. ∞

1   2   3   4   5   6   7   8   9   10

For Dawn.

For Kyle Craig, Patricia Louise, and Cheryl Anne.

For my Laguna pueblo grandmother
who carried me when I was a baby,
wrapped in her shawl, as she visited friends.

For my Navajo grandmother
who chases away the dark.

For Lena Carr, my mother, who teaches strength.

Acknowledgments

My undying thanks go to Louis Owens for his steady encouragement of my writing, and for his friendship; to Kimberly Wiar of the University of Oklahoma Press for her strong support; to Julie Foster, Debbie Harrington, Lynne Lucero, Alan Labb, and Elizabeth Wolf, who each helped me over the rough spots; to Connie Monahan and David Ceman for their magic humor; to Peggy Hessing, who let me experience the ghostly silence of the Kimo in Albuquerque; to Doris Chavez, who opened my eyes to the difficulties and great satisfactions of teaching the middle- and high-school grades; to all my Navajo and Laguna Pueblo aunts and uncles for their love and patience; to Dawn Chambers for her wisdom; and to Lena Carr for creating a warm haven filled with stories.

All errors in this novel are mine.

Eye Killers

Prologue

Eye Killer awakened beneath a shroud of soil. Sand and dead wood pressed upon his body. He worked the muscles of his arms and flexed each cord in his hands, relishing the pull of reknitted tendons. Taut as bowstrings, he thought. And at the tip of each finger, arrowheads of iron.

His consciousness soared upward, beyond ancient iron and countless stone ceilings to the night sky above. He sensed the moon in passing clouds, a reflecting disc grating his nerves. He moved a hand, thrusting his arm upward until he felt empty air. Then he concentrated on the restraining weight of soil. Dirt and pebbles rattled on wooden floorboards.

A spear of moonlight hung in the darkness; fine dust swirled in the silvery beam, as substantial as a bar of steel. He reached for it, rising from the earth. Dizziness threatened, and he swung his legs over jagged planks to stand cautiously.

The stinging moon settled in his eye. He followed the light to a window cut into rock. He touched sharp edges, cleaned away fragments and chips. His white fingers shimmered in the moonlight.

The moon, a pale eye, glared above a barren land. Blocky, buttressed towers rose above an ocean of sand and shattered rock. He remembered fragments of crossing the still, dead sea: a turning bowl of alien constellations; shifting sand hills; twin star-imprinted masked heads emerging from red boulders and white sands, sleepless eyeholes watching and hunting.

A freezing wind numbed his eye.

He remembered a lithe, dark-eyed girl; how he had howled her name when the sun's fire descended.

He remembered his name.

Crossing to a black doorway, he ascended stone steps. Smooth, carefully worked floors changed to deep sand. Cold air blew across his naked skin, and it felt like warm breath. He followed rough walls until he came to the outskirts of a glowing village. Corrupt magic worked in his body. A familiar

3

pain seared in his joints as his skeleton rearranged itself, as his skin accommodated his changing form. He dropped to all fours feeling thunder grow in his hind tendons. When he burst from his sanctuary's hidden entrance, stars glared and moonlight flamed along his spine. Below him stretched a demure, sinuous desert.

Eye Killer sniffed the wind currents. Prey. Somewhere, some shy animal grazed under the trees. And there was another smell. Rich and keening. Gazing to the south, he saw a line of delicate beads, a necklace of tiny fires pulled on string by the disc of glowering Father Moon.

Stench of petroleum waste. And the timorous scent of blood.

One

Michael Roanhorse felt the October winds eating at his body, removing whole chunks from his legs, mind, and heart, carrying them in clouds to the domain of old man Moonbearer. Stars flew in a black water sky, whirling shapes that reminded Michael of the ancient Navajo stories told only after the first snowfall. The living stories his granddaughter, Melissa, should be learning and keeping secure in her heart.

From a tin cup, the lean old man sipped a bitter Mormon tea cut with sprinkles of juniper leaves. He ignored Mount Taylor, which held up one corner of the starry horizon twenty miles away. A wind blown from the dead volcano rattled the locust tree next to him, and the loose fence surrounding his dead wife's garden sighed. He had been meaning to tighten the fence wires for the last twenty-six years—Margaret had quietly scolded him about the undone task all that time. How could he have explained (without Margaret thinking him just lazy) that the sagging fence was a breathing part of their home, like their neighbor animals—the badgers, bullsnakes, coyotes—that to fix the chicken-wire fence would be like ripping out the locust tree from the ground? Michael studied the moon.

"You know about me, too, the way Margaret used to. I'm just a dreaming old man."

Blue-edged mountain brome whispered around his feet. When the wind changed direction, he could hear the groans and shuffling of the sheep in the corral. The old collie beside him huffed at a passing insect.

"Help me to remember my grandmother's stories, old man," he said to the moon. "Come down and sit with me and Lee."

He began to recite a part of a chant that came to him:

From my walk may the pollen of yellow evening light teach me;
From my chest may the pollen of dawn teach me;

From the soles of my feet may the pollen of little whirlwind
   teach me;
From my head with sky, moon, rainbow, yellowbird pollen, may
   I be taught;
With earth's little whirlwind teaching the tip of my tongue. . . .

He couldn't remember the rest of the song, couldn't remember who had first spoken those words. And to whom.

He tasted the Mormon tea. Forty miles to the east, an orange cloud hovered above Albuquerque, and running in parallel strands straight into the city's heart were the twin lanes of I-40, another veteran of the desert. On grandfather freeway's back rode moonlit cars like bugs with lighted eyes. Michael felt droplets of moisture settle onto his face, misting the back of his hand. Snow was coming. His stomach felt warm, and for a little while he forgot the pain of his arthritis.

His brain wheeled and creaked like the windmill a half mile below the sheepcamp, pumping up clear gushes of memory. A powerful afternoon rain drummed across sandy plains, sparkled on yucca and bright sunflowers, streamed into the wash in reddish brown streaks. Rivulets of water seeped under his collar. Had it been Sarah or Melissa who had stood with him, bundled in a bulky coat, dancing about gingerly to avoid the tiny streamlets under her boots?

"But I want to see the antelope, Grandpa," the child had said; not Sarah, then. Melissa. "I want to see them dance in the rain."

"Shh, *shi'yazhi*, my little one. You must learn to stand still, learn to be quiet, or they'll all get scared and run away."

"I won't scare them!" the girl had pleaded into the rain. "Please make them come."

The rain had softened. Sunlight shifted through golden clouds, stirring up a warm breeze. Michael took off his hat and swatted it against his jeans.

"Maybe they're sitting along the mesa tops, watching us and laughing because we're standing in the rain. What do you think?"

"If they are, I'm going to kick their butts!"

"Why don't we trick them, then. You and I. See, there's your mother shouting at us to come inside. Let us turn into antelope and run as fast as we can. Then the antelope will stop

6

laughing at us when they see how fast we can run. Faster than they can, I bet."

"Faster than hummingbirds!"

Needlelike pain shot through Michael's fingers, threw him out of memory. His rheumatoid arthritis had not yet tortured him when he had become an antelope with his granddaughter and raced in the rain.

Where was Melissa now? And where was Sarah tonight? Alone somewhere like her father, maybe, trying to remember the same stories and songs?

Michael had given Sarah some of the old knowledge his grandmother, Nanibaa', had left him, hoping she would pass it on to Melissa. Only a tiny portion of those powerful Navajo songs and stories was left here on earth, if he could believe what Nanibaa' had told him before she died. And those few elders who held the remaining wisdom and stories and knowledge in their hearts were dying like butterflies in a freak spring frost.

Bitter knowledge. But the songs had been good. And useless old man that he was, he couldn't remember one song to save his life. Coyote came in many forms and old age was one of them; a creature nibbling greedily at Michael's memories, storing them away as winter fat, stealing them for his own children, or saving them for the next world above this one—the sixth world.

Michael took a last sip from his tin cup. First Warrior. First To Hurl Anger. Hunter of Memories. Good Navajo names for Coyote. If that's the way of it, Grandfather Coyote, then take my soul and heart—maybe make something beautiful out of it. For your children.

Wind answered with a terrific gust that blew sand into Michael's eyes, stung his exposed skin.

Two

"Melissa, stay home with Mama." The overflowing clump of flesh spoke from the couch. "I need you to rub my back for me."

Melissa Roanhorse silently packed notebooks into a blue backpack. Wavy hair kept tickling her eyes. She felt small and isolated in a too-large mountain jacket, a gift from her father who hadn't bothered to get the size right: the cuffs kept swallowing her fingers. Trinomial squares trilled in her brain. Algebra 1, English Grammar, spiral notebooks decorated with hand-drawn hearts and phone numbers disappeared into the pack's stained mouth. She frowned at the hearts. I'm such a baby. A stupid kid. Melissa glared at her mother—I hate you, too, mama.

"It's your kidneys pushing against your spine, Sarah. Doctor Collins told you to stop drinking so much."

"What a mouth! Calling your mother by name."

Blood pounded in Melissa's hands. The only light in the living room came from a twenty-gallon aquarium sitting on the bar counter. Silvery points darted inside glowing water— neon tetras. A gift from one of Sarah's stupid boyfriends. Why such useless gifts all the time! Melissa lifted her pack by its straps, pushed the bar stool under the counter with her hip.

"Shut up, Mom," she said. "Don't talk to me."

"Where are you going?" Swollen, glittering eyes stared from the coldest part of the room. "Stop it now, or I'll call the police and report you . . . a runaway." Sarah became vague and sulky. "My little girl, comfort me some. Hold me."

Melissa's throat tightened. She had to swallow several times before she could speak. "I'm going to Donuts, Inc. I can't study in this place."

"Get back here!" Sarah screeched. "Who are you fucking, tramp?"

"The varsity football team. None of your damn business!"

"One of these days, girl, you'll get yourself fucked up and pregnant. Just like I did."

Melissa raised her fist and watched her own shadow flowing across the faded carpet, across the cheap coffee table, falling onto the drunken woman. Sarah's teeth gritted.

"Stay away from me, bitch," Sarah whispered.

Melissa stood over her mother. Burning muscles jerked in her arms. She wanted to smash Sarah's bloated face, see the features run like mud. She threw her words like stones. "I have an algebra test tomorrow. I'm going to *study*."

Melissa retreated to the aquarium. The water's aquamarine glow made her think of ice floes and arctic waters. She thought of the hammer in one of the kitchen drawers, imagined its weight in her hand, the steel head turning as if alive, arcing for its target, striking, breaking glass clunking inward, streams of smelly water splashing, drenching her pink blouse and jeans and new jacket; all of her neon tetras strangling on the floor, including the fat one who had eaten most of the smaller ones, and her favorite, Charley, dying too.

She heaved the backpack onto her shoulder and picked up the fish food container from a china bowl shaped like a turtle. She felt suspended in water inside her bulky new jacket.

"I already fed the fish tonight, Sarah," she said. "I'm taking the fish food so you won't forget and feed them again."

Unlike Sarah, she knew all about neon tetras. They would eat and eat and eat until, without warning, their stomachs would pop open like those toy champagne bottles you got for New Year's Eve. POP! Melissa flared her fingers. A fish killed by bulimia. The fish guts were as colorful as the confetti, too. In water, though, the tetras died silently.

Ignoring her mother's weeping, Melissa hurried out of the apartment, careful not to slam the door behind her.

The wind twisted Melissa's hair into crazy tangles which she'd have to brush out later, not something to look forward to. Headlight beams swept by. Her boots echoed along the streets, and the rush of traffic joined with the chatter of leaves blown along the sidewalk. A sound of mourning for dead fish with ruptured stomachs. For murdered mothers.

Cold, invisible fingers massaged her cheeks and neck, and she opened her jacket to give them access to the rest of her body. A chain-link fence rattled beside her, and swings squealed in the Manzanita Elementary playground, where she had once found comfort playing alone. She remembered swinging inside a glass cube while all the other children—clothes as bright as candy and flashing light-colored eyes—ran closing, frightening circles around her.

Not so very long ago. Well, seven years anyway.

She wondered if the spirits of murdered people ever played on swings, imagined the wind pushing at vaporous backs, inciting shrieks of hollow laughter. Melissa was chilled by the thought. Her Navajo grandpa would have scolded her for thinking about such things—about the dead.

Funny old sheepherder. Besides, she thought, I'm only a little bit Navajo, not really noticeable at all. What does all that bullshit magic matter to me?

A sly step, out of place with the chuckle of leaves, stopped her. Instead of searching for the source of the noise, Melissa looked up to the sky. Belligerent stars, as pointed and crudely shaped as the ones in a child's drawing, pierced sponge cake clouds. Their light gleamed on cars and dribbled down a streetlamp's metal trunk. Glancing around then, Melissa couldn't make out anything definite. Too many dark places.

She played with her choices of staying under this street-lamp or running to the cluster of lamps further down the block. There, the street was brighter and more cars were passing. She dug inside her backpack for the knife she had bought several months before.

Nothing will happen to me if I'm carrying one of these babies, she had said to Veronica and Sandie, her two best friends, as they flew through the Coronado shopping mall. Why waste money on one? Sandie had asked, running ahead, dodging old people. Sandie wasn't too smart, had to have things explained to her. But Melissa hadn't been able to explain herself. She just knew it was extremely urgent that she buy one. The three of them had rushed to the bathrooms on the lowest floor of the mall, the probing fluorescent tubes making Melissa feel either guilty or excited or completely psycho.

"Maybe we should get in a stall," she said to Sandie.

"Why?" Veronica asked, grabbing for the box. "It's only a knife."

"Yes, but it's not a toy," Melissa scolded.

10   Veronica and Sandie groaned.

"Okay, okay!" Veronica twisted her red hair around her little finger. "We get in a stall to make you happy, Mel. I just hope no one comes in and catches us."

"Yeah!" Sandie grinned. "They might think we're a group of lesbos having a good time."

"Girl, you're gross," Melissa said.

"Yes, and totally behind the times," Veronica added.

"Like how?"

"Wait till you get to college," Veronica said, tapping Sandie's head (later, Melissa had told Veronica how she could've sworn she heard an echo). "You'll see."

"I don't want to go to college if I'm going to see that."

"Just shut up!" Melissa had been getting super-pissed with all of them standing in a public restroom, bickering like idiots. "Let's see this thing and get out of here."

Nudging them into a stall, Melissa uncovered the narrow, coffinlike box and unfolded the white wrapping. Revealed, the blade shivered under the light.

"Surgical steel," Sandie whispered.

They had all crowded in on the little knife as if it were the baby Jesus in his manger.

"Are you lost, young lady?" A voice rang above the roaring elm trees.

Melissa screamed and dropped her pack. She ran to the fence, gripping onto steel links and pulling herself along them until she was outside the streetlamp's cone of light.

The contradictory wind had torn the man's voice apart, making it too soft and too loud. He knelt in the blue glare of the streetlamp and began picking up her scattered possessions. His long coat rasped against the concrete, and his blond hair shimmered across his back like a waterfall.

"This will perhaps make you feel secure." Something skittered on the sidewalk, plunked into water standing in the gutter. Melissa kept her eyes on the kneeling man and bent to retrieve the object. Her fingers searched among slick fragments of ice and pulled the knife out of the freezing water.

"Now I should be frightened of you." The man's friendly voice sliced neatly through the swirling air. He stood, holding out Melissa's backpack to her.

Melissa's heart tried to wrench itself out of her chest. She unsnapped the sheath and shook the knife from it. Say

11

something, idiot! Don't give him the satisfaction of thinking you're afraid of him.

"Don't ever do that again!" she screamed.

The man spread his hands and smiled. Melissa's pack looked tiny dangling from his white fingertips. "You looked unhappy standing beneath the electric light."

"I wasn't! I mean, I'm not."

"Confidence holds a true weapon. Shall I return your satchel? Or will you retrieve it from me?"

His accent was strange. Melissa shook her head. "Just leave it there. I'll get it in the morning."

"Come. Test my mettle. You might trust me enough to share a repast. Hot drink!"

Taste his metal? Melissa gripped her knife tighter. "No, thanks. Just leave, okay?"

The man waited. White light fell on his shoulders like snow. He whispered something.

Did I notice his eyes? Melissa almost saw the shape of the question before it was blown apart by the ripping breeze.

How blue they were, like an open sky—nothing to be frightened of there.

Melissa shook her head, trying to rid herself of a fog of helplessness enveloping her. Her father's eyes were blue.

All sound died away, which was odd because the trees and the few leaves on their branches weaved about wildly as if they were trying to get her attention. Melissa gazed up, thinking she might hear the stars' passage through the frozen sky if she only tried hard enough. . . .

Her knife was plucked from her fingers. Melissa watched distantly as the man resheathed her weapon.

"This is too fiercesome for so delicate a girl," he said as he slipped it into his pocket. "What is your name?"

Melissa couldn't see the man's expression under the whirling shadows. He was so tall! She told him her name.

"Melissa." He nodded slowly. "I am sure that is not all of it, but there is time. In honor of your trust, I will give you my name: Falke."

"Fall-kah . . . ," Melissa repeated.

She saw the man now, as parts of him were revealed. Muscular, pale throat. Liquid, ocean-blue eyes, their black pupils dilating.

12

He spoke a name, and Melissa saw at once mirrory blade-like waves, pale sand, weaving anemones.

Falke took her arm in his and walked her away from the light. Strange voices hummed around Melissa, above her head, beneath her stumbling boots. She felt Falke's arm tighten around her, still gentle. The stars descended from the sky and whispered warnings to her.

But why should they?

Melissa gazed at the blond man, saw his kind, handsome profile. The street vanished, and a river opened up beside them. The sidewalk changed to grass. The streetlamps became silent trees.

It was all so romantic. "Beautiful," Melissa thought, lost in the river's chuckling course over hidden stones.

"As are you, beloved. As I have kept you always."

The trees swayed to music created by the wind. A brief thought intruded.

She had left her backpack behind.

Three

Michael woke up in his sheepherder's canvas bedding on the squeaking brass bed he had bought for his wife nearly forty years before. Beyond the stone and adobe walls of his house, he heard dull sheep bells and Lee's impatient barks. He turned from the lumpy pillow and saw a violet dawn, no hint of orange yet, through the window above his bed. The sky was cloudless and would probably become wickedly hot in the afternoon. Unless it snowed. You could never count on reservation weather for anything but being contrary. Especially in October—Coyote's month. Michael thought of Tank 19 across I-40 where he ought to take the sheep to be watered. A good two and a half miles distant. His arthritic joints burned. He hated the weakness of old age more than anything else. One of these days, he would be too weak to take his sheep anywhere.

The air was solid and glazed with ice. There was a time when he would have turned to Margaret and her warmth to soothe his aching joints. Especially during the winter months, when they would sometimes ignore their early morning chores for a little while.

Ayaah'ah, never mind, Margaret would have said in Keresan, the Pueblo language she spoke. He folded the bed's heavy canvas covering away from himself. Margaret was dead and probably happier wherever she was. Ice penetrated his joints, fully awakening his arthritis. His breath hitched at the jeering pain. He sat quietly for a few minutes, not moving. It felt as if glass knives were digging persistently into the soft cartilage between his bones. He tried to ease himself from the bed, but he couldn't.

Gradually, his muscles relaxed. Margaret had given him rubdowns with medicinal alcohol every night and again at dawn. Her loosened strands of hair had caressed his skin, and her strong fingers had easily driven the knives of pain away. Or had it been her soft humming? He used to tell her he felt like dough being kneaded and made ready for the oven. My Navajo sweet bread, she used to call him then.

Those massages had hurt like hell, he remembered. He wasn't as devout a Catholic as Margaret had been, but he intoned a prayer for her all the same. He stood barefooted on the freezing, creaking linoleum. Then he made his way to the ancient stove to brew up some coffee.

As always, Michael sat on a simple wood bench at his table, facing the 1958 July calender with Jesus on the cross and sipping a boiling-hot concoction of coffee and last night's leftover juniper brew. The picture on the calender had been Margaret's favorite of all the portraits of Our Savior she owned, and she had often scolded his attempts to remove it.

"I don't like to be reminded of death every morning when I eat," he used to tell her pretty much every morning. "Especially when I must take the sheep all the way to Sedillo grant today."

"*Ayaah'ah!*" Margaret would exclaim. "Hush up. It's supposed to remind you of the Resurrection. A very hopeful

14

thing! You would know that if you went to church with me one day instead of taking the sheep out to be watered every morning. Especially on the Sabbath. Why don't you get one of the Garcia boys to do it for you?"

"I'll try and find someone good to graze them for me next Sunday."

"You Navajos and your sheep. They're like your little children!"

He finished his coffee and sat quietly while the sun rose and flooded his doorway with yellow light. If he had known then that Margaret was going to die before him, he would have gone to church with her, and not only on the Sabbath — just to have spent a little more time with her.

He began to hum something. Not one of his wife's hymns, but a song his grandmother had sung while spinning wool. He never understood what the song was about. Nanibaa' had muttered it softly, the words flowing just beyond the reach of his hearing. He hadn't wanted to show her how nosy he was, either, by asking her what the song was saying.

Now it was gone.

Michael rose and went to the open cabinet standing next to the doorway. Melissa's brightly lettered cereal boxes flared in a shower of sunlight. He placed his cup on the dishrack his daughter had given him five years ago. "Do some dishes once in a while, old man," Sarah had said as she handed it to him. "Give Mom a break."

The sun stood directly in front of his doorway. He lifted a tiny leather bundle from around his neck, numbly untied it, and pinched light corn pollen between his fingers. He remembered the running antelope and his baby granddaughter's happy squeals, touched the pollen to himself, sprinkled it among sunbeams.

As Michael padlocked his screen door, he felt the intense light warming his hands, reminding him of a story Nanibaa' had told him when he was a young boy; one that she had often told him before his early-morning run. A story about Changing Woman. Michael searched through fifty years or so of crowded memory, but he couldn't find it. He had lost the story.

A hundred yards down a flat rocky slope was the corral where his sheep were penned. A short breeze chilled the back of his neck as he stepped carefully among sunflowers and   15 abandoned prairie dog holes. His ears began to ache from the cold. He glanced back to the northwest where blue-faced Mount Taylor sat with snow on his massive shoulders. Nothing prompted his brain. Michael still couldn't remember the story.

He tightened his belt. Several of the bolder lambs thrust woolly snouts through the gate. From a nail in a railroad-tie fencepost, he removed his favorite walking stick hanging by a leather thong. The oak wood rippled in his hands, familiar after so many years. Covering the tip was a spent twelve-gauge shotgun shell he had picked from the center of a drying puddle one summer. Michael lifted the gate and carried it several feet, wide enough for the sheep to line through. Tin cans filled with rocks rattled as the sheep jostled against the gate. He heard Lee's excited yelps from a distant patch of saltbush, and he whistled to him.

Michael decided against taking the sheep to Tank 19. All he wanted to do was sit somewhere near his home and remember the story about Changing Woman. Some songs went with it also. He whispered bits of one as he followed the older, slow-moving rams. Nanibaa' had often sung the story while she did some chore: cleaning out her blackened iron stove, giving scraps to the wiry sheep dogs, shoveling up potatoes from her small, tough garden. A strong Navajo song about racing the rising sun, chasing after a glimpse of Changing Woman, the Holy One that Michael loved the most; a woman who ran under the sun like a deer among the piñon and sage, a woman tall with streaming black hair, changing like the earth's seasons from the potency of spring to the winter weakness of old age. To the runner who could catch her early in the morning, when she was still a young girl, she would give a gift of power — the strength of the earth, which she embodied.

Michael remembered catching Changing Woman a long time ago, many seasons past, when strength sang restlessly inside his muscles and heart. And now Margaret was dead.

Pausing, he looked forty miles to the east over flat, reddish land to the distant Sandia Mountains. Above the tiny silver crest, the sun was already a good distance into his daily journey across the sky. Michael's body began to ache again. His legs lifted weakly. There wouldn't be any gifts today. His racing days were long over.

Four

"Damn nightmares remembered everything," Diana Logan commented to the echoing walls as she rushed through Lincoln High School's barren hallways, dragged down by books and bags, nearly defeated by gravity. Her sea-green Irish eyes still burned from an edgy sleep. Her usually full, reddish brown hair felt listless and clamped to her head. She wanted to confront this morning's nightmare, dissect and examine it, then scrape out the remaining dregs of fear it had left inside her. She became sodden with tears. Tangled colorless images clung to her brain, massing like a cancerous tumor. Her keys flev° out of her hand and skittered past the classroom door.

This is bad, Diana told herself, the physical part of distress, when you can't trust yourself to perform the simplest task. It's been eleven months since the divorce. Christ! Get a grip.

Swearing softly, she chased after the key ring that held not only keys but also the lost rings she had found around campus and which she always forgot to dump at Lost and Found. But she couldn't figure out how to pick the key ring up without dropping everything else. Exhausted, her defenses down, she was overcome by monsters.

Her mother, Grace, when alive, used to preen in front of a bedroom mirror, and Diana used to imagine her as a white swan idly drifting in a seamless, clear lake. Isn't Momma's wedding ring so pretty? Grace would ask, turning it under the lamp. In Diana's child-eyes, the reflecting ring had looked enormous. A fairy talisman that had held her entire world securely on her momma's finger. The fear that it might disappear had haunted her since birth, it seemed. Maybe even before then.

Ten years ago, her parents had been killed in a swift, lonely car accident not far south of Moab, Utah. Her dad had fallen asleep, or had a heart attack, or a million other things; the car had run off the road, turned over several times, snow billowing in soft clouds perhaps. . . . At seventeen, when her teenage insanity had peaked, she drove to the site of the accident and searched through all the possible trajectories of her parent's wreck, forcing herself to imagine every detail. Numberless horrifying images. And her nightmares kept vomiting new ones.

But Diana never did find her mother's wedding ring.

"Oh, crap!" She watched her carefully graded papers and texts and number two pencils spill out of her canvas bag and scatter over the scuffed, filthy floor.

Why not leave them? A monument to insecurity. A cairn to mark the passing of her once real and solid grip on the world. Then top the pile with this . . . Diana tugged off her useless gold wedding band. *God knows I don't need it anymore. Maybe one of my teen monsters will find it, pawn it, and use the proceeds toward a college tuition.*

"Right," Diana whispered, putting her ring back on, scooping her junk back into her canvas bag. *More likely it would go toward a car, a boyfriend, or a quick high. Maybe all three.*

She listened to the roar behind the two-inch thick metal door to her classroom. A girl screamed (sounded like Moira or Jenny) and the rest of them laughed. *Oh, well,* Diana thought, standing and brushing her skirt. *You never know. I should leave my ring on the floor for one of them to find—just to see what happens.*

Twenty minutes later, a moment of quiet.

Diana wanted to droop onto her desk and fall asleep, but the image of her vulnerable head brought forward her last reserves of strength. She was in no mood for surprises, especially from a horde of English 1 sophomores.

"Mrs. Logan."

A gloomy, bookish girl named Julie Mascarenas held out a folded piece of paper. Diana refrained from correcting the "Mrs." part.

"What is it, Julie?"

"It's the quiz. I've finished it."

Already? Diana just stopped herself from saying it out loud. *You mean someone actually studied for my quiz?*

"Thank you, Julie."

The girl hovered, clicked her nails. "I was just wondering," Julie began, edging closer to Diana.

"Yes?"

"Umm. It's none of my business. . . ."

Julie was slouching, but tense. Diana fought an urge to say, pull your back straight!

Something cracked among the students. A pencil, probably. Diana fancied it was a candy cane, for some reason. Julie winced at the noise, looked distressed.

"What's wrong, Julie?"

The girl stared toward the back of the room as if she hadn't heard. Diana realized that the students' focused concentration was broken. There was a shuffling nervousness in the room. Papers rustled. Desks squawked against the floor. Diana saw the concern on Julie's face turn to fear.

"Mrs. Logan," Julie said breathlessly.

Diana stood quickly, ignored her chair clattering to the floor. The kids were drawing away from a point near the center of the classroom. They were afraid. Some responded with jittery laughter. Most were wide-eyed and silent. Diana shot around her desk, ready to deal it out to whoever was scaring them.

She had to push through several boys, ridiculously taller than she, to see the cause of the disturbance. In the center of a staring circle of students, Melissa Roanhorse sat calmly at her desk, her ripped pink blouse revealing a bra strap at one shoulder, breaking pieces of pencils between her fingers.

For a moment, Diana stared with the rest of her students. Melissa's face was gaunt and sickly pale. Reddened eyes followed the pencil pieces rolling across her desk. Her thick hair was frizzed wildly as if she had showered and not bothered to comb it out.

Diana sought the nearest warm body, a plump girl named Joanie Wilson, and gripped a soft arm. "Go next door and get Mr. Hatfield." Diana looked into the girl's blank eyes. "Quickly!"

Joanie nodded, but did not move. Diana rubbed the red circles her fingers had left on the girl's freckled skin. "Take Julie with you."

Somehow, those words broke Joanie's paralysis and the two girls fled the room. Diana turned to Melissa. The girl now held the front edges of her desktop in whitened hands. She trembled violently. The desk squeaked at its joints. Pencil pieces clicked onto the floor.

19

"Melissa, tell me what's wrong." Diana touched Melissa's hands. The fingers were stiff, as if sculpted from ice. "Are you in pain?"

Melissa shut her eyes tightly and nodded. A beaded barrette came loose from her tangled hair and clattered onto the floor. Diana knelt and sidled closer. Melissa was so cold! Diana would not have been surprised to see frost covering the girl's skin.

"Please, Melissa, let go of the desk."

Melissa shook her head. The muscles of her arms slithered, threatening to lash out of the skin. Diana touched Melissa's shoulder. The flesh under the torn blouse writhed like a nest of snakes. Diana almost jerked her hand away in disgust. She hugged the girl's slight shoulders, gently massaged frozen arms.

Diana spoke quietly, "Someone get me a jacket."

A staring wall of kids ignored her request. She knew their young brains were recording this weird scene to be replayed forever after; she knew what nightmares were—merciless, stalking monsters. The door banged open. Moira Foster, a tall, red-haired girl of the calmest sort, jumped and screamed.

Bob Hatfield, the Enriched World History teacher, shoved his way through the kids until he was standing over Diana and staring at Melissa, not comprehending, his red baldness shining under the harsh lights. "Mrs. Logan, what's wrong?"

It's not Mrs. anymore! Diana wanted to scream. Instead, she gestured to her students. "Get them out of here, please?"

Bob nodded and immediately began pushing the students to the door. Someone draped a letter jacket over Melissa's shoulders.

"Be careful, Miss Logan."

"You! Come away from there."

The jacket's owner, Willard Johnson, a blond basketball jock, waved away the smaller man's hands. "Hey, man, lay off a second."

"Hey, man, get the hell out!" Bob harried Willard out the door. From the hall outside, Diana heard a swell of excited voices.

Bob squatted beside her. "What's happened to her?"

"I don't know," Diana said. "She's sick or something. We have to get her to a hospital."

Melissa's trembling had eased, but her hands still gripped the desktop.

"Melissa, honey," Diana coaxed. "Relax your hands. You'll hurt yourself."

Bob shuffled around to the opposite side of the desk. "Yes, relax, Melissa," he said as he patted her hand. "Help is on the way."

"You liar!" Melissa screamed.

Diana felt the girl's muscles stiffen. Wood crunched. The desktop sheared away from its support.

"Bob, get away!"

With an echoing crack, the free desktop broke apart in Melissa's hands. One piece swung sideways, hitting Bob Hatfield in the face. Blood spattered his immaculate shirt and he fell stiffly backwards into a line of desks. Diana watched as the other desktop twirled past her head and smashed into the blackboard. Fragments clattered across the room.

"Stop it, Melissa!" Diana tried to hold the writhing girl down.

"He hurt me," Melissa said sulkily, wrenching herself from Diana's arms.

"Who hurt you?"

Melissa's eyes darkened.

"Honey, *who* hurt you?" Diana hesitated in reaching for the girl because a voice spoke in her mind—Melissa's voice.

He said there wouldn't be anymore pain.

Diana became entranced by the girl's brown eyes. Many subtle twists lay in the irises. Fiery colors. Silence rained in invisible sheets. Particles of drowsiness descended onto Diana's head.

Sleep, Mrs. Logan.

Diana opened her eyes and saw Melissa's slender fingers curl into a fist. Too white, Diana thought vaguely. Then a bolt like an electric shock slammed into her forehead. The room tilted. Pain exploded along her back. Almost as quickly, some frantic thing squirmed into her hair. Stinging pain flared along her scalp as she was jerked up to Melissa's black stare. Diana saw no hatred in the girl's eyes, only a detached blankness, as if she were washing dishes. Melissa cocked her arm back again.

It's too early in the morning for this! Diana reached for the clenched fist. Melissa grasped Diana's hand and bit into it

21

savagely, releasing her at the same time. Diana dropped, banged onto her knees, tumbled against desks. She tried to break her momentum but her palm, slicked with blood, slipped on the tiles. She landed on her side, rolled onto her back. Melissa crouched, glanced quickly to both fallen teachers, then raced out of the room. Diana heard shouts in the hallway. A heavy object boomed against a locker. A girl screamed.

Blindly grabbing hold of a desk, Diana pulled herself up off the floor, shaking her head to clear her doubled vision. Teachers and students rushed into the classroom, gaped at the bizarre scene.

"Help him." Diana pointed shakily to Bob Hatfield. She struggled to stand. Willard Johnson came to her; his strong hands held her waist, lifted her up. "Don't let me bleed on you, Willard." Diana's thoughts cleared. "Where's Melissa?"

Not waiting for an answer, Diana unwound Willard's arm and stalked out of the classroom. Students circled around her, teachers waved to get her attention. Ignoring them all, Diana burst through the heavy doors at the end of the hall, into a chilly October morning.

"Melissa!"

The school grounds were empty of people. Cars in the faculty parking lot slept under a weak sun. Even the flag drooped. Its chain clinked morosely against the flagpole. A tight circle of numbness grew on Diana's forehead.

"God! What happened to you?" A woman in shorts with leathery brown skin squinted into Diana's face. One of the gym teachers, she guessed. The woman squeezed her shoulder painfully. "Let me help you back to the office, Mrs. Logan."

"No!" Diana wailed. "I have to find Melissa."

"Shh. Calm yourself. She's not around here."

Diana's time sense failed. All at once, a great crowd of people surrounded her. Sirens hooted. Blue and red lights fluttered like iridescent birds.

I'm going to faint now.

Many hands held her shoulders, guided her backwards. Carried aloft, Diana floated through the air until coming to rest on a soft bed. A blue sky stretched around her, as if she were inside a huge balloon. Clouds like far away sails dotted the interior.

22

Diana remembered a sensuous boyfriend at Berkeley who had owned a sloop with turquoise trim. How wonderful it had been gliding over diamond waves, sail arced above her, the wind carrying a bitter scent that always made her thirst for sweet apple cider, the sun burning her thighs and stomach, torching bare nipples.

In a fever dream, she saw herself naked and on display, a wooden figurehead, tanned shoulders back, white breasts jutting forward; a captured mermaid guiding an ancient three-masted schooner across green and blue ocean swells. The ship's hold was empty, however. The crew gone. She was alone.

A bell dinged sadly.

Diana wondered why it was so cold.

Five

A tough woman with gorgeous white hair stopped filing sheaves of paper into a tall metal cabinet. She wore a pink sweatshirt that read Oxford University in white letters, a smart denim skirt with its hem just above strong calves, and Nike tennis shoes. The woman grinned as Diana entered the office, then clicked her tongue and threw the papers onto a desk.

"Don't get me wrong, honey," the woman said brightly, "but what the hell are you doing here?"

She gripped Diana's elbow and guided her to a couch next to a potted rubber plant.

"Katy, it's good to see a friendly face," Diana said, giving her best smile. "I needed the good energy."

"I'll bet. Would you like some sweet coffee? It's not fresh but it won't turn your stomach, either."

"No, thanks. Any sign of Melissa?"   23

Katy sat on the front edge of her desk shaking her head. "Nor a word. The police have got her home staked out, so I heard. Don't worry about her, Diana. She'll be back of her own accord, crying and carrying on."

"She's a nice girl," Diana said. "I don't know what could have caused such a thing."

"Drugs, maybe?"

Diana shrugged and her back clicked. "Possibly. Did you see the desk?"

"Two policeman walked out of here with its pieces wrapped in plastic. Any word of Bob?"

"Broken nose and a slight concussion. They're keeping him under observation at St. Joseph's. I stopped in to see him on my way here."

Katy sighed. "Poor man."

"He's out for blood."

"Uh oh. Is he the only one?"

"Oh, I don't know." Diana's head ached horribly. She was self-conscious about the greenish blue bruise smack in the middle of her forehead. Her right hand throbbed painfully where a slick-haired doctor had laced up a loose flap of skin. Her upper arm was tender from a tetanus shot. "My new silk blouse is completely trashed," Diana said.

"Not the white one!"

"No, the blue one with the pocket on the wrong side."

"Listen, sweetie, go home and rest. Take next week off. I already have a sub lined up for Monday."

"My head is killing me." Burning tears trickled into Diana's lap before she could catch them in her hands. She heard squeaking steps, then Katy held her.

"I don't believe that about the drugs." Diana said, getting hold of herself. "Not Melissa."

"Why not Melissa?"

Diana shook her head trying to clear away the bleak fog that had drifted over her thoughts. "I don't know."

"Diana, so many of these kids are sweet. I know they are. But you shouldn't blind yourself to some of their antics."

I know that, Diana thought wearily.

"Please, please go home and put yourself to bed. If you need something, call me and I'll come runnin'."

24   Diana nodded. "God, I must look awful."

"You do. Which reminds me." Katy went around to the business side of her desk, opened a drawer, shuffled through some papers. "You had a visitor today."

Diana's heart began to hammer loudly. "Who?"

Katy handed her a piece of paper folded into a tiny square. Her name was scrawled on one side: Miss Diana Logan. The writing was familiar but it wasn't Roger's, thank God. How could she have dealt with him as well as everything else? She looked to Katy, completely mystified.

"Open it and see." Katy smiled. "He must've come in here about twenty times, asking after you, looking so sweet and concerned."

Diana opened the square and saw bold, handwritten lines.

> Dear Miss Diana Logan,
> I hope you get well soon. The English language won't be the same until you get back safely.
> Your friend,
> Willard Johnson

"Poor kid," Katy said. "He's been bitten hard."

Diana folded the note carefully and placed it in her bag. "Could you do me a favor, Katy?"

"Depends."

"Let me have Melissa's address. Please?"

Katy began to argue, but stopped herself. She pulled open the bottom drawer of the file cabinet. "Melissa lives with her mother near the university. A bad situation, that. Her mother drinks heavily."

"How do you know?"

"The police wanted her file. I just happened to memorize it before handing it over."

"Sneaky. What else did it say?"

Katy shrugged. "Not much. Some disciplinary notes from Eisenhower. Talking back in class, several fights—"

"Fights?"

Katy nodded and handed Diana the file. "Doozies, too. Police made a minimum of noise. And they brought the file back quickly enough. I think I recognized one of them, too; a student here once, two or three years back."

Diana leafed through test grades, pink and blue slips, absence forms, cumulative grade reports. Several photographs fluttered to the floor. Diana bent to retrieve them, but a glitch in her back stopped her halfway. Katy knelt quickly and snatched them up, gave them back to her.

"Showoff," Diana said. The photos were of a smiling girl with penetrating eyes and dense wavy hair. A vast change from the girl she had seen this morning.

"I know next to nothing about Melissa." Diana glanced at the grade reports. "And I've had her in my class almost two months. She does her work. She keeps to herself. A very private person. That's it."

Diana flicked through the remaining pages of Melissa's file. The last was a piece of paper torn from a spiral notebook. The rough edges had been shorn away; something she recognized from some of her students' dashed-off research papers.

It was a hand-drawn map.

"What's this?" Diana asked.

Katy came up beside her and held up a corner to see it in the light. "Oh. Faculty must've had her draw it when she registered last year."

"A map to what, buried treasure?"

"No, hon. Relative somewhere out on the reservation, I guess. What does this say?"

Diana looked to where Katy pointed, and recognized the neatly printed handwriting as Melissa's.

"It's a name: Michael Roanhorse."

"I'm sorry, but I don't know who that is."

Diana turned the scrap of paper over. "That's all. Only her mother's name on the registration forms and this Michael Roanhorse. See, there's her father's name on the copy of the birth certificate, John Hill, but he's nowhere else to be seen."

"What are you thinking, Diana?"

She folded the map carefully and slipped it into her all-purpose bag. "Can I take this?"

"I'm sure no one will notice. You're over eighteen, so I'm not saying a word."

Diana handed the file back to Katy. Large windows showed the main foyer, which was empty of people. Circular wood benches surrounded a trophy display case. From somewhere beyond the window's area of view, a vacuum cleaner droned lazily.

"Having been a policeman's wife makes you nosy, I suppose," Diana said quietly. "It rubs off on you."

"Oh, I'm sure you were just as nosy when you were Momma's little girl."

"You said the police were watching her home?"

"Yes. And they explained to the faculty how we're to be discreet if she should come back by chance, to make a call, and let them handle the situation."

"You mean nail her."

"Not in so many words, but yes."

"Poor girl."

"Possibly. But I'm thinking about that desk and the broken chalkboard, Bob's concussion, and your injuries."

Diana remembered being paralyzed by the sight of the desktop flying toward her. "It wasn't that close."

"She hit your hand, didn't she? Why is it bandaged, then? Is it broken?"

In the foyer, two Mexican men passed the office windows. One dragged an ancient vacuum cleaner behind him, talking with heated emotion to his older companion. The older man grinned at Diana and winked.

"No, Mom," Diana said. "It's not broken."

"There was an awful lot of blood spilt, hon. Bob is fat, but that red stuff wasn't all his."

Diana held out her bandaged palm for Katy's worried inspection. Her friend's concern went a long way toward erasing confusion and anger. It was the reason she had come here directly from the hospital. Looking at the clean bandage, Diana remembered a silvery wink of bone under a flap of torn skin. Her chest constricted angrily. She had kept the map for a reason. It damn well was her business, not just nosiness.

Katy laughed and pounded her desk. "Honey, you've got that I'll-do-what-I-want look my daughter used to get in her eyes!"

"And?"

"And I'd spank her fanny until she begged for mercy. Don't make me do the same for you."

"It's personal. Not like it's my own business, Katy. I'm worried about Melissa. I want to talk to her. . . ." Diana's temper flared. "And my damn hand hurts and I want an explanation!"

27

"I see the old Diana now, ready to kick ass and shout! I feel a whole lot better."

Katy hugged Diana fiercely, protectively. "Sweetie, you still haven't told me what happened to your hand."

Diana pulled herself away and grabbed her bag from the sagging couch. She didn't want to cry again in Katy's presence. Her enthusiasm was gone. She felt shaky and unsure again. Her hand throbbed and her headache was back. It hurt to open the door, but she didn't think to use her other hand.

Shrugging, Diana said, "Melissa bit me."

Six

Diana loved to drive. Not the actual mechanics of driving—the shifting and engines and all that—but the feeling of speed, of drifting and of flying. The car was a red, gnat-sized Toyota, a vehicle she wouldn't have chosen for herself. She could hear the road rumbling underneath her, and the front end looked as if it might someday dig itself into the road. She called her car the Mole.

A right turn came up fast, and she swerved around it a bit too speedily. The Mole's tires squealed in protest. Adobe-style houses with flat roofs under a graying sky, colorless storefronts, chili emporiums, drive-up liquor stores, empty lots filled with tumbleweeds and broken concrete, and multitudinous orange barrels all whizzed by. The dreary face of Albuquerque.

The traffic light ahead turned yellow. Diana floored the accelerator. Her pile of junk slowed down.

"Stupid car!" Diana downshifted angrily. "Stupid piece of crap!" The gears clashed. Roger had warned her about the gearbox and how its life would be cut short if she didn't learn how to shift properly.

Crap on the gearbox, Roger darling, she thought. I didn't want this thing in the first place. Diana remembered his arguments about how sound this car was, how roomy, the gas savings, its resale value, the low maintenance.

It's supposed to be my car, she had said at the dealership, almost bursting into tears in front of the salesman who wore a black, neatly pressed funeral suit. My getaway car.

"You can't beat this one, hon," Roger had said in his Texas drawl. "Look at the seams. Look how fast they are."

"It doesn't look very fast," she'd answered, kicking the tires like a moron. "I don't want it."

"It'll make a good family car," Roger said dreamily, not listening, holding her to his side.

A car honked behind her. Diana waved airily, shifted, and promptly stalled the car.

"Girl," Diana laughed out. "Get your box in gear!"

At a stop sign, Diana flipped through her datebook and checked Melissa's address. She peered at the three squat rows of one-story apartments radiating from both sides of Hamilton Street where Melissa lived with her mother. Chinese elms grew out of circles in the sidewalk. The apartment walls facing her were a uniform maroon gray. A blue beach ball sat in a gutter waiting for someone to play with.

Diana drove to the parking spaces at the last block of apartments and came to a bouncing stop. She killed the engine. Sad, washed-out brick spanned across her windshield. At her right, a tall chain-link fence separated her from a barren field. Jacketed kids played baseball in the distance.

She opened her purse and took out a brush and a lipstick called Desert Blush. She turned the rearview mirror toward her. Most of the plainclothes detective cars were familiar to her because Roger had pointed them out. She had come to find one similarity in all of them: They were all painfully plain.

Looking in the mirror, she ignored the bruised circle on her forehead and double-checked the street. There seemed to be no one watching Melissa's apartment. Diana recapped the lipstick and put it in her coat pocket. Her hair looked flattened   29 so she brushed it awkwardly with her uninjured hand. Her eyes were naked and red; she should have brought sunglasses.

Stop it! No more delaying.

She got out of the car. The wind was moist on her face. The clouds had stretched out into long silvery trails, as if enormous snails had been roaming the sky. An amorphous blob of sun was circled by a ghostly ring, signalling a wet weekend.

Diana retreated into her woolen coat and walked around to the front of the apartments. A narrow walkway lay between the building and the fence, which had green fiberglass sheets woven through it for the privacy of the residents. Before starting forward, Diana glanced at the kids' baseball game. They seemed to be playing in silence. She strained to hear them, but couldn't; the wind was keeping from her the only sound that might have comforted her. A few steps later the fiberglass sheet covered the kids from view.

The first apartment looked uninhabited. The curtains were diaphanous strips, luminous in the dimming light. Beyond them stood a bare wall and a hallway leading into darkness. Diana hurried past the door.

Along the front of the apartments, lapping against the walk, was supposed to be a continuous gravel strip. However, the people of the next apartment had raked their portion of gravel into a raised circle around a barrel cactus. In the newly cleared section lay a rectangle of dark brown earth. Someone had planted a garden, Diana realized. She recognized pansies and withered watermelon tendrils. Behind the barrel cactus lay a small compost heap of plant clippings and tree branches. An overlooking window was covered with a blue curtain. Warm lamplight glowed around its edges.

Diana felt a strong compulsion to knock on that door and to forget why she had come here in the first place. Sighing, she left the sleeping garden for the last apartment down. 324 C, brass letters said. She huddled inside her coat. Nervousness made her hands cold. She wished she had worn gloves or a longer skirt and a sweater. Her forehead felt numb. She touched the bruise carefully with her bandaged hand. A round bump lingered under her skin like a closed third eye.

She went up the steps and opened the screen door; theirs was the only apartment to have one. She knocked solidly, not hard, and pushed gently. The door squeaked open a few inches. Peeking inside, she saw nothing but the phantom outlines of a white settee and a blank TV. A strange bluish glow illuminated the settee. Ghostfire, her father's voice whispered in her mind.

"Hello?" Diana felt freezing wood under her fingertips as she coaxed the door wider. "Melissa?"

Now she could see fully into the apartment. Ghostfire, my ass. A large aquarium sat on the counter that separated the front room from what looked like the kitchen. Flashes of silver zipped inside the tank, which dominated the room like a diamond on a strip of black velvet. She entered and closed the door. She waved a hand in front of her. The air was as cold as an icebox.

"Is anybody here?" she asked the room. "It's Diana Logan from Melissa's school. I just want to talk to her."

The apartment remained silent. Diana went to the aquarium, the only source of light. Inside, silvery-blue fish were swimming crazily. Several were upside down, flapping tiny fins. She checked the temperature but didn't know whether it was at a safe or harmful level. On a bar stool set away from the counter was a spilled container of fish food.

She remembered an essay Melissa had once written describing her fish; the precise amount of food she gave them, how difficult it was keeping the water at a constant temperature, and how the fish reminded her not of neon, but of tiny, swimming rainbows.

Diana surveyed the room. The TV sat dead at her left. Pictures and Indian pots inhabited a wide bookshelf against the far corner. A long couch stretched under the main window. The white curtains were drawn, keeping out the evening light. From the kitchen behind her, a faucet dripped water at irritating intervals. Everything looked tidied. There was nothing to indicate any kind of emergency.

Maybe the fish were hungry. Diana pinched some fish food off the bar stool and searched the top of the aquarium, to find where to put the food in. She lifted the cover and hesitated. No wonder her attention had been stuck on this thing. There was no bubbling in the water. The air pump was off.

"You guys have no air," she said to the fish, and she moved the entire cover back to let in some air. Still pinching the fish food, she walked into the kitchen, looking for an electric socket. Darkness lay in a deep drift over the floor. Diana switched on the light.

The kitchen flared into brilliance. She blinked and shaded her eyes. Something on the floor caught her eye, but she couldn't see it clearly. A patch of darkness had remained after the light had come on; Diana peered under her hand at a red circle on the tiled floor. Someone's dropped a pancake and they haven't picked it up yet? She walked closer and saw, instead, that it was a pool of liquid. Strawberry syrup, maybe? Swallowing hard, Diana went to the sink and picked up a folded rag. Her heart began to thud in her throat. She soaked the cloth in an icy stream of water, listened to the water gurgling down the pipes. A window above the sink looked out to the east, to the livid Sandia Mountains set against a garish pink sky. Blue clouds hung like paper cutouts.

"Don't clean it up, stupid. Find a phone." She wrung out the cloth, refolded it, and placed it back on the counter. Shivering, she rubbed her hands together. Soggy fish flakes rolled under her fingers. She looked around the kitchen for a phone. She saw none and couldn't remember seeing one in the living room. Maybe in a back bedroom? Diana's mother used to keep a phone next to her bed. Diana's father had been a policeman, a uniformed cop, not a detective like Roger, and Grace used to call Sam at work if she'd had a nightmare or was too worried to sleep. Sometimes Diana, getting herself a drink of water or using the bathroom, would hear a slightly hysterical voice muffled behind her parent's bedroom door. On those nights, she would ease the door open and crawl into the bed next to her mother, snuggling under the blankets against a soft hip, sleeping there until her father came home.

Diana's gaze settled on the aquarium. The fish had calmed and now drifted aimlessly like floating leaves. "Oh, crap, quit dawdling," she muttered and went to the hallway entrance. On the wall were two switches. She flicked one up and a fan rumbled in the ceiling. Her skin began to crawl. "Please, God," she whispered, and tried the other switch. The hall light came on, illuminating bare walls and three doors, all shut—two on her left and one at the end of the hall. Breathing deeply to calm herself, she went to the door at the end and opened it, revealing a cramped bathroom with a bath against the opposite wall, perfume bottles, candy-colored washcloths, combs, brushes, junk scattered on every shelf and shiny rim. It was the only place so far that seemed to have been lived in.

Calmed, less frightened and more worried, Diana explored the next room. Posters and prints of animals covered the walls: Elephants, deer, baby foxes, coyotes, and an oil painting of a unicorn. The bed was covered with a blue quilt. Perched on a desk and scrutinized by a domed lamp was Melissa's backpack. Diana turned it so the front pouch was visible. Pinned there was a button that said "Hug a whale, help Greenpeace" over a picture of a blue whale hurling itself out of the ocean.

"Please, God, let everything be okay," she whispered as she left Melissa's room for the last door. Without hesitating, Diana pushed it open, switched on the light. A large bed took up most of the room, and a bureau with a mirror stood against the right wall. She opened the closet and saw nothing but a row of blouses, skirts, and dresses; on the floor lay a jumble of pumps, heels, and tennis shoes of various colors. Otherwise, the room was empty.

Diana let out a shaky breath and hugged herself. A phone. She went to the kitchen. The window was black. Water streamed from the faucet, which she had forgotten to turn off. She did so now, turning the knob tightly. On the floor, unchanged, lay the pool of dark blood. What else could it be? Diana knelt and reached to touch it, then paused. She remembered something Roger had told her about how police officers sometimes wore rubber gloves while searching suspects. On visits to the station, seeing some of the people he'd had to deal with, Diana had hoped Roger used rubber gloves as well.

She searched the drawers and found a pair of dishwashing gloves. They were cold, tight, and uncomfortable. She knelt to the pool again. An object lay hidden in it, a tiny, spiraled ridge distorting the smooth surface.

Diana touched the hard object then lifted it out, wincing at patters of dripping blood. A necklace of some sort. She took it to the sink and held it under flowing water. Red tendrils ran over her gloved fingers, as the water washed clean a delicate silver chain; at one end dangled a silver-edged turquoise cross.

Seven

Elizabeth awakened in her hidden basement. There was a familiar spiky feeling to the air—leftover droplets of glassy, stinging sunlight. Around her, blackness uncoiled. She tossed aside a silk robe, watched it snake onto the floor. Then she gathered more darkness about her, as if it were a quilt to warm herself by, and listened. Above her, the old theater was empty of humans and ghosts.

Relaxing, she let her thoughts drift. Where was Falke? Surely he couldn't find her here. She had chosen this place with care, seventy years ago when it had just been built. Thirty years later, she had wired it with alarms all by herself. John, a young boy Elizabeth had loved, had taught her the bloodlines of electrical machines and the ways of mechanical life. She had remembered his words. She was secure.

Elizabeth pictured the iron crest on Falke's chamber. A solid black anchor. She settled into her task. The darkness became impure. And the wind outside was so strong! It nudged her searching mind away from her target: Falke's sanctuary in the desert. She grasped her icy forehead, as if that might keep her on course. But it didn't. Something else besides the wind was distracting her. Her mind's eye wandered and fell into someone else's thoughts.

She saw a lamplit room that reminded her of a small adobe church. The walls held dusty windows and eroded unadorned niches. High-backed pews lined one far wall. A low ceiling of heavy logs held close shadows. Music was coming from a green jukebox in a near corner. Country music.

Elizabeth let her mind plunge into the sweet, powerful memory, and immediately, the scent of alcohol and sweat became pungent. The tiny bar was similar to those where she had sought nourishment for Falke and Hanna. Dusty people came to vibrant life and danced. Close two-stepping or the lovers' slow waltz. Within the closeness of the room, the few bodies shifted like a multitude.

34

Her heart quickened. She wanted to swirl among them, lose herself in time again. As her mind penetrated further into the memory, she began to catch thoughts. Excitement hurried her breath; someone else wanted to dance.

The memory belonged to a man. Whose was it? Why wasn't he dancing? There were women, and the atmosphere was right. She pushed deeper. The man seemed to be waiting for someone. A particular woman.

Another question unsettled her. Did the bar exist in real time? Or was it truly this stranger's memory? Human memories were so powerful sometimes, she couldn't tell the difference between them and the present.

A gust of wind blew the little place from her mind. The stranger's thoughts were gone. Elizabeth struck a match and lit the candle on the floor. She rose from the couch and searched for her reflection in the bureau mirror across the room. A nightly ritual. Her shape was lost among the pale walls.

As she knew it would be.

Putting on a sky-blue cotton dress and a gray coat, pocketing sunglasses, a comb, and money, Elizabeth left her windowless basement room, ascended narrow steps, and came out into a dark hallway lined with dressing-room doors. Passing beyond them, ascending concrete stairs, she entered the theater, which was lit only by the ghost light on the stage. The high ceiling was of dark wood beams. The proscenium was once decorated with Navajo cloud, bird, and whirling log symbols. Many years ago, an organ had droned musical accompaniments to the silent films that had played in the theater. The loud, strange music had terrified her. But she had loved the moving images of gentle, false sunlight. On the walls above the balcony, facing each other, were two sets of stylized Navajo figures—she didn't know who they were. Rows of stamped tin lamps, turquoise-inlaid cow skulls, and iron ceremonial masks dotted other parts of the theater.

Elizabeth crossed the aisles of empty seats and hurried to the back of the stage, disturbing gauzy silk cloths. She buttoned her coat, rose to a high, broken window, and dove into the fall night. The air smelled of burning rubber and wood fires. To the east, above the hump-backed Sandia Mountains, the waxing moon sailed above glowing snow clouds. The 35 traffic was breathless. Humming human thoughts were blanketed by wind. She passed new houses and buildings without straying from a hidden course, keeping her gaze on her feet and listening to the air streams. She pushed familiar distractions out of her head, leaving one memory.

One night, almost ninety years ago, Elizabeth had watched the moon swimming through messy clouds. A yellow fairy ring had formed around its disk. The night had been sunk with frost and the stench of woodsmoke; bitterly cold for the two Indian men hunched over their little fire. But how clear that night had become! The snow had covered the desert like a cotton sheet.

The men, an old man and a boy, had talked late into the night, speaking in a language of which only random parts are remembered by anybody—red or white. Certainly, Elizabeth had never heard this particular language ever again, spoken or thought. She remembered the words perfectly. But what good was that? She still couldn't understand it.

The liquid words whirled in her mind, a torrent of bright melody. The two men talked and laughed for a time. Then the old man began a mournful song, his flat eyes reflecting the firelight. The boy sat quietly and shivered.

Elizabeth had stood almost among them, as silent as a forming snowdrift. As the old man's singing became more resonant, Elizabeth had stalked among the juniper trees, listening, trying to memorize his song. Even then, newly changed, Elizabeth had understood how short a human life could be.

Now, she stood alone in darkness next to a busy intersection. Headlight beams swept over her, washing her in occasional brilliance. Her hands tingled. She saw how gaudy neon gave color to her pallid skin, unlike the moon's radiance, which only accentuated her whiteness. Manmade lights were not strong enough to needle with pain; they blew only a delicate flowing breeze, as if the reds, greens, and blues were breathing on her face.

The memory of the Indian's song often visited her, and it saddened her. At first, she had kept the memory close, as if it could give her strength and help her feel less alone. When she had first heard the old man singing to his grandson, she had imagined he was singing to her too. A lullaby of comfort and peace. Just the three of them under that starry sky painted over with moonlight.

Now, however, when the memory came upon her, Elizabeth was less affected by it, and she wondered if her mind was perhaps losing its peculiar grip on her vanishing human life. Falke had not changed her fully, as he had Hanna. Yet Elizabeth saw she was becoming more like them, less human, as the endless years wore on.

Why did that frighten her?

Elizabeth shrugged as if someone else had asked the question. Because Falke had once been strange and alien to her. Vampire. Then, slowly, during the long years of his convalescence, as she had obeyed his whisperings, endured the dreams, watched his mind's flickering images, Elizabeth had come to sympathize with his decisions. She had put aside fear and hatred to bring Falke back to life, nursing him for over a century, nourishing him as he had once nourished her own passionate hunger. She had listened to her husband's thoughts, confessed some of her own.

Elizabeth wondered, what would Hanna think of such thoughts?

Their servant would have known. He might have explained to her about this lost emotion, comforted her, if he had existed on to this time. A strange creature, but he would have told her the truth.

How would she have approached him? First, she would have taken him away from his lovely creations, the doll house cottages he had made especially for her.

"Kuenstler," she would have said, sitting his gnarled body into his rosewood rocking chair, kneeling at his side. "I'm not going insane. I think. My mind is becoming a deep muddy river with rushing topwaters and sonorous currents, with chaotic spinnets and whirlpools like somber wagonwheels."

Elizabeth laughed, wondering if she had spoken out loud.

Kuenstler had loved the old man's song Elizabeth had sung for him. Maybe Kuenstler would have understood her sadness, too, if Hanna had not destroyed him.

Cars and trucks and other strange contraptions rushed by. She shut their noises out completely, a talent she had mastered while nursing her husband and sister with stolen blood. Of all the peculiarities of the desert sanctuary, the shrieks of

37

the night hawks had disturbed Elizabeth the most. So, while holding her slashed wrist and its steady eruptions of blood over Falke's and Hanna's lips, she would concentrate all her awareness to the hidden depths inside her mind—to a private screen of silent images.

Until daylight. Then Elizabeth would find death waiting for her. A vampire's sleep that had robbed her of so many dreams of glowing trees, sparkling streams, and clear simple sunlight.

"Can I help you?" someone asked her.

Elizabeth found herself standing outside a narrow hamburger stand. Originally a trailer, the interior was steamy with the reek of frying meat. Rows of yellow bulbs lined the overhanging roof. The boy who had spoken was tall and dark-haired, broad-chested beneath a white T-shirt, close enough to touch. She heard the blood swishing in his body.

She unbuttoned her coat. "What do you have that's good?"

The boy rested both palms on the counter, glanced at her body, and nodded. "Depends on what you see as good, doesn't it? I mean, I might have it or I might not."

Elizabeth became deliberately coy. "I'm sooo hungry. And I love meat. Are you quick, or do you take a long time?"

The boy laughed. His shyness excited her.

"Depends on how you like it, I guess. Longer's better, I always say."

"Always? I like it slow, too. It tastes better that way."

The boy picked up his spatula and grinned. "How do you want it? Medium or rare."

"I want it raw. In the middle."

The boy hesitated, then turned and began to make her hamburger. The grill hissed as the meat patty touched its surface. He turned to her, more relaxed. "What's your name? I haven't seen you around before."

She traced the window screen. Lies were easy. "I've only just come here from California. Malibu, where my daddy lives."

The boy faced his grill. "Just what I figured. A runaway, huh? After I save enough money, I'm heading out of this freak town, myself. I'd like to try L.A. for a while. But the Virgin Islands are my destination. My buddy is stationed there, and he says the sun is fantastic. And the surf and beaches? Like Heaven!"

Elizabeth spoke quickly, not wanting him to say any more. "Do you like my jacket? It's real sealskin from Alaska. I hated it at first, you know? Because of the baby seals getting murdered? But it's so warm, like I have one next to me. Do you want to touch it?"

Smiling, the boy reached for the offered material.

"No!" Elizabeth fell back. The boy's hand stopped in mid-reach. "I better go."

"What about your burger? Wait!"

Elizabeth fled the trailer, her senses withering in the October night. She wondered if tears could turn to ice. They were made of water and salt. Would the salt stop the freezing process? She wiped them away quickly, noticing a red sheen on her fingertips. It was dangerous to leave tears exposed to sight.

Unsated hunger made her listless. She remembered her mother sewing the white dress she had worn on dress-up days during their westward journey, strong fingers stitching fine rows, the tough cotton and wool material, sky-blue ribbons, fragile lace. Elizabeth still kept the last dress her mother had made, hidden in Falke's sanctuary, in her emptied room. What would Emma have thought of her daughter now, more than a century later? Would she think her a monster? An evil creature to be destroyed by Heaven's vengeful fire? Would she still consider Elizabeth her daughter?

Elizabeth held out her arms and let the wind carry her into the sky. Smudges of city lights passed below. Emma had been a stolid frontier woman before Falke had killed her. Though warm and caring, her heart had dwelt too far away to reach. Elizabeth wondered if, at the end of her life, Emma had held the same core of sweet nostalgia that now tormented her daughter. Had she guarded her own private images just as selfishly?

And what about the man in the bar, whose thoughts she had swum in—what secret river flowed through him?

Eight

Wrapped in a blue bathrobe and listening to a Beatles' collection on her cassette player, Diana flipped to the next essay, a scrawled, half-page mess from Laura Sennett which was not even close to the required length. "God, Laura," Diana muttered when she realized that the fragment of essay was actually an apology for not getting the work done. Slash, slash went the angry red pencil across the empty half of the page. No apologies accepted! See me after school for makeup work!

Unable to write any more, Diana withered in her chair, cupping her large mug of coffee and absorbing its warmth into her sore hand. She hated nights. Summer nights were bad enough in her downtown apartment when there was no school. Winter nights were deadly. Fewer cars zipped below her window. No rushing people, no glittery lights or warm exhalations. Nothing to excite her imagination. Only cold nights and hot cups of coffee. And the Beatles mocking her stinky mood. She reached to the player and switched it off.

For the hundredth time, she considered pursuing a love life. Some offers—thank God—and from stable men too. But no interest. Her heart remained frozen; an ice cube, or a fish steak. The walls of her apartment offered enough protection from hurt. Why invite pain inside?

Besides, there was too much work to do. Too many worries, especially now, with Melissa gone crazy. Diana shivered. She sipped more coffee and glanced to the photographs and postcards taped to the refrigerator's side, small windows looking on a strange assortment of scenes.

One of them showed Roger's baby son, Danny, a detective shield pinned to his blanket. Diana had often wanted to explain that there were no hard feelings, only shattered ones; and that she had not wanted a picture of her ex-husband's new life. She had simply wanted a picture of a sweet-faced baby named Danny. Why bother explaining? Roger wasn't supposed to be her problem anymore.

Another picture showed her parents, Sam and Grace Logan, standing next to a bulbous Ford pickup. Dark-haired Sam wore his chinos and workshirt; Grace, her smiling face illuminating the whole photograph, pretty in a plain dress and white pumps. The sun was too bright and they were squinching their eyes as they smiled to the photographer. Behind the couple, a stop sign stood ominously amid a field of sunflowers. Oddly, the picture was canted so that it emphasized not only her parents but also the damned stop sign.

Who had taken the picture? Diana had tried to deduce the answer; examining each of her relative's characters to see which one might have composed such a picture. So far, she had only come up with more questions. Who to ask now? Certainly her parents couldn't tell her anymore.

The phone rang on the wall above her head, and she let it. Her father smiled on. Pick it up, hon, he seemed to say. It might be one of your teen monsters.

Diana lifted the receiver. "Hello?"

"Diana, it's Roger."

She picked up the week-old essays, tamped them into a straight-edged pile, and lay them down again. "What is it?"

She heard noises beyond his presence on the line. Mutterings of people and clacking machines. It was so familiar she almost laughed. Of course he would be at the station this time of night.

"I wanted to fill you in on your student, Melissa Roanhorse," Roger said comfortably, easing himself into a conversation. "Maybe ask a few questions."

"I thought you were on days, Roger. Why are you still at the station?"

"I'm at the substation on Lomas. Just making the rounds, stoking up the paperwork, is all."

Diana leafed through the essays until she found Melissa's. "Ask away."

"We found no signs of a struggle or blood anywhere else except in the kitchen. It's being tested now for type and medical complications—"

"The kitchen?"

He went on. "You saw no noticeable wounds on Melissa Roanhorse, did you, Diana?"

"Only that she was very pale and afraid."

"Afraid of what, could you say?"

41

"No. I don't know."

Diana could imagine him scribbling notes on a legal pad between questions, probably writing with the expensive pen she had given him on his promotion.

"Ever see her act like this before?" Roger asked. "Maybe smell alcohol on her breath or something?"

"No, nothing like that."

"Looking at her school files, she seems to have a violent tendency. Ever notice any behavior that would pertain?"

"Several fights don't add up to a violent nature. They were in middle school, for Christ's sake."

"Not a violent person." Roger enunciated each word. "Melissa Roanhorse slammed that teacher damn hard, Diana. Robert Hatfield? I hear he's still in the hospital. You still think she hasn't got a violent tendency?"

"It was his own fault," Diana answered. "He scared her."

"How do you know?"

"She told me so."

"What did she say exactly?" His voice sharpened.

"She said, 'He hurt me.'"

"Hmm. Did she say anything else?"

Diana remembered the whispered, almost telepathic, words in her mind. *He said there wouldn't be anymore pain.* Had Melissa spoken them? Her lips hadn't moved. Probably something my mind cooked up to confuse me even more.

"Nothing else," Diana said, feeling completely drained of energy.

"You sure, Diana?"

"What do you want from me? No, there was nothing else." She dipped her pinkie into her coffee. Cold liquid, now.

"Carl called me at home," Roger said. "Told me what happened. He's got the case."

"Carl Johns? How's Maggie?"

"She's holding up. Her cancer's been slowed some with radiation. Carl is hopeful."

"Good. I'm glad."

"Are you okay, Diana? Seriously."

"I ache. I'm going to take another bath and go to bed early." Diana picked up the angry red pencil. "How are Heather and Danny?"

"Danny's getting real clever, not like his dad."

Diana laughed, not expecting Roger to joke.

"Listen, Diana. If there's anything you need. . . ."

Ice settled inside her chest. "Please don't say that. I don't need anything from you. And please try not to call me, okay?"

"I was worried about you."

"You said Carl was handling the case. So why are you calling me and asking questions?"

Roger hesitated. "Carl mentioned you were in the Roanhorse apartment. That you were the one who found the blood."

"She's my student. I'm worried about her."

"Diana . . . ," Roger's voice trailed off. "Just be careful, all right? We'll handle it."

"Melissa's a good girl, Roger. Tell Carl to be gentle with her."

"I sure will."

Diana stared at the essay in her hand. The assignment had been a free one over any topic the student wished to write about. Melissa's had been about the indiscriminate poisoning and killing of mountain lions, wolves, and coyotes. "The Rancher's Enemy," it was called. "The real enemy," Melissa had written, "is ignorance of the life and habits of these beautiful predators. Learning about them and adjusting to their natures would be a long-term goal, but beneficial to both parties. Ignorance only helps in the killing of these misunderstood creatures. In the long run, if this random murder continues, the results can only be tragic."

"Diana?" Roger's voice spoke from the receiver.

She hung up without answering.

Nine

Time slowed beneath Hanna's bare feet, and she watched as moonlight advanced across a withered floor toward the standing mirror. Her reflection was so like a pale mist, Hanna was afraid the moon's killing rays would imprison her in the mirror's depths, holding her until the sun rose and its eyes charred her skin off blackening bones, leaving gauzy fragments swimming in air like dustmotes. A white blur filled the mirror, dominated by black eye sockets.

My eyes will anchor me to this world, Hanna thought, smiling at a distant memory of herself: Tall with red-gold hair, and green eyes.

"Corrupted," Falke said as he touched shifting moon beams. His undecipherable thoughts drifted like smoke in the decaying schoolroom; a shattered room not so different from those Hanna had known a century ago. A temporary dwelling.

Hanna shrugged. "It dries my skin. I don't like it."

A hand wove itself in her hair. She fell into the rhythm of its movement, then swooned against Falke's chest. Hanna had not heard his approach, even though her senses were almost as acute as they had once been. And she had forgotten that Falke could move as a spirit.

Fear mixed with the hunger in her belly—what else have I forgotten?

"The moon is innocent," Falke said. "It is the treacherous sun who uses her body against you."

"Whichever. I hate them both." Hanna pulled herself from Falke's grip, studied his faint image in the mirror. His shape filled the deep room behind her. Or was it a deception?

"I'm leaving you, Falke. You and your fucking wife."

Falke remained still, as if turned to rock. "I, also, might leave. East, perhaps, where the cities are vast. I have heard they are so, though I cannot believe the words."

"Who told you this?" Hanna felt a whispery touch on her skin. Gently, his fingertips explored her stomach, her nipples; his hands were like rising silk, or silken webs.

44

"No magic," Hanna said, emerging from his spell. She moved to a patch of moonlight on the floor, where she kneeled among glass shards. Falke wrapped his long coat around himself and sat against a blasted wall. City lights fluttered outside a gaping window.

"I don't understand this town in the desert," Hanna said. "A long time ago, you made these promises to me: strength, escape. And I'm still here! Wounded and hurting like some stupid animal. I don't understand why you chose a desert out of all the cities of the world."

"The search . . . a war against fate." Falke stared impassively at her. "I will tell you once, Hanna. It is a bitter song that should be remembered, kept hidden, not to be sung twice. A night, two centuries past, while wandering among sand dunes, Kuenstler gave a great shout; he had found our sanctuary. A womb inside the largest of the surrounding blood fortresses, and set within the patient caves—silent ruins. 'Ancient dwellings unoccupied for thousands, perhaps millions of years, master!' Kuenstler shouted across the red sand. 'Surely, we have crossed the Rhine and come to Nibelungland!'

"How the vassal could spin, Hanna! Break the ruins, I commanded him. Build over them a new haven, and populate it with corpses. Their drying skulls will speak of savage death; will give protection from the inquisitive Nibelungs.

"One night, a century ago, I hunted a native girl with loose, dusty hair who was drawing water from a spring. Her brown body, underneath heavy cotton garments, delicate. Her blood, raging. For one instant, I was distracted by the kill."

Falke stopped. Hanna shifted among the glass fragments and remembered glowing red arrows that had beckoned her out of the desert.

Falke continued. "As I fed upon the girl, twin moonlit masks, pale as bone and grimly chanting, rose from the sand dunes. Howling flames shot from their mouths. They opened up the sky, Hanna, brought down the sun."

"What?" She opened her eyes and saw scraps of paper flying, stripped by a sudden wind. "Lunatic!" Hanna stood and crushed fragments of glass in her hands. "Fool! Don't try to frighten me!"

Falke smiled. "Be wary of them, Hanna—the cheerless masks. For they watch endlessly, even under the moon."

Hanna became a pillar of rage. "Is this all you've got to tell me? Lies!"

Falke relaxed against the wall. "You must remember Hanna, that when last I traveled, I was under great strain to find a secure home. A place where my uniqueness would be unknown. I was tired of being hunted. I'm not accustomed to it."

"Who hunted you?"

Falke didn't answer.

"So you bled savage desert women and ended up in a rock tomb—with one frightened child." Hanna laughed. "Your wife."

"You understand nothing."

His stillness lacked surety. Was he afraid? She needed to touch him, enter his mind, to be sure. Hanna unveiled her wings and became a mist on a current of wind. She rose off the glass-littered floor and drifted to Falke.

"Have you met with Elizabeth?" Hanna asked. "Have you planned your escape with her?"

Falke sat just under her fingers. The moonlight had crept onto his shoulder. His hair became a steel river.

I could kill him! thought Hanna. If I'm quick enough.

"Leave if you will," Falke murmured. "I will remain for a time in this city and study its modern way first. Know the ways of your enemy. His lifestyle and habits. His language. You will be better prepared to destroy him."

His gaze illuminated her, pierced her thoughts. Hanna stilled her movements and tried to empty her mind. She suddenly remembered being a human child in lace-up boots and a dirty nightgown, running circles about a blood-soaked, screaming dog her father's hounds had ripped apart and dragged into a rain puddle. Later, picking through the dog's organs swelling in muddy water, Hanna had found a broken tooth. The image disappeared.

Falke closed his eyes. Hanna carefully guided a finger to his face. Slivers of moonlight burst into her eyes and she blinked. Her hand was caught and held. Instead of fighting back, Hanna kneeled on bare wood and kissed Falke's knuckles.

"You made me a vampire, Falke," she said. "Made me strong. I've protected Elizabeth. I will protect you."

Hanna nuzzled into his icy throat. Falke's pulse hammered under her lips. His hand, still holding hers, was a stone wedged between her breasts.

46

"I am connected to you," she whispered. "Your mistress. Be truthful if you can. Will my strength return?"

"You are not a frightened child, Hanna. That's why I chose you." Falke released her hand. "I made you. When I sleep, you sleep. Your strength will return. Do not fear."

"I don't understand fear."

"Perhaps separation is good, for a future moment." Falke's words nudged her away. "Elizabeth is valuable to us now."

Hanna looked into his blue eyes. They were filling with intense light, staring at something far away. She kissed his chin. "Know the ways of your enemy," she said softly. "I don't trust Elizabeth. She's been running without a bridle for too long."

"Elizabeth cannot harm us. She chooses to remain human. Vulnerable."

"I remember. She is weaker than us, and I like her that way. Don't change her, Falke!"

"Elizabeth believes that she is my wife. As I say, so will she do."

"And I?" Hanna lowered her mouth to Falke's throat, above the largest pounding artery. Her tongue licked her eyeteeth's razor-edged points; tasted her own blood. Her jaw muscle twitched open. "Do you think I'll do what you say?"

"If you would want to live more than a few hungry nights, Hanna, you will do exactly as I tell you to. Without puling."

Before Hanna could rip into Falke's throat, swift hands brought her head level with his face. She saw no rage in his expression. His gaze was steady.

"You are slow and stupid yet," Falke said. "Do not draw me out until you are stronger."

"Let me go!" Enraged, Hanna struggled against his implacable hands.

"Do you hear, mistress?"

Hanna jerked her head convulsively in assent. The ferocious pressure against her skull eased. Trembling, Hanna unleashed the braid that held her hair, allowing waves of glossy hair to cover Falke's eyes.

"I'll consider it," Hanna said. "But I want something in return."

"You want more than your life?" Falke moved his hands to the back of his head. "What is it that you want?"

47

Hanna smoothed tendrils of red hair away from his watchful eyes. His lips were cold as iron. She kissed them and licked the tip of his nose. "It can't be allowed, your having a frail wife."

Falke remained silent beneath her—a waiting pool of water. Hanna smiled and slipped a hand under his sweater, massaged the hard muscles of his stomach and chest, flicked his stiff nipples with a fingernail.

"Elizabeth won't always be valuable to you," she said. "Promise me that."

"You do not understand memory, Hanna." Falke rested his palm over her heart. "It gives when it can. We must wait for Elizabeth, and we must see what she has learned."

The tide of moonlight flared on Falke's cheek. The sudden pain of its reflected light cleared Hanna's mind. Her hunger was forgotten.

"I understand love, Falke."

Grasping his head between her palms, Hanna lifted him to her throat. Falke twisted her hair in his fingers. Hanna laughed and squirmed against his rough clothes, pulled his frozen hands to her breasts. A bolt of pain shivered throughout her body as Falke's canines slashed across her nipples. Blood misted like black water in the moonlight, dotting the walls. Flames raged in her chest, rising, as Falke licked the deep gash across her breasts and drank.

Hanna's vision cleared, and she looked toward the mirror at the far end of the empty classroom. Inside, glass knives swirled in a growing, tinkling tornado.

"Elizabeth isn't like us, Falke. For that, I'll kill her."

Make her into a true vampire, Hanna promised herself. To keep.

To cherish.

Ten

"Hanna?"

Elizabeth gathered her skirt around her thighs and sat on her coat, which she had spread out between the glistening rails of the track. Silver-blond hair settled comfortably in curls around her numb shoulders, luminous under a staring moon that punctured the western night sky. Razors of moonlight cut into her eyes, even with the protection of her mirrored sunglasses. She shaded her eyes and tried to pick out the Pleiades. The hairs on her arm flattened under the blazing light. Her skin tightened as the moisture evaporated off her body.

The moon washes everything away, Elizabeth thought sadly. And its heat was becoming hateful. She could see none of the friendly constellations; only a stinging cloud of needles descended onto her head. Even her light cotton dress, made with her own hands, crinkled woefully, its colors fading under the falling sky. Soon, she would have to leave the train yard and find shelter before the sun itself rose above the Sandia Mountains. She sighed.

"Sun, sun, go away. I can't see you anyway."

Elizabeth pulled her fist from sand, clenched it tight. If I squeezed hard enough, could I make glass? The grains cut into her flesh, marking out tiny graves in her palm. When she threw the grains into the air, new stars fluttered around her, tinkling onto the railroad tracks, ringing like glass bells. The sparkling lights of the city might sound the same if she could hear them; they, too, were disturbed and trembled nervously.

Elizabeth waited. The railroad yard wavered with rippling shadows. Suddenly, a tall woman with hair the color of autumn leaves emerged from under a concrete overpass. Bare, white legs scissored in the moonlight. Her short leather dress gleamed like black iron. Elizabeth remembered lifting Hanna to her breast and holding her slashed wrist patiently above a slack mouth, allowing a trickle of rose-dark blood to fall between pale lips. She wondered if Hanna remembered those nights as well. The silence between them would have continued till dawn if Elizabeth had not spoken.

"I know a better place we can talk."

"It's been a long time," Elizabeth said, lowering her eyes. "The years have not changed you."

Hanna said nothing, merely gazed. Up close, her hair was a languid sheet filled with coppery reds and darkening golds. Her skin seemed powdered with frost, like snow under a winter moon. Green eyes glittered from shadowed sockets. She smiled and walked to the edge of the hotel's high roof, her muscles rolling as smoothly under the leather dress as if it were her own skin. When she looked down, tendrils of her hair were lifted by crossing winds.

"Why this place?" Hanna's voice was almost lost in the murmur of traffic far below.

"The view is pretty," Elizabeth said. Illuminated by moonlight, the Sandias loomed over the city.

"There are so many lights!" Hanna laughed. "Are there as many people?"

Elizabeth leaned over the edge. Streets ran like rivers of fire, and the surrounding office buildings basked in their flame. "There are many, many more."

Hanna's long eyelashes trembled like eager black knives. "I feel I've come to paradise."

Elizabeth shook her head. "You haven't."

"You're just bored with it, sister. So many years in the same place! Why didn't you move on?"

"I waited for you and Falke to awaken. I kept myself near, to make sure you were safe."

She felt Hanna's prolonged stare and let her thoughts drift casually so that nothing could be gleaned from them. Cold fingers caressed her chin.

"You're looking well, sister," Hanna said. "I remember a little girl hiding behind Falke's coat. Now, a woman stares at me with solemn, beautiful eyes."

Elizabeth pulled herself from Hanna's touch, backing away until her hip nudged the cement wall. "You're a flatterer, Hanna. I remember a girl who bewitched my husband with searing eyes; a girl who didn't care."

"No one bewitches Falke."

"Have you seen him, then?"

Hanna shrugged. "Things are so vague. My memory darts here and there. I can't say truthfully whether I've seen him or not."

Elizabeth glimpsed the truth in Hanna's mocking eyes. "You have! Don't lie."

Hanna looked away, unsure and transparent. She cradled her breasts as if fragments of her, one at a time, might be carried off by the wind. Elizabeth believed she could easily slip into Hanna's mind, sift through what was there. She felt no superiority, only patience.

"What did Falke talk about?" Elizabeth felt her own breasts, comparing them, in memory, to Emma's. How pillowy and warm hers had been. Mine are just cold, lifeless, and empty.

"Men can't talk. All they can do is fuck." Hanna shook her head and smiled suddenly. "Falke is lost in his head. He talks of enemies and love."

"What love?"

Hanna's face became stone. "You, I suppose."

"Not me. He hasn't come to see me yet."

"Death, then."

"Death? I don't understand."

"He's courting her, Elizabeth." Hanna's eyes flashed like swords. "The warrior king kissing his Queen's frozen hand! If he's not careful, she'll strike him down ruthlessly, without mercy." Hanna looked away to the electric fires flickering against the mountains. Her voice became sad. "That's how she is."

Elizabeth drew away from Hanna, preparing herself for an attack. She gathered her senses, concentrated them into Hanna's mind, and searched with mental fingers. At that moment, Hanna whirled excitedly, her face lit up like a child's.

"I felt you, Elizabeth! You touched me! Do you think I'm healing, too?"

"You weren't injured as Falke was." Elizabeth retreated a step. "Why should you require healing?"

Hanna shook her head, puzzled. "I know I've spent many years sleeping, attached to Falke in some way. Dead. I feared my strength might have left me."

Elizabeth pushed down terrifying images. "Falke's body was almost destroyed. I couldn't wake you, Hanna. I tried and tried. I thought you were ill."

"For a hundred and ten years?" Hanna giggled. "And with what, sister, typhoid?"

"Don't joke! I still don't know what happened."

Hanna stepped back until she was in shadow, a dark slender form against the orange, polluted glow above the city.

"Let me touch you," Hanna whispered. "As a test of my strength. Will you let me?"

Elizabeth tensed her muscles.

"Be honest, Elizabeth, about what you feel."

Silence stretched around her. Then an icy fog entered Elizabeth's mind, creeping inside her thoughts, paralyzing them with frozen breath. Her soul became centered on the sinuous alien stream. Mesmerized. The fog hardened and began battering against her mind's protective walls. Her brain split open, her memories escaped out of their cracking shell, beating like moth's wings. Voices of the dead shouted, raged, wept. Vibrant colors rippled like silk under a taut wind. Across a dome of blue-silver sky, a black hole opened, a widening greedy mouth.

"Get out!"

Hanna's mind poured into Elizabeth without hesitation. Electrified fingers scurried down her spine, into her arms and hands. Stunned, Elizabeth could not fight back. Her weakening legs threatened to collapse. She was held upright only by the invading presence within her.

"Stop!" Elizabeth screamed.

As quickly as it had captured her, the fog departed. A frozen finger caressed her heart. Powerful hands gripped her shoulders. Elizabeth looked up to see eager eyes in gaping sockets.

"I'd never hurt you, Elizabeth," Hanna whispered. "I remember how you . . . suckled me. Kept me from death."

Elizabeth struggled against clenching hands.

"Shh. Calm, or you'll hurt yourself." Hanna's white face hovered closer, cruel lips grinning. She smelled of bitter, rotting leaves. "Elizabeth, I'll let you go only when you stop struggling against me."

Elizabeth took deep breaths, felt the cold air soothing her lungs and muscles. Even the moonlight helped—its needle points on her skin a reminder that her body was her own. She had lived without any real threat for so long, she had not recognized it until too late. Hanna had caught her off guard. Elizabeth relaxed and silently thanked Hanna for the grim lesson.

"Let me go." Elizabeth imagined fresh walls of defense rising inside her mind. Bits of Hanna's invading fog twitched hungrily inside her, but Elizabeth killed them easily.

"I've learned a lot since we were last together, Hanna." Elizabeth watched the vampire warily. "Don't come into me again."

Hanna drew back to the edge of the hotel roof and smiled, revealing savage eyeteeth. Her hair blew out in a fan around her head.

"Perhaps you might share some of your wisdom with us."

"Us?" Elizabeth asked shakily. "Do you mean Falke and you?"

The moonlit air around Hanna darkened. A swirling cloud of black motes erupted from her skin, like flies boiling in a carcass. Elizabeth choked on a rank, spoiled stench as Hanna's form elongated and curled into the night sky.

"Tell me!" Elizabeth shouted. She forced herself into movement. Too late. Her hand clenched at empty air.

Hanna had vanished.

Eleven

Michael opened his eyes, startled from a dream. He didn't move. He wasn't sure what had awakened him, and he didn't want to frighten it if there was something dangerous close by. Glow-in-the-dark numbers on his wind-up clock said 5:10. At first, everything was dark. Then, slowly, he could discern the round outlines of the clock and the wooden table by his bed.

He looked up and saw a window-square of purple dawn. A star twinkled in the featureless sky.

He had been dreaming of a tumble-down bar beside ancient Highway 66, the broken asphalt track a mile south of his sheepcamp. Long ago, this bar had served strong drink: mescal, tequila, and smelly, cheap rye. It had been a watering hole for burnt sheepherders, wandering ranch hands, lost city women and men, despairing old folks. A two-room adobe shack surrounded by lonely desert, the bar had been built many winters before the construction of I-40.

After receiving news of his younger brother's fall in Korea, and later, during the wake over Benjamin's wrecked body, Michael had found the bar a suitable mourning place. A church to pray and think in, more silent and more intimately human than the wide desert flats or the valleys of juniper and piñon below Madrecita, the Keresan village where his wife's family lived. On the hard-packed dirt floor, he had drunk alone and danced with other sad shadows through dusty nights and windy days, finally reaching a frozen place where his brother's pinched face vanished into the rough adobe wall.

One morning his wife and her brother had come for him, lifted him silently into their creaking pickup with the bundle of hawk feathers and sage brush hanging from its rearview mirror, and carted him to Margaret's blue house under stands of drooping apricot trees.

His Keresan in-laws endured his mourning time for their daughter's sake. Margaret found friends to care for the sheep, to help with the chores. All of her family, in the Indian way, left him alone to find his lost heart. Soon, the changing seasons healed him, and Benjamin's face became clear only in colorless pictures.

Michael lay the quilts aside. In his dream, Nanibaa' had asked him to be thankful for the Walk in Beauty that Benjamin had provided with his death. She had been sitting in her hogan, in the middle of its circular dirt floor, spinning tufts of dirty wool into four trembling strands of white, yellow, blue, and black yarn, urging him in her scolding voice to remember happiness and love, as the lines of yarn floated out the doorway.

54   Strange dreams he had been having lately.

He recalled how, thirty years ago, a Navajo boy named Square Hat had painted the image of a Navajo rug outside the bar's entrance. Michael saw the stark, zigzagged lines and blocky pyramids in brilliant reds, deep greens, and shiny blacks glowing off that painting in the desert waste. The boy had died of a burst appendix soon after. The bar had become known as the Navajo Rug. Now, sixteen years later, the shack was a pile of rock and broken adobe next to old 66. Only one section of wall was left standing, and it kept Square Hat's faded painting.

He heard snuffling at the other side of the room. A badger attacking his grandchild's cereal boxes? Maybe a bobcat sniffing at his water pail? They were the two creatures most able to unlatch his screen door. Michael rose onto one elbow. The room breathed cold air on him, and it was thick with shadows. Something moved stealthily in the far corner and whined softly.

"*Ya'at'eeh*," Michael said, giving greeting in Navajo.

A shadow moved over the floor. A doglike shape.

"Lee?"

The animal padded to the center of the room and lifted its head. Its eyes were yellow circles.

Not Lee. A smaller creature.

Ma'ii. A coyote.

Nanibaa' once told Michael that if a coyote were to cross his path, he was to pray at once. Coyotes were bad; a warning of coming danger. Not as bad as a nearby lightning strike, but bad enough.

Michael didn't feel like praying. He had always admired the coyotes' tenacity and intelligence. They were beautiful creatures. And he had taught his daughter and granddaughter to see them in the same way. Michael whistled softly as if Lee were standing in the middle of his home and not this wild creature. The coyote wagged its tail. Its large, furry ears perked up, listening. Then it turned and trotted to the blank wall by the stove and vanished like smoke on a wintry day.

Michael lay in the silence. Outside, Lee barked and scratched at the screen door.

"*Shimá sání*, my grandmother," he said to the empty room. "I'm glad you didn't see that."

Twelve

Diana got off to a late start.

Bright afternoon sunlight glared through the windshield and burned onto her lap as she left Albuquerque. She had the heater on and her window open. All the glass was clean. The gas tank was full. The highway rumbled happily underneath her feet.

Early this morning, while waiting for the coffee water to boil, sleepily holding her bandaged palm over the water and feeling a spreading spot of warmth, Diana had decided to find Melissa's grandfather. She remembered from the map that the road to his house was mostly dirt track. But even the threat of snow couldn't dampen the eager decision that had taken shape after she had found the pool of blood in Melissa's kitchen, a decision that had crystallized during her conversation with Roger. Maybe she couldn't stop her nightmares from killing her sleep, but she could try to find out what was going on with Melissa.

The land was typical New Mexico landscape: A surprise lurked behind every hill. She imagined herself driving through Texas cowlands, Nevada flats, Wyoming or Montana badlands, and lunar landscape, all in the same journey. Diana checked the odometer against the map's instructions and slowed. Thirty-eight miles from Albuquerque. The area could have doubled as Mars in a cheap sci-fi movie, complete with purple and orange mesas, black volcanic cones, and flat valleys of red sand.

Diana found the turnoff and pulled over onto a slender dirt road. Dust billowed away in a massive cloud. Large trucks rumbled on the freeway behind her. She got out and surveyed the area, glad she had worn jeans, tennis shoes, and a thick sweater. The map indicated that the old guy's house was on the south side of I-40 and that this snaky dirt track paralleled and then went under the interstate at some point further west. To the north, a half-mile away over bleak grassland, was a large, red mesa that stretched from horizon to horizon. Westward, maybe fifteen miles away, rose a single blue mountain.

Snow iced the top, making it look like an exotic dessert. All that was missing was the cherry.

Diana shivered and crossed her arms, wondering if she had any right to be here. The sky was clouded over with a gray ceiling that lowered peacefully onto her head.

Snow would arrive sometime soon. Diana got back into her car and guided it onto the deeply rutted track. Brush grass swished along the car's underbody. Something hard banged almost under her feet. Her empty coffee mug wobbled off the dash and thumped onto the carpet. She looked into the side mirror and saw her dust cloud funneling into the air.

"Mole, can we make this?"

The car, a willing aide if not very quick, plunged onward.

One Tuesday morning a million years ago, Roger had taken her car-shopping. "We'll start small," he had said. Diana, chased by monsters, had been weepy that day and had wanted a car to huddle in; anything, as long as it was fast. Roger had just started working graveyard for the Albuquerque Police Department then, and his weekend had been in the middle of the week. A boil which had burst into some pretty wild arguments.

"Why can't you change jobs, honey, or change your schedule to something that fits with mine. Can't you work days at least? I hate it that you work weekends. It's too dangerous. Imagine a real Friday to Sunday weekend. All our friends are off. Your friends go fishing then and you're missing it. You know how you love to fish . . ."

And on and on.

That had been her. Walking past teenage couples embracing before an hour-long class as if it were the final kiss of their lives, Diana had overheard many nagging phrases of gold. Innocent, at first. Diana still couldn't believe how clingy and scared she had been, as Roger had left her every evening for work.

"Girl, you had a perfect right to say those things," Diana still told herself, since no one else was likely to; although Katy had tried. "If Roger hadn't been so hard-up to be such a hotshit cop, our marriage might've worked out."

Roger eventually made detective, and now he had a beautiful home, a darling baby son, and a different wife.

A deafening, blaring horn jerked Diana from spoiled memories. She screamed, convulsively hit the brakes. A train engine blocked the sun and thundered by just ten feet from her car. An unearthly cold descended. Freight cars loomed, rattled, clanked endlessly, throwing long spikes of sunlight across her dusty windshield. The Mole shuddered and stalled.

After the train passed, silence. Diana slid her hands from her face, coughed primly, spoke to the dust:

"What would Roger think of my weekends now?"

Twenty-five minutes later, Diana pulled in next to a small rock house on a bare hill surrounded by a sea of yellow brush. She turned off the ignition. A wire hummed from a single line of electricity poles. The place seemed deserted. In front of the house was a fenced garden with nothing growing in it except one lone tree. Diana sat in her car and rolled down the window. Moist air leaked in.

She checked her watch: 3:20. She got out of the car, reached back in for her purse. The ground was rocky. The engine gurgled, resting after its groaning complaints on the dirt track. The Mole had scraped bottom several times. She wondered if there was any permanent damage. She cared only enough to hope that she wasn't going to be stuck out here.

Diana walked around to the east side of the house. Her cheeks were tight with cold. She opened the screen door, which squealed. The main door was a faded blue, and its miniscule window was covered in dust. Diana knocked and waited.

A memory of Grandma Patsy's own kitchen door, which had opened into her back garden, came to Diana. She reached up to one of the battered steel gutters poking from the roof. Whoever had built this house wasn't very tall. The roof was well within reach, and she wasn't tall herself. Diana felt a key hiding in the gutter, which had been bent upward slightly so the key wouldn't fall out. It was a brass key made for a padlock. Diana looked at the door again and saw a padlock hanging where she hadn't noticed one before.

Better wake up, Logan, if you want to get home in one piece.

Diana replaced the key in its hiding place and shut the screen door gently. Already the isolation and the peculiar silence was beginning to disturb her. If the old guy wasn't here, he wasn't here, she told herself. He's probably gone to

Albuquerque for the weekend. To visit family. Or maybe just to see people.

A mile to the north stretched I-40, set against the barren desert and the massive red mesa. It was odd, but the freeway with its relaxing drone of cars and trucks seemed to be a natural part of the landscape.

Diana wandered back to the car, imagining how easily it would be to remain here untouched by the outside world — and not care. Before opening the car door, she noticed a large corral about a hundred yards southeast of her. She glanced at her watch, then evaluated the sky. Slanted sunlight traced webs between the clouds. An hour, at least, of remaining day. She detoured to the corral.

The pungent smell of sheep hit her before she was halfway there, years and years of settled existence. Birds flitted and scolded between railroad-tie posts. Basketball-sized nests hung under the eaves of a metal roof, which sheltered stacked bundles of hay. She considered her own silent apartment.

Things are more alive here, she decided. I'll wait.

Thirteen

A mile from home, Michael leaned on his walking stick and watched three army helicopters flying slowly overhead. They looked like the tadpoles that sprang to life in rain pools after the spring and summer showers. The largest of the pools might remain the whole summer, natural mirrors dotting sandstone formations or the ridgetops along the mesas, reflecting the sky, as if a Holy One had carefully laid them out that way.

The tadpoles began breaking the surface quickly, sucking air desperately, maybe realizing how short a time they had to live. As his sheep grazed, Michael would crouch and follow

59

the tadpoles' darting movements in the green water, wondering how all those babies could exist in the middle of a dry and sandy nowhere. Living quickly, never knowing when their world was going to dry up, maybe not even realizing at all that their world was doomed, made Michael anxious for the little creatures.

The monotonous slapping of the helicopter blades faded, at times coming back louder as the sound was carried by a southerly breeze. He dug inside his shirt pocket for the container of colored gum. Around him, juniper trees sighed in the renewed silence. His toes rubbed against sand in his boots.

Michael remembered coming home to Madrecita one day, after watering his father-in-law's sheep near a sandstone bluff called the Bread Loaf, fourteen miles east of the village. *Ayaah'ah*, he thought, nearly forty or so years back. Margaret had been a young mother then, just a girl, with long black hair swinging past the small of her back, whipping up a dust storm as she beat Navajo rugs and blankets on her mother's clothesline. Dusty herself and out of temper, too, Margaret had scolded him furiously for standing useless and smiling like a good-for-nothing lizard.

They had met at a Keresan Corn Dance in Madrecita in 1937. In the plaza under wispy clouds, Margaret had danced solemnly, her luminous, dark eyes tensely concentrating on the pattern of her steps. Turning too quickly among the other Keresan girls, she spun gracefully, her plain cotton skirts stirring the yellow dust and Michael's heart. He had imagined he could hear the tiny bells on Margaret's buckskin boots ringing along the dry earth, jingling above the thudding drums and the high wailing of the singers. Maybe that's what had drawn his attention at the very beginning, since she was so tiny and almost lost among the dancers and wandering children—Margaret's ringing steps. He had followed the unique dance circle she wove, making sure he would be the first man she saw when her dance ended and she finally looked up.

The desert silence began to make his ears ring. The sheep murmured lazily. The cowbell on the big wether bonged sadly against the wood trough as he dipped his head to drink. Michael couldn't see the rest of the herd, which was below a sandy slope to his right. He stood on a table of sandstone, feeling the pain in his joints slip away as the heat from the late afternoon sun massaged them. The flavor of the candy gum receded; everything seemed to be moving away from him.

A nagging worry ached in the pit of his soul, and he reckoned it was due to the strange coyote nosing around his home that morning. To the north, across hidden I-40, loomed Mesa Gigante, its sheer face blood red in the fading daylight. Dark triangular patches corrupted the red rock like the fossil shark teeth he sometimes found. The sky above the ridge was thick with growing cloud cover.

The spiritual aspect of the mesa had always been frightening to him. Nanibaa' used to warn him to stay off its plateau. In her scolding voice, she would tell him there were witches and skinwalkers that lived and ran up there, and if he had business at the mesa's feet, to carry his rifle and to keep his tiny buckskin bag of corn pollen tied around his neck.

Of course, Michael had gone up the plateau many times to water his sheep or to find them grass. But her words had harried him all the same, agitating him when he was up there. Maybe what bothered him the most was that the miles-long plateau seemed to be empty of life. Even in the flush of spring, no magpies or bluejays ever chittered in the juniper and piñon tops, no running jack rabbits or cottontails ever flashed their white ass-tufts at him in contempt. And these were all creatures abundant everywhere else on the land. Even the trees themselves seemed unfriendly and watchful, angrily waiting for him to make an insult.

Goosepimples peppered his skin as he remembered his vivid dreams, nightmares that had forced him from his bed into a darkness extending for many miles. His meeting with the coyote seemed to be a waking acknowledgment of his bad dreams or a warning of some kind. But it was odd that he should feel afraid of a coyote. Over the years, a good many reservation creatures had wandered into his rock house, drawn by the scent of Margaret's coffee or by the good company. Some of them, like the fat badger Melissa had called Mosi, had even been regular houseguests. Michael was used to the constant visits, even welcomed them.

What was frightening, he decided, about his coyote vision was that the coyote had spoken to him, with clear words, but Michael had not understood what it was saying. He scraped his boots on the rock, wanting to sit down, knowing that if he did, his joints would swell up and keep him from returning home. Nanibaa', sitting comfortably in a purple velveteen blouse, a necklace made up of turquoise and quarters, a calico skirt, and pink tennis shoes, would have said the coyote was a messenger bearing bad news, that Michael should protect himself with a sing and a purification ceremony. He remembered night falling over her snug hogan and thought how, a long time ago, he might have been frightened enough by her words to take the advice.

However, he had set all the Navajo curing chants aside after Nanibaa' had died from cancer. Nothing, now, could have gotten him to a sing even if not showing meant life or death for him. He had thought Nanibaa' the most powerful human being alive. Her presence was enough to drive away all of his childhood's most terrifying monsters. Seeing her pray every morning in her strong voice, singing in the east-facing doorway of her hogan, hair gray as iron, Michael had believed completely in her medicines and chants—in her Beauty Way. He had felt the power of them echoing in his soul.

Then the cancer had struck her down, eating away her body until she became a fleshy bundle of skin wrapped over sticklike bones. Your grandma is dying from a witch's chant, his relatives had whispered. Nanibaa' knows who it is but she won't tell us. After Nanibaa's death, he had flung away his charred prayer sticks, eagle feathers, and bits of dried sage over the snowy edge of Canyon de Chelly.

Nanibaa' had been buried quickly and quietly . . . and forgotten. Michael's faith had followed her.

He would never return to the old ways, to the ancient ways of his people. Some Navajos would say he had forsaken his Beauty Way and would shun him. He did not care. In his heart, there was nothing beautiful about the Navajo medicine anymore. It was a dark and fierce power, powerful and frightening, something that should have never been born. He believed in its potency, but that part in which he had trusted, the beauty of it, had spoiled.

Michael rubbed at his chest with the flat of his hand. Still, after so many years, he could not heal his rage. Slow minutes passed. He began to hear the consoling hum of the traffic on I-40. Anguish had returned to his heart, writhing there like a ball of rattlesnakes settled in the corner of his house. All the people he had loved had vanished too quickly from his life. He had buried their restless corpses with stones in his heart. And now they had all come back, slipping into his thoughts and dreams.

Michael's hitched breathing subsided. He took several shuddering breaths and saw the sun sinking fast into a pile of thickening, red clouds. He realized he would not be home until after dark.

Never, if I'm going to stand in the dirt feeling sorry for myself, he thought irritably. He brushed the sand from his jeans. Fear weighed down his heart. He was afraid of the coming night again, as he used to be when he was a baby under his grandmother's wing. He whistled for Lee. The big collie bounded out from under a juniper's twisted trunk and loped towards Michael. Slowing with age, too. Michael patted the dog's stout back.

"Gather up the herd. Take us home."

Lee barked as he rousted the sheep, teasing the complaining rams, nipping at their legs, bouncing among the herd like a child.

At least I'm not truly alone, Michael thought, caught up in Lee's race toward home. He felt a powerful urge to visit Sarah, his only child, and his granddaughter, Melissa—the clever one. He needed to give Melissa her Navajo name, before it died with him. There was no hurry, he told himself. His family was not all dead and neither was he.

He remembered Nanibaa' spinning clumps of bulky sheep's wool into thin, tough strands for her blankets. She would hum quietly, and it seemed to Michael that it was her song creating the yarn under her tough, brown fingers. He had watched and listened and tried to commit all of her song to memory, knowing that she was telling him the story of the People's first journeys, their departures from the four separate holy worlds to this one, the fifth world where Changing Woman had given birth to twin sons: Child of the Water and Monster Slayer.

Red drained from the sky, and night covered him. Lee searched the darkness for predators and stray lambs. Michael sung snatches of his grandmother's song, deciphering the words and remembering their meaning, so that he could give the complete song to Melissa, for her unborn children.

Fourteen

When Diana woke up, dark hung outside her car windows, coal black. No stars or planets or anything.

"Jesus," she said out loud. The windows of the stone house were unlit. She opened the door and stood outside, shivering miserably. The sky was gray-black and heavy with snow. She hugged herself against a rising wind.

"Sleeping! How could I be so stupid?"

She heard a sharp whistle and a collie's distinctive bark. Dull sheep bells clanged.

"Thank you, God," she whispered, pulling her coat around her shoulders. She staggered from her car, then stopped when she remembered the rocky terrain. Far to the east, an orange glow rested on the horizon. The snow clouds had settled onto Albuquerque to roost.

Melissa's grandfather must have returned. Diana walked carefully down the slope. As her eyes grew accustomed to the dark, she realized she could see pretty well. A group of bleating sheep drifted toward the corral. An old man carrying a walking stick herded them between the gates.

But not so old, she thought as she approached him. He must be about sixty. Or fifty? A beautiful collie with a thick glowing coat bounded up to her, barking amicably, wagging its whole bottom like a puppy. She saw white hair mingled with black on the tip of his muzzle.

"You're just an old puppy, aren't you?" Diana ruffled the collie's neck. Then she straightened and faced the man. His gray hair was cropped very short and his face was hard and spare like the mesas she had seen during her journey here.

His eyes were shadowed, so she was not sure if he was glad to have a visitor or if he was angry at the intrusion. He wore faded jeans and scuffed hiking boots. A denim jacket covered his plaid shirt, its colors only black squares in the gathering darkness. Diana guessed he wore long johns under his clothes; her own grandfather used to, though he had lived in a heated four-bedroom house in Brigham City and not in the middle of a high desert in October like this guy.

Then he smiled at her, his white teeth reminding her so much of her grandfather's own false teeth that she felt a warm, nostalgic rush.

"Hi. Mr. Roanhorse? My name is Diana Logan." Her offered hand was held gently by his warm calloused one, then let go. "I'm your granddaughter's English teacher from Lincoln High School. In Albuquerque."

The man nodded. "Let me corral the sheep. The key is in the roof gutter. Go inside the house and warm up. There's coffee above the stove."

Without waiting for an answer, he turned and made his way back to the corral. The collie ran ahead of him, barking at the sheep, keeping them in line.

Diana watched his retreating back for a moment, then began walking back to the house.

Warm up? The house was freezing inside, almost colder than it was outside. Diana shivered as she stood in the main room, which was lit by a fluorescent ring in the middle of the ceiling. The space reminded her of a boxcar's narrow interior, but the ceiling was low. In the farthest corner a brass bed was heaped with colorful quilts and blankets. An old, stubby refrigerator was at its foot. Next to her was a long wooden table with a red-and-white checkered tablecloth, on which a tented white cloth partially covered utensils and various condiments. The screen door slapped shut behind her.

She opened the oven door of the old-fashioned stove. The interior was empty and clean. On the floor nearby were wood chips and logs in a cardboard box. Diana smelled fresh piñon. Above the stove was a shelf which held a tin can, a spiral seashell, a tiny Dutch figurine, and other odd knickknacks, all tidily arranged and covered with a fine layer of dust.

Maybe the old guy wants me to build a fire.

Diana lifted up a ring on the stove, took a log and a cutting of newspaper from the box, and stuffed them into the gap. She saw no matches. A window at her left looked out onto her car's shining hood. A tall cabinet stood next to the window. She searched its drawers and cupboard for matches, and noticed there was no sink or faucets anywhere. A large pail with a dish for a cover and a ladle was set on the cabinet. Diana removed the dish and sniffed. The water smelled sweet.

"Darn matches," she muttered, replacing the dish. She went back to the stove, searched the shelf again, found worn pumice stones, two rusting railroad spikes, and a box of dog treats. No matches. She saw a gray dutch oven sitting on the stove's back ring, lifted the heavy lid and found matches, a thin leather wallet, and round gold-rimmed bifocals hidden inside.

Her snooping had warmed her up. Diana unbuttoned her jacket, then lit a match against the stovetop and put the flame under the newspaper. Soon, she had a fire going. The screen door screeched behind her. She turned at the crackle of paper and the sound of dried dog food being scattered in a tin plate. The dog whined and pressed his nose against the screen door.

"Wait, Lee." The man opened the door with his knee and placed a hubcap filled with food on the ground.

Lee? Diana smiled. Where had that name come from? She thrust two more logs into the stove opening as the old man poured water into a pan. She saw him begin to roll up his sleeves. Diana turned back to the stove to give him privacy.

The wood fire cracked mutedly, a comforting sound. The man came to the stove and moved a large coffee pot off to one side where it would stay warm, yet not boil.

"I went ahead and built a fire," she said. "I hope you don't mind."

"You're Melissa's teacher?" He opened the cupboard and chose several cups, which he inspected and replaced. He set two tin mugs on the table. From the refrigerator he brought out a can of condensed milk.

"I'm not Melissa's only teacher," Diana said. "She has four others who teach different subjects."

"Five teachers?" The old man returned to the stove and carried the pot to the table. He poured steaming coffee into both cups. "Why so many?"

"It's the way the school system works." Diana thought of all the reasons why, but decided not to bore either of them. She adjusted herself carefully on the wooden bench, so as not to get any splinters in her butt.

The man looked puzzled. "Is Melissa doing her work?"

The hot mug felt good to her frozen fingers. Steam rose and warmed her chin. "She's a very good student, Mr. Roanhorse. She always does her work and she does it well. You should be proud."

"I'm glad to hear that." The man went to the side of the table next to the doorway and sat on a small stool, holding his mug with both hands.

Diana was unprepared for all of this. Everything indicated the loneliest existence she could imagine. The man was obviously not used to talking with people, yet his English was good and seemed to come easily to him. There was a trace of an accent, but nothing specific. She wondered how his own language sounded.

"Mr. Roanhorse, I've never been to this part of New Mexico before. Do you mind my asking how long you've lived here?"

"Since I was married." His eyes were black under his brows, except for a tiny shimmer every now and then.

"And your wife?" Diana asked.

"My wife died several years ago. I live alone now."

Diana wanted to snap her fingers. Of course! All this time, she had been expecting someone else to arrive. She began to dread her long drive back to her own empty home.

"Mr. Roanhorse, I'll be honest with you. Your granddaughter is in serious trouble at school. She attacked several teachers, putting one of them in the hospital. The police are out looking for her. No one can find her. And no one has been able to contact her mother. I came here to see if . . . if you might know where she is."

The old man gazed steadily at her, expressionless. Diana recalled other Indians she had talked to. Remarkably, she'd never had any in her own classes, until Melissa. What she remembered about them was that none of them had ever looked directly at her. She had made an extra effort to be friendly, but they had not looked at her at all. She had then read how Navajos especially are taught not to look at a person straight in the eye. To them, the book had said, it was extremely impolite.

Now, Diana sat drinking coffee with a man whom she knew, from Melissa's file, to be Navajo, staring at her as if he were trying to bore a hole through her skull. She realized that Melissa had the same piercing gaze as her grandfather.

"Did she attack you?" he asked.

Diana took a sip from her tin cup. The coffee was very strong and would keep her up all night and the next day if she was not careful. Almost savagely, she rubbed the sore bump on her forehead.

"Yes, Mr. Roanhorse. She did."

"Are you with the police?"

Diana looked straight in his eyes. "No, I'm not. I'm worried about Melissa. I want to make sure she's all right."

The man took a long swallow from his cup. "You haven't been able to reach her mother." It was a statement, not a question. He set his cup down.

"I went to their apartment. I found blood on the kitchen floor and neither of them were there. And . . . I found a little cross on a silver necklace. I don't want to frighten you, Mr. Roanhorse, by saying this, but I'm really worried."

Jesus! I'm becoming frightened enough for the both of us. Say something, old man!

"Where is this necklace?"

"The police have it. They kept it. I can try and get it back for you."

"That was Sarah's cross. Her mother gave it to Sarah when she was just a baby." The man pushed his stool back and stood. "We must find Melissa," he said. "Maybe she can tell us where her mother is. I will go with you back to Albuquerque."

"Wait a minute!" Diana stood and grasped his arm. She pulled her hand back quickly. "I'm sorry."

"You want to help. The police can't find her." The man said a word she did not understand. "My granddaughter and my daughter are missing."

"But Mr. Roanhorse, you don't . . ."

"You made a long journey here to find me; you may call me Michael. Do the police know you came here?"

"No." Diana tried to think. "No."

"We'll find the two women. You are worried for them. Now, I'm worried with you. We'll help each other. We'll search until we find them."

"It might take a long time." Diana couldn't stop herself from saying that. "What about your sheep?"

The tiled floor groaned under his boots. He took an ancient bag from under the bed and shook off the dust and spiders.

"*Ayaah'ah,* go," he said irritably to the spiders, dribbling them onto the floor. "I'll talk to my neighbors over the hill. They will take care of the sheep for me."

Diana stood by and watched his preparations to leave. There was nothing she could think of to say to stop him. She couldn't think of a reason why she should try, either. At least her own journey home wouldn't be so lonely. She felt some comfort in that.

"What about Lee?" Diana put the cups on a dishrack, lifted the cotton cloth over the utensils in a jar on the table, then returned the milk to the refrigerator. Melissa's grandfather folded a shirt and placed it carefully in his bag. From under his pillow, he lifted a tiny bundle on a string, looped it around his neck, and dropped it into his shirt. Oddly, Diana was reminded of the turquoise cross she had found in Melissa's apartment.

"Lee will stay with the sheep until I get back," he said.

Diana nodded in answer. What else could she say?

Diana watched the old man trudging up a bare hill west of his stone house. She had offered to drive him, but he had refused. The road was too rocky for her little car, he had said. The bigger rocks might puncture a tire. Lee trotted next to him, a bouncing white blob.

The land's presence deepened around her. I-40's hushed sighing made her feel uncertain about taking the sheepherder into the city. Further northwest, above the hill, she saw a huge black hole tucked into the corner of the sky. Above her, several stars peeked behind racing clouds and vanished quickly. The old guy better hurry, she thought. He probably knows more about snow than I ever will. But he was so old! She glanced to the bare hill he had been ascending a few minutes ago, thinking about brittle bones easily broken by the most innocent of falls.

69

She could not see him.

Was she crazy? To let an old man run around in the dark and climb a hill by himself? She left her car and stared intently along the slopes, trying to see him, fear making her throat dry.

Then Lee barked loudly, as if to reassure her—from the other side of the hill. Diana recognized a happy bark when she heard one. She could not find the sheepherder because he had already topped the hill and descended to the other side.

Fifteen

The first snow of the year, Elizabeth thought, as she gazed at the peculiar orange snowflakes, glowing, as if a great fire were burning somewhere in the city. The clouds were bloated with moisture. Wind in her face, she tried to fathom its direction. She followed tentative drafts with her mind, imagining them as the gentle tugs and pulls of a restless ocean. The thought of so much floating water was painful. She wished it would all turn to ice.

"Elizabeth." Falke spoke from the shadows of the houses around her. She began to walk, following no conscious path, feeling exposed and wishing she were in her room, her burrow, unseen and asleep. Her passage had been secretive, but her troubled mind had created ripples that only a vampire could see. And Falke, her husband, knew her thoughts better than anyone.

A tall figure emerged from the darkness, took firm hold of her arm, forced her to slow and to stop. Stubbornly, Elizabeth stared at a faraway streetlamp and the skeletal mulberry tree underneath.

"I waited, Falke," she said, not turning to face him. "I hoped you would've found me sooner than this."

Falke remained silent. Elizabeth heard the mulberry branches tapping against the streetlamp's aluminum trunk; joyful caresses sounded with a bold ringing. They seemed a couple, she thought, and became jealous. Falke squeezed her arm gently, then released her.

"I was occupied with wearisome tasks." He began to leave her behind. "And in ill temper, which I did not want to inflict upon you."

Elizabeth watched his disappearing shape for a moment, then followed. "I waited so many years," she said, rebuking, wanting him to beg for forgiveness. "I missed you."

Falke gave no answer. He was luminous in the artificial light, his long golden hair untouched by the wind. Beautiful and powerful like a wild animal, she thought. Pantherlike, his dark coat seemed barely able to contain his strength. Elizabeth flew to him, touched his arm hesitantly. His profile remained rigid. She stopped trying to make him acknowledge her.

"Are you healed?" Elizabeth asked.

"I easily tire. I am not yet fully recovered."

"You've met with Hanna."

"I have seen her." Falke studied her. "There were plans for our survival to be made."

He left something unsaid. Elizabeth sensed the words close to the surface, like the fat clouds ready to burst with snow. She wanted to reach into his mind and grasp the hidden thought, bring it out and examine it. He would feel her presence, of course, and stop her. Still, she was tempted.

"I've met with Hanna, too," she said, closing her mind, allowing just the words to escape. "And talked with her. She frightens me."

"Always did she worry you," Falke commented. "Hanna is harmless."

The streets began to glow with heavy electric light. Human thoughts trembled behind car windows. Headlight beams streaked around Elizabeth. The world of the living warmed and comforted her.

"I want to show you a place, Falke, where you can rest. It is quiet and private. We can talk there."

Falke's finger brushed her lips. "Take me."

Elizabeth led him to a section of the city where the oldest buildings creaked, where the lights never dimmed. She paused by a fountain gushing beneath an overhanging wall of brick and glass, and she wondered when it would be shut off for the winter. She would miss the fountain, as it seemed to be the only living creature in this part of the city.

"Everything else is dead," she explained to Falke. "I don't know how it is during the day."

Falke said nothing.

Elizabeth walked a familiar path. Not far from the fountain, they came to a tall, frightening cathedral with sharp raging spires and light-splashed flanks. Falke paused by the massive wooden doors. Elizabeth took his hand.

"The church is asleep," she whispered.

Inside, the pillars and carpeted floors along the aisle echoed no thoughts or pain. The heaters made soft breathing sounds in the empty cathedral nave, reminding her of a newborn snuggled in its carriage. Elizabeth told Falke none of her thoughts. She knew he would not understand them.

"This place does not please me," Falke said, glaring toward the choir loft and the standing podium. His voice burst against the vaulted ceiling, breaking the comfortable silence.

"I'm sorry."

He removed his coat and draped it along the back of a stained pew. He stared at her. "Sit with me."

Elizabeth wished he wouldn't look at her so frostily. She walked to the pew in front of him and sat on the cushioned seats. Above her, two statues in tall archways flanked the vast choir loft. Both were bathed in sprays of cold light. Their eye sockets were dark. She imagined Mary's carved marble hair set free to flutter in the blown air from the heating vents.

"My only fear," Elizabeth began, "is that Hanna might hurt you." She felt his questioning gaze on the back of her neck. "Hanna has secret plans and many secret places within her. I've known this since the moment you first brought her to me. I can't see into her well. That is what frightens me."

"I gave her such strength to protect you," Falke said.

"Hanna doesn't remember any of that! She wants to kill you!"

"You strike at shadows," Falke said quietly. "Hanna is jealous of my love for you."

72   "No, Falke. You never loved me. Even Hanna knows that."

Falke appeared beside her and knelt. There had been no rustle of movement. His presence was as strong and immediate as an ocean's deadly undercurrent dragging her into its depths. She rested her forehead against his chest and listened to the reassuring beat of his heart, still familiar after so many years. Scarlet tears trickled onto her knees, stained the hem of her white dress.

"Take me to the ocean . . . make love with me on the sand." Under the sun, she thought sadly, remembering the words of an old song. "You promised me once, long ago."

Elizabeth lifted her arms and held him, slowing her heart's rhythms to match his. Silently, his hands encircled and crushed her to him. She remembered the first nights of their passion, her intense hunger, the need to suckle from him, to huddle under his hardness and weight, the aching and wetness.

Falke was her husband. He was home.

Elizabeth revealed her mind to him completely, opened her fears and love. For a moment, Falke relented. Elizabeth shaped a mental conduit, and touched his mind. His hidden thoughts suddenly streamed into her.

A stranger was nestled in his heart. A girl.

Unknown, yet hatefully familiar.

The girl was staring at Elizabeth through a steady, oval flame. The candle sat on a small ornately carved table, which Elizabeth recognized as her own writing desk . . . inside the desert sanctuary. The girl was closing first one eye, then the other, as if playing some game.

The loving conduit broke.

Elizabeth grew numb, and moved from Falke.

"She is a thoughtful girl," Falke said gently. "Alive, still, as you are. She might be useful to us."

Elizabeth began to tremble with the same minute tremblings she felt in willow trees, during autumn, when confronted with the first frost. She herself had just turned sixteen when Falke had found her. And killed her.

"I want you to meet with this girl," Falke continued. "She could become our link to the daylit world. She is quick and intelligent. I want you to teach her to fly, as I once taught you."

Despair fell in a turgid sheet. Elizabeth wanted to retreat inside and never come out.

"What's her name?"

Falke did not answer. Instead, he moved to the pew in front of her. There was no squeaking of wood as he settled on the bench, his back to her. Elizabeth might have been watching him in a silent film.

"Her name is Melissa," Falke said. "I have kept her equal to both worlds as I kept you. She can move about in the sun, though it pains her."

"I can't do that," Elizabeth said. "Not anymore."

Falke nodded. "After a time, the human blood thins and . . . you become captive to my world."

"The sun can kill me now. Maybe you're right. She might be useful."

Elizabeth knew why she trembled. Her muscles were coiling. Tightening. She wanted to strike him.

"You will speak with Melissa." Falke studied his hand. "And you will protect her."

Elizabeth glared at his head, held her fists against her stomach. "Tell the girl to find me. That will be her first lesson." She rose and stormed past rows of pews and shining pillars. Doors flew open at her barest touch. Frantic anger bubbled in her arms. She struggled to maintain hardened eyes. Her hands shook. "No," she hissed and clenched them tighter. She couldn't let jealousy or despair throw her reason.

Not tonight!

She had felt Falke's diminished strength, could see for herself that he was not fully healed. Hanna had seen his weakness, too; she had gloated over it. Falke had left himself open to attack.

"Stupid, stupid," Elizabeth muttered as she thundered down wet, glittering streets. By shaping this Melissa into a vampire, Falke had overreached his strength, weakened himself dangerously. Teach the girl to fly? Of course, he couldn't do it himself; not until he was fully healed. And how long would that take? New love had toppled his senses. The long years in sleep had made him careless.

Alone, Elizabeth had lived over a hundred years in fear of being discovered, hunted, and destroyed by humans. All those years and all the things she had learned would be wasted if she embraced Falke and Hanna so easily in her heart again, as husband and sister. "Bastard!" Elizabeth loped, then

74

ran swiftly, until buildings and streetlamps became blurs, no longer solid objects to take notice of or worry about. Hate nourished her strength. The pavement shattered under her feet. Elizabeth tested plans for her defense.

The world solidified as she halted on a manmade hill above the freeway and hugged herself under a battering sleet. Her hate, along with its strength, wavered quickly and died. The loving conduit she had created trembled, sought connection. She could not stop her love or concern for the only family she had. Even though she wept at Falke's betrayal, her heart continued to beat in rhythm with her husband's. Her soul still huddled in Falke's embrace. He was as a sick child yet, not fully recovered. Helpless. And Hanna was a baby—Elizabeth's vampire sister. The thought was soothing. Of course she would protect her family.

Of course she would forgive Falke.

Sixteen

Hanna's white finger pressed the button marked 403. Faintly, coming through layers of wall, ceiling, and glass, tuneless bells rang inside the massive stone building. She heard steps and a girl's soft breathing. Hanna recognized the movements from the night before. They belonged to the shopgirl, Wendy.

Two nights ago, Hanna's mind had awakened while watching an unchanging flight of buzzing red arrows. She had circled the glowing motel sign that read "Geronimo Inn" for hours, revelling in its shower of soft artificial light. Enchanted by the flowing electrical streams, she had squeezed one of the arrows, accidentally shattering a thin glass tube. One red arrow vanished. Light contained in a glass bottle! Testing, Hanna had swiped at several more arrows, smashing them. She tried to work out the mechanics while rolling glass dust between her thumb and forefinger. Bullet-shaped coaches roared by, distracting her; lustrous machines in candy colors.

How long have I slept, she asked herself. How long did I walk in the desert? Her senses came back slowly, yet sometimes drifted away like March clouds. She soon realized she was wearing a musty, unraveling cotton dress. With sadness, Hanna left the magical sign that had called her out of the desert. Instinctively shunning the road, she walked warily under thousands of hissing, storming lights. Death settled into her brain for a time. Her blind corpse had followed a true path, however, because she had found the shopgirl the same night.

Something peeped in front of Hanna, and the shopgirl's breathy voice spoke from the wall. "Who is it, please?"

Distinctly, Hanna heard the dripping of water on flesh. She waited quietly, noticing that the apartment building had smooth walls. No places for concealment; no planters, no overhangs. The austere building looked solid and immobile. Hanna liked it.

"Hello?" said the shopgirl's voice.

"It's Hanna! Let me in!"

"Oh, Hanna, hi! I'm sorry. Wait just a second."

A buzzer sounded at the door. Is this a game? she thought. Hanna didn't know what to do. She hammered on the glass.

"Did you open the door?" Wendy asked solicitously. "Why didn't you open the door?"

"It's locked. Open up, I am freezing!"

"Oh, Hanna, I forgot. In America, when you hear the buzz, you have to open the door."

"Why can't you open it?"

"I can't. I'm still in the shower. Please let yourself in and come up."

Again, the door buzzed at her. Hanna considered ascending the wall and climbing in through the window. But she was too dizzy with hunger. Pulling open the door, Hanna flew up the stairs to the apartment marked 403. The knob was unlocked.

The room spread before her in layer upon layer of feminine comfort. Everything, except a dark window, was white. The clinging reek of oversweet lilies assaulted her senses. The rug was thick and seemed to glow with its own light. Hanna laughed and rushed to the window. Touching the glass briefly, she thought the city lights resembled a chaotic mass of diamonds, emeralds, and sapphires. "Pretty," she whispered. The shower hissed in another room. Hanna wriggled her toes in the deep shag, wanting to strip and feel it on her entire body.

The bed!

Hanna quickly searched the apartment until she found the bedroom. More of the luxurious carpet spilled inside. The bed was a fountain of white silk, gushing against the walls, shooting to the ceiling. She gave a small yip of pleasure and unzipped her leather dress. A lamp clicked on.

"Hanna?"

Wendy was staring at her from the door. She was wrapped in a towel, and a makeshift turban sat on her head.

"What are you doing?" Wendy asked shyly.

"Your apartment is so beautiful," Hanna purred, pulling off her dress, becoming naked. "Don't be frightened."

Wendy frowned, said nothing, and went to a vanity cluttered with an array of small bottles and tubes. She arranged herself on a cushioned bench and began to vigorously rub her hair with the towel.

"It's so light in here," Hanna said, coming closer to the table. The assortment of glittery things fascinated her. "The brightness doesn't hurt your eyes?"

"Why should it?" Wendy folded her towel over polished thighs. "I like bright things."

Hanna picked up a tube and read its label. "Satin gloss."

Wendy made room on the bench. "I think it would look nice on you. Your liner is a little severe for your face." She plucked the tube from Hanna's fingers. "Sit down and face me."

Hanna complied. Wendy had a pretty oval face and liquid blue eyes. Her tousled blond hair dripped silvery water. Sweet as Elizabeth, Hanna thought, and felt a slight touch on her lips as if a piece of silk were being drawn across them.

"There," Wendy said. "Look in the mirror."

Hanna felt a twinge of disquiet. Cautiously, she faced the mirror. Her body, blending with the white walls, was barely visible. Slowly, as she moved, an aureole of pale skin swam into view. Her form solidified briefly. Full, red lips appeared. Ghostly hands lifted her red-gold hair. Hanna pouted her lips seductively and winked her eye. She winked the other eye.

"I look," she muttered, "like a vampire."

Wendy laughed and searched among the potions in front of her. "It's only the winter," she said, choosing a bottle and unscrewing its cap. "Everyone who can't afford a tanning session looks awful during the winter. God knows I do! But a little of this should help."

Hanna turned her head, presenting each side of her transparent face to the mirror. I look underfed, too. "My lips are nice, don't you think?"

"Face me again, please."

Hanna waited patiently while Wendy applied something to her cheeks. The girl's face was smooth and unmarked by line or blemish. Only a small crease in her forehead indicated her concentration.

"Now, face the mirror," Wendy said.

Hanna turned and inspected herself. The makeup had given her a flush she had not seen for many years. She saw how large and dark green her eyes were, how they dominated her face. Her hair looked less startling. We look like sisters, Hanna thought. Twin, made-up children's corpses.

Wendy compared their reflections. "Much better."

"It's not real," Hanna said sadly. "I don't look like that."

"Of course you do. Look for yourself!"

Hanna turned from the mirror and faced the curtained window by the vanity. "No. Once, maybe, I looked like that."

"Hanna, what are you saying?"

Wendy looked fragile and defenseless. Hanna almost felt sorry for her.

"Come up to the window," Hanna urged gently, standing, offering her hand. "I want to show you something."

Wendy allowed herself to be pulled up. Hanna swept the curtain aside. Snow clouds rolled ponderously over the city, low enough that the tops of buildings vanished inside their misty bellies. Rain pattered meekly across the window. Occasional snow flakes pressed their images against the glass.

"It's beautiful," Wendy sighed. "I love the snow so much. Don't you?"

78   "The snow kills many things."

Wendy's reflection in the window was laid against orange and black space as if she were being projected out of the building and onto the clouds. Hanna noted how Wendy eased nervously to the bench and sat. She reached for the towel where it had fallen and began to dry her hair again.

"Who are you, Hanna?" Wendy asked quietly. "Really."

Hanna went to the bed and took the bedspread in her hands, crushing its satiny, skinlike texture against her breasts. She drew the bedspread off and wrapped herself in it, then sat. "Why do you ask?"

Wendy busily toweled off the back of her head. Blond curls glistened. "I don't know," she said after a time, draping the towel over her lap. "It's none of my business, I suppose."

"I'm flattered by your interest. Make it your business."

Wendy, eyes widening, looked for Hanna's reflection in the mirror. Hanna slipped easily into the girl's mind, caught pastel colors and a simple mood, nothing more. She soothed Wendy's growing uneasiness and spoke directly into her mind.

Ask your question.

The girl sighed. "Why are you here? Now, with me?"

"Because you invited me."

Wendy dropped her gaze to the bottles on the vanity. Straightening, she searched more purposefully until she picked up a stout tortoise-shell comb. "Not here." She waved the comb to indicate her room. "I mean here in this town."

"My husband brought me to this city. Without my consent." Hanna shrugged. "That's my life, really. I'm a flower plucked from my native soil and left to wither in this hopeless desert."

"Did he leave you for someone else?" Wendy asked gently.

"Yes. But he is dead to me."

"I'm sorry, Hanna."

"Don't be! My sister loves me. I've found new friends and a new life. They're mine, and I'm happy."

Wendy smiled, looking relieved. "I'm glad. You can count me among your friends. I won't leave you."

"That's important to me, Wendy." Hanna stood. "You helped me when I was lost and alone. Awakening in a strange world is frightening. I hope you never have to experience it."

Wendy's hair gleamed like gold rings. Almost like Elizabeth's hair. Hanna let the bedspread fall and walked to the girl.

79

"You said you're from some foreign country," Wendy said, unable to see Hanna's approach in the mirror. "But you didn't say where. Would you tell me?"

Hanna knelt facing Wendy. Wendy's eyes were trusting; her unpainted lips parted in a smile.

Hanna whispered, "I am from Hell."

She made her finger as rigid as steel and drove it into Wendy's throat. The girl's eyes bulged from their sockets. Choking, she clawed at Hanna's hand and encircling arms. Her legs kicked furiously. Feet thudded against the vanity. Bottles smashed. The bedroom wobbled in the mirror.

Hanna pulled Wendy's face into her bosom, ripped away the reddening towel. With her thumb, she stopped up spurting blood so as not to waste it.

"I'll cherish this home you've given me." Hanna's eyeteeth lengthened into curved spikes. "Forever."

Wendy shrieked into Hanna's cleavage, splattering white breasts with red droplets. Hanna licked the girl's punctured throat. Blood pulsed out of a round hole, pushing against her tongue, trickling around her lips. She let the honey stream fill her mouth, swallowed it in ecstasy.

"My sweet Elizabeth," Hanna crooned.

Wendy convulsed under Hanna's tightening bone-white arms.

Seventeen

Diana picked her watch off the nightstand and held it to the stray light coming from the hallway. 2:30 A.M. Sitting up, she reached for her robe. Having a man in the house changed life so subtly. Her sleep had been free of worry from intruders and ghosts. Her thoughts did not echo bleakly in the rooms as they usually did. She was self-conscious about the smell in her apartment, which reeked of bleach, weird detergents, pine-scented cleaners, evidence of a life spent cleaning house and not much else. Diana slipped on her watch, wondering if Michael's relatives want the clothes she did not wear anymore. Maybe they could make them into one of their rugs.

She listened to a rare sound in the living room where she had made a bed for Michael. The pages of a magazine were being turned. Yawning, gathering her robe around her and tying it carelessly, she walked into the living room. Michael was on the couch, reading by the light of the television, whose volume had been turned down. He was looking at a fossil guidebook she had found at a used-book shop years ago.

"I never went collecting myself." Diana switched on a lamp. "I bought it because the pictures were beautiful."

"There are many rocks like these near the camp," Michael answered, not lifting his gaze from the book. "I used to pick them up when I was younger, but I don't anymore. There are too many of them."

Diana noticed that the makeshift bed on the couch had not been slept in. And Michael was dressed already, in a plaid shirt, new-looking jeans, and cowboy boots.

"I hope I'm not keeping you awake," she said. "I think I tend to snore sometimes."

The old man shook his head and closed the book gently, placing it on his folded clothes stacked on the floor. "I don't sleep much when I'm in town," he said, rubbing the back of his head vigorously.

Shaking the sleep out, as her grandpa used to say. Diana checked the electric clock on the bookshelf next to the TV. Its red numbers flashed 4:16. Her watch still read 2:30. She had forgotten to wind it. Real smart. No wonder she wasn't sleepy.

"Well, I'm up for coffee if you are, Mr. Roanhorse."

After showering and putting on jeans and a turtleneck sweat-er, Diana made coffee in her seldom-used automatic dripper.

"I don't make as heavy a pot as you do, Michael," she said, taking down two inane cups with cat cartoons on them. "I guess I'm just a wimp."

"That's all right," Michael said. "Later on, I'll make us both a big serving."

"Oh, that's okay." Diana remembered grounds rolling underneath her tongue. "Actually, I don't usually drink all that much coffee."

Also, she still had the caffeine jitters from the thick concoction she had drunk at his house last night. Diana set the glass pot back in the coffeemaker and sat across the table from him. She had not said anything about his home-brewed coffee, not wanting to hurt his feelings. Not even a little joke. She was afraid he might be one of those old people who took offense at any slight, no matter how small. And what did he think of her? Diana cringed at the cat cups.

"How long do you think it'll take us to find Melissa?" she asked.

"How long have the police been looking?"

"It's only been a couple of days."

"I don't know, then. Albuquerque is a big city."

"What, Albuquerque?" Diana refilled their cups. "It's not all that big."

"I get turned around in the city," Michael said. "Tell me which way is east."

Michael had a way of looking at her that made her feel ten years old. Diana thought for a few moments, but couldn't remember. She had never really thought about which direction was where, before. Well think now, stupid! she scolded. You don't want to look like a complete wimp in the codger's eyes.

"I guess toward the Sandias." Diana waved vaguely toward the stove.

The old man glanced to the empty wall. He looked worried.

"What's wrong?" she asked.

"You have no window or door that faces the east?" He took a careful sip from the cat mug.

"No. There's an apartment next door," Diana explained. What a strange thing to ask. "Why?"

"You look like the kind of woman who would have a window facing the sunrise."

Diana wasn't sure if he was joking or not. "I remember you don't have a window facing east, either."

"No. I have a doorway that faces the east. And my wife had a picture of her Heavenly Father there. She didn't need a window."

82

Diana remembered the calender picture of Jesus on the cross hanging on Michael's somber, flaking wall. What a thing to have to look at every morning.

"Was your wife very religious?" she asked.

Michael nodded. "She was a regular contributor on Sundays. Our daughter would sometimes drive out to Madrecita, where we had our big home, and they would go to services here in Albuquerque."

"I take it you're not a churchgoer."

"I had too much work to do."

"You have two houses?" Diana asked.

"Yes. The sheep camp and the blue house where Sarah, my daughter, was born."

"Where is Madre . . . Madrecita?"

"Yes, Madrecita. It's between here and Grants. A little bit more toward Grants. Under Mount Taylor's east foot."

Without warning, Diana yawned. "Oh! I'm sorry, Mr. Roanhorse. I guess I'm not used to waking up early." Out the south-facing window, she saw the sky tinged with dawn. Michael took the cups to the sink, rinsed them, then placed them on the dishrack.

"Thank you. Just leave the pot, I'll do it later."

Diana felt calmer now that she had actually done something toward finding Melissa. Maybe the old guy would take the bulk of the worry off her shoulders, too.

"Let me put the blankets away," she said, standing. "Then we'll go get some breakfast." She gathered the blankets and took them to the closet across from the bathroom. "I'll clear out the junk in the extra room, then you can sleep in there tonight. It's not a very big apartment, but it's warm. The furnace for the entire complex is right under my floor. Isn't that great?"

"Thank you . . . Miss Logan," the old man said.

"Oh, you can call me Diana."

"Tell me how Melissa is doing in school," Michael said.

They were in a low-lit 24-hour restaurant that made nice fluffy pancakes if you happened to catch the right cook. Luckily they had. Diana's plate was a sea of golden syrup. She cut her pancake into small pieces as she spoke.

"Melissa's written and language skills are above the top for her grade level. Now, she could easily be doing college-level work. Freshman and sophomore. She's a fine essayist. Or she's going to be, once she gets the hang of it. I'm very pleased with her work. I enjoy reading it, too, which is a nice treat for me."

"Her grandmother was good with English," Michael said quietly. He buttered his toast. "Maybe Melissa gets it from her side of the family."

Diana could see he was proud of Melissa. His smile was more evident. "Yes, role models are so important to the learning process." She balked at that statement. A parent-teacher conference at six in the morning?

"Melissa always did listen to her elders. Her mother was the same way."

"Has Melissa been taught her native language?" Diana asked.

"Sarah would know that. I've taught Melissa her Navajo directions. Some of the animal names, too. I don't see her often. I don't know if she remembers her Navajo."

"I see." Diana finished her pancakes. Michael finished buttering his toast. His scrambled eggs were still untouched. Diana signaled the waitress for more coffee, then looked out the window. A blue fog drifted lazily above the parking lot. Occasional cars splashed along wet streets. White puffy clouds had settled into the Rio Grande valley several miles below the restaurant. The sky looked freshly scrubbed. Mother Nature hadn't worked herself into dropping a snowstorm yet, bless her.

"I'm not out this time of the morning, usually," Diana said. She tended to be greedy with sleep. "It's beautiful."

"That's why you need a door facing the east," Michael said. "To let the sunrise into your home. To offer a song of prayer." His voice remained steady. "And to chase away the witches."

Eighteen

Orange-red sunlight warmed Michael and deepened the color of his hands. Somewhere below his boots, the transmission gears clashed unhealthily. Diana swore under her breath, glanced at him quickly. "Sorry," she muttered as they bolted from the stoplight. "I hate Saturday morning traffic."

They passed many honking cars. Michael could taste the poisons in the air, like smoking a bad cigarette or sitting in a bar on a Friday night. He wondered why the people living in this city were not always coughing or choking. Even the sunlight with its growing heat on his arm was unnatural somehow, though it eased the misery of his painful joints.

The teacher was bundled into a big sweater, as if she hadn't noticed the sun. Air from the heater made his feet uncomfortably hot in his boots. She was too thin, he thought. Maybe that's why she was always shivering, or hunched into herself as if protecting her body from invisible punches. Michael wanted her to eat more. Their search might require some long walking. She would need good food in her belly to keep up her strength. Maybe if he pretended to be hungry all the time, she might be tempted by the sight of food.

Why was she helping him search for his family? Michael wondered if she was a mothering type who had never had anyone to mother.

"I don't know if the police have Melissa's apartment cordoned off or what." Diana brought the car to a whining stop at a stoplight. It seemed as if she was purposely treating her car badly, as if she hoped it would break.

"I vote we stay only a short while so we don't attract any attention to ourselves."

"Will they watch her house?" Michael asked.

"I'm not sure. But if we get into any trouble, I know who to call."

"You have a friend who is a policeman?"

She didn't look at him as they raced from the green light. "Yes," she said.

The small car's jolting pulled a memory out of Michael's head. "I remember this one policeman on the Navajo reservation a long time ago. His name was Benny Light House and he came from Tuba City. He was a real big man, a fat man, with little eyes like coal chips staring out of his head. He was a mean man, too."

Sometimes, Michael's memory took over all his senses as if he were taking a bath in them. Time stretched and slowed, and all sounds around him were silenced. He wasn't sure he was even talking anymore.

Everyone had called the policeman Sweet Bread. Some of the old gossiping women had given him that name because of his raisin eyes and his brown reservation police uniform. At the squaw dances, Sweet Bread could be seen stalking along the edges of the trees, watching the people, hunting them almost. As a boy, Michael was sure that this man—with his shiny black boots and his twin pistols in a Mexican holster belt—was eyeing him alone, watching and dogging his every step until striking like a rattler.

"You look at him just one time and there he is, staring at you with his rattlesnake eyes from the tree branches," his cousin, Gilbert, had said one rainy Saturday afternoon over fifty years ago.

Gilbert's battered pickup truck rocked under the force of the rain. Water slid between a crack in the windshield and trickled onto Michael's knee. The spring squaw dance had been halted temporarily. People strolled and ran to wagons, pickups, mud-streaked cars, where they ate fried bread, steaming mutton stew, cold ears of corn; or where they silently drank soda pop, coffee, or some alcoholic drink while waiting for the rain to stop.

"Don't say any more," Michael said, peering out the windshield, expecting to see Sweet Bread crouching in the shadows under the juniper trees, staring and listening. "He might hear you."

"I hope that witch hears me," Gilbert taunted. "Rattlesnake Eyes is what I call him. My grandfather says he's a skinwalker. Along with that old Centipede Woman from Shiprock." Gilbert guzzled the last of his grape soda fizzling in his nervous hand. His hair was bushy and short; everyone called him Porcupine.

Michael was scared himself, but he wouldn't show his fear, especially to his cousin. He let his can of soda sit untouched between his thighs, under his cowboy hat.

"Maybe something should be done about Sweet Bread," Michael said. Or had Gilbert said that?

Gilbert shook his head. "Witches live forever, bothering corpses, killing people. You can't kill them unless you are strong. Are you strong?"

"I don't know."

Gilbert grunted and laughed. "Shit, I don't know if I am either. How's your brother, my cousin?"

"We haven't gotten a letter for a long time."

"Talk with Tall Hat at Ganado. Billy Largo, his son, is overseas, too. He might have some news for you."

Michael blinked his eyes as if coming out of sleep, and he found himself in the teacher's stuffy car. They had stopped. He could feel her gaze on him.

"So?" Diana's thin hands rested in her lap. Michael saw they were parked near some red brick buildings that looked like army barracks. He buttoned his denim jacket. He felt chilled, and pain began to gnaw at his legs. Diana was still looking at him. "Well, what happened to this Snake Bread?" she asked.

"Sweet Bread. I'll finish later." Michael searched for the door handle. His scalp was tingling with fear. Why had he suddenly remembered Sweet Bread? Diana said something behind him as he pushed open the feather-light door. Michael rose out of the car and welcomed the smelly air. Diana appeared on the other side of the red car, grinning.

"Tell me the end, now. While we have time." She slammed her door shut and locked it. "You've got me interested."

She reminded him of Melissa. She was pretty and had the same small build; much too thin. And though her hair held a dark shade of reddish brown, it had the same wavy texture as Melissa's black hair. They both smiled in the same way, too—slowly and filled with amusement. And they were both stubborn.

"Later," Michael answered.

Diana came around the car, pulling on black leather gloves. "Don't worry. I won't let you forget the story."

The apartment was cold and silent, colder than the key in Michael's hand. Sarah had given Margaret the key, promising her mother she would never be left without a home. Losing the blue house, becoming homeless, had worried Margaret constantly, especially during her last years. Michael could never understand why. Was it a worry common to women? His own mother had been so much a part of her government house that he felt she was still there, mixing dough in the box kitchen, washing her black hair with yucca root at the outside pump.

"You're more fortunate than other women because you have two homes," he had told Margaret, saying it so often it had become a litany or prayer. Michael thought the words might comfort her, but she would turn away from him, eyes darkening, as if she had not believed him.

When he had said those words, usually at the sheep camp, he would sweep his arm out to include the whole desert. Maybe Margaret had known this about her husband all along—that he considered the little rock house their home instead of the blue house in Madrecita, which her mother had given them and where their daughter had been born. Maybe that had been the cause of Margaret's distress—knowing finally that her man's heart lived in the empty desert.

"Did you hear what I said?" Diana came close to him as if they were about to dance. Michael had heard something about the aquarium. He went to the TV, to the stuffed tiger sitting in a pottery bowl. He dug his finger into a pocket in the tiger's chest and withdrew a key.

"This was Sarah's emergency key," he told Diana, who was standing, arms crossed, in the middle of the room. "She was always losing things. I brought her the tiger when she was a little girl, to keep her keys in."

Diana remained silent. "I want to show you something in Melissa's room."

Michael replaced the tiger in the bowl. He followed Diana, who had already disappeared into a back room. Something made him hesitate. A brief shadow or movement in the kitchen. At the doorway he searched for intruders. A small container sat on the counter. Dishrags and yellow gloves hung on the wall above the faucet. The curtain was drawn. The kitchen was empty. Michael looked into the darkened aquarium. Tiny fish bodies like dried sticks floated on the surface. Someone had switched off Melissa's aquarium. He left the kitchen and found Melissa's room, where Diana was on her hands and knees peering under the bed.

"I saw it in this room the night she disappeared," Diana said, her voice muffled. "They can't have taken it."

"What's wrong?"

Diana pushed herself up and pointed to the desk. "Her backpack was sitting right there. The pack she always came to class with. It was right there when I came Friday afternoon. Now it's gone."

Desk drawers overflowed with papers, and school supplies were stacked messily on the floor. Melissa's pastel clothing was heaped on the bed; her shoes were piled carelessly in a corner. Diana picked up a pink shirt and folded it into a square.

"They could've at least picked up after themselves," she said quietly. Smoothing the shirt gently, she placed it on the bed and picked up another one.

"The police did this?" Michael asked, his face becoming hot. "They did this to her room?"

Diana gave no answer, continued folding clothes. Michael went to the open closet, where a few blouses and dresses hung, and found Melissa's collection of glass animals scattered into a shoebox on the floor. Michael remembered his granddaughter showing them to him during his last visit, when she was still fifteen. He saw Melissa gingerly carrying each fragile animal from her room, setting it on the counter next to the aquarium, telling him the names she had given them.

Looking closely at them now, Michael noticed that some of the glass animals were broken and covered with a strange white dust. He blew off as much of the dust as he could, picked up the shoebox carefully, and carried it to the window shelf. The animals glittered dreamily in the sunlight. Michael returned to the pile of Melissa's shoes and kneeled. Ignoring his stiffening joints, he paired up the shoes, found their mates, returned them to the closet.

Silence remained as they cleaned Melissa's room.

Nineteen

Michael woke up feeling warm and disoriented. Sunlight fell across a quilt covering his legs; a quilt patterned with cats, like the cups in Diana's apartment. He remembered where he was. Diana had left earlier in the afternoon, saying she needed to run some errands and finish some work at home. Huddled into her bulky coat, hair limp and falling into her green eyes, Diana had handed him this quilt and urged him to call her when he wanted to eat. Michael had made himself a bed on Sarah's couch, under the living room window where the sun would reach him. He dozed fitfully.

And dreamed.

Desert heat made his brain feel heavy and lumpish. Yellow dust rose from his slow passage among twisting arroyos, cactus, and thin grass. It was summer and the sky above him was flat and blue. Lift them higher, he told himself; the command was lost between his mind and legs. Cicadas whirred like tiny machines. Michael was carrying some kind of bag and his clutching grip on it hurt his fingers. If he didn't drop it soon, his joints would become frozen.

"Quit complaining," said a female voice.

The voice had sounded like Margaret's. Michael stopped and looked into concealing heat waves, where he saw an indistinct shape standing several yards away. Squinching his eyes, he tried to make out its features, but the dark figure dissolved into a watery blur.

"What do you want?" Michael asked. The creature had a bulky, heaving outline. It was not Margaret. If only he could clear his vision! He saw a glint of yellow teeth as the creature smiled.

"Why do you want to bother with everything, old man?" The creature spoke in a screeching parody of Margaret's soothing voice. "Go home and rest your aching bones."

Michael walked on, ignored its quiet chuckle. Paws pattered on the sand as it ran up behind him.

"You're a wreck, old son," it creaked. "You can't see that

old hogan. You can't even see the path under your own feet!"

Michael shaded his eyes, trying to pierce the unreal silver-blue lake surrounding him. He felt as if every wrinkle on his body were filling with dust.

"You're right, I can't see my grandmother's hogan." Michael recognized the grinning animal standing awkwardly on its hind legs. Even half-blinded with heat, he saw sour yellow eyes, cupped dog ears, a sharp muzzle. "But my ears are still working, Grandfather. I can hear her humming right over there to the west, where she is spinning her wool."

Michael changed direction, seeing that he had been walking too far to the north. He considered thanking the coyote. "In the future," he said, "when you come to visit, don't talk to me in my wife's voice. I don't know you."

"You'll know me good enough." The coyote's voice changed to a man's resonant voice distantly familiar to Michael. "North is where evil gathers," the coyote continued. "North is where the dead leave the hogan. Walk just my side of beauty for a little bit, my grandson. Night is coming. But remember who scattered the stars across it."

Michael woke and the first object that caught his eye was Melissa's darkened aquarium. Why let those fish die? Someone could have taken care of them, let themselves in here once a day to feed them. People now had gotten lazy.

What would his grandmother have said?

The apartment smelled of perfume.

"Ya'at'eeh," Michael called. The walls and empty spaces swallowed his voice. The apartment remained quiet. He remembered his daughter as a tidy, serious girl clutching over-size books, waiting for the bus to take her to school. She used to wear dark dresses. He supposed that was Margaret's influence because Michael also remembered Sarah's colorful socks and hair ties. Her black ponytails had always been held by some bright thing, carefully cut cloth or plastic barrettes.

Michael stood up from the couch. His joints were numb. He felt as if his bones had become disconnected from one another. Deepening worry replaced the perpetual ache. His whole soul had become one painful joint, bent in the middle. He was scared now for Sarah and Melissa. Where had they gone to?

He had no clue. He went to the bathroom and washed his face. The shelves were cluttered with closed jars. Dry towels were bunched on the shower curtain rod and held a faint soapy scent. . . .

The kitchen was a tiny box. He opened cabinets until he found a glass. Several pictures were taped to the refrigerator door. He looked into one and saw two old people, a smiling man and a woman in a blue apron standing next to a house made of rock, wood, and tin. Relics of the desert.

Michael set the glass on the counter. A weariness that had built up over many years settled onto his brain, sinking his chin to his chest. His daughter's apartment was cold. Sunlight trickling through the front window filled the living room with an icy glow. A white slash lay on the couch. Random stripes fell across the floor like fallen icicles.

Michael had truly believed Margaret would outlast him; all her relatives and all their friends had, too. During his wife's funeral, he had felt like an amputated hand. There had not been much sympathy for him, only puzzled glances and unsettled anger. The food had been good, offerings in plastic wrap, in plastic dishes, in somber pottery bowls. So much food! And many many people. Michael had been surprised at the number of people Margaret had known or been related to. It seemed as if all the villages for twenty miles around had showed up at the blue house in Madrecita. What do you know about her that I don't, he had wanted to ask them. What had she talked about? Michael had felt like the single locust tree at the sheepcamp, with not one of his own kind near him for miles.

He held the glass under the faucet, waiting for the stream of bleach-tasting water to turn warm.

It had just turned spring when Margaret had died, and the night she had passed on had been a warm one. They had gone to bed late. He had piled quilts onto his sore knees, to give them a little more heat.

Beside him, Margaret was shivering under the covers.

"I feel funny. I don't feel right," she said, again and again, until Michael's heart became cold with fear. Her voice was strong, no worry or surprise in it. She hadn't felt hot; nor had she complained of any pain or dizziness.

"What is it, Margaret?" His voice became sharp. "What's wrong with you?"

"I don't know. Bring me some water."

Blind in the dark, Michael hurried into the kitchen. A soup bowl fell and shattered on the counter as he groped for a glass. The floor remained solid and warm under his feet.

"I'm very cold," Margaret whispered when he returned with a glass of water. Her forehead was a cold stone. Michael lay beside her, held her tightly, blew shaky breaths onto her frozen neck and chest, willing his own warmth into her. Holding her became painful, like hugging a block of ice. Then Margaret grasped him frantically, fingers digging into his naked shoulders, nails furrowing into his skin. Michael felt his own blood seeping down his back.

Between two short breaths, Margaret was dead. Taken from him in the middle of the night. He held her lax head against him, her hair tickling his mouth. There had been no time for comfort. No thought or word of parting. Her muscles slackened, her fingers unclenched themselves. Margaret caressed him in a slow movement along his waist until her cold hand fell on the bedsheets between them.

Remembering, Michael set the empty glass down and watched as daylight crept from the apartment's blank walls and departed through his daughter's window.

The sound of pots rattling in the brightly lit kitchen awakened Michael. He saw a silhouetted figure pass behind the glowing aquarium. Blue fish darted like tadpoles in the murky water. Then, a shadowed, schoolgirl Sarah appeared in the kitchen doorway.

"Daddy?" Her voice sounded like crashing steel.

Hesitant, Sarah bent forward into the green glow given off by the aquarium. The skin of her broken face glistened as she stared with torn, empty sockets.

"Are you there?" she asked, frightened.

Michael tried to wipe his sweaty palms on his jeans, but he couldn't move, couldn't speak.

"Daddy . . ." Sarah began to cry. "I forgot my name."

Turning, Sarah drew back from the doorway and vanished.

His paralysis left him. Michael sat up, shading the glare from the kitchen with his shaking hand. The apartment was empty. The curtains were drawn. Michael pulled himself up, breathing painfully, until he was leaning against the couch arms. Twitching aside the curtain, he saw that it was full dark outside.

The silence in the apartment frightened him. In the desert, there was always some noise; the bony rattle of tamarisk branches, the wash gurgling against the sand, the hum of freeway traffic, a tiny plane buzzing through a blue ocean of sky. This complete absence of sound, however, was unnatural. His ears were beginning to play tricks with him. To keep his mind steady, Michael massaged his aching knees.

Back in the fifties, during one hot summer, he and one of Gilbert's sons (had it been Robert or Fremont?) had built a chicken house. Margaret's nine pullets and four scrawny roosters kept them company, clucking over the ground, pecking randomly at dried tumbleweed and bright stones. Though homeless, the birds had kept up a friendly chatter among themselves as he and Robert or Fremont set up fresh pinewood frames, which they joined together with heavy nails.

How long had it taken to finish? Hadn't Robert or Fremont been going to school in Albuquerque? Or maybe working in the uranium mine below Madrecita? The mine had been going strong back then, giving up the poison yellow dirt the Anglos needed for their secret war machines. The chicken house, anyway, had blown down in a freak tornado in 1963.

Ayaah'ah, stupid old man! It was Robert who had worked at the mine all his life. Robert was a little slow in the head; he couldn't have helped Michael build anything. Maybe the uranium dust had affected his brain.

It was Fremont then, quiet and steady Fremont. Michael thought for a moment. It had really taken them four days to build the chicken house. The memory was unbroken by food, rest, or nightfall. He remembered only unending sunlight and the two of them hammering wall planks, forming the roof over a sturdy structure, quietly talking. Michael closed his eyes, falling into memory.

A faint rasping noise interrupted. A whisper of cloth. His ears were still good. Michael opened his eyes and saw a pale child standing over him.

Melissa.

They stared at each other for a time. Half reclining and half sitting up, Michael became cramped, feeling as if a nail were being driven into his lower spine. He did not want to move.

Deer, when spooked, run for miles, over many hills, before they feel secure enough to stop. They had power. Michael had nothing.

Melissa frowned. "Where's Mama?"

Michael held his breath. The girl looked transparent, as if a scrap of wind might blow her away into the night sky. He didn't answer.

"Are you dead, Grandpa? Are you a ghost?" Melissa's eyes grew dark, almost black. "Why won't you answer me?"

"I can hear you, Granddaughter," Michael said finally.

"Touch my hand, then," she said, putting out a thin finger. "Prove to me you're real."

Michael was curious. He didn't move to touch her. "I feel your breath, Granddaughter. You can feel mine."

"I can't see you." Melissa sighed. "You are dead."

"Give me your hand, Melissa."

"I don't touch dead people. I don't talk to them."

"*Shi'yazhi,* where is your mother?"

Melissa shook her head angrily; she kneeled in front of the TV as if watching a program. She nodded to it, even laughed. Michael recognized the blue dress Melissa was wearing. She had worn it for an Easter gathering in Madrecita when she was fourteen. Small on her then, the dress looked too large now. Her thin shoulders nearly came through the oval neckline.

"Have you eaten, my granddaugher?"

She did not look away from the dead TV screen. "I'm hungry, but my stomach hurts, grandpa."

"I'll make you some toast."

"Okay. Thanks."

Michael pushed himself from the couch. His spine popped from being cemented for so long in one position. His leg muscles stretched tightly as if they might snap apart. He grunted, ignored his pain, and limped into the kitchen.

The water from the faucet was ice cold. He washed his hands and face and looked for a towel. He saw none. Dripping water onto the floor, Michael opened the refrigerator. He glanced into the living room and saw Melissa lying on the couch. He waited by the open door, cold air washing over his wet hands and face. Melissa did not move.

Michael closed the door gently and went to her. She looked like a small child who had played in an open sack of flour. Her

95

feet were bare and dusted with white. Laboring pitifully, Melissa's narrow chest hitched unevenly. Michael bent and picked her up, then carried her down the hall to her room. Her weightless body drifted in his arms. He could feel her small ribs underneath the cotton dress. Melissa moaned and shivered, as if she could feel the ground glass grating in his joints. Michael held her trembling against his chest. She was so cold! Her skin was slick and hard, and her legs were as white as frost. Michael held her gently, as he would a newborn lamb, as he had once held his stricken grandmother.

Awkwardly, he pulled quilts and blankets down, then laid Melissa on the bedsheet. Her body curled in on itself, then became still. Michael could only see her black hair and the Easter dress. Her solemn profile, her arms and legs, seemed to disappear into the white sheet.

He covered her with blankets. He would guard Melissa, not let her out of his sight. Not until he found his daughter.

Twenty

The clashing shouts of running metal vehicles faded, and the beams of their lamps, which swept across Falke, spearing him painlessly, lapsed into a background mutter like a harpsichord played in a distant room. He listened warily. There was no music. Only noise.

A droplet of memory blanketed the moon: Christiane's fierce eyes brimming with sunlight, her slender hand resting secretly in his own. Sun shafts sprayed through coach windows as if the light were as substantial as water, holdable in the palm.

The memory vanished.

Falke entered a glittering vault. He adjusted his senses to the new atmosphere. Again, he listened. He recognized sounds originating from stringed instruments, heavy drum beats.

The people of this time had changed the delicate musical sounds into the squeals of slaughtered horses, the thunder of prideful angels. The music roaring from the walls and ceiling was not music; it was mere noise, lush and overblown as a spoiled carcass.

Bright forms revolved around him. Artificial moonlight streamed onto young, mortal heads. A lurid mood greased their intertwined bodies and gave off a scent above the stench of alcohol, a scent which he could not quite fathom. There was time. He would learn from the children.

Whispers of thought billowed about him. The human bodies themselves were clumsy, but their movement and wants were caressing and erotic. Familiar. A hand stroked his arm. Falke smelled rose perfume, the only scent he recognized besides blood, and saw a girl with bobbed, purple-black hair floating away from him.

A voice shouted. "You coming or going?"

Falke turned to see a heavy boy staring boldly at him. "I am staying."

"There's a four dollar cover, is all." The boy yawned.

Falke ignored him and began to follow the girl. A woman touched his arm and spoke. "I'll get it." She was slender as the purple-haired girl but taller.

"My name is Stephanie," she said as she took Falke's hand and led him onto the dance floor, where the music was painfully loud. Falke ignored an urge to cover his ears. Stephanie glanced at him with concealed gray eyes.

"Do you want a drink?" she asked.

Falke watched as Stephanie went to a bar across the room. The walls were rimmed with curved bars of white light that made the serving boy appear cadaverous. Falke supposed that was the intended effect, and he wondered what kind of world he had fallen into. The din was suddenly silenced and a stiffening, unsure sensation fell on the room. Humans drifted by. Falke noted with approval their open, pretty eyes.

"Are you sure you don't want anything?" Stephanie took a sip of wine. She was wearing something red and short. It made her skin look vibrant.

"I do not drink alcohol." Falke reached out and touched her freckled breastbone. Her skin was smooth, like wax. He felt

97

her heart beating underneath tender flesh and bone, beckoning him.

Stephanie took another sip. Her small white teeth clicked against the glass. "You're not from around here, are you."

Falke traced her larynx and considered driving his finger through it. He tapped her chin and withdrew. "No."

"You're . . . you seem very strange." Stephanie moved closer, touched his coat. "I've never seen anyone like you before. Even in the movies. Where do you come from?"

The music started again, a deep percussive rhythm. The children began their primal dance. What had happened to gracefulness and sidestepping like water? In his absence, the world had embraced the savage's way.

"I come from a place where no questions are asked," he said, perhaps too quietly to hear.

Stephanie laughed and tugged at his sleeve. "You see that girl there? She can't take her eyes off your crotch!"

He ignored her words. "Do you have a coach?"

"Coach?"

"A carriage."

"Oh, a coach." Stephanie gazed at him speculatively. "You are a forward man."

Falke moved closer, placing his hand on her hip. The material of the dress was soft leather. Stephanie backed away, spilling some of her wine.

"I have a car," she said breathlessly. "A sports car, if you really want to know."

"This car. Teach me to ride it."

"Teach you to ride . . . you mean drive it?"

"Just as I said."

A long, clear laugh floated from the crowd. It seemed to startle and awaken Stephanie.

"Why? Don't you have a car of your own?"

"Refuse," Falked said patiently, "and I ask another girl."

"Wait! You're going too fast." Stephanie put her hand on his chest. She looked frightened and unsure. "Okay. But, right away?"

Falke kissed her dry lips. She was not beautiful, but the dress she wore fit her shape nicely. Her skin was flushed, which gave a pleasant rose color to her cheeks.

98   "Yes," he said.

"Well, wait a minute! How do I know you're not some axe murderer or a rapist?"

Somehow—and this had always fascinated him—humans always knew when death was near. Falke smiled, took Stephanie's arm firmly, steering her through twirling bodies and noise. He felt tentative touches and heard sweet whispers of invitation drifting airily by his head.

"I will be kind," Falke told Stephanie as they emerged from the noisy dance hall, into frosty night.

"How come you never learned to drive?" Stephanie asked.

Falke watched electric lamps marching past the vehicle windows. He rubbed the side of his jaw. "Where I come from, the steel carriage has not yet made its mark."

Stephanie, her eyes intent on the road, laughed prettily. "Really? I don't believe you. Where are you from, anyway? And don't say from outer space, either."

"Let us talk about you. You seduce me, then spirit me away in your little silver car. What is her intent, I ask myself."

Stephanie glanced sideways at him. "I don't know. You looked so lost in that place, I just had to rescue you."

"Do you always rescue men who look lost? It is a game of yours, perhaps?"

Stephanie bounced her dark curls from side to side as if listening to some private music. "Nope. I don't. You're my first, anyway."

The passing roads lulled him. Dimly, Falke recalled a serrated, wind-blown country, far south of his own kingdom in the Semming Pass near Vienna, where Christiane waited for his return. The sky was a veiled gold. If he looked behind him, Falke could glimpse a pale blue sea—the Adriatic. Small bells on the mounts' bridles *chinged!* merrily. Leather creaked. His knights' songs were youthful and engaging—except for the song, resting secretly, that Christiane had given him:

> A vision of truth,
> And she begged of the Sun,
> I have desired betrothal,
> A marriage in clouds of purest air.
> And the angels danced with her
> in a storm of music,

until the wings of fire
consumed her.

Falke's long shield, borne by a dusty page, had displayed a single black anchor, which swallowed the rays of a weary sun. A memory of one afternoon, nine centuries past, when he had been alive and king.

Falke shifted in the small vehicle, feeling the ancient age of the oldest cathedral.

Stephanie touched his thigh. "What are you thinking about?"

Then Falke remembered one night, over a century ago. A hideous storm of fire. A long wait. Cold trembling hands finally touching him, caressing his forehead. Falke had opened his eyes to see Elizabeth's terrified face, and the half-lidded moon reflected in her eyes. Nothing to fear, he had told her in fading whispers. Give me time.

Elizabeth's voice was soft and trembling. "What happened, Falke . . . what do I do?"

"Sing to me." Had he whispered Christiane's name?

A black mist had fallen over the moon.

If he reckoned the years precisely, backward from this moment, his secret reburial had lasted one hundred and ten years, a motionless time spent guiding the reknitting of his torn muscle and shattered bone. A healing coma in which his flesh had shed a noxious burnt shell and reformed its silky whiteness, all happening while Elizabeth held him, nourished him with her potent blood, and sung lullabies in a child's whisper.

A woman spoke at his side. "I can teach you to drive whenever you want," she said. "Just say the word."

"Stop this carriage."

"Stop . . . here?"

The vehicle halted. A lonely streetlamp peered at them.

Falke tasted Stephanie's fear. He took her hand and pulled her roughly to him, smelling the sweetness of her perfume and the more subtle scent of her body responding to him. Stephanie closed her eyes, as if waiting to be kissed. Falke brushed her cheek.

"Find a place where I can sleep undisturbed," he said gently. "A place where the sun will not find me. Do you understand?"

Falke imagined his words as some dark, enchanted cat curling around her slim neck. Stephanie opened her eyes quickly, as if finally comprehending.

"Please," she whispered, staring fearfully. "Let me go."

"Quiet, girl. Sleep."

Tears darkened her eyes. Falked closed them for her, feeling a wetness on his fingertips, and gently laid her hands in her lap. He pictured the darkness of a bottomless ocean, empty of living things, and sent the image into Stephanie's mind.

She swayed a little. "I don't . . . yes, I think . . . "

"I am going to take you, Stephanie. To a faraway place. You will not come back."

Her head droooped slowly and came to rest on Falke's shoulder. She made a small noise, as if trying to answer or object. Falke laid her against the seat, where she crumped like a sleeping child. He touched Stephanie's hair and felt in its rough texture the decline of youth.

Before killing her, Falke remembered last night.

His lungs had expanded in a sparse, icy air. The night sky was filled with glassy stars. Black pines swayed. Craggy, mountain rock lay silently as a pale girl led him to a place she had kept secret.

And she was beautiful. Gentle brown hair curling and loose about her slim shoulders, fierce eyes illuminating his frozen soul; delicate fingers touched his aching face and numb cheeks. He felt a fiery heat in her palm, a candle flame held to his face. Falke wanted more of her touch, nothing else.

Melissa rose on tiptoe and kissed him. "Close your eyes."

"Melissa, I can see, even without my eyes, whatever it is you want to show me."

The girl shook her head, undaunted. "It's a surprise! You have to close them."

Falke yielded. A slender hand crept into his, gently tugged him forward. "Don't be afraid," she had whispered. "I won't let you go."

He felt the wind changing shape, from a solid sheet to a cleansing bath, as they walked to the edge of the mountain.

"Okay." Her voice was breathless with excitement. "Open your eyes."

He opened them and staggered backward. An ocean swelled and waves glittered under a full sun. Memories from the

101

time he had been alive burst into his mind. Voices and bodies shrieked and pounded against his skull. Falke swayed from the force of them, tried to stop them. He fought against empty air. A girl held him tightly against her, true to her promise.

Christiane?

"Falke . . . what's wrong?"

After a time, Falke lowered his arms from the night sky and stared at the city, not an ocean under the sun; a cloud of spurious electric light glowed at his feet. Pinpricks tingled across his face and hands, as if the wind was throwing dry sand against him.

"I am still weak . . . Melissa." Falke smoothed back her wavy, tangled hair. Melissa gazed serenely at him, her eyes filling with moonlight.

"Why did you find me?" she asked.

Falke traced the curve of her cheek down to the unblemished skin of her throat. She trembled at his icy touch, became still and watchful. Falke had then understood why he had come to the barren desert surrounding this newly born city, the sun-tortured desert where he had made his sanctuary. And he felt as an ancient mariner, having ridden frozen waves, finally coming to a safe haven.

"It is clean here," he explained to the wind. "And there are no ghosts."

Melissa's eyes lost their abstractness. She spoke into the wind's storming, angry blasts.

"Take me with you," she had said.

Falke held Stephanie, placed his finger on the fair skin of her throat, and listened to her strong thudding pulse for a long time.

Twenty-one

It was near dawn. Still dark outside. Michael tried to move from the desk chair to check his granddaughter's pulse, but his knee joints had frozen solid during the night. He massaged the stiffness in them. Several hours earlier, he had switched the lamp on to see better, but Melissa, whimpering, had covered her eyes and made herself into a tiny ball, as if the light had been something to be frightened of.

Michael had cried then. He thought all of his tears had stayed with Margaret. He switched off the lamp and sat by Melissa, her forehead cold as if in the grip of some ice monster Nanibaa' had forgotten to tell him about. He sang to soothe her fear. Not the prayer chants his grandmother had taught him, those mighty songs containing words of gloom and power that still frightened him. Instead, he sang the story of Coyote and Arrow Lizard: how Coyote wanted the beautiful song Arrow Lizard had created, but was too impatient to learn it properly. So he stole the pouch in which the song was kept, hoping to keep it for himself. Then, fooling around as usual, he lost the song in a lake where even Arrow Lizard could not find it again.

But she had more songs tucked under her shawl, Nanibaa' would say to Michael. Arrow Lizard had patience and knew how to make songs. She remembered what she had been taught.

"Why was she named Arrow Lizard?" Michael had asked once, when a small boy.

Nanibaa's eyes sharpened. "Coyote became angered that Arrow Lizard would not teach him her song again, so he swallowed her up. But she was alive in Coyote's stomach and thinking all this time, my grandson. She was a little woman, but she had secret weapons hidden under her shawl. As Coyote trotted away, Arrow Lizard let down her shawl and showed her arrows. See! This is the lizard we call horned toad. But Coyote didn't know her true name. He had forgotten it. Arrow Lizard cut her away out of his stomach and throat and jumped onto the dirt.

103

" 'Silly Coyote!' Arrow Lizard called to the wailing animal. 'Next time, listen to what the elderlies tell you. Remember it well! And don't always think with your eyes, for the smallest creature can be the most dangerous.' "

Michael watched the walls around him turning gray with dawn light. Melissa's posters became visible. *Lóó'tsoh,* Whale. *Shash,* Grandfather Bear. *Ma'iitsoh,* Wolf. She even had pictures of some prairie dogs grooming themselves. Michael smiled as the day grew around him. Melissa would learn the song of Coyote and Arrow Lizard when she was better; today, if she woke up. He would teach her the song so she could sing it to her own children, when she had them, before they went to sleep at night.

He watched the broken form under the quilt. Hours crept past. Melissa slept on, through the morning, without sound or movement.

Twenty-two

Melissa lifted her grandfather from the desk chair. His whole body must weigh no more than a small stone, she thought. If I wanted to, I could throw him out the window and over to the next block. Melissa giggled as she carried him through darkness and dropped him onto her bed.

"Now, I'll make you something to eat, Grandpa. Eggs! I know how you like eggs." Melissa set his head straight on the pillow, then arranged his hands on his stomach. Just like the funeral home had done with poor Grandma. She jabbed his shoulder with her finger. "Time to get up!"

Michael rubbed his frowning mouth. "I fell asleep."

"I know! You must have been tired. You were really out."

"How did I get here on your bed?" He sat up, wincing. His gray hair glistened like tarnished silver.

The heat of his body had warmed her arms, and made her think of hot desert winds, swirling dust, a shimmering oasis to drink from. Melissa slid onto her knees and started to unbutton his shirt. She touched his throat and whispered. "I helped you."

A calloused hand gripped her fingers, held them tightly. "Granddaughter, how do you feel?"

Melissa drew away and studied his sharpening eyes. "I feel wonderful! Thank you so much for taking care of me. You sang to me, too. That was nice."

"Where is your mother?"

The old man glared at her, as if he was angry. Why? Melissa wondered. I haven't done anything. Her smile faltered. "She's out of town. She went to . . . El Paso. To visit a friend."

"Sarah left you alone?" His rough hand released her.

"I am nearly seventeen!" Melissa's fingers twitched freely, curled into a fist. "And what is it to you?"

"I was worried about you both." Her grandfather's gaze softened, but his words burned into her like stinging hail. "You haven't visited me for a long time, *shi'yazhi*."

Melissa rubbed at her eyes as if wakening out of a nightmare. She opened her hand, frightened at how close she had come to striking her grandfather. Cold darkness pressed at her temples. She saw the lonely desert where he had come from, the stone house on the hill, the friendly animals. A quiet place where there was no Grandma to tell things to anymore. Underneath her hand, her grandfather smelled of dust and sugarless gum.

"Grandpa, I . . . " Melissa wiped moisture off her cheeks. "I haven't brought you any gum. You must've run out a long time ago."

Michael took her hand gently and smiled. "Your uncle Samson brings me some gum, when he brings me my supplies. But he always gets the wrong kind."

Melissa laughed. "How's my horse who thinks he's a dog?"

"Your Lee still forgets his name. He wants to barrel race at the Gallup Ceremonial next year."

"And he'll win too, Grandpa. With me riding him."

Rising onto one elbow, the old man spoke. "I can't see too well in the dark. Turn on the light."

Melissa pulled her hand from him, felt uncontrollable anger rushing back. "Sleep some more. It'll do you some good."

She forced the words into his eyes, as if her mind had become a stabbing knife. Her grandfather fell backward onto the bed, eyes rolling to whites, his hands trembling at his sides. Standing quickly, Melissa felt fear prickling her cheeks.

Did I do that?

"No," he whispered huskily. "I must take you to the hospital."

Melissa leaned over him and touched his lips. "You'll be safer if he doesn't hear you, Grandpa." She closed his feverish eyelids and spoke to him again as Falke had taught her. "Imagine the words as knives cutting into the enemy's skin," he had said. Melissa pictured skull-white moonlight drifting onto breaking ocean surf.

"Sleep," she said to her grandfather.

Melissa watched as her glass filled with water from the faucet. She laughed as the water topped the brim and trickled over her fingers. The dense nausea that had blanketed her soul was gone. Her long sleep seemed to have helped her body rid itself of whatever poison had crept inside. She felt pure and light. Although, for a few minutes, she'd been frightened at seeing her grandfather asleep in her room. Stiff, like the dead.

Melissa covered her mouth and giggled secretively at the thought.

How had he come here? she wondered. When was he going back?

Anyway, her life was back to normal. Except for her eyes, which burned from the moon's disc outside the kitchen window. And her appetite was gone, too, which was a little strange. But not unexplainable. She had never liked to eat, and she welcomed this change gratefully. Any kind of fat made her shiver with disgust. The Quivering Stomach Jelly, as ditsy Sandie had called it, her one artistic contribution to mankind.

The only thing that was worrying Melissa was her incredible thirst. She turned the squeaking knob, and held the full glass up to the light. As of this second, she had filled four tall glasses with water. And she had tasted none of them. Melissa tipped the glass off her palm and watched it shatter among the fragments of the other glasses littering the sink. Maybe something richer might appeal to her. A bloody, meaty broth? A bowl of corn flakes?

Her stomach cramped. The thought of cooked meat made her feel ill again. Then she imagined a viscous white fluid oozing over yellow chips of dead skin. Skin Flakes. Gross! Melissa glanced at her watch's calendar.

Coyote October, as dreaming Granddad used to say. The crazy month when everything went funny.

Where was Sarah, anyway? If anyone could suggest something to cure this thirst, Sarah would know. Melissa frowned at the intrusive thought. She had last seen her mother several days ago, when she had stalked out Thursday night. Or had it been last night?

Oh, well, Melissa thought, shrugging. Sarah just better not call drunk from some faraway town like El Paso or Dallas and beg her "little girl" to come get her before she was raped or murdered. She had done that several times too often.

Melissa heard a click as the front door opened.

"Mom," she whispered, relieved.

She could hear a slow, thudding heart beat, different from her mother's. Falke had said her hearing would become as sensitive and discerning as a deer's. The temperature in the kitchen dropped. Melissa felt a contradictory heat rise in her chest.

"You were ill." Falke's voice was quiet behind her. His hands soothed her shoulders, pulled her against him. Melissa felt serene, as if she were floating in a pond on a hot, summer afternoon.

"I remember," she said. "You brought me home to rest and heal." Melissa loved the smell of him. Even though she knew Falke never ate, he always smelled faintly of some spice: cinnamon, thyme, or mint. His arms came around her until she was draped in his woolen coat. "But I didn't know it would be so bad, Falke. It scared me . . . as if I was dying. And the light hurts me too. Just like you said."

She realized what was happening and grew silent.

"The pain is much worse when giving up life forever." His voice rumbled along her spine. "For such a time, you need a supporting hand."

Melissa closed her eyes. "Is this what it was like for you?"

Falke stood frowning in the center of her mother's kitchen. The sweater he wore was dark gray and as soft as cat's fur. His blond hair was gathered on his wide shoulders, a waterfall under dying sunlight. His eyes were deep still lakes. He frightened her a little.

Be truthful, she thought. More than a little.

Falke kneeled. She would have run away if he had not gripped her waist firmly. A cold ache seeped into her hips.

"Touch me here," she whispered, bringing his hand up to her breast. She wondered how it would be to have him undress her, kiss her naked thighs, her waist, and neck; to have him settle on top of her and slip deep inside, filling her with heat.

"We must go," Falke said, moving away. "The night will escape and you will not have . . . nourished yourself."

"I'm cold, Falke." And my body is *alive*. "Is that how you feel?"

Without answering, Falke took Melissa's hand, led her through the wind-filled apartment, out into the shifting dark.

The clouds above them were frozen, tumbling mountains. Wind rattled in the elms, suppressing all other sounds. Melissa felt as if she might fragment into the air and be blown into scattered pieces of heart and memory. She saw the silver car.

"I thought you only rode horses," she said.

The sports car glinted on the street. Melissa touched its curved fender, ran a finger along its sleek hood.

"Very pretty, Falke. Where did you get it?"

Falke escorted her to the open passenger-side door and helped her inside. "A friend brought me here while you were asleep."

The smell of perfume and cigarettes filled the interior. Melissa slid across the seats and gripped the steering wheel. "I was sick," she said tightly. "Where is your friend now?"

Falke slammed the door.

Melissa turned the ignition. "I always did like the sports car Jaguars. That's what this is, right?" The engine was soundless. "They're much prettier than the other ones."

Falke watched her with amusement. "Which other ones?"

"You know, the other Jaguars. I've never been in one, but my mom has. She says riding in one is like flying in a cloud."

Falke settled against the door, remained silent as Melissa drove. The trees swayed. Hanging traffic lights swung back and forth. Driven paper and whole tree branches bounced along the streets. Sand particles streamed passed the head-lights.

"Falke? What else is going to happen to me?" Melissa pictured old school buildings and mossy willows. Falke answered so softly, she had to lift her hair around her ear to hear him.

"Your soul will turn to ash. And your heart will outgrow your chest."

"What? Are you kidding?"

"The changes work differently in each human."

Falke was looking at a group of kids lounging against a darkened store. "I believe you will not be harmed. You are not as I am. You bear life within you."

"I still don't understand," Melissa said. "What am I? I feel so weird. Like I've taken some creepy drug or something."

"Stop the car, Melissa."

She looked to darkened store fronts and fast food lots for somewhere isolated. She found a stand of trees behind a restaurant and pulled into it. Switching off the engine, she let the car roll noiselessly until it nudged against a leaning fence. Melissa watched as the fence creaked backward, then stopped. "Sorry," she muttered.

Falke's profile remained in shadow. "You are more spirit than human, Melissa. Finer. As silk is to cotton, perhaps." The car rocked as if they were on a boat. "Before this night, you were like flame. A tiny candle flame. You are like fire, now."

Melissa felt even more distressed. How can all this be real? "Why do I feel so thirsty all the time?" she asked, breathless. "Why is everything so loud?"

Falke's shadow was still. Melissa was afraid he wouldn't say anything. "Please tell me, Falke. I love you. That's all I want to feel." He looked as if he hadn't heard her. Or didn't care. Confusion made her angry again. "Don't tell me, then."

She stared at flashing signs on the far side of the restaurant. The lit boards held no words. She opened her window. The whisper of leaves was distant. She heard the sign bulbs clicking on and off. Falke touched her hair and the side of her neck.

"Did you kill the woman?" Melissa shivered. "Your friend?"

"Yes, I killed her." Falke took hold of her shoulder and jerked her to him. His breath burned along the back of her head. "I wooed her with sweet words and kissed her until she became naked in my arms. Stephanie scorched me like fire. Unlocked my passion. That is how I killed her."

Enraged, Melissa screamed and clawed at his face. Falke did nothing, remained silent, accepted her anger and hurt, until she became too weak to lift her arms. Then Melissa broke down and wept noisily like a baby. She didn't care. Falke held her and cradled her. She thought he might sing to her, as her grandfather had earlier today.

His fingers held her chin and turned her face toward his. Falke's gray eyes were so clear they reflected the surrounding lights as if an alien world were contained within them. He kissed Melissa with such gentleness that she began to cry again. She slipped her hand under his sweater and kneaded the stone muscles of his stomach and chest. His mouth left hers. She swayed as if suddenly let go to fall through a lonely abyss. Melissa clutched him, keeping him to her.

"My Melissa, you are tired."

She rested against his chest. His hand seemed to engulf her skull. Falke continued.

"The life of my body will always come from another. That is the truth of my existence, and yours. You must accept it. Only for you will I hunt, Melissa."

He wound his hand in her hair, leaned backward against the door, pulled her until she lay on top of him. Melissa began to feel overheated. She wanted to open the window and let the cold wind wash over them. She kissed his lips, wishing his soul into her mouth. Falke grasped his sweater's neckline. The wool purred as it came apart. Falke squeezed her index finger and brought it to his throat. The sighing air stilled. Using Melissa's pink fingernail, Falke sliced into his skin. A droplet of rose-dark blood peeked from a crescent gash, left a glistening trail as it slid down his skin.

Melissa felt a tremor of heat rise from her vagina to her face. Drawing closer, she nuzzled against Falke's smooth jawline, stretched herself over his immense body. Her lips were so sensitive even the wind's faintest touch almost excited her to orgasm. Dribbles of blood splashed onto the seat and floor, and she mourned the waste. A bitter smell filled the car. Melissa wanted to rip the gash wider, so she could wriggle inside and search out the source of the blood's flow.

Gently, she licked at his moist cut, tasted the hot liquid pouring over her tongue like honey syrup. Melissa drifted from all memory and thought, anchoring herself only to taste. She felt Falke's excitement in the rhythmic tensing and relaxing of his muscles. His hands groped into her loose hair. Melissa laughed playfully and pulled away. Falke groaned, caught hold of her arms, dragged her against him. Melissa placed her mouth over the smooth skin of his throat and sucked, again and again, swallowing the blood which quickly filled her mouth, drinking more from him, slowly and deeply.

Dimly, minutes passed. Melissa realized that as her body grew warmer, Falke grew as frozen as an iceberg.

The car jolted briefly under a sobbing wind. Then it stilled again.

Twenty-three

Hanna caught a brief image of herself in a building's towering mirrored sides. Vaporous naked arms, the frail pieces of Wendy's clothing needed to disguise the strength of her frame, the vivid powders and paints to soften her gaunt head. Foolish masks to seduce human prey. Falke had talked of masks.

Listening, Hanna paused and looked into the street. Greenish yellow lamps shooed away darkness from the skirts of glassy walls. A traffic light changed colors, but there were no cars to take notice. Suddenly, male laughter and shouts crackled against steel signs and blackening concrete. Hanna smiled as she scented blood in the nebulous air. Her own masks had worked.

Four trotting boys turned a corner and stopped in the middle of the street. They were rough-looking, muscled and hairy; but Hanna saw smooth flesh and racing hearts. They

111

saw her and bunched together, hesitating, until a light-haired boy shrugged and continued toward her. The rest followed, burst into a trotting run like young horses.

Calming her excitement, Hanna adopted an agitated walk, as if she were being hunted, as if her wings were broken. She clutched the hem of her flimsy dress as she heard boots trampling the sidewalk. A chain-link fence tinkled beside her. The building she entered echoed with jeering laughter and reeked of gasoline and oil. The floors, stacked zigzaggedly, and the scattered cars were lit by flickering tubes that only created more shadows. Hanna slowed, making sure the boys could see where she stopped.

One boy with a shaved head whooped and made smacking, kissing noises. The others spread out in a half-circle and surrounded her. They brimmed with dank, dog-yellow lust.

"Say, pretty honey," crooned a bald boy. "Pretty legs. How about giving up a kiss?"

"A *suck* for me!" yelled a fat one, darker than the others. "I've got a big surprise for you, bitch."

Hanna trembled with hunger, and knew they saw it as fear. She gripped her wispy skirt, shakily pulled it across her thigh, fueling their excitement. The boy with the shaved head grabbed his crotch.

"Man, sweet," he said. "You are luscious."

Looming figures ringed her as she backed into a concrete corner. The boys exuded a poisonous desire. Hanna made herself appear smaller, made her eyes into desperate circles. She threw an empty purse at them. "Take the money," she whispered. "Please don't hurt me."

"We don't want to hurt you." The shaved headed boy, his eyes colorless stones, spread his hands out to show he meant no harm. His smiling face hung close. She smelled cigarettes and alcohol. A memory of muddy rain pools, the shock of freezing water, awakened a glimmer of real fear.

"We don't want your money." The boy kissed her forehead with chapped lips. Fingers fondled her thigh, entwined in her skirt, lifting. A leather jacket creaked.

Or the creak of saddles. And whipping belts.

Hanna grew still. A memory from the twilight time, before Falke had killed her: A vision of drunken men dragging her through filthy water; hot pokers slashing into her breasts;

snaking belts and ropes burning into her ankles and knees; and a searing hateful pain as a glowing point came to rest in the deep of her navel.

Hanna faded as memory fogged her senses.

A sudden shout, then a rough weight fell on her, grabbing and squeezing, yanking, pulling her down. A hand hit her in the mouth. Her dress ripped. Blunt fingers pinched and scraped her body. Teeth nicked and bit and violated her.

Her memory fog vanished. Hanna's hand changed into a raging creature, slashing and biting. It flew into a chest, snapped ribs, grasped in soupy warmth, clenched a sleek convulsing muscle. The boy with the shaved head gurgled as he stared. Hanna shrieked laughter and wrenched out his heart.

The other boys, as one animal, stopped crowding and saw her. Hanna contracted her mind's power into a compact ball, felt its pressure beating against her skull. Her fist tightened. Then she let go. Bodies twisted from her, thudded onto concrete, as if a bomb had exploded in their midst. She stretched a bloodied hand out to blinking eyes. The boys made no move to rise.

"Unlock the gates," Hanna said, glaring through spiked eyelashes. "The Queen has come."

The boys wavered.

"The bitch is fucked!" The bald boy screamed and began to run. Hanna swept over the two prone boys and caught the bald boy by his jacket collar.

"I'm not finished playing." Teeth clenched, Hanna jerked the boy backward onto the concrete floor. Hanna descended and began slapping his face. The boy crossed his arms to ward off her hardening blows.

"*Bitch!*" Hanna raged, balling her hands into fists. "Where's your hard-on now?"

The boy shrieked. Hunger forgotten, Hanna exerted more of her strength. Bone and skull cracked. Mucous dribbled onto concrete. Droplets of blood and gray matter rained on her bare skin. Hanna pounded the boy as if her fists had become hammers.

Panting, she halted, wiped her face. Chips of bone rolled under her fingertips. She turned to the two remaining boys. Their eyes were frantic and fixed on the sodden bundle of skin

113

and crushed bone. The fat boy shuddered, began blubbering. She spoke to them both as if she were crooning to babies.

"Who's next?" Hanna grinned, revealing white, glistening fangs.

The boys fled, running under fluorescent bars of light. The fat one wept wildly as he blundered into thick columns and chrome fenders. Hanna decided to save him for last.

The light-haired boy was close by, hidden somewhere. Hanna could hear a rustling of boots, irregular breathing, heart quivering in his throat, veins bulging with rushing blood. Calming herself, Hanna channeled a venomous energy into her mind. She walked forward and found the boy's hiding place beneath a boatlike car. She moved deliberately toward him, no stalking, mesmerized by the boy's whining breath. A surge of power shot into her fingers. When she grasped the car's smooth fender, cold metal shriveled in her hand.

A scream uncurled next to her bare feet. The weight of the car became as light as a wisp of silk. Metal joints creaked. Hanna lifted and threw the car onto its back. She laughed at the squealing metal, popping glass, and showers of sparks. A gout of flame erupted to the ceiling. A clear, freezing liquid spread around her toes. A stench of gasoline fanned against her. The boy, lying at her feet, shrieked piercingly like a woman.

Hanna dropped onto his back, flipped him over, slammed him into the floor. His skull popped like a hollow gourd. She tore his jacket off. Using her hand as an axe, she slashed into his upper chest. Blood spewed around her in a red shower. She opened her mouth and unrolled her tongue, catching the heavy droplets which shot from the boy's gouged body.

Delirious, she drank.

Twenty-four

A rising shriek made Elizabeth pause by a deserted restaurant. The road was being stripped of dust by the wind. Light danced from a single streetlamp. A neon sign buzzed in a darkened bar window on the corner. She closed her eyes and let the breeze stir her thoughts into a kaleidoscope of swirling, distorted images. A gulf of stars waited behind green tendrils of cloud. She wanted to fly to them and bathe in their stinging rays.

But the scream held her down. Faintly, she heard laughter and the dull rip of a fiery explosion. She imagined flames licked her face, withered her skin. Elizabeth opened her eyes and began to run toward the violence.

She arrived at a fluorescent-bathed building before the wailing police cars and emergency vehicles, touching its cement walls as if they might reveal what was happening inside. She heard a child's pleading voice. Elizabeth searched the perimeter until she found a rubble-strewn hole, which she crept through.

The low-ceilinged parking lot was filled with sputtering flames and the stink of burning rubber. Black smoke curled around a column. Orange fire light flickered against windshields. She couldn't see the fire's source. Soft laughter echoed, then the sound of Hanna's voice speaking to someone—the unseen child.

The sirens grew louder. Setting aside caution, Elizabeth followed Hanna's voice. She turned a corner and came upon the vampire and her victim. At first, Elizabeth thought the two figures—Hanna and a young fat boy—were dancing with the crackling fire as their music. Moving closer, she saw instead that Hanna held the boy upright with her smacking mouth fastened to his throat. The boy's white face glistened. Elizabeth had never seen Hanna feed before. A queer, sick sensation weighed down her heart. She wanted to pounce on the glutted creature and destroy it. Elizabeth waited as if she

115

had taken root on the concrete floor. Then she heard shouting men's voices and a metallic whisper of the fence being thrown open, sounds impelling her to motion.

Elizabeth pried Hanna's fingers from the boy's oily hair, and laid the limp corpse onto the floor. The boy's pursed lips and tightly closed eyes made him look as if he had eaten a sour peach. Elizabeth took hold of Hanna's shoulder and led her carefully and quickly to the last wall of the lot, an embankment with a steel mesh fence behind it. She was afraid Hanna might fall, being engorged with blood, and not get up again. Elizabeth leaned over the embankment, grasped the fence in both hands, and methodically snapped the intertwined metal rings as if she were pulling stitches in a garment.

Soon, the tattered hole in the fence became wide enough to allow them through. Elizabeth saw Hanna sitting on the embankment, holding her head in her hands. Gripping Hanna's hot arm, Elizabeth flew them both through the torn fence just as stabbing headlights pierced the darkness, illuminating the crumpled boy and shimmering blood.

Elizabeth's feet touched asphalt.

"Hurry! We can't stop here." She tugged at Hanna and began to lead her swiftly through the empty downtown streets, hoping no one would be around to notice the red-streaked arms and ripped, bloodsoaked dress. She slowed their pace to remove her coat and wrap it around Hanna, but she didn't stop.

Hanna's gait became steadier. "Enough," she muttered, shaking off Elizabeth's grip.

They stopped in a park, which held three tubular-steel sculptures resembling a bee, a giraffe, and a fly, all designed to be climbed and played on by children. Elizabeth stroked the giraffe's belly and gazed at the racing clouds above its skeletal head. Most of the paint had been worn away by thousands of chattering children who, squirming, grabbing, and standing on the artificial creatures, had maybe hoped that the animals would magically come to life and buzz or stride away with them still captured inside.

"Why did you interrupt me?" Hanna sat on a merry-go-round and lazily spun it with her bare feet. "I would have escaped on my own."

"I heard screams and felt fire. I thought you might've needed help. And you did, didn't you?"

No answer. Elizabeth knelt in the sand and saw green eyes glittering in the rushing darkness. Hanna looked like a child herself; a child who had played far into the night and forgotten to go home. Less angular and predatory now, Hanna's features had softened into a young girl's rounded face. She seemed distracted and wistful, adding strangely to her lush beauty, as she folded slender hands in her lap and allowed Elizabeth's inspection of her. Pink lips drew back in a smile, revealing reddened, pointed incisors.

What are we? Elizabeth wanted to wail. Hanna's eldritch beauty had come from stolen blood. From murdered children.

"Elizabeth, where is your husband? Have you talked to him?"

"I saw him." Elizabeth calmed herself, tried to push out the images of wanton murder she had seen; then she remembered the familiar girl she had glimpsed in Falke's mind. "He's found a new wife."

"Falke's a man," Hanna laughed. "No use getting jealous."

"Do you know his new wife, then?"

"I don't care to." Hanna swiveled the merry-go-round until her back was to Elizabeth.

"Well maybe you should care. The girl was in our sanctuary." Elizabeth could almost see her words torn apart by the shrieking wind. In an eyeblink, Hanna was looming against the sky.

"Tell me!"

Elizabeth walked through the yellow prickly grass. Hanna's presence appeared beside her, agitated.

"You . . . saw this?" Hanna asked. "But how? I haven't felt or seen anything."

Elizabeth shrugged as if it didn't matter. "The girl is frail, apparently. Like me. Or so Falke says."

Silence followed them as they left the metal animals behind.

"Who is this girl?" Hanna asked finally.

They had come to a district of new buildings, which rose above the pallid green streetlamps. A great volume of steam hissed somewhere among the building tops. Morning was near. It crept upon Elizabeth like a deadly gas. The moving air was becoming slightly more heated.

"Her name is Melissa. And all I know is what I've seen in Falke's mind." Elizabeth did not say why the girl had looked familiar. Same thick fall of dark hair and penetrating gaze, same shadowed smile—Melissa was the mirror-image of Christiane. Falke's convent girl. A woman so dead and gone she wasn't even dust anymore. Nine centuries dead, Christiane had risen with Falke in the form of this girl. To claim him.

Elizabeth glanced at Hanna. The vampire still seemed vague, as if she were tipsy. She walked loosely in Elizabeth's coat, which barely fit her, looking emptily at the surrounding buildings. Her red-gold hair seemed dispirited too, and ignored the quickening, random breeze.

"Maybe Falke wants stronger blood," Hanna said, "to speed his healing. That's a possibility."

"Melissa is very beautiful," Elizabeth said distantly. "I think he wants something more from her than quick healing."

Hanna became still. Elizabeth hesitated, thinking she might have become dizzy or faint. Then Hanna's dark gaze fell upon her. A smile perked the corners of her lips.

"You never told me how the masks' shooting flames pierced your husband's skull, sister. Give me the story now."

"How did you . . . oh, he told you." Elizabeth tensed as memory engulfed her. "It wasn't his skull, Hanna. It went into his chest, almost into his heart.

"I can't tell how it happened; I didn't see that. Falke had been gone four nights, and you had fallen into the deepest kind of sleep. I couldn't wake you. I think it was the beginning of the fifth night when I heard him speaking to me. Not clearly. More like mind pictures. A silent film in my head. I saw billowing sand and, I think . . . two chanting angels. Then a knife-blast of sunlight. Just like that. And so much pain.

"More worried than courageous, I went out of the sanctuary to find Falke. The moon was so hot, Hanna! Its light was corrupted somehow. And evil. I guess I hadn't really left the sanctuary since I came there with Falke. And never truly reckoned what he had made me into. I walked a long way among boulders and moonlit sand. The images in my head became clearer, almost as if Falke were forming them in my brain.

"Then I found him. The remains of him. Twisted and burnt against a sandy hill . . . like a tree that's been struck by lightning. White bone and charred skin. Evil, evil, I kept saying. Same as a prayer. I didn't know what had happened, or what to do. But the night was running fast. The moonlight kept hurting me. And I was so afraid of the sun catching me and burning me into a cinder . . . or of the angels coming back. I quickly gathered Falke's remains in my arms; or tried to. Some parts of him were so slender a thread that I had to rip the hem of my dress to make a sling to carry him in. It took me most of the night to carry him home. And I wasn't doing too well either. Ash and bits of his skin kept flaking off and falling into the dirt. I couldn't help but notice that."

No tears came. A hollow ache filled her body. Elizabeth remembered how Falke's blue-gray eyes had sunk, the sockets becoming black caves.

"I feel the sun wakening." Hanna took Elizabeth's shaking fingers. Her grip was gentle. "I have a place we can stay for the day. Will you sleep with me?"

Elizabeth couldn't speak. She nodded, squeezing Hanna's hand. Together, they passed through streets that were beginning to rumble with busy cars and glowing buses.

A stranger watching us, Elizabeth thought, would think we were close sisters. Family.

The image was disconcerting. Above a mesh of shadowy elm branches, Elizabeth saw a violet wisp of cloud high in the atmosphere. As they walked through dying night, Elizabeth wished she could ask Hanna if they might wait for the sun to catch them and burn their existence to ash.

But she already knew what Hanna's response would be.

Twenty-five

At four o'clock in the afternoon, Diana sat at her kitchen table, maneuvered the phone into her lap with flour-caked hands, and dialed Lincoln High School. Katy answered harriedly on the first ring. "Lincoln High after hours. How can I help you?"

"Hi, it's me."

"Honey, how are you? I didn't expect to hear from you this weekend, but a call would have been nice."

"Sorry, Mom. I was keeping the phone free for hot dates." Diana tasted the dough on her finger. "I guess you noticed I wasn't in today."

"Yes and I'm glad, 'cause if I'd seen you in class this morning, I would've dragged you home and tied you to the bed to keep you there."

Standing, Diana dipped her pinkie into the moist soil of the spider plant on her fridge. "A little sex confession? No wonder you and George always look so happy. And I thought it was your psychic compatibilities. Hmm, maybe I should borrow George sometime."

"Brat! Go back to bed and stop being so nasty."

"Nope. I've got chores to do."

"I hope one of them is patching up the crack under your door, before you get pneumonia and die."

"Wouldn't that be a riot? Chore-wise, I mean."

"Speaking of chores, any word about Melissa?"

Diana hesitated at the refrigerator. "I think I've decided not to worry about her for a while."

"Really? That's a switch."

"Yes, well, her grandfather is in town and he may be better qualified to handle her. What do you think?"

"Do you have to ask? Saves me from worrying about your following Mr. Hatfield to the hospital."

Diana ruffled her hair. "Hey, how was work today?"

Katy snorted. "I swear the adults here are worse than the kids. Sometimes, I want to strangle them. And then spank them."

"Ahh, so it was normal. I was wondering if you'd like to drop by for a few slices of oven-fresh potato bread? If you haven't got anything pressing to do, that is."

"You Irish angel!" Katy laughed. "After a day like today, it would be heaven."

"You want to pick up some wine on the way here?"

"Wine? I don't know about that on a weeknight. How about some strong dark ale?"

"Wonderful. I've got all the makings. Just get your luscious bod over here."

"Right. Wait a minute. How did Melissa's grandfather get the news?"

"Bye, Katy." Diana hung up.

On her refrigerator was a postcard print of Renoir's "The Umbrellas," which Katy had given to her. Katy had said that Diana resembled the hurrying young girl carrying the wide basket filled with unknown, perhaps wonderful, things—hot French bread, expensive wines, foreign cheeses. Diana thought she resembled more the solemn little girl trapped under everyone's feet, clutching a yellow toy hoop in both hands, preventing it from escaping her, and caught in a triangle of purposeful women, stubbornly holding herself and her toy ring secure against rushing adults and rising, tumbling umbrellas.

Diana holstered the phone and wandered to the sink, picking flaky bits of dough off her hands. When she had been a sophomore at the university, she had mistakenly enrolled in a class called "Images of Destruction: American Wars of the Twentieth Century." It was taught by a pert graduate student named Marci Duncan, who had a button nose and a passion for old war movies. One of the assignments was a picture essay of a certain event in any major conflict the United States had been involved in since the Civil War. Diana had based her project on M.A.S.H. units along the frontline in Korea; her father had been wounded by mine shrapnel on Hill 400 during August of 1951. Like her great-grandfather Zachary, who had kept journals of his experiences fighting Indians in the 1800s, her father had kept his own diaries. Diana read parts of his diaries aloud while the sketches he had made of his regiment and the surrounding terrain were passed around the classroom.

Diana broke down sobbing halfway through, and Marci and some of the class had consoled her by taking her to the student union for coffee and pastry.

Oddly, since then, Diana had not been troubled by her father's diaries as much. She even had one of his careful sketches, a whirling Stars-and-Stripes tornado over a cross-hatched volcano-shaped hill, framed and hung in the front room next to a studio photograph of her parents as new-lyweds.

This morning, however, Diana couldn't think about anything except her father's diaries. She had taken the bundle of notebooks she kept wrapped in aluminum foil down from her bedroom closet and lugged it to the kitchen table. She hadn't opened the package. She merely sat with it in her lap and stared out the graying window, brooding, becoming weepy and depressed.

Then, like an early Christmas present, a memory had visited her: Grandma Patsy's red hands kneading a mountain of dough. Patsy, a sturdy woman with brilliant green eyes, had been briskly shouting as she used to do when her hearing aid was turned low to follow her thoughts or to avoid the telephone. The dough itself, dropped from an unseen height, pinned, twisted under blunt fingers, smashed, stretched mercilessly, had remained silent under a hearty torture. Patsy's words had given lie to her furious energy.

"How any human being ever thought, *dreamed*, of something so wonderful as yeast is beyond my imagination. But not yours, sweetheart," Patsy had nodded to eight-year-old Diana, "when you get to college. A good one. Study patiently and the stars will open to you. Just like it says in the movie with Bette. And when you do find out about yeast, come home to Grandma and her helpless sister and explain how bread was perfected."

"I will, Grandma," Diana had promised. "Momma wants me to go to Cambridge."

"Yeast!" Patsy's sister, Leslie, in a crisp lilac-patterned apron, had laughingly waved her hand in the air, unmindful of the flour covering her curly hair, cheeks, and eyelashes. "Please, my sister! Patsy, you do wonder about the oddest stuff. But you've got to help me and wonder about these young girls nowadays, going off at all hours, claiming to be working, studying and working; working where! What kind of work? Not the work you and I used to do, Patsy, raising our babies, remember? That was work! Cooking and laundering, baking, cleaning up for our babies and our men. And you wonder in modern times what people call work. Too many stores and artificial foods! Too many gadgets and clockwork!"

Leslie whirled to Diana, casting dough flakes like confetti. "You listen to your grammies, Diana. Be a doctor, too; not the new kind with shiny utensils and such gadgetry but the old horse doctors we used to have, remember them, Patsy? Who used magic emerald rings and God's living earth to cure all and sundry, and then, maybe, with faith, you can cure us sisters of our old age."

Patsy nodded solemnly, her hand roundly slapping a rump of dough. "Take my word for it, Diana. Watching rising dough is like watching the mountains grow—a bit of hard work, patience, and prayer; same ingredients in raising a child."

Remembering Patsy and Leslie in her flowered apron, Diana had made bread for the rest of the day, to ward off the horrible images that clung to her father's diaries like dried blood.

"Exhaustion," Diana said to the running water. "And weird echoes. Maybe I should get a cat. Or some fish."

Diana remembered Melissa's dead fish floating in the aquarium water like black twigs, and she quietly began to weep.

Twenty-six

Michael sat in new-fallen darkness, waiting for his granddaughter. He was remembering hunting deer down south in the Datil Mountains near Pie Town. Alone. Just married then, he had felt the need to be alone, and the mountains in that area were the most isolated ranges he could think of.

Back in those days, the dry mountaintops and valleys—even the flatlands atop long mesas covered with yucca and barrel cactus—had been overrun with deer. It was impossible not to ever feel unwatched. Moments of utter stillness, when the pine trees and brush grass echoed nothing, were rare. There had always been something moving in the brush, flitting between pines or pausing in the shadows. Carrying an old army Springfield, Michael chanted to the deer. He at once became a slight breeze or a stalking shadow; walking invisibly among the deer, he waited for the one that had chosen him.

Sarah's apartment lightened as his eyes became accustomed to the dark. The few pictures on the wall grew into square holes. Michael sat up on the couch, heart pounding. The ghostly blue light thickened. The furniture seemed to hover above the floor. Sounds ceased. The doorknob clicked free and the front door squeaked open. Freezing air blew against Michael's face, then died away as the door closed.

Melissa!

His granddaughter's name lodged itself in his mind. A woman had called to her.

"Melissa is not here." Michael spoke quietly, almost to himself. He struggled up from the couch, waited. The air stopped quivering. He thought he had been dreaming again. He was about to sit down when he saw a figure in the corner. A thin shadow watching him.

"Where is she?" Her voice was as clear as ice water.

"I don't know." Michael caught a gleam from measuring eyes.

"I am a friend." The woman removed herself from the corner, gazing at him, making no sound.

"I'm her grandfather." The temperature in the room dropped. Michael saw his breath as faint, blue clouds. He felt no fear. It was only cold air.

"Do you feel the ice, Grandfather?" The woman's eyes shivered into twin silver coins. "Does it burn you?"

"Where is Melissa?" Michael's joints, in his knees and elbows, even the littler ones in his fingers and toes, seared wretchedly.

"Maybe with friends of mine." The woman's form became solid. She wore a dark dress, like Melissa's Easter dress, but which seemed too small for her. Her naked legs and arms were the color of snow streaks hidden under rocks. Her red hair was the color of blood and spread over wide shoulders. Though slender, she seemed to tower over the room.

"I have to speak with my granddaughter," Michael said. "Maybe you can help me look for her."

The woman's eyes darkened. "Suppose I don't."

Michael wanted to lie down and sleep—just like that. His eyelids became heavy. The burrowing teeth in his joints dissolved. The horrible pain lessened. This is how Melissa sent me to sleep, he realized. His soul quaked. A fear for his granddaughter gaped inside him.

It surprised him, then, what came next from his mouth. He knew it surprised the woman too, for she suddenly became less awesome, even frightened. Her skin turned transparent.

"I know what you are." Michael's voice cut through the darkness in the room. "You don't frighten me."

A pause. "What am I, old man?"

"You came for my wife too soon. Now, you are looking for my granddaughter. I won't give a name to you."

The woman relaxed and smiled. Her teeth glinted wetly. "And I've come for you, Grandfather."

Michael stepped back. The couch cushions pressed against his calf. A memory tugged at his brain. Something brushed against his chest, as if a spider had danced across his skin.

No, he realized, not a spider. His dangling medicine bundle.

"Melissa is just a child, yet." Michael clutched the bundle. "I won't let you take her."

The woman chuckled, and its sound was a stream in a winter night, bubbling over black stones, trickling into dank pools. "You're a brave man, Grandfather. Maybe I'll let you live one more night. Would that please you?"

"You don't hold my life."

"We'll see about that."

The woman swooped toward Michael, a yowling dust-devil almost too quick to see. Her eyes grew into midnight storms. Long teeth like steel spikes lashed out of her mouth. Icicle-sharp hands grabbed his upper arms, nearly cracking the bones in half, and a putrified stink washed over him in a moist cloud as he was lifted to the ceiling. Michael retched miserably as he blindly tore the medicine bundle from his chest. The leather string binding it together came undone and a yellow cloud of corn pollen spilled out over the creature's body like a glitter of sun motes.

The creature shrieked. Its cry pierced his eardrums as if lightning had crashed into Sarah's apartment. The killing grip on his arms slackened. Michael was dropped as the woman's body clenched in on itself. He saw shrinking eyeteeth and her eyes' true color: green and glassy with fear, washed out. The woman shuddered like a frightened child. She stared as if trying to understand what had happened. Michael understood that stare, recognized such fear. He leaned woodenly and reached to console her. Snarling, the woman shoved him away. Michael flew backwards against the wall. He crumpled into the corner next to the couch. Remembering Melissa, he pulled himself up quickly, like a younger man.

"What is your name!" he demanded.

The woman clutched her stomach, choked. The name disgorged itself. "Hanna!"

"Where is my granddaughter?"

The kneeling woman sighed, unbent, stood up off the floor, smoothed back weaving, flaming hair. Blackness exuded from her eyes. The room darkened. She whispered, "No more questions, savage."

Michael began to shiver. The thunderous strength that had held him upright left him. He swayed and fell to his knees, banging them on the floor. Don't forget you're an old man, he told himself. His joints hurt, his arms and chest ached. Even his penis felt sore.

The woman rose above him, the top of her head brushing the ceiling. "One of us will find you, old man. Gut you and your granddaughter like a deer carcass."

Michael couldn't answer. His strength was completely gone; the woman's gaze stabbed the back of his bowed head. He waited for the grip of crushing fingers. Instead, he heard the squeak of naked feet, light and fragile. The steps receded, as if retreating down a long hallway. He listened. A long time passed before the footsteps vanished.

The apartment warmed quickly. Wincing, Michael touched deep depressions in his biceps where the woman's fingers had squeezed him. Michael searched the floor until he found his empty buckskin pouch. He shook it. Corn pollen dusted his palm. He sniffed it deeply to get rid of the stench of rotting meat. Then he scraped the few grains of pollen off his palm with his index finger and touched it to his lips. Corn was the essence of First Man and First Woman. He peered at the ends of his fingertips, to the whorls of his fingerprints. Wind had filled the couple with life.

Carefully, Michael folded his medicine pouch into a tiny square and placed it in his shirt pocket. His grandmother's gift had protected him from the witch. Maybe it would help him find his granddaughter.

Twenty-seven

Garish vapors twisted around Elizabeth as she walked, a tinkling menagerie shooting out puffs of carnival-colored air. Sharp under her bare feet, rainbow welts sparkled as ice formed on the fresh snow.

Falke's young mistress had not found her yet. Elizabeth knew how difficult it was for a newly taken girl to hone her mind well enough to hear a person's thoughts. Hanna once had a difficult time when learning the task. Elizabeth herself had often become lost in the maze of human mutterings. But Kuenstler had been patient. And a good teacher.

Also, they were such tiny beings in the whole span of night: Falke was still a boy; Hanna, merely a fetus. The living in their swift cars and jeweled planes were grains of dust, caught within eddies and sand bars of that particular washed sunlight which fell only in closed rooms and deep wells.

And what am I? Elizabeth wondered, stepping off a curb, leaving behind a circle of light emitted by a streetlamp. Her feet barely touched the surface of the asphalt, yet she felt with distinct clarity each pebble and broken stone embedded in the road. I am alone, she answered. And hungry.

Glancing to the flickery neon and vapid store lights, she squinted as if the buzzing glare were a fierce wind. Shadows hurried past. Cars flew by, threatening to catch her in their vortex. Imagining her arms as great wings, Elizabeth flew to a park of skeletal trees. Hovering among the elm tops, she fingered the stiff branches that clicked in the wind blown from the mountains. Below her, the circular park stared like a whitened eye. The eerie vision distracted her, broke her concentration. Elizabeth tumbled down, fell through iced branches, and collapsed against the base of the elm. Her coat had been scraped off, and it swayed high above her in a web of branches. She was wearing a cotton dress meant for summer; its pattern of tiny flowers in neat rows swept past her sight as she rubbed her face clean with its skirt. Her elbow and the insides of her legs were stinging. Her eyes went blind. A fist of raw hunger knocked her into the snow. Her mind curdled with memories collected over a slow century and a half. Falke was nine times as old. How could he stand to possess so many memories? Was he truly that powerful?

Elizabeth laughed as she rolled onto her back, opened her eyes. Maybe Falke was just so phenomenally stupid; or nine centuries dense. Age and cobwebs clouding reason. How could he let himself be so overcome by a simple girl?

Her amusement seeped away. Elizabeth slapped the snow from her skirt. Falke's power was linked to the woman this Melissa reminded him of. Christiane. What had she been? A sorceress? Saint? Something about that ancient, long-dead woman was the key to Falke's strength.

Elizabeth pressed her fingers against her temples. Christiane was alive again, it seemed, in the form of a child. And Falke had been nearly destroyed by . . . what?

Angels?

"I believe," she whispered to herself. Elizabeth nodded to reinforce her words, and remembered he had once mentioned a demon; a demon and a betrayer, and a hatred lasting nine hundred years. Maybe the hand of God was inexorably shaping Falke's destruction—by angels' hands.

Was Falke so powerful that he needed the intervention of God's hand to destroy him?

"Elizabeth?"

The voice was hushed but clear. It was no illusion or hallucination.

"Yes, Melissa. I'm here."

Elizabeth saw a tiny figure standing at the rim of darkness surrounding the park. A calm sea of ice lay between them. Blue moonglow fell and metamorphosed into lurid, orange waves. The distant shape of Melissa was wrapped in an ink-black coat. Her slender legs were bare and began to shimmer softly as she approached.

"Was it difficult to find me?" Elizabeth asked when Melissa reached her. The girl's face was blue-white, a sheet of ice, like the frozen ground. Do I look like that? Melissa glanced over her shoulder at two dogs trotting along the far end of the park. She shook her head.

"Tell me how it was." Elizabeth began to walk. No destination in mind. Ice was forming on her bare arms and legs.

As the girl walked silently by, Elizabeth noticed her bare feet. Melissa's black hair blew from her cheeks, revealing smooth skin. Her lashes were long and dark. Elizabeth could imagine they were under a spring sunset; the artificial light was toned exactly to complement the bluish tint in the snow.

Melissa's eyes sparkled as she suddenly looked at Elizabeth. "Tell me about Falke!" Her voice was quiet and ringing, like a stroked wine glass. Blushing faintly, Melissa tucked her chin under her coat collar as if she were chilled.

Tell this girl about a man who had existed for centuries, changeless, before Elizabeth had even been born? A creature of another time who had taken her as his wife? "I don't know all that much," Elizabeth said.

"But you've lived with him for years and years. No one alive knows him better."

"Maybe you should ask those he has murdered. Surely they must know something I don't."

Melissa grew silent for a moment, then spoke again. "Is he really your husband?"

"It's been said. Did he tell you this?"

Their passage was soundless over the snow. The girl touched Elizabeth's arm. "In the sanctuary, I found this in one of the rooms." Melissa dug in her coat pocket and brought out a waferlike square of metal, which she studied briefly before handing it to Elizabeth. "I'm sorry for snooping around, but I didn't know what you looked like."

Elizabeth accepted the daguerreotype, nodded. Before her family had left Independence, Missouri in 1849, her mother had paid precious pennies to have a picture taken of Elizabeth and her two brothers. Three months after her mother had died, Elizabeth searched through her mother's possessions until she found the daguerreotype tucked within their Bible. It showed Elizabeth sitting on a high-backed chair with Joseph and Ezra, the right hands of each boy on her right shoulder, both standing awkwardly behind her, the light changing their near-identical blond caps into smudges of white. Elizabeth had worn the long cotton dress with the ribbon trim around the collar and sleeves that her mother had worked on religiously, and for which her Grammy Anne had provided the cloth.

Elizabeth gave Melissa back the picture. "I don't want it."

Melissa slipped it into her pocket. "I felt like I needed to see you before I tried looking for you. I wanted Falke to describe you, but he wouldn't."

I doubt if he really remembers what I look like, Elizabeth almost said. The girl was truthful, at least. "What do you want of me?" Elizabeth asked. "What does Falke want?"

Melissa pretended indifference. "Falke says . . . that we'll live forever." She glanced at Elizabeth, hesitantly, as if she realized how ridiculous the words sounded; no matter if they were true.

"Falke himself has lived years upon years," Elizabeth answered. They left the park and strode among bleak roads. The asphalt was a river under ice. "You felt the changes. Do you believe this possible?"

Melissa shrugged. Elizabeth had seen the passing of a hundred and forty years herself. Was there any difference between that and spending one long Sunday afternoon reading in a comfortable room? Should she say this to the girl?

They walked without speaking. It was still early night, yet the traffic had lessened. Probably due to the icy roads, Elizabeth thought. The night seemed heavier without the probing car headlamps. And all the stars had disappeared.

130   "What is it like?" Melissa asked. "To live so long."

Elizabeth answered mechanically. "The most important: One must always change with grace. Another: Possessing a powerful force, you must never become too dependent on strength." She had read those phrases somewhere in one of Falke's old, brittle books. Really, the most striking thing about living so long was that you never forgot fear. Let the child learn that one for herself.

Melissa, perplexed, asked, "What are we?"

Elizabeth hesitated, feeling goosepimples rising on her arms. I don't know, she wanted to say. But that was too easy. "I think . . ."

Before she could finish, another figure intruded on them. Elizabeth glimpsed a swift shadow sweep past her. Melissa's eyes grew wide with fear.

"Bitch!" Hanna shouted, descending on the girl.

"No!" Elizabeth screamed, and tried to protect Melissa. A hand hit her in the sternum. Air swept out of her lungs. Pain burst into her skull. Green clouds spun. Numbly, ice clinging to her face, Elizabeth looked up. Ten feet away, a twisted bundle lay in the snow; Hanna stood above it, monstrously tall, as high as the woven trees against the pale clouds.

"Hanna?" Elizabeth whispered.

The vampire was shivering. Elizabeth struggled to her feet. A sensation of heat spread between her breasts. She crept warily toward the unmoving figure, careful to keep it between herself and Hanna.

"What have you done to her?" Elizabeth knelt by Melissa. The snow abraded her knees like razor blades. Gently, she turned the girl over. Ice had already formed a clear mask on Melissa's face.

"She's alive." Elizabeth pulled the girl from the frozen street, wincing at the sound; like cloth tearing apart. "Hanna, help me lift her! We must take her to Falke."

Hanna's thin face cracked into a grimace. "No!"

"What's wrong with you?"

"She's betrayed us." Her canines flashed like steel. "We must kill her."

Elizabeth continued easing the girl from the ice. "Hurry, help me! We have to get her away from here before someone comes or we'll betray ourselves."

"Stand back, sister."

Elizabeth flew angrily at Hanna, dragged at her raised arm. Hanna heaved her away.

"Elizabeth, if you don't leave her to die, then I will kill the both of you."

"Just tell me what Melissa has done!"

Hanna turned to the girl lying in the snow. "A man is hunting us. Because of her. A man is looking for her!"

"Who?" Elizabeth asked shakily. She couldn't believe, almost couldn't imagine: Hunted! After so many lonely desperate years of hiding.

"An old *Indian*." Hanna uttered the words as if they stung her insides; as if she might weep. "Her grandfather."

"Just an old man?"

Hanna held her middle tightly. "He *hurt* me."

"How?" Elizabeth went to Hanna, gently unwound her arms. "Hanna, tell me what he did to you."

A blaring mechanical whoop stopped Elizabeth. Brilliant shafts of light pierced the darkness, aimed at Melissa's unconscious body. Red, blue, yellow jewels flickered and whirled.

"They've seen her," Elizabeth whispered, as if they might hear. A single powerful beam swept across blank houses. Soon, it would illuminate the two of them.

"Hurry!" Elizabeth grabbed Hanna's hand, pulled her deeper into the shadows. A silent, white explosion staggered the dark. Dazzling light engulfed Elizabeth. A man's voice, strengthened by some device, shouted at them. "Police! You two freeze!"

Elizabeth was too paralyzed with fright to use her wings. The beam held her immobile. More voices screamed at her, running figures wavered in the streaked glare.

Rigid fingers clamped onto the back of her head and forced her into movement. Night swallowed her. Endless and safe.

Twenty-eight

Disturbed from memory, Michael answered the ringing phone. "Hello?"

"Can I speak to Sarah Hill or Michael Roanhorse?" asked a man's blunt voice.

"This is Michael Roanhorse." A chill pricked the hairs at the back of his neck.

"This is detective Johns with the Albuquerque police. We've got Melissa Roanhorse in custody down at the university hospital. Just brought her in a few minutes ago. She's a little banged up, but she's all right. We just wanted to let you know she's here and safe."

"Where is this hospital?"

"I wouldn't recommend you come down just yet, Mr. Roanhorse. Not at this time. I'm sure you know that Melissa's in a little trouble, and we'd like to have a few words with her first. Ask her some questions. Do you understand, sir?"

"Yes, I understand."

"Melissa should be up and around, according to the doctor, by tomorrow afternoon. Maybe you can come and see her then. All right?"

"Yes."

"You will give Sarah Hill this message, too, if you see her?"

"I will."

"Have a good night, then."

Michael hung up and went to Melissa's room. From the closet, he took out a crisp mountain jacket, his own faded denim coat, and his battered leather grip. Switching on the lamp, he unzipped the bag and dug out a sealed jam jar of corn pollen, which he opened. He poured light pollen into his medicine pouch then wrapped it tightly with the leather thong. The bundle danced on his skin as he tied it around his neck. He replaced the jar in his grip.

In the old days, before the warriors left to war, the path of Changing Woman's twin sons was remembered; how they came to their father, the Sun, to gain weapons to destroy the enemy monsters that were killing the Navajos' children.

Remembering, Michael left his daughter's apartment to bring Melissa home.

Twenty-nine

Elizabeth spread her arms in the darkened room. The carpet soothed her tingling feet. "Who does this place belong to?"

Hanna pulled back a curtain and the room was flooded with a bluish glow. The grim whiteness of the walls and furniture made Elizabeth think of a snowy forest. She paused at the window, next to Hanna. They were high up. Street-lamps burned far below them like stars against the snow-covered streets. The tallest buildings were toy-sized, the houses around their feet like swaddled babies. Elizabeth touched her forehead to the window and wished to be asleep in one of the houses. A normal woman, with someone beside her, a solid human back to warm herself under and huddle against.

"What should we do about this Grandfather?" Hanna's voice was taut.

"You still haven't told me how he wounded you," Elizabeth said. "I can't make decisions with such little detail."

"I told you all that happened. There isn't any more."

Elizabeth sank onto a cushioned bench in front of a vanity mirror. She pulled her legs up and hugged them. "Start again. What does he look like? How does he speak? Simple things like that are a good beginning."

"I don't know what happened! My body aches. He used some weapon I couldn't see." Hanna pulled off her dress, let it drop to the floor. She began pushing and prodding her skin, her breasts, pinching the muscles in her arms and legs.

Vigorous light speared her naked body; mistlike reflections shifted on the walls like living things.

"You say he's Melissa's grandfather." Elizabeth felt a twinge of jealousy threading into her heart. "So they're both Indian."

"Savages," Hanna dismissed.

"There are many kinds. Many tribes." Elizabeth thought of the old man teaching his song to his grandson. "Some are powerful."

Hanna sighed, as if she were dealing with a pestering child. "Elizabeth, they're all of no consequence."

"We must find out what this one knows." Elizabeth stretched her legs out, set her feet on the carpet.

"We must find a way to get rid of him."

"Why didn't you kill him right then?"

Hanna continued to check herself, giving no response.

"You still haven't told me how he hurt you," Elizabeth said.

The vampire straightened, stared silently.

"We don't have all night! We have to find Falke."

"He burned me." She shook her head. "Something in his hands burned my body. A fire appeared and fell like rain. I felt like I was being ripped apart."

Elizabeth became frightened at the room's stillness, of how Hanna's words sheared through it.

"We are the evil ones," Elizabeth said quietly. The answer she had known all along. The answer she would give to Melissa, when they met again.

The white pumps she had taken from Hanna's apartment were large for Elizabeth; they clocked on the sidewalk like horse's hooves. And the insides were too slick. They threatened to fly off with each step, or trip her. The bulky furred coat stank of perfume and made her feel hot. But they were necessary masks. Elizabeth entered the flowing dance gallery, where she knew Falke hunted.

The floor boiled with human prey. Elizabeth drifted among them, not thinking. She had found long ago that this was the best way to stalk a particular person. Falke was here, somewhere among the living dancers. She could feel his heart beating, sonorous and slower than human hearts. But his thoughts were like those of a drunken man, fogged and concealing. Elizabeth closed her eyes and let the spiraling crowd carry her to its center, where Falke waited. She opened her eyes and found herself in front of him. He was leaning against the wall with two women. His white shirt was unbuttoned carelessly. His golden hair pulsed with red and blue vapors from the stage spots overhead. Only his eyes were flawless.

"Elizabeth. How glad I am to see you."

She felt ashamed of him. "Why are you like this?"

Falke pulled one girl, a tight-lipped blond, to him and kissed her on the temple. She clutched his arm and glared at Elizabeth with possessive triumph.

"This is Andrea." Falke regarded the girl, moved back her curls, as if inspecting her skin for blemishes. "My feast companion for the evening. Perhaps, sweet meat." Then he looked to the other female under his right hand, turned her head to face him, a sullen girl with short purplish black hair and with skin almost as white as his own. "And this is Jenny. We are in the middle of courses. Yes?"

Elizabeth faced the colorful gathering massing like waves in a pool. "I came to tell you. Something has happened to Melissa."

His hand grabbed her shoulder and jerked her around. Elizabeth's rage burst. She swung and struck Falke's jaw with the heel of her hand. "Don't touch me!"

Falke wrenched her arm, whipped her around to face the crowd. His fingers squeezed the back of her neck, lifted her off the floor as if presenting her for sacrifice. The white pumps slid off her feet.

All movement had stopped. Music railed from the ceiling. No one danced. The whirling spotlights picked out gray faces in the crowd: Bloodless husks. Falke's victims. He lowered her, forced her through twitching, overheated bodies. Stretched fingers flew out and scratched at her face. A fist punched her in the back of the head. Elizabeth struggled, kicked out at empty air. She was slammed through the double doors, into biting air.

"What happened to Melissa?" Falke asked tightly, putting more strength into his hands. Elizabeth imagined her bones bending under his fingers. One contrary move, she knew, and he would break both her arms. There were other ways to taunt rage.

136   "I forgot," she answered.

"What did you do to Melissa!" Falke shouted.

"Let me go, or I'll tell you nothing!"

Elizabeth was set free. Arms throbbing, she began to run. Quickly! she panted, barely feeling the snow under her feet. A shadow paced her. Elizabeth ran faster. Stars streaked above her. The wind howled in her ears. The shadow remained with her. Elizabeth slowed and stopped. There was no escape, she mourned. Not yet.

"We are the survivors, Elizabeth." Falke was in front of her. "Only we can teach the newborn."

"What newborn?"

Falke's hands lifted her face. His eyes became blue oceans. A stark, searching finger pierced her mind. Elizabeth's brain seared open, revealed itself. Her cheeks moistened with tears. A wedge of blackness shifted inside her heart. She longed for escape from her existence, yet she was so frightened of not existing. Where would she go if the sun was to catch her? God had turned His eyes from her. All His gates were closed. Elizabeth hugged herself, bent away from Falke's hands.

"Get out," she whispered.

"We must find Melissa." Falke spoke from far above her. "Before the sun catches us. She is not far off."

"I know," Elizabeth answered. Tears like round pebbles bounced onto her hands. The hole in her heart deepened.

"Hanna was hurt, you say?" Falke's eyes became blank. "Then we must find Melissa's grandfather. Flay him, and save his skin for the savage's drums."

Elizabeth stared, feeling the first, true stirrings of hatred in her heart; but she remained silent.

The hospital corridors were flooded with intrusive light, empty of people. Elizabeth walked uncautiously; she could hear anyone before they ever saw her. Her feet squeaked along tiled floors. The air was unnaturally warm and dry. The place stank of decaying bodies. So many doors, she thought. How many would contain the people Falke had murdered? How many would contain Melissa's victims?

Or mine?

Elizabeth brushed the air irritably. Necessary casualties. Survival demanded harsh means. Elizabeth frowned. What book had those words come out of?

137

Turning a corner, she saw a nurses' station at the very end of the corridor. A young woman was standing at a desk behind the counter, head bowed, reading a book. Elizabeth went around the counter and paused a few feet from the desk. The nurse had dark hair in a complicated braid at the back of her head. She was humming softly. Elizabeth tried to identify the melody. It had been something popular. A song about roses, she remembered. An old song; much older than the young nurse wearing a crisp white uniform. The words were wistful.

"But you look like a happy person," Elizabeth said quietly. "Why such a morbid song?"

The nurse fell back, gasping, filling her lungs to scream. Her wide brown eyes were ringed with circles of fatigue. Poor thing looked harried and ill.

The woman recovered herself quickly, became angry. "What are you doing behind the counter, young lady?" She reached for a phone. "Where do you belong?"

Elizabeth laughed. "I don't belong anywhere. I'm just visiting."

"Where are your parents? Did you get separated from them?"

"They're in the terminal patient's ward," Elizabeth said, moving closer to the nurse, glancing at her book. "It's so depressing there. I wanted to talk to someone."

"I'm sorry, but I'm busy. You'll have to go back and wait with your parents." Having dismissed her, the nurse bent to her book.

Elizabeth felt the hard edge of the desk on her hip, slid closer to the nurse. "You look tired," she said. "Imagine a wide autumn meadow filled with flowers, with a stream trickling through. Lots of sunlight. Leaves against the sky. Soft grass . . ." Elizabeth touched the woman's braid. "Maybe you should sleep for a while. I'll watch the station for you."

The woman swayed, eyes blinking. "Thank you, no. I can manage." Elizabeth caught the nurse before she fell and hurt herself on the floor.

"Lean back and sleep . . . there. Just like that."

Elizabeth read the scrawls on a bulletin board to find Melissa's room. The carpeted hallway was silent as she glided along it.

Some of the rooms stank of medicines. Others reeked of flowers. Elizabeth touched a door and pushed it open. The room was dark, but it hummed with the sound of gentle machines. To her right, plastic tubes and red lights glowed around the only occupied bed in the room. Underneath a lamp, Melissa lay asleep under layers of white and near-white sheets and blankets. Her long hair was tied in a ponytail. She looked barren and gray with death.

The mistress has not fed this evening, Elizabeth observed. She laid her hand on Melissa's forehead. The skin was waxy and cold as if the girl had already died. Beneath livid skin, Melissa's heart thudded evenly and strong. For some reason, Elizabeth felt relieved. And suddenly protective.

"Melissa," she whispered, lifting the ponytail, unwinding it slowly. "It's time to go home."

Behind her, curtains rustled softly. Elizabeth whirled and saw a man standing across the room, next to an empty bed in the corner. He was old, but he held himself upright and seemed unafraid.

Melissa's grandfather.

Silence descended from the ceiling and from the rooms above, all filled with ill and dying humans. How long had it been since she'd been afraid of a man? Years. Elizabeth stepped away from Melissa. The man was still, as if he had become an oak tree. Only his eyes sparkled with life. They studied her openly.

"I have no weapon," Elizabeth said. "I won't harm you."

The man said nothing. His hands clenched, then relaxed, his only betrayal of tension.

Elizabeth spoke again. "Melissa must come with me. She, too, will be unharmed."

"Melissa isn't going with you," the man said quietly.

Elizabeth turned and closed her eyes, sending her mind into the unconscious girl. Mists and shadowy places surrounded Elizabeth as if she were in a mountain forest. She called Melissa's name and waited. Soon, she was answered. A small, pale figure emerged from gray shadows. Elizabeth took her hand and led her out of the forest. Opening her eyes, she saw that the old man hadn't moved.

"Melissa," she whispered.

The girl's eyelids fluttered open. Liquid, brown eyes settled on Elizabeth immediately. Melissa smiled, slid her hand into Elizabeth's hand.

"Your grandfather is here to say goodbye," Elizabeth said.

Startled, Melissa sat up quickly, rustling the sheets. "Grandpa! What are you doing here?"

The man walked to the opposite side of the bed. "Are you all right, Granddaughter? Have these people hurt you?"

He took her other hand and held it tightly. Melissa was stretched between them like an unwilling prisoner. Tears moistened her cheeks. "I have to go with Elizabeth, Grandpa."

The man had gray stubble on his chin. Under the light, deep furrows creased his forehead as he frowned down at Melissa. His eyes were like hard chips of flint and looked capable of long unwavering anger. "Where is your mother, *shi'yazhi?*" he asked steadily.

Melissa pulled her hand from him, swept the sheets off herself. "I don't know," she answered.

"Hurry, Melissa." Elizabeth looked toward the window, still dark. "There isn't much time."

Melissa nodded absently and stood. The man came around the bed, holding onto the chrome railings with his right hand. Elizabeth saw that he was not seeking support, but rather, that he was keeping his hand from flying out to them. She felt waves of a fierce anger beating against her.

"I won't let you go." He moved in front of them, blocking their way.

Melissa stepped up to him. "Please, Grandpa, you don't understand! Elizabeth can help me."

Elizabeth sent herself out to the man, to try to ease his rage. She stunned herself against a solid mental wall, almost like rock.

"How is she helping you?" he asked. "Look where you are!"

"It's because of *you* that Melissa is here." Elizabeth became angry herself. "Let her choose. She won't be far away from you."

"Please, Grandpa," Melissa whispered, trembling. She stared at Elizabeth. "I feel hot."

Elizabeth squeezed the girl's hand and began to push by the man. He gripped her arm tightly. Elizabeth considered throwing him off. How would Melissa, as scared as she was, take that? Elizabeth hesitated. Scowling, the man jerked her close to him. He smelt of rain and chewing gum.

"You have her now, witch." He glared into her eyes. "But I will hunt you and destroy you."

His fingers bit deeply, became painful. Elizabeth shook him off and said nothing. She led Melissa to the window and looked back at him.

"You're wrong," Elizabeth said, holding Melissa close to her, shielding her as much as possible from the spreading dawn. "We aren't witches."

She turned to the window, pressed her hand to its frozen surface, pushed lightly. The glass exploded, rained on her fingers, spilled to the toy-sized cars and streets below. Elizabeth grasped Melissa with her mind's fingers.

"Gently, now," she said to the girl, who smiled back and nodded. Elizabeth rose to the windowsill with Melissa clinging to her side, spread her invisible wings into a freezing gust from the eastern mountains, and flew toward Cygnus sailing across an inky black sea.

Thirty

Glass shards whirled against a black sky. Michael ran to the gaping window. Twin feminine shapes swirled in front of him, like blowing sheets, just out of reach of his grasping fingers. Melissa's hair unfurled, fanning out, as if she were in deep water. The small, blond witch was covered over in a mist that reached across Melissa's thin body like holding arms. Their forms shrunk with distance. They vanished into a wash of stars.

Michael pulled himself back from the shattered window, shaking away droplets of blood from his hands. Pinpoints of sour pain peppered his fingers and palms. Later that day, with a knife, he would dig out tiny slivers of glass embedded in the skin. Now, he had to follow the two girls and, somehow, bring them back. Michael paused at the door. He opened a cabinet and took out her thin dress, mountain jacket, and tennis shoes. His fingers were throbbing. Blood streaked the light dress. He tried to wipe it off, but more blood soaked into the flower patterns, corrupting them. His hands began to shake.

"Damned old man," Michael hissed, striking his jaw with the palm of his hand. A glass splinter slid into his cheek. "No more fear."

He clutched Melissa's clothes and listened. No sound came from the hallway. He opened the door fully and peered out. The nurses' station was empty. Shiny gurneys lined both sides of the hallway, as if a holocaust were expected. Michael slipped out of the room and walked toward the double doors, which led to the main lobby and elevators.

He stopped when he heard a deep rumbling sound coming from the other side of the doors, as if one of the thundering tractor-trailers which ran on I-40 were idling in the hospital lobby. His heart began to feel tight in his chest. He gritted his teeth and looked through a wire-reinforced window. A massive, hunched wolf stalked the lobby in a wide counterclockwise circle, passing between him and the elevators. Cold glass touched Michael's forehead. The beast turned and glared at Michael with furious yellow-green eyes. The double doors vibrated. Canine teeth gleamed like knives as the wolf snarled.

Michael felt his strength seeping from his body. His heart hammered miserably. A cold hatred was streaming from the beast, a noxious poison penetrating glass and skin. Michael wanted to double over and vomit. He fought his nausea desperately, panting hard with the exertion.

The wolf began to lope toward him. The girl who had stolen Melissa had at least an earthly depth in her eyes. Even predators from the desert had a gaze Michael had seen, the recognition of a competitor or of a victim. This running beast's eyes held a flat, murderous stare. It breathed evil.

Yéé' naaldlooshii. A skinwalker.

Michael pushed open the door. He gave no thought to his action. He only pictured his grandmother, hair gray as iron, sprinkling corn pollen across the doorway of her hogan, praying to the morning sun as it rose above the shoulders of Mount Taylor. The monster's black claws, screeching against the floor, tore up tile and cement. Muscles bunched under its rippling, frosted coat. The beast roared and leaped. Michael tore the buckskin bag from his throat and threw its contents over the skinwalker.

The loose corn pollen turned to luminous rain. Michael's view of the creature was blocked by a dense, rolling thundercloud blossoming in the center of the hospital lobby. Brilliant streaks of lightning shot across its billowing surface. The monster howled in frightful agony as it was engulfed by the walls of rain. Its claws skittered on the floor, fighting for purchase. Within the blue cloud itself, Michael could see the outline of a writhing man shielding himself from exploding bolts of electricity. Cool mist blew across Michael's face. He raised his hands, so the rain could wash the blood from his fingers. The creature shouted a word that Michael couldn't hear over blasts of lightning; it sounded like a name.

Michael stepped into the lobby. The poisonous stink was gone, replaced by the smell of rainwater and dust. He pressed his back against the wall as he crept past the raincloud's tumult.

Blistering fingers pierced through the mirrored, watery walls and reached to him, straining, fingernails like curved teeth. Michael felt a remorseful compulsion to grasp the splayed fingers and pull the stricken beast from its pain. Stinging droplets spattered his cheek. Remember Melissa, you old fool! Michael ran awkwardly to the stairwell, tumbled through the metal doors, and raced down to the first floor. His joints were screaming with piercing pains, but his heart felt as strong as a thunderbolt.

Michael burst through all the exits into freezing night. A sparse crowd had gathered in the snow-covered parking lot where shattered glass lay like a spray of water. High up, the stars were like rock crystal. Suddenly, a flamelike distortion flew among them, withering their light for a moment, then it was gone.

The growing morning soothed Michael's fear. Shivering, he began to feel cold, small, and hungry. His boots slipped on the ice. In his heart, he knew the skinwalker was not harmed too much by the holy rain. He had to find more powerful knowledge. His grandmother might have known the proper medicine and songs, but she was long dead.

143

Stoking his brain, sifting through bright memory, Michael strode purposefully from the muttering crowd, slipped under a covering of dawn which warmed him like a Pendleton blanket, trying to remember the ancient Navajo way.

Thirty-one

The white morning stank of gasoline and car exhaust. Snowdrifts crunched under his boots. His cheek stung. Michael walked up a familiar gravel parking space, a concrete walk, a short wooden stairway. He knocked on the wrought iron screen door. Police sirens whined across the city, muffled by drifting snowflakes, setting his mind on edge. He hadn't gone back to Sarah's apartment. After the skinwalker's attack, Michael didn't know what he might find waiting for him there.

Floorboards beyond the door squeaked and a small, wan face peeked out of the window. He had found the right one. Diana opened the door cautiously, staring at him. She was flushed in the gray morning light, though dishevelled and half asleep, and she reminded him of Sarah when she used to get up in the morning for elementary school.

"I think Melissa is in trouble," he said, trying not to scare the woman away. "I need someone's help."

Diana shook her head as if dismissing the whole situation. Then she unlocked the screen door and opened it. "I have some coffee on," she said simply.

Michael walked inside.

Thirty-two

Diana let the radio play as she drove westward, out of Albuquerque, along snow-flanked I-40. She wasn't sure what kind of music the old man liked, so she kept changing stations, hoping to catch some murmur of approval from him. So far, he had stayed quiet. Not a gesture or word of displeasure or encouragement. Maybe he doesn't like music, she told herself. But he keeps humming secret songs. Diana became slowly irritated. She left it at a country-and-western station. Maybe the inane lyrics would drive him as batty as he was driving her.

Too many things were eating at Diana. Over the past two days, she had been trying to reach Michael by phone. No answer or call back; not so much as a peep, how-are-you. Diana knew it was silly, but she had thought they were a team searching for Melissa. Sticking together, until some new information set them on the right track.

Then the old guy pops around at five in the morning, telling her they have a journey to make. Diana would have refused, too, if she hadn't been so eager for some kind of an explanation. Intuition told her Michael had found out something about Melissa. Something bad. But he had closed up as seamlessly as an oyster. He knew Diana had connections with the police. Maybe he didn't trust her.

Maybe he did trust her but needed to test her in some way. So he comes barging in at the break of dawn and demands that they take a journey together; he expects her to beg off another day at work; he doesn't tell her a word, or speak to her for two days. Now, here they are, driving out into the middle of God-knows-where. What kind of test is that?

Instead of feeling trusted and wanted, Diana began to feel a surge of disquiet cooling her stomach. Why did he feel he needed to test her?

Diana rolled down her window, turning the handle furiously. Her eyes were wet. Truth to tell, she was hurt. Not just a little, either. Oh, he probably thinks I'm just some stupid white woman who can't tell her butt from . . . from a . . .

Diana wiped at her eyes angrily. She hated when she couldn't think of the correct words to bludgeon herself with.

"It's not far, this place."

"Where are we going?" Diana gave up and changed the dial to a classical station, turning up the volume in hopes of masking her husky voice.

"To the old folks' home at Casa Blanca. I want to talk with a relative of mine there."

"I've heard of that place. It's supposed to be very nice."

"Yes."

Why aren't you there?

"Michael, why didn't you call me? I was worried something had happened to you." The nagging words spilled out before she could catch them and ram them back into her mouth. Ghosts from her married past.

"I can't tell you, yet. I have to think."

"Melissa concerns me, too. She's my student. And not just that. Melissa told me that someone hurt her. I want to know who's responsible. I need your help, Michael. And if you want my help, you have to be honest and open with me."

Diana glanced at him. The old fart was smiling, for Christ's sake!

"Don't laugh at me! I'm serious!"

"Melissa is the daughter of my daughter. My wife's daughter, also. You are a stranger to me. You talk like the three doctors who once visited with us long ago in my wife's village. Talking about little invisible creatures that were coming into our bodies and killing us. Those three white doctors were strangers to us. Even though they saved all of our children's lives and our lives, too. You sound like them and that is why I am smiling."

"Well, how do I sound?"

"Two of those doctors became my family. They cured me and my wife and they knew us. Not as bodies carrying plague, but as two stupid kids who hadn't learned to listen yet. We all of us in Madrecita finally listened, because of those two white people. And we gave those two doctors, a man and a woman, names in the Keresan language, my wife's language. It was decided by the old Pueblo men in their kiva, I think. I don't know where those doctors are now, but we still remember their names."

146

Diana remained quiet for a bit. "Are you saying that I might be concerned only in a professional capacity? Even if I am, what's the harm in that if at least one person is trying to help?"

"No. I'm saying that you must think about how much you want to help me find my family."

She mulled over that for some miles. The old guy must have known there was really no answer to that. Trying to be a slippery fish; trying to shut me up. Huh uh, baby. She'd had enough of that with Roger.

Diana turned to Michael. His gaze was fastened to the wet highway. She saw for the first time how old he looked. His face was trenched with spidery lines. His eyes were glittery and distant. His skin was too taut and shiny, and his hands were pulling in on themselves, as if the muscles were shrinking. Diana looked away, embarrassed; not for herself, but for him.

"At this old folks' home . . ." Michael began. Diana realized that the old guy still had his God-given teeth. There was no clicking sound when he spoke, as there had been when her own grandfather spoke words of longer than two syllables.

"Yes?" Diana coaxed. He seemed to have forgotten what he was going to say.

"We are going to see this woman. My father once said that she had been touched by lightning. That is a very serious thing to happen to you, if you live."

Diana smiled. "Was that a joke?"

A little color came back into Michael's face. "For us Navajos, to have lightning strike close to you is a bad thing, which requires a medicine man's healing. But for this woman, it made her different. Not bad, just different. My father trusted her. He never asked me to trust her. I think he wanted me to choose on my own. I know my mother hated her. Said she was a witch. I think my father used to see this woman, without my mother's knowing it. I didn't say anything, but I think that is why my mother hated her so."

"You mean, he *saw* her. Right?"

Michael sat up, as if coming awake. "Yes."

"Ahh, I see." Diana hesitated before saying what she was going to say next. "I thought we were going to check on some places where Melissa might be."

Michael spoke without hesitation. "I have seen Melissa."

Diana's skin became chilled, and she had to concentrate doubly on the road so she wouldn't lose control of the car. She wasn't angry, though she knew she ought to be. She was frightened. There was something in what Michael was telling her that was beginning to make her think she should go home and leave the old man to his own devices. He might be better off without her.

"Oh," Diana said casually. "You've seen her. How is she?"

"I can't say yet. I don't really know how she is. My brain is resting; remembering everything that happened. When Emily hears the story, you will hear all of it also."

Michael said no more. Diana wasn't sure if she wanted to hear any more at all.

Twenty minutes later, Michael waved his hand for a turnoff that led to a small shopping center, a gas station, and the rest home. The straight road would have taken them all the way to Sky City if they'd wanted to go there. After half a mile they turned into a parking area surrounding a compact cluster of oddly shaped buildings.

There wasn't much of a view for the old people, Diana thought as she drove into the parking lot. If she were ever sent here, she would probably die of depression. But that was silly. Presumably, this was a reservation rest home. As a latent Irish-Catholic white girl, she would probably not be welcome.

I-40 hummed to the north. The buff-colored buildings of the rest home were situated in a valley between two walls of yellow and red mesas. The yellow mesa across the freeway rose into Mount Taylor, whose bluish, snowy slopes were easily discernible in the October sunshine. The western wall of the red, water-streaked mesa began across the road and stretched south for many miles, maybe until it reached Sky City, thought Diana. The valley itself was filled with snow and barren of trees, yellow grass or any other type of normal vegetation. Only gray scrub brush and a line of skeletal black tamarisks several hundred yards away were poking through the snow.

The buildings themselves looked like sets from a 1960s science-fiction movie. Lozenge-shaped structures were grouped around a central plaza; the roofs were so low and sloping that she could see an empty space in the middle of their flat tops.

Some windows were thin rectangles; others were circles above circles.

"Do you want to wait in the car?" Michael asked.

Diana wondered if this place made him feel uncomfortable. Would this be his future home?

"No," Diana answered. "I'm coming in with you."

Michael shut his door.

"Michael?"

"Yes?" He looked back in.

"About the doctors. You said there had been three of them. But only two became friends of the Pueblo. What happened to number three?"

"The third doctor caught the plague at the very beginning. He died."

Of course. Why had she bothered to ask?

The rest home corridor was itself an alien being made up of joyless parts, Diana thought. Curving steel bars, curious eyes, twiglike arms covered with a stretched, yellowed skin. The smell, oddly, was comforting because it was utterly human. It was a wintry smell you could never cover up, ignore, or obliterate; dimming a youthful evening with washes of gray illness and death, tainting a Sunday afternoon with decay.

A girl spoke behind Diana.

"Are you here to visit someone, ma'am?"

Diana turned to Michael, unable to speak. Michael smiled sunnily.

"Little Rita Haven, hello!"

"*Guwats'i*, Mr. Roanhorse, how are you? Haven't seen you around for a while."

Rita was wearing a striped pink and white blouse, glaring white pants, and tennis shoes. Her open face and thick, black hair caught in a ponytail seemed to belong somewhere else, walking under a blue sky, or teaching a class of boisterous elementary kids. Not in this place.

Michael touched Diana's arm. "This is Diana. A friend from Albuquerque."

Rita turned her gorgeous smile on Diana, instantly making the rest home cheerier. Diana offered her hand and shyly mumbled something or other. The girl's palm was dry and smooth.

"We're here to see Mrs. Sandoval," Michael said.

"She's in her room, I think. Not in the day room, definitely! The TV bothers her. She thinks everyone in it is drunk and angry."

"How's your mother?" Michael seemed to have dropped his solemnness.

"She's doing okay, Mr. Roanhorse. You must come down and get some bread. Addie and mom made a whole batch of it yesterday. I'll tell her you stopped in and maybe she can save some for you. If it's not already all gone!"

Rita took them from the circular day room into one of the quieter hallways. Soothing blue carpet swallowed their footsteps. Ancient, sun-darkened people with iron-gray hair sat in steel chairs, glancing keenly or smiling as they passed by. Michael visited with most of them, speaking in a smiley kind of language, which he later told Diana was Keresan. She noticed that he seemed to enjoy touching people: rubbing their hands, touching their arms, patting thin shoulders.

A year or so ago, when she had been feeling particularly ignorant, Diana had gone to the university library and read up on the tribes in New Mexico. Most of the literature had lost her completely. But one thing she had learned was that Navajos don't often touch or look at people. It was considered rude.

Now, Diana saw her scant learning being thrown to the winds. Look! There he was kissing some laughing woman's cheek. Also, when Michael stopped to talk with one of the old folks, they pointed to their hips or to the backs of their arms or legs, as if they were describing their pains. Diana was reminded of a doctor making his rounds in a regular hospital.

"He sure is a friendly man," Diana commented to Rita.

Rita laughed. "Mr. Roanhorse is cool."

They entered a sun-filled room.

"Mrs. Sandoval," chirped Rita, "you have guests!"

The cozy room contained a bed, a large window, many colorful greeting cards sprinkling the walls, and a white-haired woman sitting on an adjustable chair by the window. She wore a blue cotton dress and a sage-green apron. Her long hair was caught up in a red scarf, and her eyes were closed. She sat with her hands folded in her lap and looked as if she were waiting to go somewhere.

"Wake up, Mrs. Sandoval," Rita said, touching the woman's shoulder. "Someone's here to see you." The young attendant knelt by Mrs. Sandoval and gently rubbed her arm. The woman roused herself and smiled to the room. White clouds covered her pupils.

"Ya'at'eeh," she said in a strong voice. "Who's there?"

Michael touched her hand and said something in his language. The old woman smiled and answered him, her dentures making her look unbelievably happy. Their language was rough, the words like tumbling, sliding sandstone; it was different from the language he had used with the other old people.

Diana stood back, feeling like a small child waiting for the adults to notice her; she didn't know what else to do with herself. Finally, Michael waved for her to come closer. Nothing in his language was recognizable, but she knew she was being described.

"Hello, young woman."

Diana came forward. "I'm pleased to meet you, Mrs. Sandoval."

"My first name is Emily."

"Thank you. I'm Diana."

"You teach Melissa in Albuquerque?"

"Yes, that's right. Tenth grade English." Diana smoothed her skirt, imagining wrinkles forming on it.

"I hope Melissa doesn't give you too much trouble."

"None at all. She does very well for herself."

"Good." Emily's eyes seemed to pierce through the milky clouds covering them to see Diana in her entirety.

"Michael tells me you have a story to tell."

"Oh." Diana felt a blush reddening her entire body. "I don't know. Really?"

Both of them looked at her patiently as if she had arrived with a speech prepared. Diana paused, then told of the morning when Melissa had disappeared; she described Melissa's ill appearance, the wounding of herself and Bob Hatfield, and her search for Melissa's relatives, which had brought her to Michael. Her telling became easier, and she wished she had more to add, something upbeat. Then again, she didn't want to confuse Emily with more English than was necessary. She wasn't even sure the old woman understood her narration at all.

Emily smiled absently and turned to Michael. He bowed his head as if preparing himself.

"Diana has not heard my story, yet," he said to Emily. "I will tell it in English."

"Go ahead, my grandson," she said.

Then, in a hesitant but steady voice, Michael told them what had happened to him over the past two days. The facts issued from his mouth in pictures without color: Weird dreams of some trotting coyote-man; a supernatural woman's attack on him; finding and guarding Melissa at the hospital; meeting a blond witch-girl who flew out of a window with Melissa in tow; then a confrontation with an evil man-wolf creature, which ended with a corn pollen raincloud in a hospital lobby.

Christ, Diana thought.

Outside the window, a pitiful garden of wilted corn stalks and gray tendrils of melon pushed heroically out of a patch of snow flanked by the tilted walls of the surrounding buildings. A breeze caused the corn stalks to nod and bob their heads. Already, the icicles along the roof's edge were melting in the sunlight. At one point during Michael's story (when a clawed hand reached out of the raincloud toward Michael), Emily told Diana to close the door. With me in or out? Diana wanted to ask. The hallway had emptied itself of people. A TV program droned from somewhere. Everyone, including smiling Rita, seemed to have vanished.

The walls barely had enough time to absorb his words when Emily spoke. "I cannot help you, my grandson."

Michael remained quiet and nodded, as if he had been expecting this answer. He looked like a little boy waiting to be admonished by a parent or teacher. Diana felt sorry for him, but really, did he think they would believe him?

Emily spoke to him quietly in their broken, sing-song language for a long time. The sunlight crept silently along the floor. Emily gazed often at the ceiling as if there was someone hovering there whose words she was repeating. However, though her voice was often passionate, her hands never left her lap. They were as solid and frozen as stones.

Finally, the old woman turned to Diana.

"Do you believe him?" she said firmly.

"I'm sorry . . . what?"

"Michael spoke in your language so you could understand him. Do you believe his story?"

Michael was looking out the window at the tiny, sad garden Diana had been contemplating hours before. What did he see there? Hidden signs she could never guess at? Or the one thing that had struck her forcefully about the land she had seen so far: The enormous destructive and generative power of the sun.

Of course, she didn't believe Michael's story. But she couldn't just say it. She had to figure out his reasoning in telling such a bizarre story. Emily waited patiently for her answer.

"I don't know," Diana said. She hated those same words coming from her students; she couldn't think of anything less hurtful to say.

The old woman said to Michael, "You must talk to Doris and William Pacheco. They will help you. I have forgotten many things. Your story reminds me of something from the old days, but I can't remember all of it. Talk to them in Madrecita, my grandson. They will tell you something."

"I'm not Keresan," Michael said. "I don't belong to their village."

"Margaret, *amo'oh*, when she passed away, left you a house in their village. Nanibaa', your grandmother, when she came to visit, grinded corn with me in the old days. You have kept your sheepcamp at the edge of the Keresan reservation, to watch for enemies or bad things. The Keresan are happy about that. A long time ago, the old Navajos, passing through on their sad walk, left your great-grandmother with the Keresans. Your father understood the Keresan language. After he died, when your mother died too, the Keresans took care of you and raised you to be strong. You are family with them, *ba'ba'ah*. Like me. You and William and myself are Navajo, but we are Keresan, also."

The room stayed quiet, but the sounds in the hallway commenced. Diana could hear the old people talking once more. Bouncy music issued from the hidden TV. A phone began to ring. Diana had the feeling that Michael and Emily's exchange had been some kind of a play read from a script. Emily's voice had carried the monotone of ritual. Michael would have known all that stuff about his family. So why all the somber routine? Emily turned to her.

"*Ayaah'ah!* You two better hurry and get on with your work." Emily spoke in a scolding tone of voice. "Doris and

153

William and the others are all old like me. We might not last much longer."

It was something so unexpected in this dire setting that Diana burst out laughing.

"I'm sorry," Diana blurted, trying to kill her laughter. Her face was blushing so red she could feel the heat of it. But she couldn't stop giggling. Diana wondered if the old woman would become angry. Her laughter dried up quickly.

Emily chuckled. "Come and visit me again, Diana. You have such a pretty laugh."

"I'd love to," Diana said, figuring she would never see the old woman again.

"None of my children ever laughed at my jokes. They always scolded me instead, This one—" she nudged Michael's side, "was the only child who used to. But he doesn't anymore either. I think he has turned into one of my sons by mistake."

Michael placed a hand on Emily's shoulder.

"Don't talk so much, my mother," he said dourly.

Emily clicked her tongue and laughed, reminding Diana of the young attendant, Rita. And Michael looked almost like a slender young man standing by the old woman. How old was Emily?

"It was very nice meeting you, Emily," Diana said.

Emily held out her small hand. The skin was calloused and the bones were easily felt underneath. Diana expected a strong grip, which was usually the case with other defiant old folks she had met, but Emily's was gentle and hesitant. Emily leaned forward as if to tell a secret, so Diana bent lower.

"Be careful of this young man, dear," she said confidingly. "He doesn't show much strength against pretty girls."

"We better get going, Diana," Michael said quietly.

Without hesitation, Diana knelt to Emily and hugged her briefly. The woman's body felt tiny inside the soft cotton dress. Diana didn't reflect on her action. It was probably wildly impolite.

But she was glad she did it.

They drove north in silence to the village called Madrecita. According to road signs, the two-lane road passed three other villages; Diana couldn't summon the spirit to wrestle with their names. On one road sign was an indication of just how far they had driven — Albuquerque: 45 miles.

Folded piles of ice lay on both sides of the narrow road, thrown by snowplows. Eastward, the landscape spread in a white sheet until suddenly rising up into the red cliffs of Mesa Gigante some miles away. A tinier mesa was perched on its back like a horsefly or a bell on a church. Westward, at Diana's left, another long mesa rose from a jumble of snowy boulders and green junipers, following the road pretty much all the way to Madrecita.

Soon, the road began to lift itself in lazy curves against the side of the western mesa. Water trickled from overhanging boulders onto the road. As they topped the mesa, Diana looked far to the east and saw a blackish-brown pollution cloud hanging above the earth like a hovering vulture. A sign indicated a left turn for Madrecita. Diana carefully guided her car onto a smooth single lane and saw to the northeast a landscape that had been blasted and torn apart. A huge uranium mine existed there, she remembered. Or had existed. It was only just recently shut down.

They passed peeling, unreadable warning signs. A sagging wire fence held glittering balls of snow and ice. Mine vents were overgrown with weeds. Further below, in a wet canyon, stood dilapidated shacks humbled by the fierce sunlight. Boulders were clustered at the feet of black, artificial volcanoes like disfigured toes. Nowhere could Diana see any signs of life. She had hoped to see a deer or a rabbit at least. A single blackbird flew above the wrecked, voided carcass of land.

At what level did the radiation remain? Had anyone ever bothered to check?

They came upon a grouping of rough adobe houses. A higher ridge of mountainous rock loomed above this mesa, stretching northwestward and leaving steep ravines and pine trees in its wake. Further on, Michael told her, was Mount Taylor; the original volcano. When he said that, Diana felt a chill across her face. It was as if he had tapped into her rambling thoughts of radiation poisoning and earth-shattering machines.

At his directions, they wove their way into the village. Many of the adobe buildings were boarded up, lacked whole walls, or revealed naked stone sides; no one bothered to build

155

them back up or replaster them. Some houses were plain ruins, just piles of rubble and planks. However, the other dwellings looked well-cared-for. And she could see by rectangles or squares of wire-enclosed land in the front yards that the owners maintained gardens. Though the plants and trees were withered by the winter cold, Diana could imagine lush green plants blooming in the spring, thick heads of apricot trees heavy with fruit waving in the summer winds.

Diana parked her car in sloshy mud in front of a squat, adobe house. Tidy little awnings cut from green fiberglass sheets covered the two front windows and the door. Diana groaned at the mud. She had nice leather oxfords on, and the hem of her skirt was fairly low too. No one had told her they were going into rough country. Annoyed, she emerged from her car and locked the door, urging Michael to do likewise. The village seemed deserted. Streams of water gurgled into brown puddles. Her shoes squelched in mud as she and Michael walked to the front door. She felt like a cow making its way to the barn. At least the air was fresh.

The door was squeakily opened by a little boy around six years old. "*Guwats'i*, Grandpa," he said shyly. His smile was toothy and his black hair flopped around his shoulders as he led them into a shadowy living room cluttered with photographs, paintings, Indian pots, and knickknacks of every sort. Diana recognized, with surprise, a plastic model of an antlered deer perched on a large TV set. Her grandfather had had exactly the same deer set on his bedroom bureau in his house in Brigham City. Diana remembered as a child taking the deer secretly into the downstairs laundry room and telling it ghost stories.

The boy raced ahead of them through a doorway into a green kitchen.

"*Ya'at'eeh!*" a man called. Michael nudged her forward. Chairs scraped on the floor as she entered the large kitchen. A fluorescent ring in the ceiling illuminated bare cabinets, linoleum counters, and a massive wood table. An old man and woman rose to greet them.

More gentle handshakes. The little boy vanished out the kitchen door with a yellow apple. "Come in and sit down," said the tiny plump woman named Doris. She wore a blue dress and a white apron, much as Emily had. Diana could imagine how lovely Doris must have been when a young girl. Her cheeks were full and her skin was smooth and remarkably free of etched lines and wrinkles. But it was her eyes that drew Diana's attention, with their deep violet irises and sunny laugh lines. Doris circled delicately around the table, to an oven in the corner.

The old man, William, might have been as beautiful when younger; now he was weatherbeaten as old wood. He pulled out chairs and sat himself at the table. He wore a plaid shirt, jeans, and cowboy boots. Thick glasses made his eyes into owl's eyes. His gnarled hands were settled on the table next to his coffee mug. The old couple were no more than five feet tall. They reminded Diana of those hollow dolls that held smaller and smaller versions of themselves inside.

William cleared his throat. "We were having our coffee when little Darryn came around. Michael, you remember Mary? That's her little boy."

"Did his father ever come back from Wichita?" Michael settled himself into a chair as if it were a comfortable bed after a hard day. I better keep a close watch on him, Diana thought. All this running around was surely tiring him out and, of course, he was probably too stubborn to admit when enough was enough.

"He did," Doris said, laying down cups and shallow bowls.

"He did come back, about a month ago, I think, driving a new pickup." William took off his glasses and rubbed his eyes. "He didn't stay too long. He stayed with his mother; you know Maisie, Michael? Then he left again."

"What's Mary doing for work?" Michael asked.

"*Amo'oh*, Mary's teaching at the high school," Doris said from the area of the stove. She was fumbling with a towel, trying to fold it so she could pick up a large pot.

Diana stood up. "Can I help with anything?"

Doris reached far above herself, opened a cabinet, and took down a tin of cookies. "Open this up, dear, and put them on a plate."

Diana searched through cabinets until she found a plate. On it was an illustration of a navy warship: *U.S.S. Alabama*, it read in black letters.

"Is this okay?"

"Yes. Put it in front of the men and help me pour coffee."

157

The coffee looked like black soup. Lifting the pot from the ring, Diana thought it was heavier than a regular old pot of coffee should feel. When she finally tasted it, coffee grounds rolled against her teeth.

The cups were spotless. Diana wondered about the source of water. How high was the water table here? On the slopes of the ridge above Madrecita, she had seen the green of forest cover. Mountain-fed streams? Surely there must be water coming from somewhere. Maybe there was an underground spring.

Diana poured coffee, stirred a meat stew in a big pot, and hunted for napkins and spoons. After a while, she sat down and regarded the plate of cookies in front of her. Thick butter cookies and gingersnaps.

"We haven't seen you for a long time, nephew," William said, winking at Diana. "What have you done since, gotten yourself married?"

Diana felt a blush creeping up her face. These people were so old! They made her feel like an awkward teenager. Diana laughed with them and sipped her coffee.

"I was in to see Emily for a bit," Michael said. "I have trouble that I need to talk to you about."

Doris muttered something Diana couldn't understand. Diana was reminded of how Grandma Patsy would utter prayers to herself when some tragedy or evil struck the world.

"Tell us, my nephew," William said.

Michael told them his story. Nothing was changed. All the details were in sequence and relevant; like listening to a tape recording. The caffeine Diana had absorbed over the past few days was mixing together, making her jittery and anxious and more irritable. She was becoming increasingly embarrassed for Michael. And for herself.

When Michael finished, he took a long drink from his cup. William and Doris were silent. Doris was humming softly, her hands folded in her lap. After a time, William spoke, smoothing back his short gray hair.

"It's been a long time since I heard such a story. I think it was Shorty Red who said something about that north mesa, Mesa Gigante." He turned to Doris. "Is it?"

Doris nodded. "Yes," she said dolefully, looking across the room. Outside the window, Diana saw swaying mulberry branches. "It was the night his brother was killed. Struck by a train, *amo'oh*. That snowy December. Such a bad thing to have happen near Christmas."

"That was Jimmy," William said. "You were a young man then, nephew. I think it was the same year you were living in Albuquerque with Margaret and Sarah."

"I remember Shorty," Michael said. "I hunted with his sons one year above Pie Town. He had a big mustache like a Mexican."

"Yes." Doris turned to Diana and smiled. "Jimmy had the same kind of mustache. We used to call them the Bean Brothers."

"The Mexican twins," Michael said. "That was a long time ago. My father, I remember, didn't like them."

"They were good men, amo'oh," said Doris. "It was hard on Shorty when Jimmy was killed."

The old people grew silent. Diana smelled the dusty air and felt suddenly sleepy. She reached for a gingersnap.

William spoke quietly. "The elderlies used to say Shorty's mother was a witch."

His words, said in such a casual way, made the hairs on the back of Diana's neck prickle.

"What the Navajos say is a skinwalker," Doris whispered, crossing herself. "A person who runs as a wolf."

The two men nodded somberly.

"What was it Shorty used to say about that north mesa," William said, closing his eyes, squinting them as if that might help his memory.

"I remember my grandmother saying things about it," Michael said. " 'Stay away from that place, my grandson,' she used to say to me. 'That is where the skinwalkers run.' "

"*Haah'ah.* Many years ago," William began, his eyes still closed. "There was some Indians who lived there. I don't know where they came from or if they were related to us. I think there was something evil that hunted them. *Kwoo-yishuuko*, around that place, nephew, where the mother is. Do you know that place?"

Michael nodded grimly. William continued.

"My own father said that his grandfather showed him where that place used to be. It was a big cavern. 'There is nothing in that place, son,' he said to me. 'Only some broken

159

pot shards and grinding stones. It is an old place.' I never asked him where it was." Turning to Diana, William laughed. "I was too scared."

"*Haah'ah,*" Doris said. "My father said that when he was a boy, they used to, my father and his uncles, they used to pick up the potteries that were there and hide them and bury them. They used to sing over that place to bless it. But the old elderlies said it could never be blessed."

"*Ayaah'ah!* too," William said, opening his eyes. "It was good land. They wanted to make it safe for their herds."

Diana put her half-eaten cookie down. "Is this the big mesa next to the freeway? Where the railroad passes under I-40?" Across from where Michael lives, she wanted to add.

"Yes," Doris said. "That north mesa."

Diana retrieved the coffee pot from the stove and poured them all another cup. Had anyone at the university heard about any of this? An undiscovered pueblo! A place even the Indians wouldn't go to. She could imagine the entire anthropology department wetting its pants over such a thing, crawling over it like termites. Or like the earth-shattering machines. No wonder the Keresans had kept it such a secret.

Diana studied the old folks. They really shouldn't let information like that fall into conversations with just anybody. She was a stranger. How did they know she wasn't some creep ready to exploit such juicy tidbits? Diana sipped her coffee and wondered what the "mother" they had mentioned was.

Michael pushed his cup away. "You know all of this. The whole story of it. Will you help me to find Melissa?"

His voice carried such a tone of weariness and defeat that Diana wanted to reach to him and comfort him. Instead, she held her warm cup tighter. They must help him! They're his relatives.

It was William who answered Michael.

"No, my nephew. We can't help you."

Michael remained still and quiet. Diana bit back her anger, barely. She had no right to be here, to witness this callous refusal of a plea for help. How could she say anything?

Oh crap and to hell with it! as Granddad Stephen used to bellow. Diana unclenched her jaw to speak. "Melissa may be in serious trouble. My student." Diana tried to control the

160

unsteadiness in her voice. "The least you people can do is to offer him sympathy. Or suggest someone who can help."

"We sympathize, dear," Doris said, laying her hand on Diana's. "But there is nothing we can do."

Diana's face burned. She hated her face because it displayed all her emotions, especially embarrassment.

"It's all right," Michael said, wincing as he rose from his chair. He couldn't quite stand up straight. "We better go."

Diana stood up, reproachful. At least say you believe him! she wanted to shout. She kept silent.

Accompanying them into the living room, seeing them off, William shook her hand and retreated through a doorway at the back of the room. Was he embarrassed, too? Angry? Diana wished she could figure these people out.

Doris hugged her. Diana caught a whiff of some soap smell. A delicate, familiar kind of scent that was gone as soon as the old woman let her go.

"Come see us, Diana," Doris said smiling. "Call first, before you come. Then I can make you something good to eat. A pot of chili, maybe."

Doris held Michael. "Everything will be all right, *ba'ba'ah*," she told him. "Melissa is a strong girl. Like her grandmother used to be."

They were all waiting for something. Diana didn't know what. A cabinet door slammed in a back room. William emerged from the doorway he had left through, carrying a small white square in his hand. As he gave it to Michael, Diana saw that it was a photograph of a young boy.

"That's Jerry." William beamed. "My own granddaughter's new baby boy, though he is three years old now. His godfather is Samson White, who is Keresan. He stays in Margaret's house. Your house, where Sarah was born and grew up. Always remember it, my nephew. You, Emily, and me are Navajo, but we are Keresan too. Tell Samson your story and he might help you."

Oddly, Michael smiled, and straightened. Diana sensed some kind of a communication or ritual happening again; as she had with Emily at the rest home. She was missing something, and she knew it. Michael placed the small photograph in his breast pocket and patted it. "Thank you," he said.

161

Once more, William approached her. Diana thought he was going to hug her, but he didn't. She cleared her throat. "I'm sorry I spoke to you in the kitchen like that. I'm worried about Melissa. We haven't found out anything yet, and it's frustrating."

The old man nodded.

"Don't worry. We'll get Melissa back." William leaned to her. By now, Diana recognized the confiding gesture as one just before a joke. She moved closer to him, too.

"Don't let the skinwalkers catch you, Diana," he said quietly. His owl eyes remained unblinking.

Diana smiled uneasily. Was that a joke? If so, no one else in the room was laughing either.

Thirty-three

Diana dropped Michael off at Sarah's apartment. He could feel her curious gaze on his back as he struggled out of her cramped car.

"Do you want me to wait with you?" Diana asked, jingling her car keys.

"I'll wait here alone. Melissa might come back."

"I also would like to speak with her. But I guess you have your own agenda." The car racketed into gear. "I'll make us something to eat. Call me to pick you up."

"Thank you," Michael answered. He watched the red car turn from his sight, then he walked to the dark apartment. He noticed the frozen stars, so distant, not a glimmer of their heat penetrating to him. The front door of the apartment was open, but nothing inside seemed out of place. Throughout the journey back, Michael had slept fitfully, just on the verge of some release. His mind was buzzing with too many memories, sparked by what Emily had told him.

162

He warmed himself under a hot shower and, afterward, toasted some bread. There was nothing in the refrigerator but spoiled milk and half a bottle of wine. Michael opened the bottle, poured himself a little, then settled himself on the couch, in the dark, to wait.

Sooner than expected, he heard the front door open. Michael waited, saw memories gather of dark forest pines and a hushed wind sighing through them. Some quiet animal, a deer maybe, was watching him.

"I knew you'd be here," a young girl said, the witch who had taken Melissa. "They waited for you this morning before the sun rose. You never came. I told them you wouldn't."

Michael did not move, not even to set his glass on the floor. "Where are they tonight?"

The girl crossed the room and stood near the kitchen doorway, next to the aquarium. She glowed faintly as if lit by a calm fire. He could make out her features clearly, though there was no real light in the room. Her blue eyes were solemn and she had a waifish build. She reminded Michael of a girl he had seen in a film many, many years ago, a silent film lost between the thunder and song of a matinee showing of Tom Mix and Gene Autry films. Her hair was a gentle silvery gold, like evening light on a cloud. She was not as imposing or threatening as the other woman, the one named Hanna; she was looking away from him, toward the floor, as if enduring his search of her.

"Falke is with Melissa, tonight," she said. "Hanna is out . . . somewhere. I can't feel where she is anymore."

Michael sat up and set his glass on the floor. He felt mildly dizzy. The alcohol had numbed his aching joints, and he wiggled his fingers to keep them from stiffening up.

"You are speaking as if you trust me," Michael said, almost to himself.

The girl shrugged. "You cannot hurt me. No matter how much you want to."

"Why haven't you tried to kill me?"

"How do you know I won't?"

"Because I trust you."

The girl stilled, gazed at him speculatively. This girl, like the other one and even Melissa now, froze like deer when an unfamiliar sound reached their ears. It was disquieting. Michael knew these were not ordinary people, whatever Diana tried to tell him. She had to be warned more forcefully.

"Why do you trust me?" the girl asked.

"You have not hurt my granddaughter. You hold her life carefully; I have seen this."

"Hanna wants you dead."

Michael shrugged. "I don't like her, either."

The girl became still again. "You're not afraid?"

"I am afraid."

"I will tell you something. Hanna is afraid of you."

"I'm an old man," Michael said. "My arthritis pains me. My eyesight is poor. Hanna has nothing to be afraid of."

"I'll tell you something else." The girl stepped from the doorway. "I don't think Hanna's afraid of you enough."

"Where is my daughter?"

She shook her head. "Falke would know. He doesn't tell me much anymore."

"Is Sarah alive?"

"I don't know."

"What do you think?"

The girl paused. "I can't tell you now."

Michael was overcome with weariness. His strength drained from him; he felt anger rooting in his bones. He wanted to smash things. He wanted to grab this girl and hurt her, demand that she take him to his grandchild. But he was tired. He felt a thousand years old.

"Get out," he whispered, bowing his head into his hands. Silence drizzled around him. He lay back and saw the trailer Margaret and he used to live in just before Sarah was born, a silver thing, parked in a sand lot somewhere, a forgotten area in the big city. He remembered the ponderous way it had rocked during a thunderstorm; how the rain had crashed against flimsy aluminum walls. Or how the summer sun had cooked them slowly inside its guts; that merciless sun, always more vicious in his memory than anyone else remembered, creeping along the trailer's sleek, rocketlike sides.

They had been a newly married couple in their first home. Wide-eyed kids. Giddy with freedom and just as afraid. How were they to make all the payments? Caught in a gem-like city they knew nothing about, that cared even less for them, and with a baby on the way. Until now, Michael had never felt such tormenting fear in his life as he had then. A winter storm of fear was shaking his soul, crushing his heart, turning all his hope to ice.

Michael pictured Margaret gazing out a window of their little trailer, watching moveless sand hills and hollow yellow grass, big in her belly with baby Sarah. Their daughter.

He walked to his wife and held her.

Thirty-four

After retrieving Michael from Melissa's apartment and putting him in the back room to nap, Diana tackled the dishes. Emily fascinated her. When I'm old and alone, Diana thought, I hope I'm as sane as that lady. If I'm lucky, not as blind. Diana was glad the woman had refused Michael her help. Really, what could Emily have done? What was Diana doing herself? Providing room and board for an old man searching for his granddaughter, maybe keeping him out of trouble.

It was 8:20 by her watch that sat in a soapdish. Diana let her hands relax in the hot, soapy water. No, I'm not just ferrying him around and cooking for him. Or paying for our breakfasts. I'm searching for Melissa, too. In my own humble way.

One of the reasons, she'd decided as Michael had spoken with Doris and William, was that Melissa resembled herself a little at the same age—which wasn't so long ago, Diana realized. No real family except for an old man and woman; distracted in a gloomy kind of way; lost in a safe world of printed matter. Did Melissa have a boyfriend?

Diana's gaze drifted to a gray and white marble rolling pin a boyfriend had once given her—in high school, for Christ's sake! Diana was an able cook. A tomato casserole would come out of the oven looking like the picture in the cookbook. Nothing compared to what old Patsy Logan could conjure up,

165

though. Diana's grandma had been a white sorceress in an immaculate kitchen.

Flicking bubbles from her hands, Diana went to the windowsill and picked up the rolling pin. Heavier than she remembered, she had to use both hands to keep the thing from slipping out of her wet fingers. She carried it into the living room and set it on the sewing table next to her mother's old swing-up sewing machine, close to the front door. In case any skinwalkers come calling.

Michael snored briefly in the back room. Diana changed her mind and brought the rolling pin back to the kitchen table. She sat down, and listened to the soap bubbles popping in the sink behind her. Then she picked up the phone and called Katy. Lots of rings buzzed in her ear. Maybe Katy had gone dancing.

A man-wolf in a hospital lobby. A supernatural monster imprisoned in a blue and white cloudburst. Howls of anger echoing through hospital corridors. Twin flying girls.

"Diana!" puffed Katy. "I know it's you! I ran from the back garden. Let me get my breath."

Diana pressed a finger to an eyelash, and touched her forehead, probing her vanished third eye. "I called to say the swellings on my head have gone down finally."

"Well, of course! That's expected. I hope you're getting plenty of rest? Can I hope for that too?"

"Enough rest. Any news about Bob?"

"Out of action, as far as I can tell. He's been in contact with some lawyer people, or so I've heard."

"*What?*"

"He wants Melissa's hide up on his wall with the other trophies he's shot to death."

"He has dead animals on his walls?"

"So I've heard. Bob fancies himself a big-game hunter."

"That's ridiculous."

"I don't know if he's got a case or not, but he's working at it." Katy snorted. "Maybe you ought to get on his wagon, Diana, make a little horse money."

Diana felt a sudden urge to visit Mr. Hatfield with her rolling pin and crack it over his head. "How's the sub getting along?"

166   "No injuries so far! Any luck with the old man?"

Diana made the decision quickly. "No. I haven't seen him much. He's worried, of course."

"Poor man."

"Yes, really." Diana wasn't sure why she had lied to Katy. Following pure instinct, it seemed. "Michael seems pretty healthy to me, though," she added.

"Melissa'll turn up, Diana. I'm sure the brat is holed up with friends. Maybe it'd be best if we didn't find her for a while, if she just skipped town for good."

"What an awful thing to say!"

"Have you been reading the papers?"

"No . . . I can't."

"Some are speculating about an international drug ring." Katy snorted again. "People are getting so damned uptight. We've got the Kid Police sniffing around the campus, some pretending to be students. Detectives check in on the hour, asking about Melissa. The faculty's getting paranoid. However, the kids are pretty much amused by all the attention. And yours keep coming around the office to see how you're doing."

Diana grinned. "And what do you feel?"

"I'm worried that you're not getting a proper vacation. I think you've been spending too much time over this." Katy paused. "And, just between you, me, and the walls, I think you're holding out on me."

"I'm worried, Katy. And when I worry, I fidget."

"Nice way to squirm out from under the truth. For your sake, honey, don't hold out on me too long. I'm hoping the girl does turn up somewhere. But it's going to be hard on her when she does."

Diana shook her head firmly. "We'll be okay."

There was a silence on the line. Diana rushed to fill it.

"Look, Katy, I have to go."

"Oh, I've told the sub he can finish out the week—you can bitch and moan later. And keep in touch! I'm finding myself sitting up at the phone, nights. I haven't done that since my oldest was in high school. And I've taken up knitting again."

Tears made Diana's kitchen sparkle. She thought of Michael's hands and how trembly they moved sometimes. "Knitting's good for your hands," she said.

"Sounds familiar. It's what my sister used to say."

167

"I'll call you tomorrow afternoon, Katy."

"Whatever you're up to, Diana . . . well, you know. If you need help with anything, give a holler and I'll come runnin'. I may be old, but I'm still spunky!"

The air wasn't so dead anymore. The familiar sensations of having another breathing person in the house, of having to be quiet during the day, concerns about how nice the place looked and even how she looked, and wanting something good in her stomach and not the quick-to-prepare junk she usually ate, had all returned. And Diana was enjoying their return.

She began taking down various ingredients kept in small Tupperware containers, mixing bowls, and bread pans. Her movements felt unhurried and familiar. Comforting. As Michael slept and walked in whatever dreams old Indians had, Diana made bread.

Thirty-five

Her heart a small stone, Elizabeth watched as Melissa and Falke strolled in a frozen park, moving gracefully among frozen waves. Clouds scraped the stars, abraded them into coarse, brittle jewels. At Elizabeth's approach, the girl broke hurriedly from Falke's encircling arm.

"Elizabeth," Melissa breathed. Falke's face was marble. Elizabeth ignored him, confronted Melissa. The girl's face was chalky and wary, not with illness or fear, with exhaustion.

"You're tired." Elizabeth took the girl's hand. "Come."

Melissa lowered her eyes. Elizabeth thought she would refuse. The girl followed after a few moments, glancing only once at Falke as she accompanied Elizabeth toward the rim of the park.

Melissa pulled her hand back. "What do you want?"

Elizabeth smiled to soothe her. "You must start learning a different way: The way of holding strength. My husband will only shelter you. He will teach you nothing."

"I have lots of time to learn," Melissa said sharply.

Elizabeth lifted her face to the falling clouds and basked in the wind, which filled the elm branches with chattering life. The threat of more snow had emptied the streets; for that, she was grateful. Elizabeth unbuttoned her coat and let it fall to the ground. A gift for Old Man Snow.

"Those are Falke's words," she said. "Already, he's playing truth with you. His favorite game."

Melissa stopped, her face vibrant with angry color. "I know what you're trying to do."

"I don't even know what I'm doing myself."

"You're trying to make me not trust him."

"You shouldn't."

Melissa smiled, taunted. "You're jealous!"

A wild rage flooded Elizabeth. "And you're a child!"

Melissa's reflexes had quickened since last night. She swiped viciously. Elizabeth picked the girl's hand deftly out of the air. Melissa screamed and tried to wrench herself away. Elizabeth squeezed the fingers tighter, wanting to crush the delicate bones.

"Do you know how much pain a vampire can take?" Distantly, Elizabeth felt her eyeteeth growing into fine, needle-like points.

"Let go!" Melissa wept in outrage.

Elizabeth shoved her brutally. Melissa twisted and sprawled on the sidewalk.

"Get up!" Elizabeth shouted.

"Leave me alone!"

Elizabeth pounced on the girl, jerked her up, shook her savagely back and forth. The girl began to sob hysterically.

"You *listen* to me!" Elizabeth couldn't stop her outpouring of jealousy and hurt. Melissa pulled a hand free and struck Elizabeth across the face. Elizabeth had never felt such a murderous storm of hate growing inside her. The sighing clouds turned to molten iron. She caught the inviting scent of blood in Melissa's arteries.

Melissa is nothing to me, thought Elizabeth, muscles thrum-

169

ming with strength, lashing, preparing to kill. And she has stolen my husband. Elizabeth's white fingers flew open and reached for the girl. Her teeth became too sharp. Melissa's eyes widened into startled circles.

Elizabeth cried out and whirled away from Melissa, held her violence in. She let it thunder uselessly against her skull.

I promised! I promised Melissa's grandfather, in my heart, to keep Melissa safe. Walk! Walk and walk until exhaustion numbs emotion, until hunger fogs memory.

Lots of time! the stupid brat had said. Melissa's arrogance sickened Elizabeth. Yet it was not Melissa who had stolen Falke; it was Falke who had stolen the two of them . . . from everything.

A waiting silence stretched behind Elizabeth. She turned back and saw Melissa watching her, as a child will watch when trying to reckon with something. Elizabeth's muscles slowly relaxed. Her body shivered as rage slipped from her soul. She let her arms swing loosely at her sides.

"Follow me if you want. I don't care." Elizabeth chose the darkest street. Her stride lengthened until she was nearly running. In time, soft steps joined with hers.

"Tell me what you have done," Elizabeth said.

They were in a section of the city overgrown with bright fast-food emporiums, lush neon forests, and artificial grass.

"Since the hospital?" Melissa perked with interest.

"Before then."

"I don't remember it too well, that time." Melissa shrugged. "I threw up a lot."

Elizabeth paused under one of the buzzing neon signs, holding her hand to it, letting the electric lights drizzle over her fingers like rain. "Try to remember."

"I think my grandfather was afraid of me."

"Are you sure?" Elizabeth continued walking, wishing she could slough off her clothes and run and run and run. "I spoke to him earlier. He strikes me as a man not afraid of much."

"Oh, he's not. That's why that night sticks out in my mind." Melissa seemed perplexed. "I could smell his fear, almost. I think."

Elizabeth paused, saw the eager light in Melissa's eyes as she watched the people in the shops and in the passing cars.

"Right now, Melissa, you're like a cheetah, or a leopard. A predator. Fear excites you. Maybe that's what bothers you."

"I smelled his fear," Melissa stated. "I can hear better, too. Sometimes . . ." Her voice became hushed. "I can even hear things that aren't there."

Elizabeth ignored what the girl had said. "You were with your grandfather a night, a day, and half a night. What did he say to you?"

Melissa laughed suddenly and ran ahead, looking as if she might bounce off the planet. She called back, "I was pretty sick, remember? He sang to me a lot. Some old Navajo songs. He told me a story."

Elizabeth felt her chest tighten. How had he sung? She pictured the man's voice under moonlight, a river of soothing song.

"What story? Do you remember the songs?"

"Not really. Parts."

Elizabeth quickened her pace until she came abreast of Melissa. "Tell me what you remember!"

Melissa stopped and peered upward. "Why?"

Elizabeth followed Melissa's gaze up the tall lines of a black building leaning over them. She marked the progress of cleaning ladies in some of the lighted windows.

How to explain the power of memory?

"Melissa, you must learn to memorize the thoughts of your enemy."

"What enemy? My grandfather?" Melissa walked away quickly. Elizabeth followed behind at an observing distance. How well can the girl hear?

"You are my husband's mistress." Elizabeth thought the words more than spoke them. "Therefore, you are my enemy."

"Your enemy." Melissa's whispered reply came on a breeze. Her slight back was exposed. Elizabeth went to her and touched a tense shoulderblade.

"Don't turn your back to me, or anyone else, ever!"

Melissa faced Elizabeth, serious. "I trust you, Elizabeth. I'll remember what you say to me. My mother says I'm a quick learner. I even skipped a grade."

"See everyone as your enemy," Elizabeth said. "Trust your motives. Trust your heart more than your mind. Instinct! Remember, you are more predator than human."

"Will I be able to fly soon? I would like that."

Elizabeth shook her head, wanting the girl's warmth for herself. The heat of life. There was a tiny bit still left in Melissa's body. It shone from her eyes.

"The moon will steal your strength," Elizabeth answered. "First, you must learn to hunt."

"You talked to my grandfather?" Melissa asked. "How is he?"

Elizabeth kept walking, not caring anymore whether the girl followed or not, and held the man's image firmly in her mind. He had been tired, almost transparent with exhaustion, but solid, too. Again and again, she had tried to penetrate into his thoughts, but his defenses had kept her out, as solid and opaque as rock. Elizabeth had caught waves of emotion from him beyond anger, but she could not give name to them; they were complex and fascinated her.

"He's worried about you," she said.

Elizabeth was reluctant to meet with Falke again. What would she tell him about Melissa's grandfather? The man was dangerous to them, and she wasn't sure why. Maybe later, Hanna might give up something other than confused talk.

"What is your grandfather's name?" Elizabeth asked, testing Melissa.

The girl answered quickly. "Michael."

Elizabeth considered telling Melissa that it was dangerous to let names fall so easily from the tongue. Names, she believed, were filled with secret, dangerous powers. She paused under an immense streetlamp near the freeway and brushed its rough aluminum trunk. Behind her, the traffic's mechanical roar was threatening and hostile. Looking up, she saw the glowing circle that resembled a sun-washed daisy. The lamplight fell slowly and in large chunks. She imagined it falling on her bare arms and upturned face like snowflakes.

"The light of day is dangerous to us," she explained to Melissa. "One time, try to endure the sunrise. You will feel yourself burning, even when there is hardly any light to be seen."

Melissa came next to Elizabeth, marveling. "We really are vampires."

"The sun tries to kill us. The moon hates us too."

"I love the moonlight," Melissa said, faltering. "I mean, I used to, before . . ."

"I hate him," Elizabeth said, not caring who heard.

Thirty-six

Diana changed from a workshirt and jeans to a stiff cotton dress, and she combed her just-washed hair into a ponytail. In the kitchen window, stars swam in condensation. Her hot soup of meat and vegetables could survive a while without her attentions. She sat at the table and cut herself a slice of the potato bread left over from the day before.

Slight creaks, rustles of clothing, clinks of a belt buckle came from the back room where Michael had been sleeping. For the hundredth time, Diana wondered how old he was. He didn't seem to sleep much. A symptom of old age? she wondered. After her shower, when she had replaced the towels, Michael had been awake and staring at the ceiling. He hadn't spoken. She had wanted to ask if he was all right or if he needed anything. Maybe it was too hot in the room? Was she being too noisy in the kitchen? But Diana hadn't asked him anything. If she averted her eyes, she could imagine he was not in the room at all.

Firm steps in the hallway. Diana looked up to see Michael in a green flannel shirt and jeans standing straight in the doorway, rubbing his cropped hair — silver hair cut so short he looked like a soldier.

"Smells good," he said, smiling. "It woke me up."

"Sit down." Diana offered her chair. "I think I might've made too much food." She began gathering silverware and bowls. Not the plain everyday stuff, but her nice china dishes from the top shelf.

173

After they had eaten, Diana carried cups and a tin of cookies she had found lurking in the back of a cabinet into the living room. Michael settled onto the couch and picked up a magazine. Roger used to say that particular magazine was a waste of time to read; it had no real news in it, so why waste money on trash? Diana had never seen anything wrong with the magazine, although it did make world tragedies into dramatic, unreal stories with happy endings. Or hopeful endings.

It's my money, Diana used to answer. Besides, some good always comes out of the compost, as flower-loving Aunt Leslie—Patsy's spacey sister—used to say.

"I was thinking," Diana said, pouring out coffee for them. "I'll check around some of the crisis shelters tomorrow. Homes for battered women? I'll have to go alone. Melissa might be hiding out in one of them."

Michael nodded. It was quite late night, now. Traffic noises had died down completely. Diana got up and pulled the drapes tighter. Then she made sure the iron safety door was bolted. A cockroach caromed off the step. White clouds blew out of her mouth. Diana held herself against the freezing night.

Several days more of sick leave, the weekend, then back to work. Diana wished, for an instant, she could drop everything and live in a desert. Or become a stewardess. She was still young and thin enough. Diana saw herself caught in an endless horizon of land or air. No more attachments or driven worries about love-struck ex-husbands or nutty teenage kids.

Ugh! Diana thought. No thanks. Imagine spending ten hours a day six miles in the air, fielding glistening stares; or forty miles in the middle of a desert with a bunch of smelly sheep, detached from everything she had ever known, from everyone who knew her. Diana returned to the old man, and to her hot mug of coffee.

"So, tell me more about Emily." The question had been waiting all day to be asked.

"I don't know much about when she was little," Michael said, setting his empty cup down. Diana poured him some coffee and placed a cookie on his saucer. It was a ploy she had used on her granddad when she had wanted him to talk or explain something. He had never been able to resist butter

174

cookies; apparently, Michael couldn't either. Now the association was making her uncomfortable.

"Emily's a strong woman," Diana said. "My arm is still sore where she squeezed it."

"Emily used to weave her blankets when her eyesight was still good. That's why her hands are so strong. Beautiful rugs, I remember. She sold them at the trading posts in Navajoland and at Gallup, but only if she knew who her rugs were going to. Some of the traders were understanding, and she was good friends with them. I remember her rugs were really something.

"She mixed her own colors, gathering them when she used to herd sheep. Sometimes, when she was about your age, Emily used to ride her brother's horse up into Beautiful Mountain for several days, maybe even a week, to gather colors for her yarn. She always went alone. Emily was not afraid of anything. 'My mother scolded me again', Emily used to tell me. 'She keeps saying it is a man I went to visit. Tall Hat, maybe, or Toothless Man.'"

Michael laughed and broke his cookie in two, offering one piece to Diana. He leaned closer to her, as if to tell a secret. "A little time after that, after her mother told her to look somewhere else for her colors, Emily's first son was born. Not to Toothless Man, but to his younger brother, Keeps His Teeth, who was better-looking. That's what Emily told me."

Something like falling papers rustled in the front room, as if a stray wind had blown into the house and was leafing through the pages of a book. Diana wanted to ignore it, wanted to laugh and learn more about Emily, but the sound seemed urgent and odd. All the doors and windows were shut. How could a wind have come inside?

Michael's laughter died. He was staring past her into the front room. Diana turned and saw a wispy girl standing in the doorway between the front room and the living room.

Scalp rising, Diana stood up. "Who . . . can I help you?"

The girl said nothing, stared through her with fierce blue eyes as if Diana weren't there. She was frail, almost ghostly, about Melissa's age and eerily beautiful. Her skin was creamy-white, no peach or rose color anywhere except in her lips. And her hair was the type of shimmering blond that reflected every particle of light that struck its surface. Her dress was mid-length and of thin cotton. A summer dress? Her white legs were bare. She wore no coat.

"Michael." Her intense eyes glanced down as if containing a surge of excitement.

Diana backed toward Michael, waving a hand behind her so she wouldn't bump into him. He grasped her shoulder, and she almost jumped out of her skin.

The girl stepped further into the room, hesitated into stillness, looked up at him. "Come with me."

Diana realized who the girl was: the witch who had spirited Melissa out a hospital window, into the stars.

Michael moved in front of Diana, as if shielding her. "Where is Melissa?"

"She is in safe keeping," the girl said. "For the present. Please, Michael, I want to . . . talk with you."

"Then talk."

"Not here. It's not safe for her if I stay. I haven't been invited." She looked at Diana for the first time. Diana felt, almost heard, a crackle of electricity sizzling into her eyes. The room blurred slightly and darkened, as if she were going to faint. Diana shook her head.

"Michael?" Diana's eyes cleared. "What's going on?"

"Wait for me. Don't go out! I'll be back later."

"Wait, I don't understand," Diana stammered. "Where are you going?"

Michael's hand left her shoulder. Diana's eyes burned.

"Wait a minute, damn it. Michael!"

Diana grabbed hold of his arm, wrenched at it. Michael did not shake her off, merely looked at her. "I'll come back with news of Melissa," he said. "Wait for me, and pray."

Convulsively, Diana pulled her hand away; let him go. She wanted to slap him—for leaving her. "Go then."

Michael went to the girl, hesitated. Together, they left Diana's apartment.

Thirty-seven

Michael is with me now.

His presence was familiar to Elizabeth, a contradiction; she knew next to nothing about him except his rhythm of movement, his body's quiet language. Where to take him? So many places. For the moment, it was enough just to walk with him.

He kept abreast of Elizabeth, occasionally watching her. He moved silently and dark against the snow. His eyes were black and steady. Elizabeth felt strangely awkward, like a schoolgirl walking next to a deep and thoughtful river.

"There was a time when I might have been afraid to walk next to you," Elizabeth said.

"I have nothing for you to be afraid of."

"I know. I know it now."

"Is Melissa afraid of me?"

"No, she loves you, Michael. I sense it in the way she talks about you."

"She talks about me? What does she say?"

"Not much. I don't think she really knows enough about you to say anything." Elizabeth gave him a smile. "Perhaps that's why she isn't frightened."

"Why does Melissa talk about me, then?" Michael stopped. The full moon waited in his eyes; not predatory. A curiously gentle moon.

Elizabeth hesitated. "Because . . . I asked her to."

Thirty-eight

Diana stood immobile in her doorway. A strong wind chilled her. Nothing moved among the snow-covered houses. Electric light rained along the icy street, shimmering like broken glass. Michael had gone wearing only his plaid flannel shirt, jeans, boots. His denim jacket hung from a brass hat stand she had recovered from a flea market. Mist, like a living being, caressed her face. Shivering, Diana closed the door.

She gathered up the empty cups and closed the tin of shortbread cookies. She had not liked that moment of recognition between Michael and the girl, especially if the story he had told was true. Maybe she should call the police.

Diana dumped the dregs of coffee into the sink and rinsed out the cups. She hated coffee rings. They were so hard to get off without bleaching, and she didn't trust bleach. It was too clear, too green; it did weird things. She had told Roger a million times, at least, to rinse out his cup after he used it. A simple enough operation, she thought. Had he ever bothered to do it?

Almost unconsciously, Diana took the phone and dialed Roger's home number. She sat at the table, looking away from the tilted composition of her smiling parents standing in a field by the side of some unknown road. More to the point, Diana avoided looking at that damned looming stop sign.

Roger answered, as she had hoped. Why was she calling anyway?

"Hi, Roger." Diana's stomach became a bottle filled with moths—that hadn't happened for a long time—and her hand was trembling. Diana held the receiver tightly. "Can you talk?"

"Yes, of course I can," Roger said. "Are you all right?"

"Kind of. Well, not really. I'm . . . you know. I'm still worried about Melissa."

"Yeah, I know. After that scene at the hospital, we haven't heard a thing, either. I wish I had more for you, Diana."

"I know you'd call if something came up."

"Diana, are you sure you're okay? You don't sound very well."

The words tumbled out before she could stop them. "I feel good, Roger. That's why I called you."

There was an uneasy silence between them. Usually the self-assured talker, Diana thought. I wonder what he's thinking.

"I appreciate that, Diana," Roger said.

"How's your Danny?"

"It's way past his bedtime. His mother is reading to him now to try and get him to sleep. I can hear them upstairs."

"Oh." Diana tried to wipe her tears off the phone; they kept falling and burning. Too many to dry all at one time. She hoped she wouldn't get electrocuted. Diana had read somewhere that you could get fried talking on a phone while an electrical storm was busy shattering the sky. So maybe crying into the phone was like putting a wet finger into a socket. Diana was afraid to say anything more; her voice was out of control.

God, what's wrong with me?

"You better go up and tuck them in," Diana said.

"I could come by, Diana. I want to, to make sure you're all right."

"No!" Diana pressed her eyes shut with her fingers, awkwardly, because of the receiver. "I mean, I can handle myself. I'm sorry I intruded on your life."

"Don't . . ." Roger began to speak.

Diana hung up and thought, I've got to make a connection. *Connect.* Diana rose and went to the bathroom, washed up, brushed her hair carefully, trying not to look too closely into the mirror, then chose a demure lip color. Men like demure women, don't they? Diana wondered. Diffident, maybe. Nothing too fancy or wild. She left making up her eyes for last; her hand was still shaking. And her reddened eyes were dripping like leaky faucets.

"Oh, crap on it." Diana ran steaming hot water and scrubbed off all her efforts. She got her plain dark coat out of the closet and checked the fridge quickly to see what was needed.

I should make a list, she thought. Twenty miles long.

Diana grabbed her keys from the cup by the back door and left the apartment. The back screen she left unlocked, in case

Michael should decide to come back. Serve him right if I locked him out. The air was painful against her face. The car roof stung her fingers. Shivering, Diana hoped the car would start.

Thirty-nine

"Why are you with me?" Michael asked. The girl's feet, he noticed, were covered with red cloth shoes. The white skin of her ankles moving against the snow made it seem as if the shoes were walking by themselves.

"I'm searching, just like you." Her voice was soft and blended well with the crystal stars glittering above the reaching trees. "I don't belong here, either."

Michael thought of his house on its bare, rocky hill; the ruts of dirt road leading up to it would be covered with deadly ice. And the lights of Albuquerque would be a warm smudge of orange above the eastern horizon.

"I don't like the city," Michael said.

"No." The girl nodded as if she understood. "There are worse places, though."

Michael couldn't think of any. There was the Hell that used to frighten Margaret, but even that seemed to be a city. A city of grinding, wailing bones.

They walked a time in silence. Michael's boots crushed delicate ridges of ice. The crunching feel was satisfying, as if he were hunting on dried pine needles. The girl's steps were soundless.

"Why did you come to me again?" Michael asked.

The girl shrugged, muttered something too softly to hear. Maybe he wasn't meant to.

". . . and I'm afraid," she said.

"I'm walking with you because I'm afraid, too. I'm afraid

for my daughter, and for my granddaughter. Are you afraid for them?"

"I'm too selfish for that. I came for you because I was afraid for myself."

"What did you think I could do for you?" Michael's legs were now moving by themselves, numbed to the ferocious pain that slowly crept into his hands.

"When Melissa talks about you, I can picture you in my mind: A lonely house made of stone. It's a strong image. But, maybe, I'm wrong to say it."

"Melissa doesn't know about me that good. Those are your words. How can she speak so that you can see me clearly?"

"Her heart, Michael, speaks for her. I see into people's hearts. And their souls."

"What can you see in my heart?" Michael thought of Margaret in her coffin, hands puffy and frozen.

The girl glanced at him and frowned, as if studying the question. "I'll keep my conclusions to myself, for a time."

"What are you scared of?"

The girl stopped walking, looked at her feet. "I'm scared of my husband. And of my sister. I don't know why I call her that. She isn't my true sister."

"Sister and husband. The two people you should trust the most."

She glanced sharply at him. "Why do you say that?"

"In private times alone with my wife, she used to say the same to me. I don't know why. She had two sisters and one husband, so I believed her."

The girl looked away. "Lucky woman."

"Margaret is dead." Michael remembered the press of Margaret's small hand on his shoulderblades, kneading his spine. Her strong, calloused fingers.

The girl stood in front of Michael. He hadn't seen her move. Her eyes were as clear as pools of rainwater freshly fallen into sandstone crevices. Michael remembered Margaret finishing her joyful dance, folding her yellow shawl, pulling stray hair over her ears, her sun-touched eyes watching the other dancers drifting away as the dust rose into the sky, then seeing him and smiling, maybe knowing him as her husband even then.

"Walk with me a little more," she said, coming close to

Michael. Her smile was sad and gentle. "Melissa gave me your name. I think she trusts me."

Michael hesitated, saw the pale girl and the night surrounding her. Her cool hand slipped into his, tense, waiting.

"I don't know what to call you," Michael said.

The girl stirred, a pansy waving in a soft wind. "My name is Elizabeth Mary Washburn."

Forty

Diana checked her watch as she drove into the 24-hour supermarket parking lot. Almost two. She had driven most of the last hour, not thinking, making no conscious decisions; she couldn't even remember where she'd gone. Diana parked, thrust her checkbook into her pocket, and emerged into cold night.

The supermarket was empty of people. As she walked in, her eyes adjusting to bright lights, she didn't see any checkers in any of the lanes. Creepy, she thought. Diana grabbed a basket and went to the center aisles first.

Her shopping was done in a sleepy daze. She heard people talking, but the two times she had seen anybody, they had been lone employees shelving products. As a freshman at U.N.M., she'd had a work-study job as a bookshelver at the medical library—the worst job she'd ever had. It was the terminal quiet that had bugged her; trying to shelve books extra-quietly so as not to disturb anyone's studying. Eighteen years old and already worrying about destroying someone's medical career by wrecking their concentration. Diana used to carry Three-in-One oil in her sweater pocket in case her cart had squeaky wheels.

Ridiculous to think about now, she thought, still remembering the horrible anxiety that used to grow and grow as the work hours slowly passed.

Diana wandered into the fruits and vegetable section. First looking around to make sure no one could see, she thrust her hand into a large vat of pinto beans. The sensation of being swallowed gave her goosepimples along her arms. She cruised the vegetables next. Diana picked up a tomato and squeezed it, extra-hard, just because she liked the feel of it collapsing in her hand.

"Like little heads, eh?"

Startled, Diana dropped the tomato. Looming over her was a tall, smiling woman with luxuriant auburn hair draped around her shoulders like a cape. She wore a black leather minidress and nothing else. Her skin was chalky and her eyes were green-black, like liquid bruises.

Diana turned away and walked quickly toward the checkout lanes. An employee was busily wringing out water from a mop. Diana thrust her basket at him. "Can you help me, please?"

"I'm not a checker, ma'am," he said. "But I'll get you one."

"Hurry, then."

"Don't rush so into the night, Diana," the woman said into Diana's ear, "where it's frozen. And dark."

"Look," Diana said, clutching her basket against her chest, glaring up into predatory eyes. "I don't know who you are or how you know my name, but I'm not in the mood for bad jokes. Go away."

The woman stopped smiling. "I'm afraid that's impossible."

An older woman, wearing a store uniform, came up and took Diana's basket. She began to ring up each item. Diana moved to the register.

"It is possible." Diana took out her checkbook and held it out as if she was holding a pistol. "See those doors? Walk straight through them and keep on going."

"Eighteen-ninety-four, please," said the clerk.

Diana wrote out a check. The red-haired woman appeared in the next lane and grinned wolfishly at Diana. Something in the store lights made her teeth metallic and pointed, as if made of steel.

"See you soon, Diana," she said and strode toward the glass doors, making no sound as she left the store.

"Is that girl bothering you, ma'am?" The clerk gave Diana her receipt. "I can call the police, if you want."

183

Diana shrugged and gathered her groceries. "Just some bored kid. Thanks, anyway."

Before leaving the store, Diana surveyed the parking lot through the store windows. Only her car and several others, probably belonging to employees, occupied the lot. Diana carried her bags out to the car and set them down. Digging in her pockets, she came out with the car keys twisted in wet tissue.

"Yuck," she muttered.

Enormous shadows surrounded her.

"Hello, teacher," a man said behind her. Diana turned quickly, backed against her car. The man was tall and had blond hair, which flowed around his throat and across his wide shoulders. His face was shadowed except for piercing blue eyes. Diana felt she was facing a wall.

Diana held her keyring up as if it were a shield. "What do you want?"

"A talk, introductions made." He took her hand. His fingers were like cave icicles. "I am a friend of Melissa."

Fear swallowed Diana's heart. Her mouth dried. "Melissa? What you done with her?"

The man let her hand go. "With Melissa I have done nothing. She is well-kept and safe in my home. You need not fear for her."

Diana heard a sly movement behind her, the girl she had met in the store. Diana didn't turn to face her, afraid the man might try something while she wasn't looking.

Oh, yeah? Diana thought hysterically. What are you going to do if he does try something!

Fear was making her giddy. This scene was familiar; catching some kids smoking pot behind the portable classrooms or some teenage couple getting a bit too passionate; try to discipline one child, and his friends and any passing peer group member would surround Diana, perhaps lending support, perhaps trying to scare her into submission to their superior powers. *High School Domination Terror! Horror of the Peer Group Monster From Mars!*

Diana began to laugh.

The man in black—perfect!—did not move, but seemed to tower even further into the night sky.

184

"Did I miss a joke?"

"I'm sorry," Diana snorted into her keys, "but I almost did."

Iron fingers slammed into her face. Diana swam back to consciousness, knees stinging, hair in her eyes, the underbody springs squeaking next to her ear. Asphalt grated on her palms. Her laughter was gone. Ice grappled her heart and squeezed.

"God, please help me," Diana whispered as someone grabbed the collar of her coat and yanked her upright. The world bounced and began to darken. Her legs quailed. She began to fall. Diana was lifted and thrown against the car. The man came up, waved the woman away.

"I am sorry myself, Diana," he said, leaning close. "I had not finished my introductions. And I hate to be interrupted."

Diana's brain focused. She struggled against the woman holding her. Fingers grabbed both her elbows and screwed them into her back at a ferocious angle. The woman nuzzled into Diana's hair.

"Not laughing now, pretty eyes?" The woman twisted Diana's arms further.

"Hush, Hanna," said the man. "Diana, the woman is Hanna. Be careful of her for she sees everything. Perhaps the old man has spoken of her?"

"*No!*" Diana lied. Her arms were burning. Tears of anger stung her eyes.

"That is no loss. Hanna and Melissa are family, as I hope soon you and I might become. In hopes of that night, Diana, I will give you my name. It is Falke."

Her head was tingling. The world began to gray. Diana wanted to make some kind of fearless, snappy comeback. Her mouth opened but no words came out.

Falke smiled. "You must think about it, I understand completely. Perhaps then we should have a talk while you are still with us." He held her chin between his fingers. "And when you see the old man, you can tell him of our visit."

His accent was odd. Diana couldn't place it. It was foreign, certainly, but where from?

"Is Melissa all right?" Diana asked.

"You should be proud of her, teacher. Melissa is learning a new way." Falke gathered his coat around him and glared at the full moon. "I am her teacher now. You see the few pupils I have? Tragic! And I should have flocks around me."

185

Diana's arms were numb from the angle at which they were held. If only a car would come! "What are you teaching her?"

"That life is a dream. Inside, you walk; somnambulistic. Your life is a nightmare, perhaps. Other's lives are blissful dreams. At the end of each lies death; and there I wait. Melissa has awakened. A newborn! I am holding her hand and guiding her."

Diana gritted her teeth. "What about the other girl," she hissed, "with Michael. The blond. What is she teaching him?"

A ripple of thoughts seemed to pass over her head.

"Perhaps, Diana, it is that you do not want to understand." Falke caressed her forehead with his thumb, touched her chin. Diana saw a flickering of fire deep in the iris of his eyes. The flames seemed to leap out, reaching for her. A rigid line of white, like the peaks of faraway snowy mountains reflected in a dark lake, descended to her. The world of storefronts and stinging knees began to slide away.

"The old man understands." Falke's words rumbled against her bones. "Even without Elizabeth. Or, with passing time, I believe he will understand that he might become a true adversary. You will tell him I said this, girl."

A faint siren woke Diana, made her turn to the empty parking lot. Behind her, bare feet scraped the asphalt. Out of the corner of her eye, Diana saw Hanna glance to the intersection across the lot. Without thinking, Diana raised her foot and stamped down hard where she thought Hanna's toes might be. There was a surprised gasp. The grip on her arms loosened. Diana pushed herself into Hanna, hoping they would both fall backward, but it was like hitting against stone. Diana wrenched free her left arm, cocked it so she could jab it into Hanna's midsection; Falke caught her wrist easily and pulled her toward him.

"*No!*" Diana screamed, watching her opportunity fail. She made a fist with her right hand and rabbit-punched Falke in the throat, the way her dad had taught her.

Falke gripped her face and tossed her backward. She landed hard, and the air swooshed out of her lungs.

Heaving to catch her breath, Diana heard shouts from the supermarket. Confused, she saw several men in bland store uniforms and the woman clerk who had offered to call the police running toward her. Diana rolled over, stood shakily,

186

and dug frantically for her keys. She staggered to the passenger's side door. Her checkbook fell from her quivering fingers, her gloves followed. Finally, her keys! Breathing became possible. The store people seemed to be screaming in her ear. Diana unlocked the door and fell into her car, slammed the door shut, locked it. The car began to rock crazily, its springs squeaking like a distressed animal.

What are they doing to my Mole!

Bounced viciously, Diana almost lost the keys again. Clenching them, she righted herself in the driver's seat, stabbed the key into the ignition and turned it. The engine roared. A flitting shadow crossed the windshield. Diana hesitated in reaching for her seatbelt.

Hanna was poised in front of the car, bouncing a grapefruit in her palm. Diana's hand wavered at the gearstick. Her foot was paralyzed above the clutch. The grapefruit that Diana had bought flew from Hanna's hand. Before Diana could react, the windshield shattered inward, throwing glittery shards of safety glass onto the seats. The immediate, sharp tang of citrus made her think of childhood breakfasts. Saturday morning treats. Diana depressed the clutch.

The side window exploded and a white hand streaked into Diana's hair, twisting and pulling. Diana felt herself rising from the seat.

"No!" she shrieked, and threw the car into gear. Please God, Diana prayed, don't let me stall it. As if impelled by some mighty hand, the car lunged at Hanna. The woman stopped smirking and threw herself out of the way as Diana's little red car stormed past.

The storefront windows whirled in dizzy circles. Diana spun the steering wheel to straighten out the car's forward momentum, then floored the accelerator. The car raced out of the parking lot, past the intersection, onto flat uninterrupted road.

Diana shifted gears automatically and flung her hair out of her face. Her fingers throbbed painfully; blood moistened them. Her lungs and throat felt like popped blisters. The freezing, whistling air felt heavenly on her face.

"Thank you, God," she whispered.

"I'll rip you to pieces, little *bitch!*"

Diana screamed as Hanna ran up beside the car and jumped onto the roof. The car growled and swayed as Diana wrenched the steering wheel back and forth. Tires screeched. Diana gagged on clouds of burning rubber. Something pounded on the roof. The ceiling collapsed with each hammering thud, then ripped open. A white face leered at her through the gash. Hanna's fingers wriggled into the ragged hole and pulled it wider. Metal shrieked.

"I'll tear your eyes out!" Hanna shouted.

Diana thought, This is not happening.

"You'll have to catch me first, *shithead!*" Diana hit the brakes with both feet. Black and gray smoke billowed from under the car. Squealing, the Mole convulsed and shuddered.

Hanna was thrown off the roof onto the road. Diana shoved the gearstick into reverse and pressed the gas pedal to the floor. The transmission screamed like an angry bee.

"Come on, baby!" Diana yelled, bouncing in her seat. "Just a little faster!"

Smoke rolled out from the back tires. Burning metal and rubber forced tears out of Diana's squinted eyes as she guided the reversing car. She glanced through the hanging windshield in time to see Hanna rise from the road and chase after her again.

"Oh, shit!"

Again, the car echoed with a heavy boom as Hanna threw herself onto the front hood. Diana turned the steering wheel sharply, sending the car into a sweeping slide. The front end of the car swung around too quickly to control, but Hanna had disappeared.

Breathing hoarsely with fear, Diana braked the car, shifted into first before the car stopped fully, and accelerated again. She shifted automatically through the gears, oddly realizing that things were easier and worked better if you just didn't think about them. Darkened buildings swooped past. Moist air poured in from the torn, flapping roof. Diana reached out to the dashboard and patted it.

"I'll never complain again, Mole," she promised.

Jesus, she thought, those are the people Melissa is hanging out with? Diana reached to adjust the rearview mirror, but it had vanished along with the rest of the windshield.

Forty-one

Diana's living room was dark and too hot. She reached out and switched on the reading lamp, then checked her watch. Almost five. The light hurt her eyes. She switched off the lamp and sat up from the couch, looking to the window where a gray dawn formed an amorphous blob.

"Michael?"

Diana realized she was still dressed. Her clothes stank of sweat and oil. At first, she was puzzled, then memory flooded her brain. She touched her knee where she had scraped it on the parking lot asphalt; the skin was tender and covered with bits of debris and dried, crusted blood.

"Michael, are you here?" Her voice was hoarse.

Diana stood and immediately stepped on a hard, ridged object. Dizzily, she bent for it, frightened because somewhere in the back of her mind, she already knew what it was before fumbling at it. Her pistol.

Footsteps echoed in the hallway. Diana grasped the gun in both hands and raised it to the doorway. A gray figure stepped into the kitchen. Illuminated by dawn glow, Michael watched her warily. Both remained silent.

"Put down the gun," Michael said gently.

Diana saw that she still had it aimed at him. "Sorry," she muttered, plunking the gun down onto the coffee table. Whirling images from last night flickered in her eyes. Diana rubbed at them. Stay out, she pleaded. I'm not ready to deal with you.

"When I came in," Michael said, not moving, "I didn't recognize you."

"Thanks."

Forcing herself into movement, Diana pushed past him to the sink. She ran water into the coffeepot. The icy stream dribbled soothingly on her hands. She rubbed water onto her face and the back of her neck, and touched several cuts on the left side of her throat. Probably cuts from flying glass, Diana thought placidly. Good thing the jugular wasn't slashed.

"I went out," she said, shivering. "It's cold out there."

189

"What happened to your jaw?"

"Nothing."

Diana set the pot on the ring, but didn't switch on the flame. She went to the refrigerator and took out a loaf of potato bread, then absently stored it in the freezer.

"I want to take a shower," Diana said. "Then I'm going to rent a car. We can get something to eat when I get back."

"What happened to your car?"

"Somebody broke it." Diana almost burst out with insane laughter. "Probably some bored kid."

Michael said nothing as he left her alone in the kitchen.

Diana was afraid of her car. Most of the windshield was gone, smashed in, and glass crunched under the gas and clutch pedals as she started it up. Deep creases broke the hood's red finish. The roof was torn open to the pink morning sky. A firm wind drummed on her head as Diana approached the car dealership. The sky to the west reminded her of an ocean sky; puffy clouds and a soft blue pastel.

Fingers of steel caressed her mind. Falke. Diana massaged her aching jaw; the skin felt clammy and hard. Falke touched me and now I can't think straight, Diana thought, as she reached to the carpet and picked up the rearview mirror—is that possible? The car interior stank of burned rubber and something clunked ominously by the front wheels as she swung into a parking space. She climbed out of her wrecked car and noticed peering glances from the men standing inside the dealership. What are you all staring at! Diana wanted to scream. However, she closed the door carefully, so the rest of the windshield wouldn't cave in and reached through the broken side window to retrieve her purse which she had almost forgotten.

I need to call Roger, tell him what happened to me. Diana's trembling fingers opened her purse to make sure she had her credit cards. The morning sunlight streaked across her hands and face like angry flames.

A cup of hot coffee nestled in her hand. Diana thought of Katy, who was probably off to school by now, and she held her cup tighter, moving it under her chin, savoring its warmth. Diana wanted never to let it go.

Michael spoke. "What happened to you last night?"

Diana shrugged and took a tiny sip of coffee. "I met Falke and Hanna."

Michael placed his copper-colored hand over hers. Diana almost smiled, thinking: Indians do have red skin. She supposed her great-grandfather Zachary might have told her something else; how Indians were called redskins because of the colored war paint the warriors used to decorate themselves with. Diana remembered reading Zachary's diaries, staidly kept by her aunt Susie—the same aunt Susie who had kept measles-ridden Diana in Albuquerque while her parents were busy visiting angels in Moab—and being surprised the old Indian-fighter had taken time off to write anything at all.

Do Indian's still use war paint? Diana wondered. Or was it all just decoration now? Have to ask Michael sometime.

"Did they hurt you?" he asked.

Diana shook her head. Michael's eyes were bleary from lack of sleep, but they were mostly sharp with concern. She squeezed his hand.

"Not badly. They hurt my car. I feel . . . I don't know, like I had the flu or some bug. I know it's silly, but it is the truth."

"Did they touch you?"

Diana nodded, dismissing. "Who was the girl you went off with last night?"

Michael spoke without hesitation. "She is one of them. Elizabeth, who is the skinwalker's wife. I learned his name too. And I know Hanna already."

"Wonderful." I am going crazy, Diana thought, but at least I'm not going alone.

"Falke is making Melissa into what they are," Michael said.

Diana gripped her cup. "Why?"

"I don't know why."

"That makes two of us. Why Melissa?" Why me! Diana wailed mentally.

Michael didn't answer. His plate of eggs, toast, and ham lay untouched. Diana wanted to tell him to eat, that good food should not go to waste. But he must be nearly three times her age! How could she tell him anything!

"This girl, Elizabeth," Diana said. "What else did she tell you?"

"That she is afraid."

"Of what? I thought she was one of them."

Michael glared at her, his bleariness gone. His eyes were chips of flint in a sandstone mask. "Elizabeth is afraid because she is still living. Still a little bit human. Like Melissa."

Diana felt her insides shrivel into whimpering, dried husks. She winced at a stark image of Hanna ripping through the Mole's ceiling as if it were aluminum foil. Not human—Oh, really?

Diana straightened in her seat and searched for a waitress to refill her cup. "Here's my next question: What are they going to do with Melissa?"

A young waitress came and refilled both their cups. She took Diana's plate and looked at Michael's. "Is his food all right?" she asked.

"I don't know," Diana answered.

"Maybe I should have the cook heat it up for him," she said to Diana, as if Michael weren't there.

"Michael?"

"Today, we will visit Samson White," Michael said, looking up to the ceiling.

Diana's mind-gears clashed. The waitress shrugged and left.

"You've lost me," Diana said. "Who is Samson White?"

"The Keresan man William said we must talk to." Michael dug inside his shirt pocket and pulled out a white square of paper, which he handed to Diana. It was the photograph William had given to Michael yesterday of the little boy, Jerry. The kid was bundled inside a thick, sky-blue sweater. His smile was a tad goofy, and his ears were too big for his head.

Poor thing.

Diana began to cry. She didn't even know it was coming. Her entire body was wracked with choking tears. Her mind shut down and her heart felt as if it were wrapped in a swiftly unraveling, silken cocoon. Everyone in the restaurant was staring at her, she just knew. She tried to stop up her tears with her hands, but she couldn't. Diana sat hunched on the slippery benchseat, seeping like a wrung dishcloth.

The clattering cups and dishes eventually brought Diana back to a solid world. Several old people, sickly pale, were staring at her unsympathetically, perhaps trying to figure out the situation. Good luck, Diana thought.

To Michael, she nodded, ". . . newborn."

This time, the trip to Madrecita did not take as long, did not seem as far. Maybe, Diana thought, because I don't want to arrive at wherever it is we're going—like childhood trips to the dentist, or to the clinic for annual shots. She realized that the childhood memories that were easiest to catch were the ones in which some horror had been done to her body, her mouth, her teeth, her middle, or her arms. The clearest, however, she had to admit, were those memories immediately after the painful episode; when her mother or Patsy or Leslie had presented Diana with a salubrious cheeseburger, chocolate shake, and fries.

Diana braced herself mentally; she glanced to Michael at one point during this exercise. His head was bobbing and swaying gently. He was asleep. The sleek rental car climbed the curving roads easily. The day was thickly overcast, undecided whether to drop snow or rain. The passing adobe houses filled Diana with vague, uneasy premonitions.

"Is this a ghost village or what?" Diana prodded Michael's shoulder with her finger. "Everytime we come here, there's never anyone around."

"Take the steep road." Michael pointed to the right. "That way."

The adobe ruins looked more ruined than they had yesterday. Diana took a turn onto a narrow road, which rose sharply between a rock cliff and more ruined houses. Most of them stared emptily at her. A few gazed respectfully as the car passed deeper into the village. After several twisting turns, Diana saw a large blue house sitting alone in a partly snowy field, like a fragment of turquoise set on a white beach.

Diana emerged from the car. The surrounding quiet surprised her though she hadn't really known what sounds to expect. The smell of woodsmoke made her feel colder. The sound of the car door shutting exploded like a shotgun blast. A dreadful silence entered her heart.

"I doubt if anyone's home," Diana muttered, more to herself than to Michael, who didn't seem to be listening anyway.

The house brooded. A white door faced them, shining dully as if made from shell. The turquoise-blue house was massive, like a church. It was simple adobe with a high roof of

193

corrugated metal. A small attic door was padlocked shut. Michael walked to the front door and knocked. The sound was brittle and lonely.

"Try again," Diana urged.

"There's no one home."

"Maybe they didn't hear."

"There is no one home."

Irritated, Diana walked around to the north side of the house, which stretched into a smooth wall interrupted only by two windows and a door at the far end. She wiped dust from the nearest window with her gloved hands, and she peered in. An old-fashioned coal heater stood against a green wall. A TV faced the window. Dotting the wall were several photographs she couldn't make out, shadowed like tiny, dark caves.

Diana came away from the window and buttoned her coat. A mile or so to the west, the flat shelf of rock Madrecita lay on rose up into the mountainous slope she had seen yesterday. She noticed a wide saddle in the ridge and wondered what its name would be—probably The Saddle, or something equally subtle. Further north, she knew, the heavy brow of rock stretched toward the blue slopes of Mount Taylor, a dead volcano lost beyond the impatient snow clouds.

We better find this Samson White quickly, Diana thought, or we'll be here until the spring thaw. The next window revealed a large bedroom. A brass bed lay against the west wall and on its mattress was stacked a pile of blankets and quilts as if guests were expected; the thing probably squeaked like a rabid mouse with every twist, bump, and turn, Diana mused. Across from her, against a blue wall, was a bureau with a round mirror reflecting only black. Various bottles shining like rock crystals sat on the bureau's surface.

As Diana's eyes became used to the dim bedroom, prosaic details became more apparent: the floor was covered with faded green tiles, which were worn through in a few places; a closed door beside the bureau had a white porcelain knob; a stiff-backed padded chair sat in the corner . . .

No, wait! Diana cupped her hands against the glass to block out her own reflection. Someone was sitting in the chair—an elderly woman who appeared to be thinking. Her elbows rested on the arms, her hands were folded in her lap. She was wearing a light blue dress, which nearly swallowed her up, and a gingham scarf tied over her white hair. The woman was smiling to herself.

Diana retreated from the window and walked to the front door, where Michael was sitting on its step.

"There's someone inside, Michael. I told you they didn't hear you."

Michael looked up at her, not saying anything.

"I said I told you they probably couldn't hear you," Diana said. "I knew there was someone here."

"Who was it?"

"What do you mean, 'who was it'? How should I know? An old woman."

"An old woman?" Michael frowned.

"Yes." Diana felt electrified tingles scurrying down her back. "Come and look, see for yourself."

"No. You shouldn't look at such things."

Diana moved away from the house, closer to the parked rental car. "At what, Michael? Are you trying to scare me?"

"No," he answered, nodding toward the road. "Someone is coming."

Diana turned and saw a thin old man wearing a cowboy hat, jeans, and a red sweat jacket. He seemed to have noticed the coming snow, too, Diana thought. The man was shuffling quickly, kicking up faint clouds of dust.

"Is that Samson White?"

Michael nodded and held out his hand. Not understanding, Diana simply looked at him.

"My arthritis is bad in the cold wet," Michael said.

"Oh." Diana hurriedly helped him to his feet. Michael, though not fat, was heavy and solid.

A canopy of black clouds had appeared over the village. Samson approached and Michael greeted him in his language—Keresan or Navajo? Diana was beginning to get confused. The two men talked as she stood by. Intermittent splatters of rain began to fall, rattling against the tin roof and pattering in the dust. Diana saw dark tendrils of rain and imagined she could see each individual droplet as it came hurtling toward earth.

"Maybe we should get inside before we get soaked," she suggested, silently praying they didn't get stuck in Madrecita. 195

Samson nodded and spoke some words to her. His teeth were white and straight.

"Pleased to meet you, too," Diana muttered grumpily as the rain turned white.

More burnt, turgid coffee. Diana rose from the table and went to the wood stove. The kitchen, into which the front door opened, took up a good third of the house. The high ceiling was made up of huge logs that had come, Michael said, from the slopes of Mount Taylor. Dark, glass-fronted cabinets guarded either side of the front door like standing bears. Running the length of the south wall was a counter with twin sinks. Above the sinks, a window looked out onto a piece of hardened dirt, where a propane tank lay like a beached submarine. From a studied inspection at the window, Diana had seen that the house was a large L-shaped building. The door with the porcelain knob, in the bedroom where she had seen the old woman, led into the bent part.

Bored, Diana searched in a cardboard box next to the stove for dense logs. The rain had stopped, and a fierce wind had started. Blown sand sighed against the metal roof. Diana turned to the two men to ask if they wanted more coffee. They were sitting across from each other, speaking in their language. Their cups were sitting on the edge of the table nearest her, waiting to be filled.

"I'm going to find a restroom," Diana said as she poured coffee. No one answered her. Michael was listening intently as Samson chanted a hushed song.

Diana went into the next room, the living room, she supposed. Everything was set just as she had seen it earlier. The coal heater stood at eye-level, like the squarish robots in the science-fiction serials of the thirties. She looked at the photographs. In one, an old old man, as wrinkled as a mummy, leaned on a cane under a juniper tree. In another, a small, raggedy boy grimaced into the camera, behind him was a dilapidated hen house with openings in its sides big enough for wolves to steal through.

Diana sighed. I can't honestly believe I'm making a difference to Melissa's life by standing in this dusty old place while two old men sit in a forgotten kitchen guzzling coffee. I can't even understand what they're saying, much less plan any kind of strategy, break bread with them, make medicine, or whatever.

Frustrated, Diana rattled the door to the bedroom. It was wedged shut as if the wet weather had welded it to the frame. She forced the door open and a musty, woody smell engulfed her as she entered the room. The smell would have been pleasant, being slightly nostalgic, if it hadn't been so thick. The cold was different in here too, deep and thickly settled. The kind of cold that existed in caverns in the deepest earth. The room was shadowy. Diana saw a white string dangling from a naked bulb in the center of the log ceiling.

Such a long way to walk to turn on a light.

Taking a deep breath, Diana walked steadily across the bedroom and pulled quickly on the string. She sensed that there were eyes following her every movement, whether pleasantly casual or frighteningly calm, she couldn't tell. Then Diana heard a squeak behind her, like seat springs moving, where she had seen the old woman.

"Hello?" Diana's voice was a squeak itself. No answer. "I guess I shouldn't be here."

She saw the room under a weak glow, which only created more shadows. Peering into the darkness, Diana saw with relief that there was no one in the chair, only a pile of blankets. She walked to the chair and touched its velvet arms. Impelled by her hand, it rocked studiously.

"No one but Samson lives here now," a voice said behind her.

Diana gripped the chair with whitened fingers. "Michael! Don't sneak up on me like that. You'll frighten me into early retirement."

Michael was standing next to her. "There are no ghosts here."

"Of course there aren't any ghosts," Diana said sharply, thinking: Of course there were ghosts. In this room. Everywhere.

"This was Shirley's favorite chair. Samson's wife. She used to keep the door in that corner open all the time, especially during rain storms. Some of her relatives said that is why she died."

Diana could see how this room might be a woman's favorite. You could sit here sewing or thinking quietly, the door opened to the north mountains and brisk air—believing this was heaven.

Diana closed her eyes and imagined the door standing wide to weaving apricot trees; a moist breeze stirred the room, filling curtains, cooling face and hands. All the little ones grown-up and gone, raising families of their own. No one demanding anything of you anymore, except your cherished grandchildren and the corn and apricots demanding their prayers and offerings. Your body once again your own.

Diana was annoyed by the men's presence. Leave me alone, she wanted to tell them. Let me sit in peace.

Then she realized these thoughts were not her own, couldn't possibly be hers. I don't have grandchildren! And I don't have any right to be here either.

"There's another door," Diana said quickly, glad that Michael couldn't see her face. "Where does it lead?"

Michael called out in his harsh language. Samson answered from the kitchen.

"It's not locked," Michael said as he opened the door.

Diana followed Michael into a darkened room. It was longer than the others, but not cramped. At the far wall was a curtained window, which let in a hesitant light; a bed lay to the right of the window and a redwood cabinet of drawers stood opposite. The rest of the room was in gloomy shadow. Michael opened a door in the east wall. Immediately, a rush of mountain air bathed Diana's head, washing away some of her dread. She stood, relishing the wind, hoping it would never stop.

And the whole room was revealed: an expansive ceiling, flawless adobe walls, two simple chairs side-by-side at the foot of the bed, a redwood bureau with a large mirror standing next to the open door, a squat coal heater under Diana's left hand, another bed under her right, and bunches of woven baskets on every level surface. Diana felt oddly comfortable in this room, as if she had stepped into a place that had been set aside just for her.

"This was our bedroom." Michael cleared his throat. "Margaret's and mine."

"You lived here?" Diana asked.

"Yes."

"Is Samson a relative of yours?"

Michael hesitated. "No, not what you would call related. I call him uncle because he was my mother's friend."

"It's a lovely room, Michael. Thank you for showing it to me."

Michael walked to a chair next to the standing cabinet and sat, disappearing in its shadow. Diana felt alone. She crossed the room to the bed and touched the quilt covering. The springs creaked. Her face grew hot, as if Michael had seen her thoughts. She stepped to the window and drew the curtain back. Diana saw the back of a green building beyond the surrounding apricot trees.

"What is that building?"

"The church."

"Oh." Diana touched slick, vibrating glass. "What will we do if we find Melissa?"

"I don't know how powerful these creatures are. But finding them won't be hard."

"They want us to find them."

"Yes."

Outside, the wind's rustling became a comforting drone, nothing strange or scary. October weather.

"Michael, what are we going to do?"

"I don't know how to destroy these skinwalkers," Michael said. "I don't know if they can be destroyed."

Diana had unconsciously expected those words, and she felt a deep withering of her soul. "You have to find a way, Michael. Somehow. What I saw last night . . ." Her hand trembled as she splayed her fingers on the glass. "I remember your asking me why I was getting involved. How deeply. I can't answer that now. All I know is that I want to find Melissa too."

Diana heard a slight moan of floorboards as Michael stood and walked toward her; or so she thought. The air smelled of pine and of moisture on dust.

"Come into the kitchen. We must talk about these creatures with Samson."

Diana turned at his voice and saw Michael closing the east door. The echoes in the room had deceived her.

"There is a story about creatures such as you're describing to me." Samson's gold bifocals made his brown eyes intense and wary. "Before Albuquerque was such a big town, before the Mexicans came, there were some hidden settlements of

Indians all around this land. Inside the big mesa north of your sheepcamp, there was one such settlement."

Michael nodded. "My grandmother told me not to go up there."

"Yes. Those Indians in that old settlement had visits from all kinds of bad things: Evil, twisting winds; creatures that ate babies. *Ayaah'ah*, things like that! The skinwalkers you're telling me about sound like what I heard about when I was small. There is one story that I should have listened to and remembered. My mother told it to me when I was a baby." Samson leaned toward Diana, smiling. "When I was being bad."

"Is there someone we can talk to?" Michael asked.

"Morris James at the old village will know what to tell you. I cannot help you, *amo'oh*. But Morris will know something."

Diana was getting irritated with the chain of people they were supposed to talk to. Pretty soon, the whole pueblo would think Michael and she were a couple of loons.

"I thought you would be able to tell us something," Diana said to Samson. "I'm beginning to think no one wants to help us."

Samson blinked ominously at Diana. "I will tell you not to go up that north mesa after dark! There are bad, strange things up there. Killing things. Things that breathe evil and badness. Evil songs. Bad talk! I will tell you, *ba'ba'ah*—do not go up there!"

"Okay, okay," Diana said.

As they drove along the wet road, Diana heard Michael humming some song.

"What is that song you're singing?" she asked.

"It is a chant I sing when I want to rest." Michael closed his eyes. "You have listened to me talk these past two days. You can tell our story to Morris when we get to his house. To see if you remember it."

Diana nodded. "Agreed. If you promise me you'll rest a little."

"I promise."

"Samson slipped you something," she said. "What was it?"

Michael dug in his shirt pocket for a moment, then handed her a black, spherical stone. "You have sharp, suspicious eyes that see everything," he said. "Good."

"What is it?"

Michael took the stone back and dropped it in his pocket. "It is something for your medicine bundle."

Diana drove on, saying nothing.

The sand-colored house that they arrived at was one of about twenty similarly shaped houses standing on a cleared shelf of land overlooking a river canyon. Further south, trucks and cars passed on I-40. The tidy house Diana parked in front of had a yard full of playing kids.

"Sounds like a nursery," said Diana as she stepped out of the car. One fat boy wearing a stained jacket ran up and shot her with a toy gun.

"I got you, you're dead!"

"But I'm still standing, aren't I?"

A tiny girl with fierce, black eyes came up to her. "Are you a cop?"

Diana laughed. "No."

"Then what are you?" Her ponytails bounced with each word.

"I'm a high school teacher from Albuquerque. Why aren't you in school?"

"School's out!" a boy yelled behind Diana.

"It burned down!" a running girl shouted.

The little girl took Diana's hand and walked with her to the front door. "Don't listen to them," she said. "They're stupid. It's the asbestos in the school. The people are cleaning it all out so that it won't kill us when we're trying to learn."

"I see. What's your name?"

"Melanie. Come out when you're done and talk to me?"

Before Diana could answer, Melanie ran off and proceeded to mow down the others with her plastic gun.

"That's a remarkable story you have told me."

Morris James was a bony man with heavy turquoise bracelets hanging from his wrists. His black hair was slicked back with some kind of oil and a fancy, gray cowboy hat rested on the table next to his elbow.

"Yes it is remarkable, Mr. James. Very." Diana shifted sleeping Melanie into the crook of her left arm and sipped the tenth cup of coffee she had drunk in the last two hours. Her nerves were well past the breaking point with all the remarkable stuff happening to her anyway; another cup couldn't do much harm.

"I don't know how your people take to such things, Diana, but us Indians tend to take these supernatural things seriously."

"Yes, I understand that."

"Especially when a little one is involved."

Diana nodded encouragingly, she hoped. Michael, sitting beside her, seemed to be asleep.

Morris continued. "Our elderlies tell us that our children are the only real treasure we have now. Our land is being chopped into bits, scattered away. The uranium mine is poisoning our brains and bodies with sickness. I read and understand things. That is also the most important thing to us now. The ability to read."

"Yes, it is very important. I agree, Mr. James. But we are very worried about Melissa. Anything you can tell us will be helpful in our search."

"These young boys nowadays don't care nothing about reading nor writing correctly. Least, the ones I have seen. I've talked with our Indian physicists and doctors and teachers and my heart just busts with pride. But these other hotshots are just wanting to fistfight and complain. Their only concern is telling off the white man for stealing our land; whilst standing by useless and watching it happen!"

Michael was looking at the TV in the next room. He was nodding gently, either at what Mr. James was saying or at what Big Bird had to say about friendship.

Morris James spoke. "Learn to read the legal documents, understand what they are saying, learn to twist them to our needs, I tell these boys. Just like the white man can do. 'Stay quiet, old man!' they shout to me, 'Go on home and sit down with the women and let us handle things.' And then they do nothing! Damn it! Let the women have the damn nomination if you're just going to sit on everything, I say back to these boys."

Morris James was shaking with anger. Diana tried to remember the basics of CPR, just in case the old guy's heart decided to 'bust.' Melanie's forehead was a feverish dome against Diana's sore throat.

"Wait," Diana said. "What do you mean, give the women the nomination?"

"Diana, women are still not allowed to nominate in the elections! The women know also what's needed for all of us! 'That's not the way it's done,' the boys tell me. 'It's not the traditional way,' they say to me. Well, I shout at them back, we're driving ourselves into the dust and the whole U.S. government is laughing as we do it! I tell them; we better make it the done thing, otherwise all you yahoos will drive us and our children into a big ditch!"

"Are you in the council?" Diana asked.

Morris James laughed. "With this big mouth of mine? No! They rubbed me out pretty quick. But I keep on talking! Maybe someone will listen."

The eastern horizon was a sooty black cavern. On the way back to Albuquerque, the landscape flowed under a solid sheet of snow.

"I thought at least Mr. James would help us," Diana said, remembering only Melanie's strict demand: 'Auntie, when you come back, talk with me and not with Grandpa. Okay?'

"They are all old and impatient. Just like us. But it must be done in this way." Michael smiled. "It's the traditional way."

"What 'way'? Why doesn't anyone want to help us?"

Michael remained silent. A dozen or more big semis thundered past. Diana hated the way their ponderous bodies shook the earth and road, dug dangerous grooves in the asphalt, threatened her life. Tonight, however, she could almost hear them murmuring their sympathy. Diana cleared her throat.

"Michael . . ."

Diana felt she needed to present her life to him, explain her broken life with Roger, so that Michael could understand why she was busting her tail searching for a girl she knew nothing about, one student out of the thousands she was bound to have in her rapidly-becoming-nullified lifetime. But maybe she shouldn't. To lose a granddaughter was light-years away from anything Diana had ever known, might ever know. Roger had left her because she couldn't, *wouldn't,* give him a baby. Why would Michael want to hear that?

Diana remembered the wake for her parents: The twin coffins they had lain in—twin silver rockets eager for Heaven; the horrifying stench of funeral flowers; the hole that had

203

opened in Diana's heart when the patch of sun she had watched that endless afternoon slid onto her mother's open coffin, settled on her puffy face, and her mother had done nothing about it: no movement to turn away, no lifting of a graceful, ringless hand to shade herself, nothing. And her father had lain against a silk wall, his stilled face somehow . . . not right; misshapen, but not in a grotesque way — he had become a stranger. Not the lightly freckled man who had loved cats, who had loved to sketch the mountains under every type of sky. Diana remembered their long hikes together, her routine search for a warm flat rock to sit on to watch her father draw. The rough whisper of pencil lead. The sigh of chalk. His thin face would become more gaunt as the day wore down, as his life and energy flowed onto the paper. At day's end, Diana would drive them back to Albuquerque — when she was old enough to drive — buying them each a milkshake and a cheeseburger out of her allowance money, and watching relieved as his gray eyes filled with light once more. Then she had taken her father home to recover; again and again for precious years. Drawing pads propagated, alive with breathing sketches.

Until the angels had descended in Utah. Then, Diana's heart simply died. Her father's misshapen head resting on a silk pillow was drained of life, his cold hands no longer recognizable, merely things engorged with a stinking, alien fluid. No more sighing mountains or comfortable flat rocks. No more stories.

Diana shook her head violently as she drove. That is not a gift I want to give any child, she had raged at Roger. One or both of us dying. Killing a baby's love forever.

But who would truly care if I died now?

The freeway became a river, and quadrupled itself. She wiped hot tears away, but more dripped out of her eyes. Diana braked savagely. The sleek rental car squealed and swerved and bumped onto the shoulder, shuddered, then died.

Diana hid her tears from the old man. Acid droplets scalded her fingers, enflamed and crinkled her blouse, seared into her breasts. Her chest caved inward. She wanted her heart to burn and crisp away too. However, like the stout veteran it was, her heart tripped on, ignoring old wounds, keeping her alive.

For a long time, Diana kept her eyes hidden. Cars and tractor-trailers roared. Headlight beams filled the interior, fled. Immovable, Michael waited beside her. He didn't touch Diana. He had left her for that faraway land he traveled in so often. Diana wondered at it. Was it ever stormy there? What kind of rain fell? Was it like the vivid landscape in her own heart; did the rivers eat and eat and eat at the soft contours, twisting them into unknowable, frightening shapes?

Was Michael ever afraid there?

"I'm sorry," Diana whispered, breathless.

Slowly her madness passed. She let her hands fall into her lap. "Are you afraid, Michael?" It was the only logical thing to ask him. His answer would reveal the truth.

Michael answered, "Yes."

"What are you afraid of?" Diana's voice hurt, as if there was an open wound inside her throat. Did I scream? She touched her skin and felt twin, hot scars beneath her left ear.

"I'm afraid of my granddaughter. I'm afraid of being so old and weak in my legs." Michael's voice was unrelenting. "I'm afraid of dying alone."

Diana nodded painfully. "I was nearly killed last night . . . but I feel nothing. No anger. Just cold. That's what I'm afraid of. I don't want to die alone, either."

Diana reached to him, touched the calloused skin of his fingers. He gripped her hand with firm strength. Diana hesitated before looking at him. She didn't want to. Old men were ugly when they wept. She had to meet his eyes, though, to see what truth they carried.

Michael's face remained in darkness until a passing semi illuminated him. His dark, hawklike features seemed to swallow all light, dampening it as an eclipse of the sun kills all light and heat. His eyes were as black and dry as shadows in a cavern, or in a tomb.

Diana shuddered and looked away, almost cried out. Her skin crawled. Michael frightened her, his strength and his murderous gaze at the secretive night.

All at once, as if a heavy stone had crushed her heart, Diana believed everything.

Forty-two

"I feel trapped, Michael," Elizabeth said, head bowed. "Enemies on both sides. I'm not as strong as they are. Once, I was equal to their threat. I was newborn and strong. Muscles tight. Now, I'm old and afraid."

Silent buildings lined the street, surrounded them like moonlit, snow-covered mesas. If he hadn't seen the enemies for himself, Michael would have laughed at the girl's words. I'm the old one, he wanted to say. His hands were numb from the cold and a horrible fear gripped him—he couldn't move his fingers. Calm, he said to himself. The muscles in his fingers became supple. Michael reached into his pocket and took out his container of gum. "Don't make fun of me," he said, offering Elizabeth the candy.

The girl laughed lightly, declined his gift. "Michael, I wasn't making fun. I'm being honest."

"I'm not good with people," Michael said. "Maybe I shouldn't have stayed out in the desert alone, after Margaret died. My own ears have gotten creaky to people's talking."

"I don't believe that," Elizabeth said, smiling. "Your whole body is one big ear. You know exactly what I'm talking about."

"Maybe. You listen to your wife's thinking at night, then your cousin arrives in the morning to visit, then your aunt would like some coffee, then your nephews and nieces come; all of them talking and thinking. Sometimes, it's very painful."

"It's painful because you care. You let all these people in, and their words turn into a great flood." Elizabeth spread her hands. "If you listen to a crowd of people, and you have powerful senses like mine, you can catch the currents of people's thoughts, flowing like water against soft sand; hatreds and longings, real laughter . . . and love. You catch all of it, Michael. You might think a life like mine would be tedious. But it's not. There are so many things to watch."

"Does your sister listen to things in the same way?"

Elizabeth's hands described a wide circle. "Hanna's like a sheet of steel. Thoughts ring against her; I think they're painful to her, too. But she can turn her senses—suddenly! Then she becomes like a knife. A stabbing weapon."

"You protect yourself from her?"

"I've always protected myself. And challenged myself. Never choosing the safe course, I fall into everything."

"That toughens you," Michael said. "My grandmother, when I stayed some winters with her, would throw us all out of bed when it was still dark morning. 'Run!' she would say to me and my cousins. 'Make yourselves strong. Jump in the stream and bathe in the ice, with the bears.' But I never saw any bears with us."

Michael noticed Elizabeth watching him, and not watching him, as if curious; the way Margaret used to watch when she wanted him to explain himself.

"Once," she said, "I remember Hanna moving among a crowd of humans on some dance floor, like a white tiger among a herd of gazelles. I've seen tigers on the television screen, prowling under a strange, lusterless sun. My body doesn't revolt at that sun. That particular sunlight, burning from the glass screen, is artificial. Once, I took the back off a TV set and felt the wires and glowing tubes, all the connections. Nothing magical, I found, but still impressive."

The girl stopped abruptly. "I don't know, Michael, but it wouldn't surprise me if Hanna was afraid of that television sun. As a real tiger, I heard, is afraid of fire." She clenched her hands together as if they were cold. "The sun in movies is frozen. It's not a real sun at all. And the movie landscapes are frozen. Artificial. Not like ghosts. More like paintings. I remember a theater that showed silent films, about eighty years ago, down by the railroad tracks near the center of town. The Orpheus it was called, or something. And all the time I watched movies there, I wanted to shout to the audience: There's nothing on the screen! Can't you *see*?" Elizabeth laughed, as if embarrassed. "I wanted to rip into the silent images and show the people that all of it was only empty light and air.

She tugged at Michael's sleeve. "You see, I thought it was some weapon to weed out people . . . yes, people like me. Or creatures like me, I should say. I thought all of those people were trying to trick me, and kill me."

Michael, his heart thudding faster, silenced his movements. The girl continued.

"Of course, they had no idea what I was. I was just some sickly girl with no family, who lived out in the sticks somewhere and liked movies. Several of the town sons wanted to marry me, even." Elizabeth smiled distantly. "What kind of children do you think I would've had, Michael?"

The snow clouds had turned into steep canyons rising on all sides of the sleeping city. They had walked most of the night, with only brief pauses to watch the sprinkling of city lights through falling bits of ice. Michael had a craving for a tortilla sprinkled with sugar. The girl spoke.

"Many years ago, in my family's two-room cabin in Boone County, Kentucky, the rooms would smell better than roses when my mama baked bread. Even the sounds were sweetened: the sigh of the opening door, the creak of floorboards under our feet. My mama used to want nice rugs to cover the rough wood. I was always getting slivers in my feet. We could never afford rugs, though. I tried making some out of straw one summer, but the bits would spread out all over and then I'd have to clean, and there would be more slivers for my feet to catch every morning." Elizabeth covered her face.

Concerned, Michael touched the girl's cold arm. Elizabeth looked up, eyes bright. He realized the girl had been laughing.

"I'm sorry. Here I am, talking and talking. This long life of mine is so bottled up inside of me, sometimes I want to burst. And I'm bursting now, like a pregnant bubble."

Michael told her the truth. "I like listening to you."

"Where was I? Oh. But here, the sand swallows your feet, even if you're like me. My feet hardly touch the sidewalk or tiled floors. For some strange reason, though, sand catches me. Not in a bad way. And I don't feel certain things very well. At first, when Falke took me to his sanctuary, when we married, I thought I had died and become a ghost. The bedsheets felt like air; doors and wood furniture crackled under my fingertips as if they would burst in my hands.

" 'Gently,' my husband would whisper, taking my arm. 'The door has done nothing to deserve such punishment.'

"I then learned to touch things more with my mind than with my physical body. Blowing at things with the air out of my lungs does no good. I didn't think anything came out of me at all when I breathed. But something does come out. And I don't think it's air."

Elizabeth spoke quietly.

"Falke's servant built me a doll's village. To ease my restlessness, I suppose. Not on order, you can imagine. Falke was not as sensitive to a girl's heart as this strange creature was. Kuenstler. He had huge hands. His next task, he once told me, was to construct a piano from stone, wood, and panther's gut. I begged him not to; I couldn't bear it to have music coming from broken things. He wiggled his fingers like this. They were gnarled from all the cold and hard stone.

"I remember walking among my little cottages and thinking how lovely they all were. Some had furniture. Others were bare. And some I wasn't even allowed to enter. During the long nights of Falke's absence, I made curtains with sashes and hundreds of long skirts and dresses for myself. Before his death, Kuenstler made sure I had plenty of cloth in many, many colors. I was never frightened of him, though he watched me all the time. I remember he frightened Hanna when she first came to us. Then, later, she laughed at him and teased him horribly."

Elizabeth stopped on a snowdrift. Michael saw her thin form wavering against the stars, like a dim candle flame, and wanted to cover her with his coat.

"I don't understand how Hanna came to us. There was rage in her laughter. Her eyes set fire to things. Falke was free with her, I remember, and it sparked me to jealousy. He needed a warrior, he said, and his fragile wife needed protection.

"When Falke was away, I used to watch the dust falling for hours and imagine it as snow or rain. I never left Falke's side when he would finally come back to me. His slow heartbeat was the company I wanted, and I would prattle on to him about the most useless stuff I could come up with. I remember my mother talking to me when I would get feverish, and it always comforted me to know I hadn't died. I would have sung to Falke too, but he told me my singing was like a wandering child's. I was sixteen when he took me away from my family, made me into his wife. In our passion together, I was a woman. That was the cruelest thing he could have said to me.

"It wasn't till later that I found out what he had made me into . . . what he had stolen from me."

Michael felt cold fingers touch his hand.

"I can see the real landscape, that you can see under the sun, by starlight. But I can see colors that you probably cannot see. From the murmuring heat waves off a living body, I can tell its emotion. Pale yellow fear. Electric arc-blue from an angry person's skin. Humming, vapory purples from an orchard of apple trees . . ." Elizabeth paused. "I can remember, from when I was a true little girl, the land's water being lifted from the ground by a lonely sun. Moisture like a vibrating sheet, disappearing into the sky's blue well."

Elizabeth glanced upward, rubbing her arms. Michael became aware of a tenseness falling out of the sky.

"If you listen carefully, Michael, the light from the stars bounces off everything, and you can hear it. Like a sigh. Or the moist *plip!* a bubble makes when it touches a wood floor and explodes. I believe it is the actual light particles breaking upon the surface of real objects. Moonlight cuts me like a razor or broken glass. Starlight, though, from lonely suns, teases me with needle-tipped fingers."

Forty-three

"Michael," Diana said as she opened her door to the fierce morning sun and to the old man on her doorstep. "We've got to stop meeting like this. The neighbors are going to start gossiping."

Michael walked in, without comment on her pitiful try at humor. Diana shaded her eyes and closed the door, pushing in the tangles of old shirts and pants she used to cover the crack underneath the door. Every fall, she promised herself some proper weather-stripping material—and every winter, she was always too cold or too busy to do anything about it.

210   "I've got coffee on," she said. "You know where the toast is."

"Thank you." Michael wandered off to the bathroom. The old guy sure liked his showers, she thought. The phone rang. Diana went into the kitchen, arranged herself in front of her mug of coffee, answered the phone. "Hello?"

"Diana, it's Roger. Some things have come to my attention that I'd like to talk to you about."

Diana recognized the voice of officialdom. "What's wrong?"

"I didn't know you were conducting some little investigation on your own. Why don't we share information? Parcel out leads. Since you've decided to become an amateur detective."

"Roger, it's early and I don't know what you're talking about."

"Okay, how about this? Why don't you just give me what information you've got and leave it at that? Before more people get hurt. What is it? You don't trust your neighborhood cops to break a case? You think you can do better?"

"Roger, calm down." Her voice was trembling. "I really don't need this now."

"Diana, what you need is for someone to tell you to mind your own fucking business."

All warmth left her. "You mean someone like yourself?"

"Yes. Someone official. Though you never were good at listening to anyone."

"Never listened to what, Roger? What are you talking about?"

"You've got Melissa Roanhorse's grandfather staying with you, don't you?"

Diana felt betrayed. Roger has someone watching my apartment, she thought. "So?"

"You've been running around, asking questions, poking your nose where it's not wanted, causing disturbances. Lying to me. I have a report here about some teenagers joyriding in a supermarket parking lot. One of the checkout people identified you as the joyrider."

A terrible calm settled in her mind. Her jaw and throat began to ache. Michael's shower hissed merrily on.

"Diana, you can't deny this. I've got your damn checkbook right in my hand!"

"I'm not going to deny it." She sounded to herself like a sulky teenage joyrider.

"It was you, then, that . . ."

"Yes, Roger, it was."

"Diana, what the hell are you up to? I called Katy this morning and she says you're on some kind of vacation. That you cannot be bothered—doctor's orders? I tried to get her to elaborate, but the stubborn old cow was shut up tight."

Diana bit her lip to keep from laughing. Thank you, Katy, my tough, dear friend.

"And don't thank her, either, goddamn it. Katy's doing the exact, the perfect, thing to help you get yourself killed."

"Roger, is this an official call? Are you going to arrest me?"

"God, I ought to. Keep you in lockup for a few days to let your marbles settle down."

"You're not going to arrest me, then?"

"No, Diana. I can't."

"Then I don't have a darn thing to say to you."

"Will you listen to me? I have to say something to you."

"Are you going to swear at me?"

"No."

"Go ahead, then. Talk."

Diana held her hand out flat. It was steady.

"There've been a rash of homicides in this city over the past week. And another one was found last night. Messy. We have witnesses and statements. Nothing definite. Now this is closed information, all right? I want you to know that some of our witnesses have identified Melissa as being at several of the homicide locations at the time they were being committed."

"It's not her, Roger. I know it's not her."

"Keep out of this situation, Diana. I don't want to see you get hurt. That's why I'm calling you."

Surprising, really, how steady her voice was; with the world crashing down around her. "I'm not promising anything."

"I expected that," Roger said quietly. "Lord knows, I ought to have you brought in for questioning. All we need is for some English teacher to muddy up the water."

"I can't stop now, Roger. I don't really know what's going on, but I do know that I will help Michael as much as I can; which isn't much, I'm afraid. Please, Roger, trust me just a little more?"

"That would be Michael Roanhorse, right? The girl's grandfather?"

Diana nodded. She almost felt her thoughts stretching to Roger's mind, snaking along telephone wires, soothing his worry, caressing him. A large sigh drifted back to her.

"I must be getting senile in my own old age." Hesitation on the line. "You are still a stubborn bitch, you know that?"

Diana laughed. "I know."

"I'm not going to regret this, am I?"

"I like being alive, Roger. I'll be okay. And I promise to let you know if I find out anything."

"I've got Jesse and Carl keeping shifts around your perimeter. And you're not going to talk me out of that one." Papers rustled distractedly. "I'd like to drop by. Maybe this evening. To make sure you're staying out of trouble."

Diana pushed all distractions out of her head, and answered with the first thing that came to mind.

"I'd like to see you, Roger."

Diana felt her face becoming hot. Why was she baiting him? Why didn't she tell him she was almost killed? She hung up, her brain yammering, her heart burdened with the bleak premonition that it was going to be another wonderful day.

Diana poured coffee.

"Thank you," Michael said gratefully as he sunk onto the kitchen chair. "That feels good."

Diana began making toast. "Where have you been all night?"

"Walking with Elizabeth." He held his fingers over his cup as if it were a campfire. "Talking about things."

"What things? Why are you being so mysterious?"

"There have been murders in town."

"Yes. What has that got to do with us?"

Michael glanced sharply at her. "Elizabeth talked about them last night. The killers."

"Does she know who they are?"

"I know them. You know them too."

Diana set a plate of neatly squared, buttered toast in front of him. "I *don't* know. I don't even know what we're doing."

"We're learning about the strength of our enemies. Medicine is being gathered. You and I must stop them."

"You're kidding, right? Me and you? That's crazy!"

"I know." Michael nibbled at a piece of toast. "Your bruise looks bad."

Diana shook her head, irritated. "We have to find Melissa, first. That's what I'm helping you do. That's it. We save the rest for the police, okay?"

"If we tell the police, do you think they can stop the killers? And get Melissa back?"

"All these questions you ask!" Diana snapped. "Why can't you answer one of my questions?"

Michael mulled over his cup of coffee. Diana sat opposite him. Stew over that for a while, she thought.

"We must go back to my daughter's apartment," he said obliquely.

"Why, for heaven's sake?"

Michael chose not to answer her. "Eat something. It's going to be a long, hard day."

Diana adjusted her sunglasses in the rearview mirror and touched her spreading bruise. Pain came in a swift rush.

"You have some inside information, right?" she asked, coolly navigating the rental car across sleek patches of ice. "This is why we're going to Melissa's apartment again."

She looked at him to see if he was even listening to her. Maybe he was. Michael was watching the snowy world pass by. Diana herself was in a strange, perky mood. She felt puffed up and overdressed in a wool skirt, silk blouse and heels, as if she had planned on going to an exclusive brunch instead of to a spooky apartment where she had once found a puddle of blood on the kitchen floor.

"You know, Michael." Diana pulled at the loose pantyhose bagging at her ankles. "You never did finish your little story the other day. Do you remember?"

"I remember."

Eastward, in the direction they were driving, a milky sinuous cloud oozed down the Sandia Mountains as if God had spilled sour cream onto the rocky slopes. Diana knew the old man wasn't about to continue with any story. She began to shiver, and turned up the heater.

"I like this car," she said, jerking the steering wheel back and forth. "I'm kind of glad that woman ripped a hole in the Mole's roof. I never would have gotten any work done on it otherwise."

"Hanna almost killed you," Michael said. "Is your wound making you sick?"

Diana grinned. Her mind was humming. "I never felt better. You know, I think we're finally on the right trail. We just might get Melissa back within the next couple of days."

Gloomily, Michael waved his hand to the north. "The right trail is over that way somewhere. This is not the right trail."

"The right trail is in Santa Fe?"

Michael shifted in his seat, as if he were suddenly uncomfortable. "Why are you talking this way? Do you want to stop looking for Melissa?"

"No. What does Elizabeth say?"

"Many things."

"She's very pretty. You two spend an awful lot of time talking. Where does she come from? What do you two talk about?"

"I listen to what she tells me."

"Like what?"

Michael remained silent. Diana could feel his anger rolling off him in dark waves. I'm teasing him, she realized. What's wrong with me? Maybe I am sick.

"I'm sorry, Michael." Diana rubbed her aching throat; the skin felt covered in ice. "I'm not dreaming too well. I heard that's bad for you."

"You're not eating enough," Michael said, unsympathetically. "I'm getting worried about you. What we must do requires a lot of strength. And respect."

Diana's temper snapped. "You try sleeping through a bunch of nightmares and see if you get any rest!"

"I'm an old man. I've lost much of what strength I used to have. This arthritis is killing me. I can't hunt for Melissa alone."

"Bullshit, Michael. You run around all night with that young thing, and then drag me all over the place as if I were some little kid. Well, I'm not, all right? I'm doing this because I want to, because . . . I'm scared for Melissa. And if I don't eat or sleep to your satisfaction, then too damn bad!"

Now the car was too hot! Diana jerked the heater lever back and the plastic knob broke off in her hand.

"Crap!" Diana pried open the ashtray, popped the plastic thing inside and slammed the tray shut. She rolled the window down furiously and didn't say anything until she saw the familiar row of red brick apartments approaching. Then she parked clumsily, killed the engine, clenched her keys in her hand.

"I'm scared, Michael. I don't know what's happening to me. I don't know how to deal with this stuff. I'm not even sure *what* I'm dealing with." Her voice was hoarse from shouting. "You say we're gathering strength and medicine, whatever that means. I hope we are, Michael, because my head hurts and I can sure use all the strength I can get."

Michael's hand rested on her shoulder, not moving or wanting or demanding. It was just resting there, warm and friendly. Diana covered it with her own.

"Put your gloves on," he said, opening his door. "We're almost finished here. Can you feel it?"

Everything in the apartment was the same, except for the smell of stagnant water. And the air seemed colder; much colder than the whirling snowflakes outside. Diana removed her sunglasses.

"Michael," Diana whispered, hands deep in her pockets. "Why are we here?"

"I don't know. I had a dream."

"It's freezing in here."

They both headed for the kitchen. The aquarium was dark and cloudy. Diana didn't look too closely into it. She stopped only to let Michael go ahead of her. The kitchen itself was filled with a muted, gray light. The floor was spotless. A stream of water hissed into the sink.

"I hate running faucets," she said and turned it off.

Diana tightened the knob. At the bottom of the sink rested a purple, glistening object. Diana stared, trying to make out what she was seeing, debating whether to pull the curtain or switch on a light to see better.

"Michael," she said, breathless.

Michael was beside her in an instant. "Move away, Diana! Go into the other room!"

"What . . ." Recognition, then horror, washed through Diana. Her first few days of student teaching a class of spacey eight-year olds had been taken up by a simple lesson: What Lives Inside Your Body? The expensive-looking guidebook had been dreadful; written for stupid people, not sturdy elementary kids. However, the accompanying life-sized come-apart model of a human torso, which her class had named Max, had been excellently designed. Even Diana herself had learned a thing or two. What she hadn't realized, until now, was how large a human heart actually was. Now, close enough to touch, a plump human heart was drying in a streaked, bloody sink; discarded carelessly as if it were nothing more than a bunched-up dishrag.

Michael grabbed her arm and pulled her away. Diana shook him away violently, then reached for the heart.

"No!" Michael held her against his side. Diana tried to throw him off her, but his arms were too strong.

"*I know what it is!*" Diana screamed.

"Come away! We must search all the rooms."

Michael's grip was making her arms numb. Diana couldn't tell him this because her voice was gone. They searched quickly through Sarah's room and the bathroom, as if expecting to find nothing. The door to Melissa's room was shut. Diana realized this was where the freezing air originated from. She immediately reached for the knob. Michael stopped her hand. Diana wrenched it from him.

"No," she said, glaring into his black eyes. "I have to do this."

Michael stepped back. Diana's fingers turned the knob without conscious control. Her face tingled. What if there's blood on it? Diana shoved the door open, cringed as it rattled mockingly against the wall.

The room was dark except for a white square hanging in black air. The daylight was fading fast. Diana wished she had brought a flashlight.

Light burst into the room. Michael had flicked on the light switch, a device Diana had forgotten about. Melissa's room was tidied, all the clothes folded or hung away, the shelves put back in their slots, the glass animals huddled on the few shelves, shoes paired and safe in the closet. Only the bed was disturbed. Someone was hiding under the covers.

Diana stood paralyzed.

"I can't," she whispered hoarsely. Michael took her hand. Together, they approached the bed. Michael grasped the blankets and whipped them back.

217

Diana's mind went blank. She thought all the lights had been switched off. Then her hand was set free to hang in empty space. Swaying dizzily, she blinked her eyes open and saw a broken young woman lying in Melissa's bed. Blond hair was spread over the pillow among spatters of dried blood. Not Melissa and, presumably, not Sarah either. Diana had never seen the dead girl before.

Michael bent over the corpse and rubbed its bare shoulder as if warming up a cold spot for the girl. The skin bunched and wrinkled like thin cloth.

"Don't touch her, Michael. She's dead."

He looked at Diana oddly, then nodded.

Diana's eyes were drawn to a ragged hole between the girl's breasts; she tried to ignore the nipples which were flattened and transparent, like pressed flowers. From out of the large hole itself, rib bones emerged like stiff fingers.

Michael straightened. "The girl has been dead for three or four days," he said. "The cold weather has kept her full."

"Full?" Diana resisted a powerful urge to touch the corpse's puckered knees.

Michael pulled the sheets off the bed. The corpse was nude. Her gray skin was withered and crinkled, hung like wet laundry on the emerging skeleton. Her feet were small and pointed downward. Diana imagined the girl as a spinning, graceful ballerina.

"Who is it?" Diana asked.

"I don't know."

"Did you know she'd be here?"

"No. I had a dream about . . . something."

Vertigo shifted the room under her feet. Diana steadied herself, held desperately onto Michael's shoulder, not wanting to fall on the corpse.

Michael gripped Diana's arm. "Leave the room. Call the police if you want. Only let me search the body for sign before you do."

"I want to stay with you," Diana said.

Michael knelt beside the corpse again. He pressed the gaping wound with his fingers. Diana saw how resistant the flesh was to his touch. The corpse's neck was ripped and blotchy. The room began to circle around her.

218   "I won't call the police, yet," Diana said, covering her eyes.

"We'll call when we leave. But not tell them we found her."

"Why not?"

"We have too much else to do yet. We'll answer their questions later."

"What are you looking for?"

Michael shook his head irritably. He caressed the girl's face gently, pushed away matted blond hair, which covered her open, sunken eyes—blue eyes, once. Diana shuddered, her own eyes burning. No tears came. Her shoulders convulsed with weak, dry sobs. She felt scraped and sore. Her stomach and leg muscles quivered.

A monster had murdered this young girl, she thought. Those things William and Doris had called skinwalkers.

Tears slipped out of her eyes. And Diana moaned as Michael closed the girl's papery eyelids forever.

Forty-four

Diana and Michael sat in the truck-stop cafe, not talking. Michael prodded a cooling hamburger with a fork. Diana clutched her mug of hot coffee for warmth, never wanting to let go. The girl's corpse had seemed unreal. A shattered mannequin. Diana's mind replayed an image she had not remembered till now: The dead girl's gray feet and painted toenails.

"What are we going to do?" Diana asked.

"You must go back to Doris's house. They'll all be waiting for you."

"Michael, I'm too tired to try and figure out what you're trying not to say. What the hell are you talking about?"

"I will leave you there with them. They will perform a sing for you, maybe heal you."

"Heal me? Keep me out of trouble, you mean."

219

"I'm not going to let these creatures hurt you. I will go on without you."

"They'll kill you at the first opportunity," Diana said, only just remembering to lower her voice in the restaurant. "I know that. Falke told me so."

Michael stared at her. "What else did he tell you?"

"That Melissa is a newborn." Diana paused. "And that you were a true adversary. Whatever that means."

Michael leaned closer to her. "Falke's head is getting too big for his hat."

Diana laughed. "*What?*"

Michael shook his head and turned his cup upside-down. "With Elizabeth helping us, I might get Melissa back."

"Elizabeth? How do you know she isn't playing some game with you? Maybe she's just trying to throw you off track, or ease you into a position where she can get rid of you."

"She's had many chances. I don't believe she's one of them."

"Oh, really? From what she says or because she doesn't look like the murdering type?"

"I follow my heart." Michael's voice roughened, became dangerous. "What else can I believe?"

Diana returned her attention to her coffee. Katy had once said that Diana didn't really drink coffee at all—just hot, sweetened milk with a few dashes of coffee in for spice. Diana wanted to talk to Katy, tell her what she had seen. Could she do that and expect a sympathetic ear?

I doubt it, Diana thought, saddened. Not anymore.

"I'm not going, Michael. This has gone far beyond you, me, and Melissa. These creatures are murdering people. God! I don't know why I didn't believe it before. Some complete mental idiocy, I suppose."

"Belief takes patience," Michael said.

That sounded familiar, Diana thought. "Well, whatever."

"What are you going to do?" Michael asked.

"I don't know. Go to the police. Call out the National Guard."

"You've seen what these creatures can do. Guns aren't going to stop them. These are not natural creatures. They live outside of here." Michael rapped the table. "They walk in the spirit world."

220 "Why can't we just drop a bomb on them," Diana said,

"assuming of course we can find a bomb. And if a bomb can't destroy them, how do you know your medicine is going to stop them?"

"My corn pollen was painful to Falke and Hanna. This I saw with my own eyes."

The magic corn dust, Diana thought. What I need is one of Aunt Leslie's magic emerald rings. "All this stuff is being set into motion. The killings, the journeys, the songs. Even the old folks are getting into the action. But one thing I still don't know—what are they?"

"Elizabeth explained this to me. They are creatures who must take blood, steal it, from living people. That is how they keep moving for many, many years. And one other thing which I can't explain. Elizabeth talks with sadness about her lost life, says to me how Falke stole her life, and how she wishes to see the sun but is afraid of it. I asked her about this, but she will not speak of it."

Diana gripped the table. "Michael. You say they're afraid of the sun. They drink blood. I don't believe I'm going to say this . . . you're describing a vampire."

"Vampire." Michael rolled the word on his tongue. "Explain these things to me. Maybe they're not skinwalkers after all."

"Michael, only lunatics believe there are any vampires walking the earth."

"You saw a ghost," he reminded her.

"Ghosts are different!" Diana stammered. "Ghosts are pretty harmless and you don't have to be insane to see one. Ghosts don't drink blood, Michael. They don't tear roofs off of people's cars. Vampires do!"

Diana thought, Jesus, I believe it myself!

Michael spoke. "The one named Falke is not from this country."

"So?" Diana felt like a bullying adolescent with no real understanding of anything—but who cared anyway?

"So," he explained patiently, "the medicine we are preparing might not destroy him. I don't know but it might kill him also . . . all of them." Michael hesitated. "We need to try it. But if he is so different from the evil things running here, if he is a vampire, how are we going to hurt him?"

"I don't know." Diana didn't want to mention how vampires were usually—*usually?*—killed.

"I might know," Michael said quietly.

Dishes clattered, inside her ear it seemed. Diana needed more coffee. Gallons of it. She didn't want to sleep ever again. The restaurant was empty of people, and the few waitresses and cooks on duty were talking in an animated group across the room, behind the register.

"Well, how?"

"I can't say. Not yet."

"You mean you know, yet you don't know?"

"I have a strong feeling that I know, but I don't want to break it."

"Wonderful."

Michael paused. "Go back to Doris and William's house. Hear what they have to say. Wait for me."

Diana sipped her coffee-tainted milk, and grimaced. She felt nauseated.

"Sure," she answered. "Whatever."

By the time they left the restaurant, it was completely dark. On the freeway, Diana eased her car behind a massive semi carrying a tan, military-type vehicle, stubby and flattened like a cockroach. The vortex was less dramatic here, at the trailer's tail.

"About this Sweet Bread character," Michael began suddenly, opening his window a bit. "A lot of my family and neighbors believed he was a witch. He was mean to people, always harrassing them for no reason, even the old women and men. The people began to talk about Sweet Bread, even far-away in Shiprock. Who is his family? What clan is he? What tribe? for he couldn't be Navajo, some people said, though he could speak it with conviction. Navajos are more respectful than that, my uncle said to the others."

Diana imagined a bunch of dusty old geezers sitting in the sage somewhere in the desert, the hot sun boiling out all the green from the junipers and the blue from the wide open sky.

Michael continued. "They were all talking, late at night, in my mother's government house. All of us were drinking coffee and feasting on fried bread and hot mutton stew. It was a war meeting, I knew, though my maternal aunt, Daisy, kept telling me it was only a quiet discussion. Why did they invite me? I was real young then, only a boy. My uncle, Red Man, said it was so I could stir coffee and heat stew.

"I listened to them discussing Sweet Bread. I knew they were coming up with some war plan, all these adults talking around me. I think I was scared. I kept thinking Sweet Bread was running fast around my mother's house under the moon, listening to what the people were saying about him, looking in the windows and staring at me. I saw him not as a man, but as something four-legged. A coyote, maybe, or a fox. One of those creatures the Navajos say are bad."

Diana felt her body's heat departing and thought: Why are you old Indians so spooky? In front of them, the semi's cargo began to writhe on the trailer, like a nest of squirming snakes, as it passed underneath the orange freeway lights.

"I was happy to be with the adults in their war meeting. But I wished I wasn't there, also. Then early morning came, and I was woken up by Red Man. He called to me by my war name. I knew something serious was up. He gave me my clothes and stood in the doorway as I dressed. He was chanting, or maybe the radio was on. He sprinkled corn pollen across the door- way, and on my forehead.

"The stars were still bright, and it was winter-cold. I walked steady with him to his truck. There was another man inside of it, but I can't remember his name right now. Between his knees, he held two rifles. One of them I recognized. It was my uncle's.

"We drove on the dirt roads for a long time. I thought we were moving in smaller and smaller circles. We stopped where the trees were thickest. Morning light was coming up around us. The three of us walked silently into the trees, not far, and then we came to a ridge. Down below was a dirt road. On the other side of it was an old hogan with a hole broken into its north wall. That is a Navajo sign for death. A hole is made in the north side after the person who lives in it dies, to let his spirit out. But no Navajo ever goes back inside. No one touches the dead man's things, for they are his. Only the witches and skinwalkers are not afraid of the dead. They will touch his things, use them to make their evil medicine. I knew this. I began to get scared. The sky was clouding up and filling with gray light. We sat down and the other man took out some cold bread and mutton jerky wrapped in tin foil from his pockets. We sat there and began to eat.

223

"In a little while, we heard a car driving slow down the road. It stopped next to the old hogan. A fat man got out and he whistled three times, like an owl. I got more scared, for it was Sweet Bread."

Diana looked at Michael. His face was in shadow and his large hands were clenched onto his knees. She tried to imagine him as the boy in his story, but couldn't. Carefully changing lanes, Diana slowed and pulled off the freeway onto the dirt shoulder. She left the engine on, but turned off the headlights. Reaching under the steering column, she switched on the emergency blinkers.

The old man spoke. "My uncle stood up tall on a rock and shouted down to Sweet Bread, 'Why have you come here? This is a witches' place. Drive home fast and rest with your family.' Sweet Bread looked up to where my uncle was standing and answered him, 'Red Man, my family is coming to greet me! Go away, so I can speak with them here.'

"My eyes were watering very badly. I was afraid for my uncle, but I couldn't talk. My throat was paralyzed. My uncle picked up his rifle from the other man and looked down to Sweet Bread; 'Drive away fast, or I will shoot you,' my uncle said. 'This is an evil place and we shouldn't be here. Don't keep us here any longer!'

"Sweet Bread only laughed at him: 'Red Man, my family is coming.'

"I looked into the flat valley. From the north, I saw three black shapes running toward Sweet Bread. I couldn't tell you what they were. They weren't like any animal I ever saw. The other man told me to keep my head down and to pray. My neck was paralyzed. He put his hand on my head and pushed my cheek into the sand. I saw my uncle standing against the gray sky, and my fear left me. He raised his rifle. I heard Sweet Bread laughing below us. Soon, some other people began to shout at my uncle. Men and women. The other man sat up and aimed his rifle also. They both began to fire. My paralysis left me, so I could cover my ears. I didn't want to close my eyes, so I looked at my uncle as he cocked his gun and fired, kept firing, until all his bullets were gone."

"Dear Christ," Diana whispered, and remembered red-faced, Irish-Catholic Patsy crossing herself with calloused fingers.

"I didn't see those people. Not the bodies, either. My uncle and the other man left me with the rifles while they went down into the valley. They were gone a long time, and it wasn't until I smelled smoke that they came back. This happened to me many years ago, after my father died."

Slowly, Diana turned the ignition, and nearly screamed as the already running engine screeched. She was furious. "Why did you tell me this? As if I wasn't frightened enough already!"

"Last night, I dreamed about Sweet Bread. Only this time, I walked down the ridge with my uncle and the other man. The four witches' bodies were burnt up when we got down to the valley. Their eyes were staring at us and their black hair was waving in a winter wind. They were trying to get up."

"Michael," Diana said, grasping his sleeve. "Please don't. What is the point?"

"I heard feet pattering in my dream. Soft paws running in sand. In my dream, I saw a little hungry coyote go to the body of Sweet Bread. It grabbed his hair in its sharp teeth and tore some of it out. Then it began to run away. My uncle gave me his rifle and shouted: 'Go! Run after it and kill it!' I never heard my uncle shout at me before.

"I ran after this coyote. Then I felt like I had wings. I flew over the little, running coyote and aimed between its shoulderblades. Under the spine, I knew, its heart was there. I shot the little animal, and I killed it . . ."

Under Diana's hand, shifting as the earth shifts in an earthquake, Michael began to shudder. Unbelieving, Diana saw that Michael was weeping. Tears moistened his stony cheeks and ran into his hands as he tried to wipe them off.

"Oh, Michael," Diana whispered, smoothing his shirt down his hard shoulder and arm.

He gained control of himself and said, "Sarah is gone."

"You can't know that, Michael."

"Go to Madrecita. Stay there. Protect yourself. I don't want you to get hurt."

Shaking her head, Diana gently held him. Held onto him.

Forty-five

Elizabeth had no clue where Michael might be. Wrapping a long coat around herself, she left her basement room, watching carefully for hidden enemies. The air smelled of burning rubber and wood fires. The sky billowed with orange clouds. To the east, above the Sandias, the moon sailed into coming snow. Traffic was light and the hum of human thoughts was depressed.

Strange images, not her own, had filled her dreams; the sizzle of burning wet wood and the glow of red coals. Elizabeth was frightened for Michael. It was silly, of course. Old age would kill him whether she protected him or not. But her heart had become focused once again, allowing her to pierce other thoughts, of those she loved and of her enemies. And her memory was sharpening, impenetrable as crystal, as when she had first realized she was alone. So long ago! she thought. After Falke had met the angels and vanished into healing sleep.

Elizabeth passed buildings and streets without straying from an invisible path, keeping her gaze at her feet, listening to the currents of raucous wind, and concentrating hard. She pushed familiar distractions away, keeping one memory close.

Over a hundred years ago, during a June night shortly after Falke had been ripped apart by Heaven's vengeful fires, Elizabeth had stalked among the tamarisk and cottonwood trees along the intimate Rio Grande. Then, she remembered, Albuquerque was a fragile town, newborn itself, the Rio Grande its suckling mother, and its swampy valley populated by nomadic criminals, defrocked priests, Mexican *brujas* limned by glowing fires. Elizabeth had listened to lovers talking in the cool shadows along the riverbanks and watched children scurrying like chipmunks through mottled darkness, busily fetching water from the river in wooden buckets. Unseen, Elizabeth had observed the old witches in brown head shawls and dusty skirts whispering sing-song incantations and performing complicated rites; she committed their words and gestures to memory. She could still hear the clear female voices against the crackling of magical fires.

Elizabeth hesitated on a gravel lot. Snowflakes tickled her forehead as she examined the memory. Something eluded her. A simple line from a lover's poem or a child's song, perhaps a whole spell uttered in frail whispers. Elizabeth pieced together and broke apart that night by the Rio Grande, and all of the similar nights hunting corrupted men, killing them for Falke and Hanna. Always listening. Waiting. Nothing had interrupted the stillness of those nights. A sliver of moon sparkled on gray waves. Even the beams of reflected sunlight, glittering from choppy waves, had not stung her. It was all soft river mist dampening her dress and frozen cheeks; and droplets of red-tainted moisture, tiny boulders, trickling down her chest and stomach.

Elizabeth shook her head, driving away the memory, and forced herself on. She realized what was happening. Someone, Hanna most likely, was trying to glimpse into her mind, searching for rents in her brain's fabric. Very gently, and with slender feminine hands, as if Elizabeth's brain were being teased open and coaxed, not raped.

A night of contradictions. Elizabeth could expect the morning to come quickly, without apology. She had to find Michael and urge his escape into the concealing snow, before Falke and Hanna found him.

Railroad tracks lay like silver lines flying from her feet. There were few lights around. Huge warehouses with broken windows sat alone in darkness, exhaling black air. Elizabeth called to Michael, both in thought and voice, picturing his black eyes and the determined set of his mouth. She heard only cars splashing along the freeway. There was no answer to her call.

Elizabeth continued in this way, following the twin lines until they reflected only cloud light. She had forgotten her directions and couldn't be bothered to set her course by the smells of the city. Soon, she heard the rattle of branches, flames sizzling, and a man's voice carried on a shy breeze. Elizabeth followed the sounds.

Three men surrounded a small fire in a clearing near the river. Tamarisks and cottonwoods leaned over them protectively, trembling in the fire's light. Michael sat among the men, 227 hands out to the flames. Elizabeth watched him, without betraying her presence. He was listening to an ageless man in a camouflage jacket and a comfortable beard. The other man, lying on the snowy ground, his back to her, wearing overalls and an oily cap, was either asleep or dead. His coal-black hands were motionless. Elizabeth pushed herself from the trees and approached them.

The bearded man saw her first. He nodded, saying nothing, his twinkling stare returning to the fire. Michael noticed the man's pause and looked to see what had disturbed him. Frowning, his face shifted with the flames. Elizabeth walked to the clear spot next to Michael, noting the lack of fear or curiosity in the other men. She sat on an icy hump and joined them in watching the fire.

"Do you know where Melissa is tonight?" Michael asked.

Elizabeth shrugged and followed unraveling smoke. "I've seen no one."

"What are you doing here?" His voice was tight and angry.

Tears tripled the flames, made them fly across the windy trees. She wanted to tell him about Hanna's prying fingers, but only shook her head.

"You can't stay, Elizabeth," he said, gentler. "It is dangerous to be with me."

"I know," she whispered, refusing to acknowledge her tears by wiping them away.

"Do you know what I saw today? A murdered girl. My hands are bloody with innocent blood. My heart tells me otherwise, but my eyes tell me I've killed her. An innocent life, not a warrior's."

"No, Michael. She was Hanna's victim."

"She was a young girl. I think Melissa is lost to me."

Elizabeth stared at him. "You can't stop! You're the only one who believes."

Michael's hands clenched into fists. Maybe he's imagining me in their grip, Elizabeth thought. She longed to flow inside of him, comfort him; she was too afraid of what she might find.

"They're hunting you," Elizabeth said.

Michael nodded. "I must become invisible, like you. There is a way, but I have forgotten it. The Chiricahua Apache down south still know the way, but there isn't time."

"You know how to protect yourself. Falke and Hanna are afraid of you, Michael. I can feel this. Their fear . . . it's stinking up the air. Use it."

"Will you betray me?"

Elizabeth had already formed the answer in her heart. "I wouldn't."

"There will be more deaths before sunrise. I must rest."

Elizabeth rose silently, gathered her coat around her. "Please walk a little with me, and I will show you a place to rest."

His gaze pierced into her. "What if I find you?"

During the day, she thought. That's what he means. Elizabeth imagined him leaning over her, waking her, sunlight bouncing off the walls behind him. She would see Michael as he was meant to be seen. But only for a few seconds. She would see what kind of light his eyes held, their true color. Then, he would set her free.

Michael waited beside her. They left the old men to their fire.

So many cars on the freeway, Elizabeth thought. Below the overpass on which Michael and she were standing, tires thrummed and engines roared with their insistent mechanical life — sounds reminding her of a river swollen with broken ice.

"You found a girl's corpse," she said, penetrating into Michael's mind a tiny bit, to see what he had seen. It was a trick she had often used on Falke, a guessing game — catching images in the shallows and trying to decipher their true meaning.

Michael whirled on her. "Stay outside of me!" The glare he struck her with was hard as jet. "If I have something to say to you, I will say it."

Elizabeth drew back, noticing only then how close she had been to him. She knew she deserved the rebuke, but it made her angry in return.

"I'm sorry, Michael. Maybe if you trusted me more, I wouldn't have to dig in such a way to find out what you're thinking about."

"We found the girl. Diana was nearly broken by what she saw."

"Diana's an innocent, I suppose. A virgin? As opposed to what you or I are used to. But are you sure of this?"

"Diana is a young woman who isn't familiar with evil or death like that. She must be protected."

"Protect her, Michael, and you will destroy her. If she's to be your companion in all this, you can't keep her from such things. It'll weaken her . . . fatally."

"These enemies are beyond her. She's not strong enough. Maybe I made a mistake in getting her help."

"Maybe she was chosen, Michael. She's not a child."

Elizabeth walked away, across the overpass lanes. She was ravenous, and needed the effort it took to pull herself from Michael to forget.

"I was a young woman too," she said when he joined her. "Years and years and more years passed. Time never stopped for me, to let me catch my breath or so I could hide myself from what I am. Now, tonight, I'm an old woman imprisoned inside this girl's body. I shouldn't be here, but I am. I don't understand it, but I accept it."

Michael's steps were measured evenly beside hers; almost matching. Or had she adjusted her pace to his?

"Diana told me that your husband touched her," Michael said. "I felt something different about her. I didn't know what it was. She said it was like the flu."

Elizabeth stopped. "You know how death leaves a residue? It's like a cloud that gathers darkness about itself; the day turns black and your bones ache. You know how that is, Michael? My mother explained it to me when I was a little girl huddling against her dead body. I listened to her, laid my head on her chest, listened as hard as I could. I couldn't hear anything. Only the rain spattering on the canvas roof of our wagon and splashing in a million tiny steps outside in the mud.

"We moved her body off the hard planks and carried her to her grave. My brothers carried her feet. They were small boys, yet. Just little things, but they were stronger than me. I always hated them for that. My momma's hem fluttered in the wind. I was too weak to carry her; I kept her skirts out of the mud. We reached the grave, me holding my mother's skirts and the men puffing and panting. Death had settled into her. Her spirit was gone, I thought. But then, she spoke."

Elizabeth felt nothing. She only remembered the horror that had twisted her father's face, her brothers' screaming as they dropped her mother's feet, and her own sad, awful hope that her mother had awakened from death.

"'Wake up, momma!' we children cried. 'Wake up, wake up!' My father cradled her head gently and spoke very sternly to us. I didn't hear his first words. The rain was too loud. He told us to pick up our mother's feet out of the mud and to help him lay her to rest in her grave.

"'But she's alive! Momma spoke to us!'

"'Your mother's dead, children. She didn't speak.'"

Elizabeth looked at Michael. "It was only a little air trapped inside her lungs, he told us later. None of us believed him though. All we knew was that he had killed her final breath."

They resumed walking and passed houses whose windows were lit with rainbows. Elizabeth continued.

"Only now do I realize that Falke killed my mother. He killed all of my family, and me too. I don't know why he wanted me, why he felt he had to kill all of us to possess me. It's the way he is. As I am, Michael. I can understand his motivations now. Falke is a force empowered to kill. Everything he touches withers. The love I once felt for him changed. I don't know what it is now; I know it isn't love."

"We are trying to find your husband, to do him harm. You've spent many more years with him than I have with Margaret. Yet, I don't ask you for forgiveness."

"I would forgive you if asked me, Michael. I live only with memories. Falke is no longer my husband."

"You protected him for those many years, searched his mind. I was with Margaret for many years and yet, sometimes, she was still a stranger to me."

"But you were both alive. You shared the sun, had a child together. Falke and I share only night." Elizabeth laughed grimly. "And Hanna."

Elizabeth had stopped again. They were standing in a green-lit parking lot. Peeling signs advertised it as open twenty-four hours. Elizabeth felt exposed. Naked. And someone was watching her.

"I don't want to be here," she said.

Avoiding Michael's eyes, Elizabeth stepped into his calm presence, listened to the familiar beat of his heart.

"Michael," she said, taking his hand. "There is a place I want to show you. Will you come with me?"

He gripped her hand firmly and followed.

Elizabeth sat next to Michael on one of the pews of the breathing church. Mary hadn't changed position since Elizabeth had come here with Falke. The podium microphone was a silver tulip. The pew creaked with every movement Michael made. Elizabeth rocked sideways a little but made no noise.

"Churches were safe places to me when I was growing up," she said. "I knew I could always find food and comfort in one. Even now, when I'm inside one, I see this strange light. It falls from the ceilings and spirals out from the walls. Is it God? Angels? I don't know. Perhaps the captured emanations of people long gone. Ghosts."

"Maybe it is you," Michael said. "And maybe you're not the only person to see this light. Margaret might have seen this light, too. Perhaps that was what drew her to church."

Elizabeth nodded. "I like that. I'm glad you think your wife and I would see the same things. Perhaps we do. Maybe all women see things . . . that their loved ones can't. Secret, wonderful things. And the joy of life is to decipher it for ourselves, to reckon it out so that we can give it to our loved ones as a gift. 'Here, this is what I see. Share it with me.' Do you think this is true?"

"I think you are a special woman."

"I know you won't use my given name. I don't know your true name, and I wouldn't use it either if you did give it to me. I call you Michael because that's the way I speak. I understand. No one knows my real name, except for you. I don't think it really matters to most people: The special power a name possesses."

Michael smiled. "My father took me hunting one day when the snow was deep. Very deep. He taught me my directions and the names of the animals. Then he spoke my warrior name and told me what it meant; 'My son, don't ever let this name out of your sight. Always know where it has been and where it is going. Always know who speaks it and make sure they are good people. Never give your name to an animal, for their minds are not like ours. They are to be respected always, but we must not trust them all the time. Share it with the Holy Ones for that is the name they will know you by and no other.' "

232

"I have no special name to give . . ." Elizabeth's eyes lit. "Or maybe . . . maybe there is. I remember my mother talking to me as we rode in the wagon. The benches were hard and I was crying, I don't know why. My mother sung to me a lullaby in a language I had never heard her use before. The words were carried out with the wind and placed among the treetops. Then I remember seeing a faraway country; I wasn't dreaming. I saw a long lawn of grass and flowers like little blue bells."

As she spoke, Elizabeth let her tears fall unheeded.

"Then my mother touched my head and spoke. 'You see the country where I come from, Eliza? Far across the ocean. My father is still there, I think. I see him in dreams more often now than I used to; maybe he's trying to tell me something.'" Elizabeth felt Michael's warmth next to her. "That's what my mother said to me. My true name is there, in that place. I feel it in my heart. Someday . . . I will search and find it."

Elizabeth knew of a hidden place where Michael might stay, unburdened by cold or worry. She led him there. Snow patches lay about them, colored a strange luminous blue. Morning was still far away; she couldn't feel its heat. Her mind was calm as she spoke.

"Imagine watching the stars drawing circles across the night. You have to wait patiently for them to do it, sometimes years. Then, slowly, white circles will fill the whole sky, and all revolving around one point: Polaris, the North Star. That's how powerful memory is, Michael. If you are like me."

Elizabeth lowered her voice, as if talking to herself.

"Then, imagine the sky gold and the shadows black and long. Sometimes, the sky is silver and hard; it hurts my eyes. My body feels the sting of flame, even when I'm just remembering. Streetlamps are seductive. They make me wonder if I am immune, or can be, to true sunlight. I'm unnatural, I know. Yet, I wonder. And hope."

Elizabeth watched Michael's form agitate the darkness under a bleak, artificial glow, then vanish completely into the night. She turned and walked alone.

Imagine Michael under a clear sky, she told herself. A sunflower raised up in a field of blue. Why do some people remain as ghosts, and others go so far away?

Forty-six

$\mathbf{A}$ knocking at the door woke Diana from restless dreams. She sat up from the couch, listening, hoping the sound had been in her imagination. The doorbell rang this time. Groggy, she went to the door, straightening her jacket, and looked through the fisheye peephole. Roger was waiting on her front doorstep, bundled in a wool coat. Diana switched off the outside light and unbolted the door.

"What time is it?" Diana didn't know what else to say. "I don't have my watch."

Roger smoothed his sandy hair, then checked his watch. "About 9:10. How are you, Diana? I came as soon as I heard."

"Freezing! Come inside."

Roger cleared his throat. "My boots are dirty. I don't want to track any snow in."

Diana studied him. He didn't seem cold. Steady puffs of mist blew from his nostrils. His face was thinner than she remembered, and he seemed agitated. Roger was watching her frank study of him.

"Take them off, then," Diana said, unlocking the screen door. Roger's presence made her apartment feel too small. Too echoey. She knew he was trying to be quiet, but he was so big. The floorboards groaned under him in a way she had never heard before. And she had forgotten how tall he was, how awkward he could be in cramped spaces. His boots thumped onto the carpet. His coat gave off blue sparks as it hugged a chair.

"Come into the living room," she said, leading him. "It's warmer in there."

"I'm sorry, Diana. I brought you out into the cold without even thinking. It's just been that kind of night." He nodded ruefully. "You know."

Diana sat next to him on the couch, holding herself tightly, feeling chilled. Roger was a shadow next to her. The room's only light came from an outside streetlamp, filtering through patterned wooden screens on her windows. When Diana had

234

first come into this apartment, she had held her palm up to the incoming light to study the silhouetted decoration. Now, a peppered pattern of tiny four-leaf clovers was spread over Roger's cheeks and forehead. His hands were somewhere below the falling shapes, in the darkness where she couldn't see them.

"Carl came by," Diana said. "I gave him a message for you not to come."

"I was worried. It's terrible to find a body, especially one that's been . . ."

Roger was staring into her face. Diana drew back, afraid he was going to lunge at her. Had his gaze always been so piercing? She honestly couldn't remember.

"Diana?" He squeezed her hand and fumbled at the lamp. Light sliced into her eyes. "Jesus . . ."

"Not very nice, is it?" Diana hid the bruises that covered the lower right side of her face. "I told Carl not to say anything."

"What the hell is going on!" Roger shouted into her face, as if she had done it to herself. "Who did this to you?"

"No one. I fell down."

"Off the roof? Don't lie to me, Diana."

"Never mind, Roger! I did this all by myself, no one helped me."

"What were you doing?"

"Just leave it, all right!"

Roger shook his head. "You've changed, Diana. I'm not wrong, am I?"

"Why did you come here?"

Ever so gently, his hand covered her cold fingers. "The way you sounded on the phone this morning, I figured you wanted to see me too."

Diana felt a circle of warmth forming in her middle. "Please don't, Roger."

"Honey," Roger spoke quietly, moved closer. "I miss you."

A familiar fire burned against her throat and soothed the tender skin of her battered face. Oddly, her teeth began to ache. Diana lifted her hands and pushed Roger away. His heavy cotton shirt brought her senses back. I should do some washing, she thought wearily. Towels, sheets, curtains, bedspreads—floating objects paraded past her inner eye. Clean everything that wasn't nailed down.

235

Her confusion cleared. Diana caught fierce waves of sexual heat and violent emotion rippling through the air in confused directions. Her skin tingled from their pulsating strength, as if her whole body had become a quivering radar dish: A human emotions satellite drifting ever doggedly onward.

"You're looking at me, finally," Roger said. "Not much."

"I can't, Roger. It might spoil everything."

"To look at me? I'm no Cary Grant, but I'm not bad."

"Don't joke. You're not listening. If I see how deep your eyes are, follow them all the way into your heart, I might see that you don't really care for me at all. That maybe all you wanted was a quick screw with your ex-wife."

Roger's hands tensed on hers. "That's not nice."

Diana pushed him away. "No, it's not, is it. We had all that love before, and it still didn't work out."

"We were just kids then, honey."

"I guess you're pretty settled with Heather now. You know all about women from me — stupid, gullible Diana. But it's not such a long step from prom night, is it?"

"Diana, I made a terrible mistake. I don't feel sorry about Danny, not one bit. But I wish to Christ he was yours and mine."

Diana trembled. "Do you want me to forgive you? Is that what you want? You want someone to hold when you can't handle life? A mistress? You couldn't work things out with me. You didn't even bother. You had to . . ." Diana's voice broke as she remembered a deep blackness that had swallowed up her soul and mind; all light vanishing in a blank abyss. "You had to find someone else to make a baby with."

"Diana . . ."

"Why couldn't you wait for me, Roger?"

"Sweetheart, please."

Diana stood, struggled from his encircling arms.

"I'm sorry," he said. "We could start all over. Make a baby of our own."

"*No!*" Diana hit his hands away.

"I love you. I love my Danny, and I love you."

"I wasn't ready and you couldn't wait for me."

"Diana, come back here."

"*I loved you!*" She screamed.

Sense of movement. Large hands reaching, missing by inches. Walls rushed past her tunneled vision. A massive, shifting cold. The door nearly stopped her, a stable and protective thing. She slammed it out of her way. Sudden freezing air slapped against her face. Bright points of light wobbled above her and under her stockinged feet. A man shouted after her.

Diana ran faster.

Forty-seven

Elizabeth found the teacher wandering in a snow-covered park wearing only a light overcoat; she thought for a moment that it was Hanna, until she noted the diminutive size. The young woman was shaking and pale, with a yellow-green bruise flaring along the side of her face like ghostly flames. Her haunted eyes were red-rimmed and streaked with tears. Elizabeth spoke to her gently.

"Diana, come out of the cold. Look at your feet. This isn't a place for you."

Diana whirled, straightening. She became very still. Her hand strayed to her coat pocket.

"It's you," she breathed. Her voice was raspy and she swallowed visibly, wincing. "Where's Michael? What have you done to him?"

"I haven't done anything to him. He's resting. Diana, I must speak . . . wait."

Elizabeth bent, removed her shoes, scraped off clinging ice, held them out. "You know what I am. I don't need them."

The teacher nervously crinkled her coat together, then snatched the shoes, as if she thought Elizabeth might grab her. She shook them out, cautiously slipped them on, and waited. Her long hair was tied in a careless ponytail; floating strands, which she kept pushing irritably away, bobbed in her face. Her eyes, despite the redness, were deep green and beautiful.

"What do you want?" Diana asked roughly.

"I want to talk about Melissa."

"Where is she? Why are you holding her against her will?"

"She isn't being held."

Diana scanned the park as if searching for hidden enemies. She keeps tugging at her pocket, Elizabeth thought. It hangs heavily there. Does she have a gun?

"I won't harm you, Diana. There's no one in this park. You, though, might hurt me. I leave myself open to your weapon, if you choose to use it against me."

Diana's jaw was set. Her hand stayed in her pocket. "Say what you have to say."

"Melissa is becoming more distant to Michael. She's said this to me; not in so many words. I'm telling you the truth."

Diana clasped her trembling fingers and blew into them. Elizabeth noticed again how thin her coat was.

"We can go somewhere, Diana. Somewhere warm and well-lighted." Elizabeth reached to help her. Diana skipped back, hand flying to her pocket.

Be stubborn then, Elizabeth thought.

Snow crunched under Diana's feet as she moved closer. "How do you know Melissa doesn't trust Michael? He's her grandfather, for God's sake."

"Have you spoken to Michael about this, asked him any questions? Have you listened to his answers? You'd know then, too."

"Where's Melissa? You're doing your best to make me trust you. Tell me where she is."

"I don't know. I haven't seen her for several nights. Michael hasn't seen her either, and it's . . . worrying him." Elizabeth's breath caught in her throat. "He's beginning to lose faith."

Diana nodded tearfully. "Michael's wearing himself down. He's not sleeping at all." She lifted the wayward tendrils of hair over her ear. "I don't know how to help him. If only I could speak to Melissa."

"I don't know if that would do any good. Melissa's becoming . . ." Elizabeth hesitated, ". . . enchanted with the darkness."

"Who are you people?" Diana asked, exasperated. "Why did you attack Melissa of all people?"

"It concerns a history which I've been slow to understand myself. Falke's history." Elizabeth saw Diana shrink, become paler. "Michael said you two met, and that Falke touched you. I can see the signs, Diana. Michael has told you something about us. I can add more . . . it would only confuse you."

"Sounds like some New Age double-talk to me. Michael says that you're . . . skinwalkers?"

Evil monsters, Elizabeth wanted to add. "What do you believe?"

Diana pressed her fingers against white temples. "This is a dream, I know it. Or I'm losing my mind." She looked up, scowling. "I won't tell you what I believe."

"Whatever you believe about me, Diana, you mustn't give up looking for Melissa. You have to help Michael find her. Bring her back to him. Alive." Elizabeth wanted to grab the young teacher, shake her bodily, scream at her, make her understand that Michael was slowly killing himself. Elizabeth gripped her hands together. "I think that Melissa still has a chance to come out of this alive."

"You *think?*" Diana's tone was acid. "And what about her mother? Where is she?"

"Michael knows."

Elizabeth watched as the young woman's anger became stronger, as she grew less pale and watchful, as she started to approach unafraid. Diana's eyes were chips of green stone.

"Melissa's only sixteen," Diana said. "Have you considered how a sixteen-year-old girl might react to all this? All the harm it's doing to her?"

Elizabeth retreated into darkness. Safe darkness. "If you find Falke, ask him those same questions."

"You bet I will." The teacher's eyes flashed from behind thickening snow flurries. "What about Michael?"

"I'll try not to let any harm come to him, Diana. I promise."

Forty-eight

The night wind swirled around Diana's little car as she drove slowly west on I-40. Snow lay unbroken for many miles until lifting into ghostly blue mesas. There was only one cleared lane for eastbound and one for westbound traffic running dangerously close to each other. Giant truck wheels rumbled by, almost crushing her car. Twice, grating airhorns had yelled at Diana to keep to her own lane. Intense, quadrupled lights flooded the interior from another semi close behind. Several tumbleweeds bounced onto the freeway and disappeared beyond the reach of her own headlights. It was three in the morning, and the world was alive.

Her brain whizzed about light-years from the planet. Roger was stuck in her vitals, apparently forever, a nail in her heart, tearing in deeper by the minute. And the damned vampires too. Diana breathed the word to herself several times, not wanting to believe, yet remembering a strand of light shifting against the trees in the park, the shape of white arms and the folds of a pale dress emerging from a slit in the air, then Elizabeth standing watchful, untouched by the snow.

Diana opened her window and reveled in the sensation of the fierce wind mussing her hair and hot air blowing on her aching feet. She tried to bring up something good in her life to blot out the emptiness settled inside her, but none of what she remembered was really powerful enough to do the job. A lot of it was nice—Christmas mornings, for example. As a child, she had crept through the darkened house, sniffing brisk pine needles, plugging in the family tree lights, pulling the drapes, and watching as the decorations twinkled and sent friendly messages out to a silent, arctic world.

Diana had loved to imagine her family home as a fairy castle, a fortress against a dark, surrounding forest populated by gentle ogres in the shapes of her parents and the terrible dragons across the road which were the grumpy neighbors— their tall, blond son a captured prince whom Diana must rescue, then marry. Singlehandedly, Diana must have slain oceans of armies; married dozens of princes in intricate ceremonies gleaned from library books; rescued dogs that were unicorns, cats that were purring banshees, and mulberry bushes that were stray cows from evil sorcerors. Diana remembered hours spent in one or another of those intense fantasies until she had graduated to a crazed preteen pummelled by sadistic hormones.

Diana left the freeway, nervously passed a grader, then, barely glancing at the road signs, made her steady way toward Madrecita: Michael's own childhood haven. What kind of fantasies had filled his brain during the long days herding sheep? Maybe killing the monsters and witches of his own people's legends?

Diana smiled at that, remembering the story he had told to Emily and herself.

Michael probably joked and made friends with every creature, real or imagined, that he met. She felt a brief, deep sadness at his absence from her, and she toyed with the idea of driving all the way back to Albuquerque. Diana had grown so used to his grounded presence beside her, his quiet listening to whatever inane thing she had to say or think, that, bereft of him, she felt like a baby spider ballooning in a sky of dangerous crosswinds and updrafts, lost from the touch of a steady world under her feet.

The car tires rumbled over ice as she came to a stop in front of Doris and William's house. A warm glow behind calico curtains made Diana think dismally of her own coldly lit apartment windows back in Albuquerque. Don't old people sleep anymore? Maybe they were having a party.

Diana had to force herself out. The car door was ripped from her hand. The hinges creaked as a whirling, snow-laden wind tried to escape with the door into the sky. She stepped onto hard-packed snow and shut the door without locking it. She gathered her father's old mountain jacket around her. The surrounding adobe houses, with their darkened windows, were hunched like miserable ghosts. Looking up, Diana saw a bulbous roof of clouds, illuminated from within by a shifting blue light, stretching east to a black horizon. The snow reflected the odd glow and Diana felt as though she had fallen into one of her fairy tale forests. Above the western rim of

Mesa Gigante, easily seen in this light, white tentacles of snowfall caressed a shadowed ridge.

Diana shivered as she made her way to the front door. She had never imagined it could be so cold, even in Brigham City, where the snow fell in massive lumps. The air stung her exposed face and hands, yet soothed her throat and aching back, ridiculous contradictions she couldn't be bothered to work out just yet.

My whole life has turned into one big contradiction, Diana mourned. And what am I doing now? Running straight into the heart of it, with arms and eyes wide open, blindly accepting.

"Stop being so selfish all the time," she muttered. "Remember Melissa, and shut the hell up."

Diana knocked on the door and tried to smell the wind. There was nothing to smell. The cold had killed everything, all the freshness and comforting tinge of woodsmoke. The door opened and a tiny, wrinkled face with owl eyes appeared in a shaft of golden light.

"Come in, Diana," said William, opening the door wide. "We were waiting for you."

A smell of strong coffee struck all her senses dumb, as if she had fallen into a pool of winter water. Diana entered the house and shut the door carefully behind her.

Diana's chilled muscles were beginning to relax. William and Doris had led her straight into their green-walled kitchen lit by a fluorescent ring, sat her at the table, and rained food upon her: a thick, meaty stew, sweet bread, an assortment of sweet and bitter pies, and lakes of coffee. Diana ate politely. Now, she sat back and cuddled her hot mug, her stomach tight and bilious.

"I wasn't expecting to find anyone awake," she said to Doris, who sat next to her.

"We don't sleep much anymore, do we?" Doris said, nodding at William. "We go to bed at seven-thirty and wake up around about two in the morning. There's nothing to do at that time. Maybe a little cleaning or something like that. So we have long breakfasts."

William rubbed his face with his gnarled, weathered hand. "I remember when I was just a boy, around about winter, my mother and grandmothers stayed up all night, cooking food for the hunters who were coming home. Me and my friends would sit around a big fire at the edge of Madrecita and watch for the hunters' fires burning along the ridge, telling us to expect them soon. There was always a lot of food being made, and a lot of meat coming home to us."

"Michael told us you were coming, dear." Doris inspected Diana's bruise. "*Amo'oh*, he told us about your wound."

"Yes," William added. "We told him everything was prepared. Send Diana to us, I said. We'll have food ready for her when she comes."

Diana touched the old woman's hand. "You're all being so nice to me. I don't know what to say."

William laughed. "Don't say anything. Eat some more!"

"If I eat another bite, I'll explode. I don't think I've eaten this much since I was a kid."

Doris scolded. "But you've only eaten a little bit. Not enough to strengthen you. You look the size of some of the smaller children here in the village. Not a real hunter's size."

"Hunter's size." Diana chuckled as if Doris had told a joke. Then she realized both old people were gazing at her steadily, without a trace of a smile, the way cats do when they expect you to open the door for them. Doris reached for Diana's hand and covered it with her own; a warm, likable spot.

"It has been decided, dear," Doris explained. "You are the one who must seek out this creature, find its shelter, find Melissa, and bring the captive girl home."

Diana's mind whizzed along a freeway of its own, with no stops in sight. "I don't understand."

There was a puzzled silence between the old people. William cleared his throat and began to speak.

"Me and Michael and Emily are not members of this tribe; the Keresan. We come from outside, from the Navajo land. We are Navajo. When my grandmother was a little girl, her and her family and all the Navajos were driven from their hogans and sacred land and made to march many miles to the east, to a fort the army had built there. We call it Hweeldi. Many of the people died, from heat and from starving. But some of them, like my mother, ran away to the Keresan people they met along the way. The Keresans gave beautiful necklaces made of corn kernels to the Navajos, to eat on their walk. And the

243

Pueblos took in some of the Navajo's children, to protect them. 'The soldiers are always watching,' my grandmother warned my mother before leaving to Hweeldi. 'We will come back for you, my daughter, on our way home'. But my grandmother never came back."

Diana listened uneasily, saddened by the sound of the wind creaking outside the house; a lament for William's narrative about heat and death. What she knew about death was that corpses were cold and alien and hard when you touched them. Corpses spoke of a winter that defied any natural change of season.

William continued. "The Keresan people here raised us Navajo children as their own, and they were careful of the government agents and soldiers who would take us away if they found out we were Navajo. That was a long time ago. Many passing winters. I don't know, but I think that the government will send us three old folks to Hweeldi if they found out we were here—as old as we are. So we keep many things secret.

"One of these secret things are the old, old stories kept by our grandmothers and our grandfathers. These are not stories of fun, but stories that are powerful medicine. Such powerful medicine that you have to go into ceremony, to be blessed, to protect yourself before you can sing even one word. That is how powerful they are."

William paused a moment, looking to the ceiling, as if the images he saw would appear above his head.

"We will take you to the Mother's home, around where Sleeping Woman is, to a ceremonial hogan we keep secret there. You will hear and learn one of these stories and its songs. Emily is our medicine woman. I remember some of the words that my mother taught to me. We will teach you these things, to give you power and strength."

"Me?" Diana smiled weakly. "You've forgotten one thing, William. I'm not remotely Indian. Not even one-eighth."

William and Doris remained silent.

"I mean, I'm not ungrateful for what you're telling me. I'm very honored and flattered that you've considered me so important. But I think I'm in over my head here."

Doris cleared her throat. "You've seen much more than what we've seen, Diana. You know of these vampires. You are

244

not Pueblo or Navajo, but you've told a story that Emily recognizes. And it's not only Melissa that needs healing. It is you, too."

Diana sat up. "Emily didn't want to help Michael in the first place! So look who he had to turn to: A lousy teacher who can't even get her own life in order. I've ignored everything I've been taught and stuck my nose into everyone else's business. I'm not the person you want, Doris."

"Touch your wound, dear. You cared enough to risk your life for Melissa," Doris said. "We see how much Michael cares for you. It's time to heal the wounds that the government soldiers caused us, time to heal the hurt, the weeping, and distrust that still lives between our people. Emily has seen this in ceremony, Diana. You must accept it now."

Diana shook her head. "I'm sorry, Doris, but I don't have to accept anything. I'm only just learning to handle my own life, to do things I thought were impossible. I'm finished with accepting things I once thought couldn't be changed. Some things, anyway."

Diana couldn't face the old couple. Maybe they would accept her honesty as a gift of some kind. A consolation gift for rejecting them. But wasn't that a betrayal of their trust? Maybe they'll think I'm offering my honesty as a pledge that I'll get Melissa back. Diana thought carefully, and spoke as if she were thinking out loud.

"This is hard to say, Doris, but I think I have to. Tonight, I've only just realized that I still love my ex-husband. When he left me, I hated him. So much hatred lived inside me that I never knew existed. It ruined me, and a lot of friendships I had then. They saw what was happening to me, but they couldn't give me any comfort. Not the sort I needed. They listened patiently to what I said. I think I might have said too much. But I didn't care. I only wanted them to hate Roger as much as I did.

"Now this stuff with Melissa comes up, Doris, and I'm really confused. I fear for Melissa so much, I can't think straight. Just like it used to be with Roger. My life is falling to pieces again. Love on the rebound, if you know what I mean."

Doris nodded gently. Her eyes moistened with tears, and her hand stayed on Diana's.

"You have to understand, Doris. I have to protect myself. I have to accept that Roger is gone, that he has a new wife and a little boy I couldn't give him. The truth of my life is that I am alone; and that's something I can change. I have to begin . . . start a new life or something. This time I have to be ready. I wasn't with Roger. I have to heal myself first, before I start caring or being afraid for someone else." Without meaning to, Diana bowed her head. "I'm really not ready to protect Melissa. I'm afraid I might do her more harm than good."

The fire in the stove crackled hungrily for more wood. Doris and William were so still, they might have turned into trees.

I'm all washed up. They probably think I'm a fool, which is probably a good thing. Maybe they'll find someone else, one of their own tribe, a Navajo, to find Melissa.

Diana looked at William. "Do you understand now why I can't go on with this? I couldn't tell Michael. He's too far away, wrapped up in his hunt. I don't want to hurt him."

Scowling, William stirred into life. "I have brought Emily back to Madrecita. You must stay with her for a while, to tell us what you know about these vampires, and to gather your strength. I ask this of you because Emily is very old and I don't think she can stay long without help. We'll find someone else to help Michael."

Diana swallowed. "The police have decided it would be a good idea if I stayed away from Albuquerque for a time. So that would be perfect."

William rose quietly and walked out of the kitchen without saying another word. Doris struggled up and chuckled.

"I'm getting so weak, now. Help me with the dishes, dear, and then you can go to bed."

Diana smiled and rose. She let her tears fall, not wiping them away. She didn't want the old woman to notice her useless crying. Diana only wiped her sleeve across her cheeks as Doris' back was turned. She had never felt so alone in all her life.

Forty-nine

"Michael Roanhorse."

The empty, moonlit room dimmed. Then Falke appeared, as if he had stepped from a coiling mist. "With what weapons shall we do battle? Sword, axe, or spear?"

Michael rose from the cot in the dusty room Elizabeth had hidden him in. "I don't have any weapons with me."

"No rifles? Hidden knives?"

"I have nothing."

"You come ill-prepared, my friend."

"I see no weapons on you."

Falke smiled and lifted his hands. "As naked as the day I was born, I was never better equipped."

"An old warrior's song," Michael said.

"Older than you can imagine, Michael. When, as a boy, I first walked this earth, there were creatures about in the forests and lakes that you would have never dreamed of. Evil beasts that hunted men for sport. They, also, held no weapons—save ripping claws, teeth, and sinews of steel. Potent blood."

Michael nodded. "In the old days, we Navajos fought with such creatures. Stories of our wars with them are remembered, carried, in many hearts. Maybe you and my grandfathers and grandmothers walked in the same land."

"Perhaps. A warrior as yourself could only have come from a race who knew of such beasts. Yet am I a creature from that age who knows from sweet experience. Your knowledge and your blood have passed through many hands. It is tainted and weak. My hands are strong and calloused, drenched with human blood, toughened as dragon hide. Peel the flesh from my head, and you will find a skull as hard as dragon horn. Between you and myself, Michael, it is an uneven battle. There is no challenge."

"*Hágoshį́į*, we'll see. Let's talk until then, *ma'iitsoh*."

"While there is night left, old savage."

Michael sat back on the cot, hands on his knees, ignoring his blistering, screaming joints. Falke remained standing near a far window, just outside a shaft of moonlight. His blond hair flamed like an electric arc.

"Where were you born?" Michael asked.

"I awoke upon a dusty bier. Flowers covered me. An endless stone corridor stretched into darkness. In the candlelight, everywhere, the flowers were drenched in blood. Nine centuries have passed since that time. Tonight, I am here as you see me. And you are waiting for Melissa."

"Yes."

"The girl has made her choice."

Michael stood up again, swayed from the nauseating pain in his body. "Our strengths are not the same, you say. But I will still fight you anyway. For my granddaughter."

Falke shifted among the moon beams, his eyes fragments of broken silver. "Then you would break upon me like water, old man. I am the stone cliffs."

"Water and wind carve away the rock. Look at the desert. All that sand is broken rock."

"A thousand million years it takes the water and wind, but you don't have that long to live."

"I'm an old man, as everyone keeps telling me. My joints hurt me with a pain like breaking bones. My eyesight is leaving me. But I still feel a warrior's strength in my fingers. I would be very honored to be killed by you. If it happens. It would be the end of much pain."

Falke gazed at him, examining. "Where do you come from, old man? From what world?"

"I might tell you my name. And from that, you would understand my weakness. But I'm not ready to die, yet."

"I would not recognize your world, savage."

"You come from the same place, *ma'iitsoh*. I know you."

Falke seemed to gather a shadow around him. "Melissa, as my wife, would live forever. With limitless strength. Wouldn't you wish that for her?"

"You're not alive."

"If I returned her to you, she would exist in a short lifetime of suffering, then break apart from old age."

"Melissa's Walk in Beauty," Michael answered. "She still has many songs to sing. Let her sing them."

Falke stopped in the center of the room. "Melissa is mine, old man. And I will keep her songs."

"Then you better kill me, now, before I begin the song of my hunt."

"You know this, Michael, that death is no solution." Falke's sad face was motionless. "And that the search is everything."

Black clouds enveloped the tall figure, then slid under the moon shafts. Michael stood alone among squares of moonlight. He clutched his medicine bag tied around his neck.

My Walk in Beauty is ending, Michael thought, unable to stop a needle of anger sliding into his heart. He remembered Elizabeth's small, powerful hand in his, remembered each distinct fingertip.

It was time to make a final song.

Fifty

When Diana awoke, she felt as if the bed, blankets, and sheets, like river ice, had frozen around her. The heavy canvas cover popped with her movements and the layers of quilts smothered her comfortably. She remembered Sunday mornings before her parents awakened; the house was silent and the cold was similar to this mountain chill, with a stillness in it she had never been able to fathom. In her darkest moments, Diana had imagined the stillness as what a corpse might feel as it lay alone in a morgue, seemingly forgotten, as relatives and friends worried over their own grief.

Shiver! Not a happy thought.

Diana threw off the covers, swung herself from her warm spot on the mattress, and settled her feet onto a threadbare Navajo rug. The air felt so clean it was painful, as if the air itself had been scrubbed and rinsed, tugged through the rollers of an old-fashioned washing machine, then hung to dry.

She hoisted up her suitcase from the floor, popped it open, and dug inside to see what was there. She vaguely remembered the numbness and disconnection her brain had experienced the night before. An undeniable sapping of spirit. Rage waited inside of her—a black, coiling, hissing snake. But Diana mentally crossed rage off her agenda. She had to keep her wits up and as clean as the air around her.

Diana pulled on some jeans, a sporty T-shirt, several layers of sweaters, and her old hiking boots. The sweaters hung on her strangely, making her feel like a kid experimenting in daddy's clothes. She took out a pair of bundled socks and stared at them. I don't recognize these as my own, she thought. Where did they come from? The wrapped ball rasped in the palm of her hand. Her toes were icing over. Who the heck cares whose socks they are?

I do. She sat with them in her lap and tried to think whom they might belong to. After several unsuccessful minutes, Diana finally put them back in her suitcase. She rooted a bit more and found a year's supply of panties, a box of animal crackers, a bar of chocolate, a new blue silk blouse—price tags dangling. But no more socks. I must have packed this while I was asleep. She dug deeper, below the underwear, and touched cold metal. Her pistol.

Diana glanced around the room. From a window, gray, brooding light trickled into the room and revealed a redwood dresser piled high with baskets, pots, trinkets. The sky outside was featureless, what Diana imagined a baby chick might see before pecking itself out of its shell.

Why no curtain on that window? she wondered.

Diana stood on the groaning floor. A hand-held mirror lay on the scratched surface of the dresser, along with several empty perfume bottles, rosary beads, and about ten intricately patterned Indian pots. Diana lifted the heavy mirror. The scrubbed air had given her skin a soft blush which she actually thought looked nice. Her hair was a fluffed mess; she hadn't tied it back before going to bed. Her eyes were somewhat bloodshot. And the colors of her bruise were truly brilliant; a rainbow plastered to the side of her face. The hard bumps under her ear had gone down, leaving only a patchy red rash—the flesh was no longer tender. Diana propped the mirror against one of the largest pots, ready to tackle her errant tresses, when someone knocked on the door.

"Coming!" Diana yelled, assuming generally about old people's bad hearing.

"Get up and have something to eat, dear," Doris said, her voice muffled by the door. "Your breakfast is getting cold."

"All right, all right." Diana rummaged quickly through her purse for her brush. God, what's the hurry? I thought Indians were supposed to be patient. Diana ran the brush through her auburn hair, enjoying the lusty crackle of static. Her hair began to rise on tiny currents of air. She brushed more vigorously, and smiled at her image in the mirror—a tawny catwoman, disguised by winter clothes. Diana made a cat claw with her free hand and hissed.

"Just some coffee for me, please."

The food smelled wholesome, but the thought of eating made Diana feel full, as if she had spent the whole night devouring mounds of food. The kitchen looked brittle under the fluorescent light. The fire in the oven popped thinly. Diana drank strong coffee and felt the chill in her middle relocate to her hands and feet.

"You're so thin," Doris said, laying a plate of stacked pancakes next to her elbow. "You must eat something."

William ate silently across the table.

"I'm not much of a breakfast person," Diana answered.

"Here." Doris nudged the pancakes closer. "Have just one pancake with some butter and syrup. There's some leftover stew in the refrigerator. Heat yourself some, if you want."

William put his fork down and took a swallow from his cup. "You better eat something, Diana. She won't leave you alone until you do."

Diana blushed under his hoary gaze. "Maybe I'll have one, then." She speared a pancake and laid it on her plate. Only then did Doris stop bustling, and sit herself down.

"Here, have a little syrup," Doris said, handing over the bottle. "It's too sweet for the both of us."

"Yes, I can't have any, with my diabetes," William said, wistfully smiling. "But I sure like the smell of it."

"Then I'll have some syrup, William, just to please you."

"*Ahehee'*. Thank you."

The pancakes were so good, Diana ate a couple more, along with some bacon and a serving of scrambled eggs. The

251

ghostly sensation of being filled vanished, and Diana realized she was ravenous. A round, domed loaf of bread waited in the center of the table, just brown enough to look healthy and delicious. She tried a toasted slice with some sugar sprinkled on top—William's suggestion—with yet another cup of hunters' coffee.

"Any more food," Diana said happily, "and I really will explode!"

Sunlight on white frozen waves. William's round lenses sent occasional flashes of lightning into Diana's eyes. She threw the last batch of quilts into her car and closed the hatch smartly. William had loaned her the blankets for her stay in Emily's house.

It was nine in the morning. All the school buses had gone away, lurching and groaning from Madrecita, carrying their bundles of bright little kids to whatever school they were bound for. Earlier, Diana had heard shouts and laughter and scuffles outside the house. Looking out the main window as Doris and William were collecting the quilts, Diana had seen many children gathering in front of a long, blue building, which Doris had said was the village meeting hall. Diana had watched the kids for a while, trying to perceive any differences in their behavior from the children in Albuquerque. None, of course, had been apparent from such a cursory glance. Kids were kids, wherever Diana had found herself teaching.

"I hope this is all, William," she said now to the old guy who was studying her car as if he might buy it. "Any more heavy blankets in there and the axle will break."

"Those are bedrolls we take hunting with us," he said. "They're made to keep you hot in the deep snow. Until you can get some coffee into you."

"I can believe that."

The air was sharp. Diana looked to the northwest, where the wind was blowing from, and saw the deep canyon gouged into the ridge, leading her gaze into shadowed layers of overlapping pine-covered slopes. We're so high, she thought, pines are growing there. No wonder it's so cold. The trees looked like tall people wrapped in green cloaks ascending the slopes; a sprinkling of snow on their shoulders. Diana was amazed at how far she could see. I'll bet if I stared long enough, I could see deer.

"Are there deer up there, William?"

William looked up with her. "Not as many as there used to be. I haven't seen a deer come down for many years. Nor Barbary sheep, either."

"It looks like there should be thousands up there."

"I think the mine scared them all away."

For a moment, Diana hadn't understood him. "Mine?"

William pointed back toward the east. The part of the village they were standing on was set on a massive sandstone shelf. William's house was situated back from the edge, but Diana could still see what he was pointing at.

"Oh, the mine." Now she remembered.

There was a ponderous haze in the sky, which made the horizon silvery and way too bright. Below this odd sky and the oil-tanker form of Mesa Gigante far away was a white-sheeted valley dominated by three unnaturally smooth mesas. Their sides were stippled and striped with red and black sand. Ice-flecked surfaces glittered, as if the whole area were sprinkled with shattered glass. Diana saw an image of Hanna smashing through the Mole's windshield as if diving into water, sending out sprays of razor-edged slivers into the night sky.

"They have taken all of what they needed," William said, "and left us a bunch of money, but they haven't shaped the earth back into what she was."

Diana shook her head and gripped her keys. Something dark and powerful was welling up inside her, like a growing ocean wave poised to smash hard, granite cliffs. She forced her rage down, again. One day, it's going to be too strong to push away, she thought—then what are you going to do?

"Well, William, shall we go see Emily?"

By now, Diana could recognize a pattern in the directions around Madrecita. Houses and ruins sat in familiar places. Bare trees appeared where she expected them. Diana was only a little surprised at their final destination.

"Isn't this Michael's house?"

The house they pulled up at was the large blue house where she had seen the phantom woman. Diana had heard enough stories about haunted houses to be certain she didn't want to be near one — and this house was certainly strange. She killed the engine and listened to its ticking as William shook the car getting out. Just looking at the structure of the house made her uneasy; it was built like a fortress, as if intent on keeping its occupants in and enemies out. Enemies, Diana thought wearily. Vampires. Hunched inside his arctic jacket as if pushed down by the cold, William walked to the screen door and knocked. Diana waited to see who, or what, might answer.

The front door opened and old man Samson White came out and greeted William. He was dressed in a thermal shirt, the sleeves pushed to his elbows, along with jeans and unlaced boots. Diana braced herself and opened her door. Her legs tingled as the wind whooshed up her pants legs. Shuddering, she tapped the ground gingerly, then stood up. Her mountain jacket was bulky. She zipped it up, becoming warmly engulfed, feeling like an astronaut making an Extra Vehicular Activity on some unknown planet. Both men turned to her. Diana waved and staggered around the car, through deep snow, to retrieve the blankets from the trunk

Soon, they were all standing in the huge kitchen made hot by a roaring fire trapped in the stove. Something bubbled in a dutch oven, and next to it stood the resident coffee pot, forever simmering its dark, frothy liquid that could quench both thirst and hunger.

"You can put those things in the back room, where you'll be sleeping with Emily," Samson said, pointing with his chin to the doorless doorway.

"Thanks."

Diana carried the blankets to the next room and hesitated. The television stared blankly at nothing. Funnily, this room seemed to be inhabited. It was a comfortable feeling, like a gathering of friendly people; Diana became nervous anyway. There are no such things as ghosts, she repeated to herself as she moved on to the next room; just vampires.

The floor squeaked and almost shifted under her feet. She kept her eyes on the bulb string dangling from the dark ceiling like a life line. Once under it, she realized she couldn't pull on it with her arms carrying heavy blankets. "Oh, crap." Diana turned unwillingly to her left, to the bed in the corner

254

and approached it. No ghosts are here, stupid. Probably just a massing army of spiders. Diana dumped the blankets onto the bed. The springs squeaked loudly, scaring her more.

Gathering her courage like sticks of firewood, Diana turned to the corner behind her, to the ancient wingchair where she had seen the phantom woman. Of course, nothing sat there. No woman or ghost. Diana felt silly, but relieved.

She was touching the bed covering, groaning at its texture, like a broad sheet of river ice, when the floorboards creaked behind the closed door next to the wingchair, inside Michael's old unused room. The porcelain doorknob turned and the door cracked open. A frozen draft fell across Diana's cheeks. An old woman emerged from the room.

Diana clenched her breath in her lungs so she didn't scream. The old woman stood in the doorway and scanned the room, moving her head first one way, then another. Her irises, Diana could see them from this distance, were cloudy bluish-white spots.

"Emily," Diana whispered, then cleared her throat. "Emily, it's me, Diana Logan."

The old woman turned toward the sound of her voice and smiled, teeth straight and perfect. "Yes, the woman from Albuquerque. Michael's friend."

"I'm sorry, I hope I didn't frighten you."

"I thought there was someone walking in here. I was unpacking my things, but I can't remember where all the cabinets are. Can you help me, dear?"

Diana rubbed her arms against the chill. Emily was wearing a simple turquoise-plaid dress and an apron. Her white hair was in a tight bun. Her arms were bare, no coat or shawl to keep away the cold. Diana wanted to go to Emily and hug her, to make sure she was real and not an apparition; she felt she needed to make some kind of connection with this house, with the whole village and with its people.

"Of course, I'll help you," Diana said, hugging herself.

She didn't know if William had left, or even if Samson was still in the house. She suspected William wasn't and found she didn't really care if both men were here or not.

So Emily and she spent the morning sorting and folding clothes from the cabinets and drawers in this comforting room that had once housed Michael and his wife. Periodically,

255

Diana shoveled a block of coal from a wide-mouthed pan into the tall coal heater standing in the corner next to the door. It was very efficient, filling the room with near-visible waves of heat, and Diana soon became comfortable enough just in jeans and a borrowed plaid shirt.

The larger of the two brass beds in the room, by the window at the furthest end of the room, held a growing pile of brand-new clothes and towels; bright shirts and pants which Emily explained were to have been Christmas presents the previous year. They had never been wrapped and distributed because Emily had to be taken to the hospital then. For what, she didn't say.

"We could get some wrapping paper and wrap them now," Diana suggested as she folded a boy's striped T-shirt. "You could give them away this year."

"I'll give them to the village elders for distribution. There are needy families who could use them. You can take me there later on."

"Okay."

They continued folding and cleaning until the early afternoon. They did not speak much, and Diana liked that. She felt they were becoming familiar with each other's patterns of movement and breathing; and Diana began to feel less conscious of herself as an intruder and stranger.

The room itself was lovely, just as she remembered. The adobe walls were thick and featureless, yet smooth as polished wood. Diana took more time poring over the details of things. The gauzy curtains, delicately printed with unfolding spreads of roses, resembling an old Japanese painting Diana had once seen in a friend's home. A gentle pile of lace doilies, folded just off-center enough to tell her they had been sewn by hand. A broken piece of a white, flat rock that held the outlines of a fossilized fern. A woven basket filled with pine cones. A dusty oil lamp. As Emily silently moved around her, Diana took these objects in her hands, felt their textures and their weight, trying to glimpse some meaning from them.

A little more time to stay, she thought. That's all. What is this house like in the spring?

Eventually, Diana pulled the curtain back from the east window and was surprised to see it was late afternoon. She patted the bed and sat. She was hungry and didn't know how to broach the subject with Emily, not wanting to disturb or irritate the old woman when there seemed to be so much still to be put away and cleaned.

"How about some coffee, Emily?"

The old woman turned from her task of sorting clothes into undecipherable piles. "I wondered when you would want to eat. I didn't want to disturb you. You seemed so much into your work."

Diana helped Emily navigate through the doorways between the separate rooms until they reached the kitchen. The house was indeed empty. Diana guided Emily to a chair and went to the front door. Through the window, she saw her car sitting alone in the snow.

"William and Samson must have gone," Diana said. She picked up the iron handle of the stove, stuck its end into a notch in one ring and lifted it off. Gray ashes fluttered about the stove's interior. Diana blew on the coals until they flared a fierce red. She searched in the box on the floor for several narrow logs, which she placed among the thin wisps of flame. Soon the fire was crackling noisily. Diana peered into the coffee pot. Fresh coffee had been made for them already.

At Emily's urging, Diana began to search the cabinets and shelves for something to eat. Emily sat and hummed a soft song to herself.

"I feel like I'm being fattened up for the kill, Emily."

Diana followed Emily to the woodpile about fifty yards in front and slightly left of the house, beside a huge tank lying on its side, which might have once sat on the back of a railroad car. Behind the woodpile stretched a plain of snow, broken only by a single leafless tree. A mile to the east, the open pit mine was gun black and poison yellow beneath a ceiling of building clouds.

How many roentgens or X rays or whatever am I receiving right now? Diana imagined the yellow patches of the unnatural mesas shooting lethal rays straight into her skull. Wood chips crunched. Emily had just turned over a large branch with her foot to expose the drier sticks and shavings underneath the snow-covered woodpile.

Diana kept having to convince herself that Emily was indeed blind. For a while, the old woman had moved carefully about the house as if she had never been there before. Diana had to point out the danger spots and lead Emily by her thin arm practically everywhere. Now, though, Emily moved about easily and without hesitation; she seemed to see things that even Diana had missed, like the hordes of tiny spiders that lived in the old house with them. Emily knew that the little creatures were shunned by Diana and took patient care in showing her likely spider spots to avoid. Diana had begun to feel blind herself. Maybe the old woman was listening to the air currents, hearing them as a scholar might hear the subtle inflections and accents of an unfamiliar language, which no one else bothered to understand.

Or had forgotten.

Emily's clear voice broke into Diana's thoughts, over a sudden gust of wind. "I'm glad that you are beginning to eat. It reminds me, too, of how good food warms you up."

"It sure does. I'm getting fat." Diana knelt and began picking up the larger pieces of wood, which she prodded first with a long stick to make sure no deadly arachnids were waiting to pounce on her. "Soon, I won't be able to get into anything."

"I'm not trying to change your mind, dear. William and Samson have gone looking for someone else to help us. William told me how much you needed to be out of Albuquerque and out of danger. I'm glad that you are here to help me clean the house. And to cook."

"I meant getting into clothes, Emily. Not other people's business." Diana straightened and looked above the adobe and rock houses to the canyon beyond Madrecita. Snow flurries began to creep over the ridges, softening the harsh contrasts between black and red stone, green pine trees, and bone-white snow. For some reason, the healed spot where Melissa had bitten her began to throb dismally in unison with the new bruise on her face.

"Potatoes are easy to cook," Diana said, looking at the woodpile, pondering the novel idea of using an axe to break the wood with. "I wouldn't mind trying something a bit more complicated. I need to get us some more food, anyway."

Not moving, Emily seemed to be waiting for Diana to say more.

"And I did need the vacation," Diana added.

"It is more than a vacation," Emily said solemnly. "We are learning about each other. I will teach you some words in Keresan, if you want."

"That's what you and Doris and William . . . and Michael speak?"

Emily prodded wet logs with her foot. "Michael and William and I speak Navajo. Keres is a Pueblo language. Like Tewa. We only speak Keres because this is where our home is. But the stories and songs we keep are Navajo."

"I better learn to speak Navajo, then," Diana said quietly.

Emily turned to her, almost casually. "Really?"

Diana sighed, exasperated. "Oh, I don't know! Yes, I would like to learn Navajo, and Keres, maybe Tewa, too, if you have the time. For my own knowledge."

"If you have the patience," Emily said. "But I can't speak Tewa, or I would teach you that also."

Diana laughed. "And what could I teach you, Emily? In exchange."

"Maybe . . . you could teach me to speak better English."

Diana began to feel weepy. "I think you speak perfectly fine English."

"I don't know. Sometimes I don't understand the children who come to visit us old folks. They talk so fast anymore, like the TV. I guess I'm just getting old, and too slow."

"I know what." Diana stood next to Emily. "I can teach you some of the words the kids use nowadays, and you can surprise the children when they next come to visit."

Emily laughed. Diana imagined teaching her the slang that changed so much during the course of a school year.

"Maybe I can even bring some of my students from Albuquerque and we can all teach you folks how to speak real cool."

Cool? That was a moldy one.

Emily touched Diana's arm. "Maybe you can teach all the little ones at the Head Start to speak cool, too."

Emily, laughing, moved back toward the house with a stack of kindling in her arms. Diana watched her. The old woman walked straight to the doorway of the house, without a stumble or break in her stride.

Fifty-one

Melissa soon discovered that Falke's sanctuary was large and labyrinthine. If she started walking, following one stone corridor into another and another, she might find herself in the same spot an hour or six hours later; even if she was careful to retrace her steps. Ornate lamps gave off a soothing, dim light. The walls were polished to a sleek finish, with pretty wood shelves and carved niches at strange places, such as a niche set on a level with her ankle.

Some of the rooms were doorless, and mostly the same size, except for a bewildering room she had named the planetarium, writing it in dust in the center of the stone floor. A few rooms were furnished with simple chairs or the skeletons of beds with a few stacked blankets, never any sheets; no mirrors. And the sanctuary was soundless. If Melissa stopped for a time, an hour or half a night, the only sound she heard would be her own heartbeat echoing off the walls, growing in volume until she had to shut her ears from the painful, dense rumbling.

Very strange place I've inherited, Melissa thought wistfully. And funny sometimes.

In one room a green, silk curtain covered an unseen window. Melissa had watched for an entire night to glimpse the action of some breeze, but the curtain hadn't twitched. Finally, she had eagerly tugged the sash cord, ready to learn the mystery of where this sanctuary lay. The curtains had silently drawn back, revealing an unworked cavern wall and a deep well of blackness just below the stone windowsill. Melissa had perched on the sill, leaned her palm against rough rock, and peered down. Far below, a single lamp burned above a wooden door and a narrow step. Years of dust covered the step. No one had crossed that threshold for a long time.

And where was Falke, anyway? she wondered angrily.

Melissa paused in a blank corridor, trying to work out exactly where that secret back door was. She wanted to be the first person to set foot on that step and to find where the door led. Maybe it was some kind of escape tunnel to the outside world. To another world! Or maybe it led to a private room that Falke did not want her to find or to ask about. Just how much had he told her about this sanctuary, about the rooms with the unfinished furniture, who had first set the lamps into the walls, or who had built this entire place?—Nothing! And how was she ever to find out anything if she was left alone all the time?

While Falke was busy making new friends.

Melissa hesitated, then made up her mind. Tonight, she would return to Albuquerque. She checked her digital watch. No, not enough time for what she planned.

Okay, she thought. Tomorrow night.

Melissa retraced her path back to her room. She opened a creaking vanity and pulled out her backpack, which she had retrieved from her mother's apartment . . . she couldn't remember when. Then she tied her hair back and pulled off the long dress she had borrowed from Elizabeth's room. Melissa draped it over her bed where another dress lay waiting: A white cotton dress with ribbon and lace trim. Reworked, it might fit her.

A sewing needle lay in her palm, like a tiny sword. Melissa remembered vividly the morning she had escaped from her grandfather; drifting across the glowing city, smears of light spinning under her feet, tatters of warmth peeling from her body, sliding down an invisible dome as Elizabeth flew them to an old theater that Melissa recognized at once.

"This is your home?" she asked.

"Come upstairs," Elizabeth whispered.

Corridors unfolded, cement steps flickered under their feet, until they came to a dusty darkened room with echoey wood floors and old-fashioned door knobs. Ponderous buildings shivered like mist as Melissa walked to a window and pressed her forehead against the glass.

"Hanna scares me shitless," Melissa said. "And it doesn't seem as if Falke's too eager to keep her away from me either."

Elizabeth was standing in a corner, almost invisible against the white walls. "Why?" she asked.

"He told me so: He said it would strengthen me."

"Falke says and does many things. Who's to say whether he acts from his storehouse of knowledge, or from boredom?"

261

Melissa stared at the slow-moving cars below. "Do you really have an idea about what he says and why? If you do, I'd like some advice."

"I don't claim any secret knowledge into his heart. Only the knowledge a . . . wife has into her husband's behavior. Mixed with a little intuition."

Melissa looked at her. Among the stacked boxes and dusty office equipment, Elizabeth was hard to see, even with her new-and-improved night vision. "Falke said that you two were never properly married."

"Yes," Elizabeth agreed. "He would say that. Would it matter to you, Melissa, if he once said to me, after love; 'Beloved, we are joined forever by the self-same blood flowing in our bodies and hearts. The only marriage our kind will ever recognize'?"

"What kind is 'our kind'?" Melissa asked, already knowing what kind of 'love' Elizabeth meant.

"A marriage of gods, Falke says. Or angels." Elizabeth's smile was fragile.

"Falke is no angel."

"Neither am I, or you. We're devils. Satan's instruments. But Falke and I were joined in that eternal marriage he described. Can you say the same to me?"

Melissa mulled over everything he had said to her; remembered the truth in his eyes. Falke does love me, she thought. I can see that much, with or without new-and-improved vision.

"I can feel his wanting me," Melissa said, not realizing she was speaking her thoughts. "I see myself in his heart. It scares me, sometimes, what I see inside of him."

Elizabeth approached. Melissa prepared herself for an attack; she saw no violence in the woman's quiet steps.

"I saw you in his heart, Melissa, before I met you. Maybe before he even knew you existed."

Elizabeth's eyes were sun sparkles on ocean waves, and Melissa felt like a kid under her scrutiny, as if Elizabeth held the power to illuminate the hidden depths of her soul. Falke had never exposed her like this, had never made her feel so naked. Melissa glanced down at the woman's small, bare feet.

"I know," Melissa said, choosing her words carefully, so that Elizabeth would understand what she was saying, without explanation. "I saw Christiane in his mind, like seeing a face underwater. When he was sleeping. Falke holds my hand when he sleeps with me. And I think that makes it easier to slip inside his dreams. The connection, you know?"

"Memories, Melissa," Elizabeth said. "I don't think Falke dreams."

The third-story office rooms and hallways of the theater were unoccupied, Melissa remembered. She felt as if only the ghosts and mice were listening to her.

"In one of his memories, I saw Falke against a window. A forest was passing behind him. There was sunlight outside, and we were moving. He was holding my hand, not squeezing or anything, gentle and warm. I felt like I became someone else. It wasn't you. It was Christiane. I felt creepy; lost in memory. *Her* memory. I don't know how I knew this. Then this hand reached out to touch his face, Elizabeth, and . . . and Falke was warm. So warm."

Elizabeth spoke sadly. "It's a thing vampires can do, Melissa. I don't understand it either. Lost in memory, you say? I think it's more like we become lost in time."

Melissa let her words stream past. "He was going away. And I wanted him with me so much. I felt his passion; I could see it in his eyes. But that day, I was the stronger one; I was betrothed to the Son of God. I made him go away. Falke let my hand go, but he promised he would come back for me. To win my hand, he said. I knew I wouldn't be so strong then, Elizabeth. And I hoped for that so much.

"But Falke never returned to me. Into whatever dark place my God had thrown him, Falke never emerged. My soul became gray stone. My knight never came back to me."

Melissa blinked and came out of her trance. She felt distant from herself. All at once, Melissa realized she was kneeling on the floor with Elizabeth.

"That's Christiane," Elizabeth said, drawing a straight mark in the dust covering the wood floor. "I used to drift uncontrolled in Falke's memory, and I'd see her in a similar manner when I was new to being vampire. Like you, Melissa. I used to *become* Christiane. Falke never spoke to me about her. I had to steal into his brain to get the truth."

Melissa felt shaky. "I feel like I'm her all the time, now."

"When you become stronger, the visions go away and come back only when you need them." Elizabeth's eyes darkened. "I think Falke truly believes Christiane has come back to him. In you, Melissa."

Melissa sensed Elizabeth's honesty. "Falke sees me but then he doesn't. He sees her!"

A breath of wind blew in her hair, caressing her. Tears slipped out of her eyes and dripped onto her lap.

"These memories are weakening him," Elizabeth whispered. "They are making him careless. Hanna sees this, and I think she's planning something evil against him, against all of us. She scares me shitless too."

"Falke's so far away," Melissa said. "I don't know if he can hear me in that secret place he goes to."

Melissa felt herself suddenly falling, the support she had been leaning on was gone. Elizabeth was standing by a window.

"The sun is rising," she said. "Come downstairs. You can wait out the daylit world there . . . with me."

Elizabeth held out her hand. Melissa was pulled up, steadied. And it was funny, because Elizabeth was smaller and more fragile. She looked like the lost child Melissa felt herself to be.

Elizabeth glanced at her, perplexed. "What's so funny? We're talking about the end of the world, and you're laughing!"

Now, Melissa flung the needle at the sanctuary wall where it stuck, shivering. The white cotton dress she recognized from the picture of Elizabeth as a child lay draped across her lap. And the stinging sensation was real, too. Her bones were beginning to ache.

Morning was near.

Nothing funny about that, Melissa thought.

Melissa stuffed a brush, cassette tapes, and some money into her backpack. Had Elizabeth walked the same steps, wandered in the same corridors, waited for Falke, like me? Melissa wondered. Had she explored every possible route and niche? Maybe Elizabeth knew where that secret door led . . .

"I'll find Elizabeth," Melissa said to the empty room, already feeling less lonely. "And I'll ask her."

264   They might even become friends.

Fifty-two

Night enshrouded buildings, and streets streaked past Elizabeth at light speed. She had seen gazelles on television, had been entranced by the animals' sprightly, graceful movement against desert trees and blue space. Elizabeth imagined herself as one of those creatures, and she ran faster.

Michael had shown Elizabeth her death. There were no more attachments. No one close to her who might understand the fading pattern of her history; her lonely secret life beneath flickering electronic suns. She was going to die alone.

But there was one chance with Michael. He elicited strange feelings from her. Unsafe, unpredictable emotions. Elizabeth longed to whisper inside of him and learn the truth of his being. Where had he come from, this sunflower raised up in a patch of blue? What were his intentions?

Love warms me too, she had wanted to tell him in the brief time she had seen him; but she hadn't.

Elizabeth had awakened at twilight, dressed eagerly, flown up dusty stairs, and found him sitting on the narrow cot in the abandoned office room where she had hidden him last night. Seeing him sitting alone in the dark room, Elizabeth had been struck by how the streetlamps outside had given Michael's skin a glowing, bluish cast, making his face and hands into a night sky holding a full moon and only the most vital stars.

My Blue Angel.

"I remember when the desert all around us echoed only of nighthawks and wind," she had said to Michael, settling comfortably next to him. "I know you can say as much. What do you remember?"

He had not answered. Elizabeth watched his shadowed profile. His eyes were far away and thoughtful. Familiar. Her mother's eyes had been like that sometimes, a century gone, when gazing at the line of the approaching Sangre de Cristo Mountains.

He finally spoke. "I remember heat, and nothing but a lonely quiet. I remember the first automobile I ever saw. I

thought it was some monster I had dreamed up and set to
life."

Elizabeth smiled. "I remember a wooden wagon that I
walked behind," she said. "My family's prairie schooner with
our name 'Washburn' printed along the side. Not very often
did I ride; every little bump and stone near to cracked my
spine, and come nightfall, I lit off the back with a pain in my
rump when we stopped to camp. Not a very restful sea back
then . . ."

Michael gripped Elizabeth's arm forcefully. Elizabeth had
not been angry, only bewildered. And frightened.

"Are you okay?" she asked, terrified that he had become ill.

Michael remained silent as he ran his hands into her hair,
soothing, his thumb hot on her forehead . . . then hesitating.
She felt a tiny, sharp pain in her scalp.

"What?" Elizabeth touched her head. Michael held something out to her—a single strand of gray hair, almost the color
of his own.

Plucked from her head.

Elizabeth felt a gathering anger raining from the dark sky and
vibrating in her bones. She had left Michael alone, to sing his
anger and blend it with strength, as he had explained. His
heart had gone farther away than the most distant star.

Bridges swooped above her, black trees formed a continuous, snaking line. Pockets of hot and freezing air burst
against her face, her bare arms and legs. The true sun continued his climb through space; his arrival was imminent. Elizabeth felt the sky churning, heating up. Air molecules, no
longer lazily spinning, were sloughing off cold mist. Find
cover! instinct urged.

Elizabeth ran faster. Michael was a man who had lived his
life as a human. With time, she believed, and with long life,
comes truth. If nothing else, that is what she had learned:
Truth. She was a woman, no longer human. But not quite
vampire, and Michael had touched a core of burning life
hidden within her heart. He had seen her soul, reached for
and touched it; where everyone else, including herself, had
forgotten that it existed and had turned away.

Tears blurred the gray morning. Elizabeth forced herself to
stop. Her surroundings were bleakly visible. She was stand-

ing in a large park with rolling snowy hills and oblong bowls filled with ice. A golf course. If Michael were with her, they might have remembered together how a sandy mesa had once stood here — before the gloating houses and sullen flatness — tunneled through with rabbit and prairie dog burrows, stalked by hawks and coyotes. Now, the freeway below the golf course rumbled with cars, as always, but its voice was pitched differently; maybe it was complaining at the increased load of cars rushing along its back.

A wisp of steam began to hiss from Elizabeth's forearms.

Michael would not understand what I'm doing at this moment. He has lost so much in his own life. Would he mourn my death? He doesn't know Falke and Hanna as well as he might, and they will kill him for his lack of knowledge.

Elizabeth grew anxious.

I would mourn him greatly.

Her skin was beginning to harden. Elizabeth looked around quickly. Above the mountains, a few remaining stars were covered over in a violet sheet. Heat began to penetrate her, tear at her insides. In ten or fifteen minutes, her skin would begin to blacken and char, just as she had always pictured it happening.

But it would not happen today. Michael would not have understood why I tempted death. Why should he? Why should he understand or care anything about me?

Elizabeth flew quickly from the strange, artificial hills back to her hidden sanctuary. Death was a cocoon. A haven. Nothing to be frightened of. There was no floating on it, or above it. Silent leaves covered you. Dust, not carried by the wind, thickened on your corpse, grew heavy on your chest, closed your eyes . . .

She remembered an old song:

> The sun, he passes by, and shouts "How rude you've become!
> You," he quiets, "a woman who once loved me to distraction."

Elizabeth had loved a young man once, dark-haired with gentle hands, almost forty years ago. John had loved her, had constructed the secret room she huddled in, given her sweet songs, taught her the habits of machines, offered his life and protection. What had she given him? An ache somewhere? Vague memories? Nothing as solid as time.

267

And now, once again, love stalked her under a circle of blue. What had she to give this time? Only small gifts: The destruction of her sister and husband, and their spawn; then herself, to the sun.

A song of her own making—decaying evil and a little love.

Fifty-three

Diana woke up. Across the black room, she heard Emily's slow breathing. Something else had awakened her. She listened, heard only elm branches scraping across the roof. Diana moved from the warm spot on the sheet to the colder regions of the east window and moved aside the curtain. Her car had disappeared under a white sheet. Snow flurries twirled into moving shapes, almost human figures. The clouds reflected a salmon-pink as if a great fire were burning somewhere below the east horizon. Diana ignored the cold and sat up, touching the window. Tiny flutterings of air from the cracks around the panes blew against her fingertips. She shivered and pulled up the blankets and quilts and wrapped them around her.

I can't stay here any longer.

Hiding out in Madrecita was beginning to have a calming effect on her besieged heart. The people were conspiring against her resolve, making her want to stay. The innocent mornings and the pillowy dark were healing ingredients that she might soon become dependent on. And it wasn't right that these old people, who held no real connection to her, should treat her as a member of their family; too long a time had passed for Diana to feel a part of anyone's family. Roger's mother, father, brother, and sisters had all stayed a comfortable, expected distance, nonintrusive and undemanding. That was something she could understand.

Here, however, there were all kinds of demands! Working at simple chores that soothed her befuddled mind, becoming intimate with people she might never see again, learning tidbits about Navajo and Keresan life. She was leaning rather heavily on Emily to help untangle the nightmares in her life and to strengthen herself against the evil she had encountered. Emily was making her fat and healthy, and demanding that Diana not worry so much.

Diana closed her eyes, listening to a disruptive wind among the branches above the house. She imagined each snow crystal touching her arms and thighs, threads of water trickling into all her crevices, soothing hot rage. Diana remembered the ridged shrapnel scars that had spiraled around her father's calves like massive trees roots. She remembered massaging ointment into them on hot days and nights when he was brooding and silent.

Far from sleep, Diana worried at a corpse of her own making, her wedding ring; she felt it gnawing at her finger. Then, brick by brick, she began to raise deathless, opaque walls around her heart; fortifications which Melissa and Michael had nearly broken through. The work was not easy. Diana had to struggle at it. She ignored the dancing shapes outside her window and lay back down on a frozen sheet, covering herself completely with mounds of blankets, shutting out gentle silence. Dreams became distant friends again as Diana toiled with bricks.

A red light slipped into her brain. Diana opened her eyes, blinking, and glanced at the glowing outlines of the room. Emily's bed was neatly made. The mirror across from her reflected dark curtains. Diana shivered on the sheets and saw that all the covers were squashed into a bundle at her ankles. The coal heater's belly crackled noisily, almost glowed with heat, but the room's temperature seemed below freezing. Diana stepped onto the floor and quickly pulled off her sweatshirts, thermal undershirt, and sweatpants. She chafed her goosepimply skin, cringing at the new layer of fat she had developed, then walked to the heater. Standing in red, pulsating heat, she raised her arms and stretched luxuriously.

That ought to wake up the ghosts.

No longer shivering, she moved to the dresser. She ignored her shadowy image in the mirror and looked at the photographs tucked into the frame—school pictures of grinning dark-haired boys and girls, none older than elementary-school age; about the time it became uncool to send away pictures to the grandparents, Diana supposed. She noticed one in the far corner and took it down. The face was familiar.

Diana stared into the mirror, moving closer so her face was illuminated by the heater's glow, and she pushed her mass of tangled hair from her face. She held up the photograph and compared images: Same wary eyes, sharp nose, big ears. No bruise, though. Of course, it's not me. Diana turned the picture over and read the scrawled name.

Melissa Roanhorse, fourth grade.

A gray morning squeaked through the windows. Diana dressed carefully and made the bed. She kept within pockets of the icy light, avoided shadows, to illuminate the decision she had just made. Her movements felt solid. A strengthening wind pushed into her heart. She removed her suitcase from the closet, dug out her purse, and brought out her wallet. It burst open—too easily—and Diana thumbed through plastic and paper cards and folded bits of paper with old phone numbers on them until she found the picture she was looking for: Roger's son at four months. Gently, Diana slipped Melissa's picture into the clear plastic where Danny's had been, closed the wallet and placed it back into her purse. She returned to the mirror and tucked Danny's picture in the space left by Melissa's.

Emily, Doris, and William were sitting around the table, eating. Diana walked to the cabinet and took out a cup for herself.

"There's some cereal in the cupboard, dear," Emily said. "Help yourself."

William offered his chair, took Diana's cup from her, and poured them both coffee. Diana settled uneasily among the women.

"It snowed pretty good again last night," William said. "I don't think you'll get back to Albuquerque in that little car till spring."

Diana sipped the bitter coffee and spoke words that she forgot immediately. She held the cup under her chin, hoping the fumes and heat would unclench her knotted brain.

"It's almost six," Doris said. She peered through gold-rimmed bifocals. "Are you feeling all right?"

"I'm a little frightened," Diana answered, thinking—Big lie. "And I don't know what to do."

William stood upright. "What to do about what?"

Diana sighed and committed herself. "About Melissa. And Michael. I don't know the right . . . songs. Will someone teach me?"

Emily laid her hand on Diana's. "Why are you talking this way? I thought you already decided."

"Not really. I've decided now."

Diana caught faintly a gathering of thoughts between the three old people, like hearing telephone wires humming on a windless day. Doris then spoke.

"There is much for us to do then. Many songs and prayers must be sung over you, to give you strength. We know of several men and women who are beginning to learn their medicines and strengths, but they have not seen what you have seen. They have not touched these creatures, what you call vampires. And none are as close to Melissa as you. That is part of why Michael chose you and sent you to us. That is why Emily is back home."

William coughed and spoke from where he was standing, by the stove. "We must sing in ceremony this day, Diana. Emily will guide you and shield you from one of our most powerful chants. Even though you are not Navajo, you will do good, *shi'yazhi*. I know you will bring back the captive girl. I understand some of your fears, but maybe not too much. I'm an impatient old man, and you must forgive me."

Emily patted Diana's hand and spoke. "My oldest sister, when I was small, taught me things that her grandfather taught to her. Old Navajo prayers that I have taught to William and to Michael. Songs we have kept to ourselves all these years. They are powerful songs and dangerous if mistakes are made—or if you have no faith. My dear, I think that you have faith. I have thought about you since I first met you, held you in my prayers. I have decided, too. I will teach you our old medicine. To keep in your heart forever. I know, in the time we've been together, you have thought seriously about things. Now, you say you have decided. I believe you."

Diana felt as if a great weight had been lifted from her mind. "I have done a lot of thinking. I'm glad you believe me, Emily."

"I won't say that you'll be all right, dear," Emily said. "For these coming days, we will not have left the old days when our warriors fought and were killed. Not just with the white soldiers, but with all of our enemies and the evil creatures that hunted us. My sister told me, when I used to sit on her knee, that I must never forget my grandparents, what they prayed about, and how they died. I didn't forget."

Doris was weeping steadily, holding a handkerchief under her glasses to wipe her tears. Her weeping and the fire in the stove were the only sounds in the massive house. A wave of comforting heat washed through Diana. She felt as if she had come home.

"What do I have to do?" Diana asked.

William, pausing in a chant, switched off the truck's battered radio.

"The sun will not show himself today," he said.

Diana glanced at him and saw a bemused light in his eyes. She didn't question him; she was trying to keep her mind filled with the song he had been singing. A precarious light shifted in the cab as the pickup truck glided swiftly across a snow-covered sea. Diana wondered if she might be warmer walking outside. She opened the window and was immediately hit by tremors of freezing air. She rolled the window up a bit and held her hand out to the wind, which seemed to tug at her fingers.

"Always remember the wind," William said. "You are one of his own. You have breathed him inside you. Look for him in the ends of your toes and in your fingertips. He is all around inside of you. He is speaking to you right now. Listen to him."

Diana was only partly listening. Stark images of the murdered girl she and Michael had found bludgeoned her eyes. Tears squeezed out of them, and she tasted warm salty water on her lips. The unknown girl still remained nameless. No one seemed to know to whom she belonged. And more nameless mutilated bodies had been found since Diana had left Albuquerque.

Diana shook her head and listened to William.

"This is one chant that goes to the Whirling Logs part of the story . . ."

More words followed, but her whole attention was caught by that sentence. She tuned everything else out.

Whirling logs. And a chant to their part of the story.

Diana idly frizzed her hair, trying to raise sparks. It was something she had done as a child, a kind of nervous disorder, she supposed. She changed her position on the sprung, uneven seat. The passing snow made her want to fill it with some kind of wild color.

"They're not human, are they," she finally said.

"Navajo witches are human. Skinwalkers are evil humans. They eat stew and fried bread just like you and me. The Holy Ones are not human. They don't understand us people too well; or maybe too much. Coyote is one of our greatest teachers, yet I don't consider him to be human. But his stories are about people. He knows about us and teaches us the good and bad of our ways. I think these vampires that have stolen Melissa are to be respected, as we respect the Holy Ones and Coyote; even though we fear the vampires and hate them."

A thought almost popped out of her lips, but Diana kept it close and examined it as the truck slowed and descended into a yellow, high-walled canyon.

Did Melissa hate and fear what she had become?

Around mid-morning, they rattled to a stop. Diana emerged from the truck, wrestled shut the hollowed-out door, then slipped and fell into the snow. Muted laughter bounced among the canyon walls. Unruffled, Diana picked herself up and swatted the snow off her jeans. She looked up. A hundred yards away, a circular structure sat almost unseen below a rocky knoll. Blue smoke spiraled out of a smokehole in the center of the domed roof. A hogan, she remembered from Michael's description. Two men were walking toward her. As they came closer, she saw that one was younger than the other, about high school age, and had long hair tied in a ponytail. The other man wore a denim jacket and a tall, black cowboy hat; he carried a short-barrelled shotgun slung over one shoulder.

"What's going on?" Diana asked William, who had dropped down the tailgate and had begun unloading supplies.

"Those are my nephews," he said. "Harrison and Peter. They will help us with the ceremony."

"I meant with the gun."

William paused. "Harrison is here to protect us from any witches who might disturb our sing. When you fall into the song, you are wide open for attack."

The two came around the other side of the truck to help William. Peter, the younger one, smiled winsomely at Diana, briefly shook her hand, then lifted a box of potatoes and pans and began lugging it to the hogan.

"Came as quick as I could," the other one said; Harrison. "Blew in ahead of the winter storms."

Diana kept her gaze on Harrison's hand—blocky and hard—as it gently held hers. "Thank you," she said.

Diana paused in front of the hogan's doorway, where sand the color of the canyon walls had been shaped into a small mound. Feathers tied to sticks decorated the crest, along with strips of animal fur and a stubby piece of wood wrapped with string. The doorstep had been cleared of snow, and the Navajo blanket that covered the entrance was tatty but colorful.

Emily was kneeling on a rug at the other side of the cozy, circular room, laying out small objects on the blue silk blouse Diana had given her earlier, as an offering. Emily wore a woven wool dress patterned in a single red and black stripe, which left her arms bare, and a wide sash around her waist. A turquoise-colored shawl covered her bare legs. Her white hair was loose around her shoulders and she seemed younger somehow. The patchy grayness in her face had vanished, replaced by healthy color. Her cheeks had become more rounded. Her eyes, still covered in milky-white clouds, were less sunken and seemed to see things. It certainly looked to Diana as if the old woman was studying the objects before she placed them on the blouse.

They were the only people in the hogan. Diana hesitated in the entrance, wondering if she should take off her shoes. The floor was hard-packed dirt. She looked at the hole in the ceiling above the potbellied stove and watched smoke streaming into a dark sky.

"Emily, are William and the others going to stay outside all day?"

"They have to watch for enemies," Emily said, not looking up from her task. "They'll come in to sing, when they are needed."

Diana touched the curved wall, which was made up of interlocked, smoothed logs. "What's going to happen first?"

"We must purify you for the chant. I have already finished the sandpainting."

"Sandpainting?"

"We don't have much time." Emily smiled, picked up a coffee can, and dipped it into a five-gallon tank next to her. Over one knee lay a long strip of yellow-white material. "Come in now, *shi'yazhi*. I want to tell you a story."

Fifty-four

The door under Michael's fingertips vibrated like the leaf of an aspen tree blown in a winter wind. His entire body shook in sympathy. He could hardly summon the courage to push open the door. He finally stepped into a white apartment. A pale sun flew over Albuquerque, but the curtains in this room were pulled shut and taped down, as if night lived here. Michael closed the door gently and waited in a moaning darkness. Light crept around the edges of the curtains after a time, and he was suddenly on the snowy slopes of Mount Taylor, the trees around him lit only by starlight. He moved to the soft outlines of a lamp and groped for a switch but stopped himself before turning it on. It was soothing to imagine that he truly was on Mount Taylor just before dawn, listening to the pines and thumps of falling snow.

He hesitated, too frightened to move further.

All day, he had waited for some kind of sign that would lead him to the skinwalker's home. He had watched a patch of morning sun making its circuit across the old office floor. He had not slept or daydreamed, yet he had suddenly stood up and began walking. The old theater, where Michael had taken little Sarah to see running horses and where he himself had seen singing, shooting cowboys on a white screen, was now a shadowy, echoing cavern. Red carpet cushioned his footsteps. Longhorn steer skulls watched him quizzically from the ceilings. Tiny, faint images of Monster Slayer and Child of the Water, the twin sons of Changing Woman, painted under one passing lamp on the wall.

His vision guided him. He eased his legs down cement stairs and switched on the flashlight that Elizabeth had left under his cot. A circle swept before him, revealing yellowed posters, rooms with mirrors and more mirrors, all kinds of odd junk. He came to a concrete room filled with bundled cables and pipes, steel boxes and humming electrical works. Dust fell onto his hands as he shifted aside an iron girder made to look solid and immovable. Then he crept in darkness for hours, it seemed, until he came against a small door. Michael steadied his flashlight, then turned the knob.

The room he entered was private and dark. He was reminded of the odd roomlike openings in the walls of tamarisk down by the wash near his sheepcamp. In the flashlight beam, he saw a candle sitting in a dish in the center of the floor. A search through his pockets turned up matches, and he lit the candle. Old movie and circus posters surrounded him. Silks hung on strings created a blue sky with puffy clouds and a demure sun. A chair and bureau of dark, inky wood stood across from him. A propped mirror sent back a dusty, ghostly image of himself. The only other piece of furniture was a small couch. At first glance, Michael had thought a shawl was draped across the cushions. Then he realized someone was wrapped in the cloth, asleep.

Her solemn face illuminated by candle flame, her head resting on a cotton lace pillow, Elizabeth slept on, without breath or movement, for many silent minutes. Michael kneeled next to her and touched her shoulder, to wake her. Her skin was so cold it burned his fingers.

Michael pulled a chair over and sat. He remembered that Margaret's coffin had been sleek and shiny, like the darting airplanes that often raced above the sheepcamp. The massive thing had been solid and strange. What was Margaret doing in it? Get out! he had wanted to shout, all during the wake and funeral. Come home! This isn't a place for the both of us.

"Margaret liked the old Navajo stories. Stories of Changing Woman and her twin sons. I think she wanted more children, but something happened in her belly after Sarah was born. I don't remember what exactly. Only that it was a creeping, hurting thing."

Michael placed his flashlight on the floor and shifted in the chair, making himself more comfortable as he spoke to Elizabeth.

" 'Tell me how Changing Woman protected her babies from the enemy monsters,' Margaret used to ask in an angry voice. I don't know why she was so angry. All the time, she was angry. Maybe, I was angry then too. Two angry young people.

"*Ayaah'ah!* that's not a story to bring out in anger,' I would tell her. 'Quit thinking that way about things. Angry. It will bring in the bad out of the dark.' I was right. When Margaret wanted to hear that story, I could hear Changing Woman's lies to the monsters who would eat her sons if they found them, good tricks she used to protect her sons: 'I made these prints in the sand with the heel of my hand' Changing Woman said. 'You monsters have eaten all the children. Now, I am lonely. I make these tracks in the sand and think there are many children running and laughing around my home.'

"I think I believed that Margaret's wanting that story would bring the monsters back, start them to breathing in our home. I got scared, for there was no one to kill them off anymore. But I was young, and didn't know things too well then."

Michael smiled and leaned to Elizabeth. "Those monsters sure were stupid. They believed they were so powerful that they could kill all the children."

He massaged his sore knees. Who had Elizabeth talked to, he wondered. Who had sat in this chair? Who had she listened to?

Michael sought Elizabeth's cold hand. "Can you hear me? Maybe, if I keep talking, the words will give you dreams to watch and listen to. Maybe that is the way with your kind. 'That is the way of Sleeping Woman,' Emily once told me when I was a young man. 'Even though she is made of earth and stone, she listens.'

" 'Go to her, my grandson,' Emily would say. 'Go to Sleeping Woman below Red Rocks Coming Together and tell her your story. Sing her your songs, *ba'ba'ah*. She will help you to remember them. And she will enjoy listening to you.'

"So some days when I was herding, I would sit above the valley where Sleeping Woman lay, and I would tell her the stories I had learned. Emily was right. She helped me to remember them."

Michael rubbed Elizabeth's hand, to warm it. He tucked the shawl tighter around her shoulders.

"I say all this to you now, Elizabeth, because I want to tell you my warrior name. But I don't think it is proper if I tell it. You are my enemy. The sister and woman of my enemy. The enemy of my children. The song of my hunt tells me that I must destroy you. Yet, I have brought no weapons with me. I have only brought you the name that was given to me when I was small and hunting with my father, with only the pine trees and deer to listen. I know you will understand its life. And I know that you will remember it always, even after I am gone."

The door to Elizabeth's room squeaked open. A slight breeze touched the back of Michael's neck. He turned around and saw the standing sharp-nosed coyote staring at him from the darkness beyond the candle light, grinning with yellow teeth.

"Come, my grandson," it said, "We have a long journey to make. And we are both of us old and creaking. . ."

Michael removed his pouch of corn pollen from his jacket pocket. He unsheathed his knife, wet his thumb on his tongue, and rubbed the blade with his saliva. Then, remembering his warrior name, he walked into the throat of a dark hallway, which swallowed him like the entrance to a mountain forest.

Fifty-five

Patches of skin on Diana's face itched where Emily had applied paint. She was standing near the center of the hogan next to a rectangular bed of red coals, wearing a skirt borrowed from Emily and nothing else. The room shimmered with heat waves. Diana touched her face, where broad stripes of yellow lay across her chin, blue across her nose and cheeks, black across her eyes, and white across her forehead and parts of her bangs. The paint seemed to be crawling over her skin.

"Don't rub off the paint," Emily said. "It will dry soon." She continued painting a sinuous figure on Diana's left foot; a stylized snake, to match the one on her right foot.

"I have learned to do this ceremony," Emily said, "but I have not heard of these vampires before. So I must make good my memory and change some things of this chant for it to work against them. What my sister taught me is very old. Much of what the other Navajos do has changed. I don't know what songs they sing now, but this one is powerful medicine when it is done correctly. There is another chant, which is almost forgotten among the Navajos. That one I know better, but it will wait. In it is the reason we Navajos must pay for our healings, which you must hear. And I have changed things to protect both of us. For with this chant you must be purified properly. This I have not done for we are in a hurry. But the Holy Ones will purify you after your work is completed. That is what I promised to them. I say this now, so that you will come back and finish it properly. Now, sit here and face the doorway."

Diana touched the area between her breasts. A blue circle was painted on the skin, with stripes the same colors as on her face radiating outward, over her shoulders and across her waist, until they met in another circle on her back, a white circle, Emily had explained, representing the moon.

"The moon will help us in the hunt," she had said.

Diana lifted her arms and quietly studied the designs on the insides of her elbows: Thunderclouds.

Emily took a pinch of herbs from a pouch and sprinkled it over the coals. She hummed quietly as she watched the ceremonial fire. Diana furtively touched her painted face, which had begun to tingle. She felt light, suspended in space. Dizzy, she closed her eyes. Images swooped past, looping gracefully like iridescent hummingbirds.

"I see something in you," Emily said cautiously. "Woven threads around you, colorful ones, flying out the doorway. It is how your visions are traveling."

Diana opened her eyes. Emily waited.

"I didn't like to cook when I was married," Diana said. "I liked more the idea that I was cooking for someone else besides me or my grandparents. That what I was creating with my hands and imagination was sustaining a stranger; who happened to be a man. Like having a baby, I guess." Diana closed her eyes. "I'm remembering all these things, now, and they seem to be good thoughts. Does that make any sense, Emily?"

Tiny wisps of purple flame danced across the coals, like waterspouts touching the surface of an ocean. Diana's eyelids began to droop from the pulsing heat waves. Then a loud cracking sound woke her up. Diana thought someone had broken a piece of firewood. She looked up and saw a middle-aged woman wearing a woven dress similar to Emily's standing in the doorway. Her graying hair was tied back in a solemn ponytail. The woman beckoned Diana to follow. Without thought of Emily, or of the snow, Diana rose and followed.

The sun was a white orb in a turquoise sky. The snow had disappeared, replaced by yellow grasses rippling in a breeze. Diana walked further, until she came to a place where heat waves were hung like rugs made of water, where a mirrored lake swallowed distant sand dunes and mesas. Diana couldn't see the woman clearly anymore. Only her curved, white earrings were vivid. They looked to be made of shell. The woman spoke.

"Eye Killer didn't let me say goodbye to my daughter. I would wish that I could kill him with my bare hands. But that is a truth which needs proper healing. I can't kill the monster now."

Diana's face began to ache. "You chose the wrong person," she said. "I know who you are."

"Water is all around us, teacher, though it isn't raining. Be my child now and listen to me. Eye Killer ambushed me and killed me. I had forgotten my warrior name, and I paid for it. But I saw something in his body that was weak. The old Salt Woman is shaping good weapons. You must carry them to Eye Killer's home. Do not doubt them. Guard them, as Changing Woman guarded her children, and they will remember why they were born a long time ago."

Diana bowed her head. She couldn't look into the woman's eyes. "What if I mess everything up?"

"You won't, if you remember your warrior name."

"I don't have one."

"The sun house colors flowing on your body will help you to remember it. You are carrying the sun and moon. You will carry the Warrior Twins. Be respectful of them, for they are powerful beings."

The woman stepped closer and touched Diana's hand with gentle longing. Diana saw her clearly now, saw where Melissa's fierce, dark eyes had come from.

"My daughter is far away from me. You must explain to her why I went away. You must tell my little girl that I love her. She is crying for me, and I cannot help her. Please, teacher. Help my little girl to come home."

Diana's feet began to tread by themselves. She moved silently through rainbows and fountains of gushing, clear water. The woman's figure became blurred and small, but her voice remained strong.

"Tell my daughter to look for me in the soft rain when it stands beside her home, for I will be in it."

Diana opened her hand and saw the necklace in her palm. A reminder of the enemy facing her.

"Eye Killer," she whispered.

Outside the hogan, the wind was trying to force its way inside. Tiny spats of dust drummed against her cheek. She tried to change her position, but she was too tired. William handed Diana a white buckskin bundle.

"These are the warriors you must carry," he said. "Unwrap them."

"Like this, dear," Emily said, helping her.

Diana unrolled the bundle as Emily showed her until two

flattened sticks, one black and one blue, each about fourteen inches long, were revealed. Both were heavy and thick in her hands. The ends of each stick were sharpened into a flat blade, and both were decorated with a similar white-shafted arrow, except one had a yellow and white feathered end and the other had two white feathered ends. The sticks' wood was silken, as if they had each been handled for many years.

"These two prayersticks were shaped long ago by Emily's grandfather. This is what her older sister told her. They traveled with the Navajos to Hweeldi, but decided to stay here. We don't know why. So Emily kept them at Madrecita; she kept them a secret for all these years. They passed to Emily when her sister died and now they will pass on to you. In your hands, they will become warriors to fight Eye Killer. These prayersticks carry songs with them. I didn't remember them too well; Emily helped me with the words. I will give you one song now, to keep. Listen to the words well. Put them next to your heart. Make them your words."

The old man leaned back and clasped his hands in his lap. His skin was so red in the firelight, he seemed to have vanished into the dark log walls of the hogan. Diana listened as he began to sing. The melody was intricate and reminded her of morning sunlight flowing through juniper trees and over boulders blanketed in snow, changing the shadows from black to raging white. She cradled the prayersticks in her trembling arms, held them close, kept them secure. Tears welled in her eyes, changing the bed of coals into a red sun. The paint on her face began to itch again, but she remained still. She listened and memorized the prayersticks' song. Her mouth struggled around the Navajo words. Her heart swelled with the song's deepening beat. Blood pounded in her body, forced her to stand, frightening her, as if it had never happened before.

Fifty-six

Michael walked in a mountain forest until he came to three doorways hung among spectral pine trees and lit by pre-dawn starlight.

"The girl is four grounds up," the coyote had told Michael as it had led him to this building. "Behind a kind of door I have never seen before. Evil rests there, my grandson. More powerful than skinwalkers. Eye Killers. Go up as if you were hunting on dried pine needles. Wash the girl as you have done before, when she was a baby, with this." The coyote gave Michael a bundle of yucca root. "Be strong, prepare her, and I promise to take her home with me, without fail."

Heart frozen, Michael walked to each door, touched the painted wood, until his fingers trembled at the last door. He took the pollen pouch from his breast pocket, untied the drawstrings, and sprinkled corn pollen onto his palm. He opened the door. An angry cold bit him as if it were a living creature. Michael swung the door wide.

Across from him, a small figure was lying on a silvery bed of ice. Still holding the corn pollen in the bowl of his palm, Michael walked to the bed and stood over it. The small girl lay quiet, eyes closed as if she were sleeping, almost blending into the folds of ice. She was on her back, arms at her sides, and her long black hair was tied in a ponytail which snaked over her throat. Michael touched her sunken eyes and the bony ridge of skull under the sagging cheeks. Not a girl, but a dead woman.

"My daughter, I have found you."

Sarah's gray skin seemed to ripple under the faint light as Michael removed his denim jacket and lifted his medicine bundle from around his neck. Suddenly, he saw the morning sun flickering above vivid pine trees. He was climbing Mount Taylor again, and somehow he had found a rushing stream. His little girl kneeled beside him and watched him work. Michael smiled as the yucca root lathered in his fingers.

283

"I haven't yet told you, *shi'yazhi*, how I am going to make a cradleboard for Melissa's first child. I will find its planks here, on the back of Mount Taylor, settle beside this stream, and carve the wood gently. Make it soft.

"'There, granddaughter,' I will say to Melissa when I show it to her. 'This is a good cradleboard. Once, the back boards and the footrest were made of sunbeam—the glow of the sun from after a gentle rain. I can't do work like that. But it will be strong enough to hold your firstborn.'"

Michael felt a gentle touch of wind on his face. He unwound Sarah's hair and began to wash it with yucca root and clear water.

"And then, I will curve the arch of the cradleboard under my fingers. It should be made of rainbow, but I don't know where to find that. I made a cradleboard for you, *shi'yazhi*, a long time ago. It was the first and the best one. Margaret was happy with it. But now that I have knowledge with me, I will make an older one for Melissa. I will find a rainbow, from somewhere. And the lacings will be zigzag lightning, as they should be. But I don't know where I will find them. I don't know where to look . . ."

Around him, the morning-lit pine trees vanished into winter clouds. The stream at his knees iced over, covered his hands in white, swept up his arms, swallowed his body. Michael saw a swollen, blackened cut across his daughter's gray throat, just under her jawline. He stared as the yucca root lather crept into her scalp, under the hair roots; he frowned as a dark fluid ran across the ice. He lifted her cold body and cradled her.

"When Melissa's baby is born, we will wrap it kicking and crying in the blankets that were given to the Navajos. The blankets of beautiful darkness, of dawn, of blue day sky, of yellow evening light, and of sunlight. The baby's pillows will be of mirage and of heat. Melissa's baby will sleep under their protection."

Michael settled Sarah on the ice. He lifted his medicine bundle and untied it. He chose a flat, black stone and a white arrowhead from the pile. Then he retied the buckskin.

"These I found when I was a boy herding my grandmother's sheep. The flint I will leave with you, *shi'yazhi*, to shield you against any monster's weapons. This white arrowhead, which

Margaret and I found sitting on a sand hill, will protect you from all lightning. I don't know if there is lightning where Grandfather Coyote will take you, but keep it anyway. Beside your heart."

Michael placed them, one each, in Sarah's stiffened hands; he curled her fingers around them as best he could.

"Sarah, go to sleep now. Sun's jewel and turquoise arrow I don't have with me. It is said that the Warrior Twins memorized the arrow's name, before the four were taken back to the sky. I was given a part of that arrow's name. Here, I will make you the pattern of it, and give you its name, *shi'yazhi*, in a circle around you; to protect you on your last journey."

In an hour, Michael was finished. His fingers ached from the concentrated work. The intricate, whirling circle he had drawn on the carpet flickered softly as if filled with white flames. He watched the light shift like water waves on his daughter's corpse, now covered with a fine drift of yellow corn pollen, all that had remained in his pouch.

The room's door squeaked open, gaped wide like a grinning mouth. Three shadow figures moved in, surrounded Michael.

Eye Killers.

The tallest of them smiled redly.

"Well, old stone, shall we go to it?"

Fifty-seven

Deep inside her jacket, Diana held the prayerstick bundle tight against her stomach as she picked a safe trail down a snowy slope.

"Are we in any danger from . . ." Diana couldn't say the words. "Is there any danger here?"

285

Up ahead, Emily stepped purposefully through the snow, her form almost blending into the shadowed juniper and piñon trees.

"This is one of our sacred places," Emily said. "Most of the Keresans and the three of us Navajos know about this place we're going to, but it's kept secret among us. You're not allowed to show anybody this place until they've been purified by ceremony. You are with us now, Diana. That's a good thing, and requires your respect and strength. You must keep the animals of the land sacred in your heart. Respect them always. Don't lie to them, for they will know the truth. The land is ours to live on, but the animals are the true guardians of it."

The wash they now followed snaked into a narrowing canyon. Juniper branches brushed their shoulders. Diana took a clump of snow off one branch, packed it tightly, and nibbled at it. Her stomach growled. She finished and gathered snow off another branch to snack on. The canyon walls closed in rapidly. Diana touched wet stone walls and had to follow behind Emily instead of walk beside her. Now there was no snow along the floor of the wash. Deep sand slowed their steps. Diana looked above the darkening walls and saw orange-black clouds in a jagged strip of sky. The cold air soothed her eyes. She felt as if cedar woodsmoke had been ground into her skin permanently—a mark that separated her from the rest of the world.

Then Diana smelled something so out of place yet familiar that she hesitated before moving on. "What is it we're coming to?" she asked.

Emily didn't answer, continued humming quietly to herself. Diana ceased to worry. If Emily had heart enough to walk and sing, they were both doing okay. Diana followed the old woman without asking any more questions.

An image came to her: The ocean. Diana sniffed the breeze. Definitely salty. They passed through narrowing turns then came out into an open space surrounded by close canyon rock. Across from them and almost hidden among dense boulders, Diana saw a glowing cave. The ground at its entrance had been scooped out to form a wide, shallow bowl. And almost seventy feet up, the sandstone ridge had been eroded naturally into a gouge through which rainwater—

when it rained—could spout and fall into the bowl at Diana's feet.

A small fire murmured on her right as Diana entered the cave. The fire-lit walls were rough and of a type of grayish rock different from the canyon sandstone. The cave itself was the size of a two-car garage. Inset into the center of the floor was a circular pool of water two feet across. Diana kneeled and touched the steaming, bubbling water. Green algae covered miniature shores and felt soft and vibrating, like the fur of a purring cat.

Emily sat on a boulder that had obviously been brought here. Deep niches had been carved into the rock and several of the higher niches held wrapped bundles.

"Emily, it's beautiful," Diana said, not moving from the spring. The cave was all so wondrously conceived, she wanted to kneel here forever.

The old woman smiled. "I haven't been here since I went into the old folks' home to stay. My eyes are getting so bad; I wanted to come here before my sight goes away for good. And before I die. The Mother is good company for old people."

Diana wiped her moist fingers on her jeans. "The Mother?"

"She is behind you."

The cave entrance, by nature or by human hands, had been fashioned into a perfect circle. Outside, the cloud bottoms were tinged with a dusky red glow. Her gaze was drawn back to the cave entrance. The gray wall on the right, opposite the intense spot of fire, held a series of regular markings like magic runes. Diana stood up and moved closer. A pattern began to emerge.

Stretching fifteen feet across and almost stepping out of the wall was the fossil outline of a prehistoric creature. Shaped into a humpbacked turtle, with all of its dark-brown bones and joints vividly preserved and distinguishable, the fossil seemed to be swimming inside the rock. The stubby tail was curled around a group of small, smudged blobs almost at ground level. Diana couldn't make them out clearly, and she kneeled down.

The delicate shapes were tiny replicas of the fossilized Mother. Four of them lay snuggled within the Mother's protective embrace, as if the family had decided to nap for a hundred million years.

"Babies," Diana whispered, touching their bared grins and tracing the Mother's armor plates. "Fossil babies with their mother."

"The land was different back then," Emily said, coming next to Diana. "There were no people, the elders say, when these animals were walking and breathing. But there were children and grandparents. Brothers and sisters. Fathers and mothers. I think there was love then, too."

Diana became aware of the prayerstick bundle pressing into her middle. She reached for the old woman's wizened hand.

"Newborn . . . ," she said.

The wind threw silvery particles around her feet, tugged playfully at her jacket. Diana huddled against it as she stumbled along an arch of dense snow. She remembered the wind's touch from inside the hogan; the wind was male, she knew. His strength was brutal. She would tell this to Emily, if she saw the old woman again.

Hands planted over the hump on her stomach, Diana struggled on. Ice rained against her painted face, soothed her aching bruise. Tendrils of hair, which escaped from under her woolen cap, seemed drenched in woodsmoke, and the smell made her feel warmer. Diana removed her gloves and touched the snow. It was gem hard and prickly on her fingertips.

"It's not so cold," Diana said to the wind, putting her gloves back on, adjusting her cap. She continued walking. Ignored, the wind bellowed among the lonely junipers.

Diana stopped on the crest of a low hill. Waves of snow washed around her, colored a ghostly blue when the moon appeared for brief moments through cracks in the clouds. Diana felt stranded on an ocean of ice, many millions of miles from any human beings, and she reveled in the sensation.

"No, not sense dead," she said to herself, to the junipers, to the warm hump under her hands. "Not a fish steak, either."

Just . . . waiting.

Diana topped another hill. Away to her left towered a dark rock face, several hundred feet high; moonlit clouds were piled on its sandstone ridge. This mesa extended south for a bit, then curved away eastward, toward regions unseen. Diana recognized the oil-tanker shape: Mesa Gigante.

How many times had Michael seen this view? she wondered. Had he ever shared it with anyone? Diana stood as still as her sore body would allow and watched her breath curling in fragile plumes. Of course, he had seen it with Margaret. Maybe they had walked in the moonlight, to scare away predators from the sheep, or to find lost lambs. Or maybe they had walked here simply because it was so beautiful.

Diana looked down into a shallow valley. A drift of snow lapped at her hiking boots, foamy silent tides urging her out into an open sea. She pointed to a thin trail along the valley floor. Right there, she thought. Diana could imagine Michael and Margaret walking together, talking, moving with a simple grace. Two people who had grown old together. The deep night would be familiar to them, nothing scary or sad.

Michael tried to tell me that, I think.

This precise moment in time was suddenly vaguely familiar. Had Michael described it before? His stories had been full of distant things she couldn't really remember, until she found herself in a similar place or situation, like dreams that wake you up laughing or crying-sad with tears on your pillow, and you can't remember why. It felt as if Michael's stories, their hidden ingredients, were sitting deep inside and waiting for the proper song to set them free.

Wind whispered. "What are they, teacher?"

Diana answered out loud as if a person had spoken: "They are the memories of those people or places we once loved that have passed away, caught from another world or plane of reality, and shared out now in painfully small doses."

A breeze lifted her hair. Diana touched her head. She had lost her cap somewhere. The growing wind became insistent, hard. It pushed against her, as if urging her toward the mesa.

She unzipped her father's jacket partway. The wind's strong hands reached inside and almost lifted her off the ground. His breath tickled on her exposed throat. Diana's hair billowed. Her sweater, filling with rushing air, fluttered along her nipples, her breasts, her waist.

"Run with me."

"Where?" Diana asked.

She let the wind enter through her mouth. He swept into her lungs, and her chest widened to accommodate the large volume of thrusting air. Her leg muscles twitched. In an instant, she was running.

This is nuts, her brain warned. Remember the rabbit holes and hidden trees ready to break your legs? Diana, stop this!

The thoughts annoyed her, and she shut them up. Then she realized she was no longer alone.

Diana stopped and listened. In the distance rose a faint, ululating cry—like a lonely, weeping, fairy-tale goblin. Several more voices joined in from various directions surrounding her.

"Are they dangerous?" she asked. "Should we stop for them?"

"Wait, they are coming."

Diana stared westward, in the direction of the first cry, and saw a bushy-tailed, doglike animal prancing across the snow. As she watched, several more of the bouncy creatures swooped in to join the first. They barked happily to each other, as if in greeting, then began running in tandem toward her.

"Who are they?" Diana backed away.

"Race them!"

A flare of energy burst from her heart to her legs and she began to run. The twin prayersticks clicked together under her jacket. Soon, the animals caught up and ran alongside her. Diana heard their panting breaths and soft paws thudding into the snow. Every once in a while, one of them would utter a small, excited yip as if they were laughing. Diana recognized them now.

Wind roared in her ears, which began to ache from the cold. But if she covered them, she would lose her balance, fall, and lose the race. Snow-sheeted land flew under her feet as she ran faster. The revealed moon flickered in her eyes as she leaped from hilltop to hilltop. She knew, though it was not possible, that her running feet were no longer touching the ground. The landscape flattened out. The sparse scattering of junipers became dots below her. I-40 appeared like a brightly jewelled necklace across the snow. In a short while, she was able to glimpse the flat top of Mesa Gigante itself. Diana kept her gaze on the falling landscape, ignoring all pain, and was just barely conscious of the coyotes racing beside her.

Fifty-eight

Elizabeth emerged from her theater's secret door into the alley and pressed her back to the frame, hesitating. Behind her, vibrating into her bones, shaking them apart, rumbled percussion and electronic instruments. The alley seemed almost like a stage itself with the bits of wood and broken bottles arranged to send sparkles of light across the enclosing walls; and the debris carefully sprayed over with a surreal, corpse-colored spraypaint.

Darkness prodded her into the street. Her thoughts were disarrayed. She couldn't concentrate well enough to fly, so she ran, following sun-lit memories stirred by a strange, unknown wind. A line of graves stretched out across a bleak, gray land; headstones had been beaten into the dust, carved inscriptions worn away by wind and sand. Elizabeth felt herself turning into a husk of dried corn, and she ran blindly. But the images needled into her skull, pricked at her brain: All the graves had been dug open, the sand strewn about as if the ground had exploded, dust swirling among deep walls—all the graves were empty of corpses.

Elizabeth suddenly knew where Michael was, whom he was with. She passed muted streetlamps and clicking traffic lights until she came against a sagging chain-link fence. She grasped gauzy diamonds, felt them collapse in her hands, as she stared at the abandoned school building.

"No," she whispered.

"Sister, we expected you sooner."

Hanna's voice sifted from one of the topmost windows like glass dust. Elizabeth heard a man's wavering breaths and the murky sounds of shallow lung pulls; she heard the ghostly echoes of pounding feet, children's nursery chants and bright laughter. The fence began to tinkle under her hands, then fell silent as Elizabeth stormed into the building.

She ascended rotting stairwells. A dank mist rolled along the corridors. Elizabeth found the large classroom from which Hanna had spoken and searched for possible exits and weapons. Broken glass wove about her feet. Across the room, a streaked mirror reflected the tattered ceiling.

"Now, Elizabeth Mary, we can finally sit and talk."

Hanna emerged from the darkness as if it were a fall of black water. Elizabeth didn't answer. She tried to pierce the hanging smoke to find Michael. She wanted to scream his name.

"Where's Michael?" Elizabeth said. "Why did you bring him here?"

"Why does the moon do anything?" Hanna's porcelain-white face broke into a smile. "You've been so distant these nights. I wanted to get your attention."

"You have it. Now, speak!"

Elizabeth blocked the invisible fingers worming against her brain, seeking doors of entrance into her mind. There were always unguarded ways, Elizabeth thought. Secret passages. She searched for her own weaknesses, to secure them, before Hanna could find them and exploit them.

"Where is Falke?" Hanna's giggle cut into the darkness like spears of acid light. "Your husband."

"I thought he was with you. I thought you two had removed yourselves from the world like true lovers."

"Sister. Always the romantic. Love is sweet tragedy, isn't it? We women all find ourselves slaves to it."

"I don't see anyone fawning at your knees, *sister*. What would you know about love?"

The groping tentacles of Hanna's mind-force vanished. Elizabeth swayed dizzily from their release, and from the force of energy she had used to keep them out.

"I know love as a powerful web," Hanna said. "A soothing narcotic. The final lie."

"You're the final lie, Hanna."

Hanna's impassive, almost sad, face flushed, but not with anger. She burst into raucous peals of laughter. "Oh, I like that! I'm the final lie. You make me sound like the devil himself!"

"I'm not flattering you."

"No?" Hanna pouted. "Then how is the old man, your lover?"

"He's not my lover."

"Isn't he? No man ever sang me any songs. And no man ever built me any dollhouses either. I might've filled them for you, too, if I had wanted. And I will! An army of slaves to worship your pretty feet."

Elizabeth shook her head, taunting. "I can't see any sense in what you're saying, Hanna. Is this how a warrior speaks? With words like silly mice scampering in the snow?"

Hanna chuckled. "The two of you make such a pathetic couple. You, the estranged young wife; and he, the demented adulterer."

Elizabeth shuddered in desperation. "You wanted to talk, so talk!"

"I will offer you nothing, Elizabeth. Your wistful human existence has come to its end."

The glow of the outside world's streetlamps, headlights, living room lamps, rained upon Hanna. Her black leather dress glimmered dully, as if made of iron. Elizabeth hugged herself. Her laugh sounded strained to her own ears.

"Am I supposed to wait for my destruction?" Elizabeth said. "I won't make it easy for you."

"But you have, sweet sister!" Hanna laughed, delighted. "Love drew you to him. The trap is sprung! You walked straight into it, both eyes open."

Hanna pointed to the doorway. Elizabeth fell back, then stopped. Three figures entered the classroom—two pale women holding Michael by his arms. They dragged him across the floor to Hanna and turned his still body toward Elizabeth. His head hung limply. His white shirt, his dancing shirt, was blood-soaked and ripped across his bruised chest. One of the women grasped his hair with a white hand and pulled up his head. Michael's face was gray and caked with blood and broken glass.

"Such easy prey," Hanna said, glaring at Michael. "I don't know why we were so afraid of him."

Michael's hands clenched and he groaned, as if caught in the storm of nightmare.

Elizabeth began to panic. Her mind raced frantically, but along all the old tracks, unable to jump from them. Something beat at her mind, a memory that had covered her over in layers and layers of darkness.

Hanna caressed Michael's throat.

"Let him go." Elizabeth's voice slipped. "Take me instead." 293

"Such a noble woman." Hanna nodded to the two women. "These are Rachel and Jenny. New to our way of existence. I shaped them with my own heart, sister."

Michael's chest began to heave. His jaws clenched. He opened his eyes for a moment; like black stones, they swallowed all light. Elizabeth tried to remember other humans and their ailments. All she could remember was how her mother had been wracked with convulsions as she died, how the whole wagon had shaken in sympathy, and how the rain had pounded into the mud and the canvas roof.

"Please . . ." Elizabeth whispered.

The two vampires holding Michael, a slender black woman and a sullen girl with short, purplish-black hair, edged closer to him as if they might crush him with their knees. Michael struggled weakly, not against them. He was fighting something in his mind.

"Let me help him." Elizabeth began to shake. "He's dying."

"Elizabeth." Hanna looked at her. "I will let him live. For as long as he wants, and more . . ."

"What do you *want!*"

"His soul."

Elizabeth's heart twisted. Her hands tightened into useless fists.

"His miserable soul," Hanna said. "And I want you to give it to me. Prove your love, Elizabeth. To both of us. Make him live forever!"

Only one way out . . . for both of us.

Elizabeth's rage withered, leaving her powerless. She felt frail and old. Her eyes ached, but healing tears failed to come. The vampires holding Michael, their completeness, slammed against her as if bolts of lightning were hitting her. Their energy was too powerful. Inhuman. And she was still a little bit human. And weak.

"You'll leave him alone then?" Elizabeth stared at Michael, willing him to look at her and condemn her.

"For all time." Hanna stepped away from Michael. She glanced to the others. "Leave them."

Elizabeth flew the short distance and kneeled at Michael's side. Slivers of glass cut into her knees as she lifted Michael and held him. His medicine bundle dangled between them. Elizabeth tore a strip from her hem and wiped the glass and blood from his forehead and cheeks. Glittering fragments remained embedded in his skin.

"Michael," she whispered hoarsely. Elizabeth drew him against her. His weight was comforting. "Michael, you must listen to me."

"Elizabeth," he said, so faintly, she might have heard his thoughts. "Coyote tricked me. Led me to my dead child, so the monster could catch me." Michael smiled. "I won't trust him again."

"My love, you must sleep. I won't leave you."

His hand found hers. "Listen to the Eye Killer. Save yourself. Even as you are, you remember love. That is your strength."

Tainted, red tears moistened his hand and Elizabeth wiped them away. "Let me save you, Michael." She offered him a smile. "Death is painless."

Michael opened his eyes, and Elizabeth saw clear into a blue sky where the sun flew and wrapped her in hot arms.

"No," he said, sitting up slowly and crossing his legs, Indian style.

Elizabeth squeezed Michael's hand and pulled at it, to help him stand up. Michael turned and gazed into a far corner of the classroom where darkness gathered. Elizabeth wanted to shout—Come away with me! Michael remained sitting.

"I see what you're doing, sister," Hanna said. "I do believe the old man likes my company." Her form moved against the shattered walls, counterclockwise, circling them wolfishly. "Maybe it's my supernatural beauty that stays him. Is that it, old stone? Colder than bones, you will lay, sooner than you expect."

Elizabeth stammered, "Come with me, Michael."

Michael tightened his grip on her hand as he followed Hanna's slow circuit around the room. "Eye Killer wants to talk. I want to hear its words."

Elizabeth relented. She straightened at his side, ignoring her stinging knees, and watched Hanna closely. Hanna smiled ferociously.

"You want to say something to me, old savage? Out with it! Or should I squeeze it from you?"

"I'm the man listening. I have nothing to say."

"A wooden Indian. That's why you don't speak."

Hanna paused, standing over them. Elizabeth noticed a red stain on her right index finger.

"What is it you desire most, old man? Freedom? Room to wiggle your toes?"

Michael said nothing.

"Hold me spellbound with your talk, the way you do with her." Hanna pointed at Elizabeth with the bloody finger. "Babble about your life, the sun dancing in the trees, the stream waters whispering their songs. Yes, old man. I know what my tiresome sister wishes. And the inane shit she loves to hear."

"You teach me," Michael said.

"I know what you really want." Hanna sidled closer.

Elizabeth's fingers tensed into a rigid weapon, a flesh and bone spearhead.

"You want my little sister," Hanna crooned joyfully. "Her innocence! So fragile and vulnerable. And such a pretty, blond head." Hanna stood upright, smiling. "I see Elizabeth as your lover and protector, but remember—she's as evil as Falke and I."

Michael was unmoved. "Teach me your medicine, Hanna. Is it more powerful than my people's?"

"There's no savage's magic harmful to vampires," Hanna said.

"The mountains are worn down by the rain. It is spoken by the Holy Ones. And there are other worlds than this. Other cures."

"And different evils, old man," Hanna said. "We occupy all of them."

"With time, you will die out. Even if you destroy Melissa and Elizabeth and me."

"And Diana? I'll kill her, too. Time creeps like mud. Even the stars will shine differently; I'll still be walking on this planet."

Michael's face hardened. "I'm not a healer of time. I will die soon. But my children, and their children's children, will learn about you, gather the proper medicine, hunt you, and destroy you."

Hanna's voice became grating. "You've forgotten, old man . . . you've got no daughter left."

Glass rattled under him and the room creaked as Michael stood from the floor. Elizabeth absorbed his pain, felt her muscles grinding against razors, felt all the joints in her body turning into knobs of ice, then cracking. Her breath rushed out in dry spurts. Drawn up by Michael's hand, she reached blindly for his arm, to help steady him. But she quickly realized that it was she herself who was being steadied.

Michael's voice speared above Elizabeth's head into the swirling darkness.

"I won't forget Sarah. You're trying hard, ghost of a woman, but you have no power. I'm still not afraid of you."

Elizabeth caught a scent of musty, empty air from Hanna. The scowling vampire grew livid, her form became denser, as if a blanketing cloud of dust had been blown away.

"Michael . . ." Elizabeth said.

Hanna's eyes spouted black fire as she staggered toward him. Before Elizabeth could shield Michael, clawed hands fell on her shoulders and wrenched her away from him. Hanna raked Michael's dancing shirt away with red fingernails. White arms slashed out of the darkness, coiled around him. The vampires holding Elizabeth laughed into her ears as Michael's throat was torn open by canine teeth. An outraged shout blasted against the peeling walls, waking Elizabeth from shock. Blood spewed around her in a hopeless rain, spotting the walls and floor, drenching her arms and dress. Elizabeth looked up. Hanna's mouth gaped wide to catch the red droplets, then fell to the dying man. Held back by crushing hands, Elizabeth reached for Michael, and she shrieked as his life was taken.

Fifty-nine

Diana settled onto the cave's cold sand, listening. Blackness filled her brain. She touched her eyes to make sure they were open and held her hands in front of her face until her arm muscles began to twitch with strain, and still she saw nothing. She tugged at the pocket of her fanny pack and pulled out a flashlight. She covered the glass end with her hand, aimed it down, and switched it on. A spear of light flashed onto her tennis shoes. The rock crystals in the buff-colored sand sparkled. She wiggled her toes.

"Still alive," she whispered, lifting the beam to the low ceiling. The rock there was an orange and black mishmash and seemed to be imprinted over its entire surface with hieroglyphics. Diana stood to get a better look. Not writing, but a whole panorama of fossilized plants. She touched them, felt their sooty outlines; the ghosts of ferns, primitive bulbs, and segmented stalks.

Does anyone know about this cave? Diana lowered the light beam onto the floor, illuminating a wavy, beachlike surface, and began to walk, noting that the smell in the tunnel was a musty kind of odor, like an upstairs attic or the stacks in a library. Something quick and slender squeaked over her feet and skittered away. Diana reached up to muffle her scream and hit her forehead with the flashlight instead. She bit her knuckles to stop a fit of hysterical laughter. After a few minutes of deep breathing, she relaxed.

Diana switched off the light and tried to think. The air seemed to be freeing itself of water; her skin was tightening over her bones. She felt a new bruise forming where the flashlight had hit her. A pale fish darted past her eyes as she reached to massage her forehead. She realized there was a light in the cavern.

A dizzy swoon of terror rushed into her. She dropped the flashlight and clung to the nearest boulder. Breathless, she listened and heard nothing, but stayed under the boulder's shadow anyway; then she closed her eyes and imagined days turning into years and centuries, the formation of fossil ferns and the slow-moving tides of rivers and oceans. Her heart began to throb less wildly. She opened her eyes.

A stealthy, yellow light touched the folds and wrinkles of the cavern ceiling. Diana picked up her flashlight and put it in her jacket pocket, then she stood cautiously, brushed the dust from her jeans and continued forward. She looked back and saw her shadow still crouched into a tight ball. Diana straightened and looked around her. Pinpoint sparks winked along the walls as she moved. Diana placed her hand on one wall to steady herself. Flakes peeled off under her fingers. She began to see more of the cavern as the furtive light became denser. The cavern floor rose into a gentle slope. The deepening sand caught at her feet. Up ahead, the crest of the slope almost touched the lit ceiling.

She hesitated just before she reached the crest. What if there's some kind of a guard watching the entrance? she wondered. And what am I supposed to tell them if they capture me—that I'm lost?

Exhausted and hungry, she staggered up the last couple of yards, then stopped. She groped hurriedly for the nearest wall, lowered herself to the ground, and stared, unbelieving.

Below the crest, the cavern opened into a wide expanse the size of a football field. Ringed along the encircling cavern walls were hundreds of burning lamps. Twinkling dust motes dove and circled in the air just beneath the domed ceiling. The floor was a flat sea of sand extending into a dark distance, and scattered along its surface, rising up like giant gravestones, were open-roof cottages made of gray sandstone. Diana swallowed and her throat clicked in the dry air. The scene was like an expressionist painting of a spare village lost under the foot of forgotten mountains, illuminated by swimming stars. Diana pressed the prayersticks hidden in her jacket for comfort.

All the windows in the cottages faced her, and behind several dainty curtains glowed a steady circle of lamplight, as if nameless people were waiting patiently to welcome her to their home.

Sixty

The half moon, a frozen eye, watched through a window as Elizabeth pushed herself from a corner, where dark walls keened like wounded animals, and crawled across broken ice to the broken corpse. Moonbeams split and wheeled under her fingers. She fell across the body, listened to its chest. Dust motes flew into a bar of light and flamed into ringing crystals, mocking a cavernous silence. The head lolled as she pulled the corpse into her lap. She sifted through icicles on the ground and chose the clearest one. She held her wrist to the light, slashed an artery. Elizabeth knew where all of them lay; she remembered what she had been taught. Black jewels appeared on the corpse's chest and face.

"Michael."

Elizabeth lifted his head to her breast, held her bleeding wrist over his mouth, guided him to the falling stream. She called to him. His dead pupils began to fill with tears, trickling like rain pools forming in stone.

"Drink for me."

Time creeped. She heard a sound like paper rustling and looked down. Michael's eyes closed, blinked open. Elizabeth smiled emptily as his fingers grasped onto her arm. She continued to smile even though it hurt when he began to suckle the blood from her body. To ease their shared pain, she whispered parts of the chant the old Indian man had sung to his grandson on the plain of living ice. The words felt like shifting stones in her mouth. Then Michael began to whisper with her. His fingers loosened and dropped from her wrist. His eyes, glassy black spheres, found her.

"Don't hate me, Michael," she said.

Elizabeth stared at the hunched figure sitting just outside a square of moonlight, and she listened to the glass rattling on the floor.

"Michael. Your eyes have changed. Your heart is different. Even your soul, now, is in a wasteland of darkness."

She moved to him and touched him. His muscles were jerking so violently, she was afraid they might rip themselves apart.

"Hanna drained everything from you. She killed you. And I made you drink corrupted blood. I've betrayed you. You feel as if God's eyes have turned away from you, dearest. I know this."

Michael stirred next to her.

"Hold me," Elizabeth whispered. "Or don't hold me. Stand away, or take me. I can't decide, Michael. I'm too weak. I'm not an earth woman, and we must remember that."

Pale, cold hands gripped her shoulders. Familiar eyes stared at her through shafts of moonlight, searing with a dark flame. They tore into her heart and stirred the ashes of her forgotten passion, a thing she had killed long ago.

"Help me, Michael," she whispered against his sleek, cold chest. She felt the heat of blood thundering under her lips. Raging torrents of sweet wine. All of him. All hers, for a kiss. She pulled him against herself, fell back under his weight. His fingertips traced spirals across her stomach, her breasts, her neck, describing hidden places she had never dreamed of before. Elizabeth began to weep at their beauty. She guided his mouth to a place where she had not been touched for many years. His kisses were gentle, lingering. Then a searing, releasing pain filled her.

Elizabeth cried out, overwhelmed. His fingers drifted in her hair, soothing, as he pulled her head down to his throat. Elizabeth moaned and kissed his hard jawline, descended, hunger opening her heart. Michael touched her lips, caressed her small, needle teeth. Elizabeth bit deep into him, felt his throat muscles writhing under her tongue. Hot, sweet liquid poured into her mouth; his life became hers.

She opened her eyes and watched Michael's transformation into a vampire. His hair surged out under the moonlight, grew into a black sea; soft, thick waves washed through her fingers, wove around her breasts and hips. His skin became silken, smoothed by invisible fingers, like stone smoothed by water and wind. His eyes became twin mirrors reflecting a distant sun. They swooped close to her now, at once piercing and gentle.

"Come inside my home," he said.

Lightning streaked across his irises. Her heartbeat quickened to the rhythm of her running steps. Water splashed under her feet. Mud squelched between her toes as the earth pulled at her. The thunder surrounded, almost lifted her. Lithe, tan shapes swept past, washing her in rainbows. Elizabeth ran faster—tried to run. The gazellelike animals caught her in their powerful vortex and twirled her among dandelion seedlings. Wind like a silky cloth billowed around her. Thunder pounded into her body and wailing voices carried her and taught her a complicated dance. From somewhere, a man was watching her. She concentrated on her steps, to make them beautiful. He sang his name to her. She listened and memorized it.

Then the sky darkened. The voices and pounding thunder ceased, replaced by a silent tension growing in the atmosphere. Something swelling and heavy and kicking inside her body mimicked the tension, reminding her of its living presence. The air pressed against her as she walked to an old screen door. The shadows in the corners and under the table and stove fled. She touched the rough screen and looked outside.

A rocky desert greeted her. Sunflowers swayed. Dust rose from the ground and swirled in tiny whirlwinds. Then an orangish-pink circle crept into the sky, and solid arms encircled her, warmed her, filled her home with light; the home she shared with her husband . . .

Just as quickly, night descended again. And the arms left her.

Michael lifted away from her, as if taken by a sudden wind, his skin a sighing river passing under her fingertips.

"Don't leave me," Elizabeth said, holding onto him with all her strength.

"Morning light is near and it hurts me." Michael was trembling. "I must bring back Melissa. My daughter is dead."

Elizabeth closed her eyes, clenching all of her muscles, and looked into his heart. She saw herself there. And a terrible pain. A pain she could never understand. She couldn't speak.

"We were born in separate worlds," Michael said. "And I have felt you through all of them."

Elizabeth hesitated. Time was passing quickly. The stars had resumed their journey. She might destroy everything if she waited any longer, held him back. Never enough time. And I made a promise.

Gently, she pushed him away.

"Just words, Michael. Before you know it, they've vanished into thin air. And gone."

Elizabeth sagged wearily and gazed at the blood-spotted floor. "You can see Falke as I do. Follow your sight and mind. Trust them. And sing the song the old man taught to me, without knowing. It helped me to find you, through the different worlds. Though I don't know what the song says."

"Sing it to me again."

Elizabeth looked up to a broken ceiling, imagined the moon's circle flying among reefs of cloud. The entire song tumbled out of her soul, streamed past her lips. Tears like hot stones rolled down her body. And there was a vast hole in her heart where the song had once been.

Michael spoke, "This is what it means. It is not a song of war, or of power against enemies. It is a healing song. A prayer. One my grandmother taught to me when I was a little boy."

> Changing Woman's child I have become
> With him I walk
> Now restored to beauty I run
> All is well again
> All is well again
> All is well again
> All is well again.

Remembered sunlight streamed into Elizabeth. She clutched at it sadly. Then she listened to his departure. His steady steps. The rhythmic pulsing of his fading heart. She engraved it into her memory as she had done with his name, more real than any wedding ring. But she wouldn't look at him. Elizabeth only held his emptied medicine bag against her cold stomach.

Sixty-one

Diana pushed herself from the boulder and stood up. The scene below her had not changed, as she had hoped it would. The crazily arranged cottages rested quietly under a circle of lamps in the cavern. No one, so far, had come to investigate her presence. One of the lamps was close by. Wriggling her fanny pack around until it rested on her hip, she unzipped it and lifted out her pistol, trying to remember how it worked. She held the gun as Roger had taught her and pulled back the slide, fitting a bullet into the chamber. She checked the safety to make sure it was on, took several deep breaths, and walked toward the lamp that hung from the cavern wall.

She saw that the lamp was merely a wide bowl filled with oil. The thickly braided wick was held by a ring and supported by three metal fingers. She opened her hand next to it; the whole lamp was the size of a cantaloupe. Diana studied the fixture, never having seen anything like it before. The scored metal bowl and the ring holding the wick were decorated with faint engravings. She thought about using her flashlight but decided not to. She could see parts of the deeper sketches, and the images made her skin crawl: A man on a table with his chest cut open, and thin lines indicating the organs and their names written in . . . what? She couldn't recognize the language because the characters had been worn to thin scratches. Diana reached out and waved her hand over the guttering flame as if weaving a magic spell. Leaning closer, she blew out the flame.

Diana descended to the ground level of the cavern. There was no discernible draft, but she felt as if she had stepped onto a glacier. Diana held the pistol out in front of her and walked to the nearest cottage, surprised that it was not very far away. Her perspective had fooled her. The cottages' real size had deceived her into thinking the cavern was much larger than it actually was. She could reach the top of the wall with her hands. If she wanted to.

The ruler-straight stone was unnaturally smooth and unmoving beneath her fingertips. When she pulled her hand away, a drift of dust fell, revealing perfectly edged layers of porous, black brick. Diana switched her pistol to her left hand and wiped her fingers on her jeans. The gray dust had an oily feel she disliked.

Diana listened for sounds of approaching enemies, then she slowly followed the perimeter of the small cottage. The cavern remained quiet; no squeak of mice or bats or any other living thing. Had anyone ever lived in these houses? She could imagine it, incredibly enough: No interruptions of sun or moon or passing stars, no wind or storms. No rain, no roofs. How would you measure time? Diana glanced at her watch and was frightened to see how much time had passed.

Three A.M.

She peered around the front corner. The other cottages stared. Only two held black gazes. The rest glowered with square yellow eyes. Diana unzipped her pack again and took out her flashlight. She turned the corner and walked toward the front door, which came up only to her lowest rib. She stopped to peek inside the window, but the curtain was drawn. Not a twitch of wind moved the fabric, and there was no glass either. She could have easily stuck her hand into the blackness beyond. But what if something grabbed her hand and pulled?

Diana's skin shivered into hard goosepimples. Don't think about that! She huddled at the door, closing her eyes. Her heart thudded evenly inside her chest, and that was the only sound she heard. "Okay," she whispered, relieved. She moved to the front of the open doorway and switched on her flashlight; only then, did she see how dim it was in the cavern. The beam cut into the cottage room like a straight razor. A skeleton in ragged clothes and gray dragging skin sat at a flimsy wood table, grinning at a tin plate set in front of it. The curtains glowed with a luminous fairy light.

Diana backed out of the cottage and switched off the flashlight, deciding it was probably best not to announce herself with an electric spot. The next cottage was about twenty yards away; its windows were lit with a sour glow. Breathing deeply, Diana walked towards the glow, wincing at the rustling her jacket made. She leaned against the wall of

305

the cottage and listened to the freezing stone. She heard no murmur of voices or movement from inside. Maybe something was lying in wait, still as a hunting tiger, ready to pounce on her and eat her.

Her face became numb. She slipped the gun inside her pocket and cupped her hands over her painted face. The air was not only cold but dead. The pistol was a comforting weight tugging at her side. She blew warm breath into her hands and rubbed them together. Then she swallowed a fresh gulp of water from her canteen.

Is there any sense in checking out every one of these cottages? Or am I just being nosy? Again, instead of walking straight for the front door, she went around the corner of the cottage and waited. One purpose for having the lamps in a circle around the cavern, she reasoned, was that no concealing shadows existed anywhere. Intruders like me would be exposed on all fronts. She stared at the other cottages surrounding her, hunched gray ghosts with glowing eyes. No movement near any of them.

Might as well check this one out, Diana thought, gripping her pistol. Since I'm here.

She looked around to the front of the cottage, saw that nothing was entering or leaving, then crept to the front door. This time, the window was at the other side of the doorway, so she couldn't look inside first as a precaution. The door was open slightly, however, and she could see the interior opposite wall. The lamp glow was unwavering. Diana touched the door with the pistol barrel, pushed slightly. The oak door moved on silent hinges. She could now squeeze herself into the cottage—if she wanted to.

Do I want to?

Diana crouched and went inside.

Sixty-two

The room was sparsely furnished. A simple oil lamp was set on a wide table. A bookcase with three leatherbound books rested against one wall. In the corner was a solid-backed rocking chair, facing away from her. Diana entered slowly and found she could stand upright in the room; of course, since there was no roof. Rough cavern rock loomed above the four walls.

The massive oak table occupied the center of the cottage. On its surface were scattered sheets of paper, thick envelopes, an ink pen in a bottle of ink. Diana picked up a sheet of the paper. It was of a heavy bond and felt more like stiffened cloth than regular paper. She plucked the pen from the bottle and felt its tip. The ink was caked and dry.

Diana set the pen down and looked at the rocking chair. The arms were curved into scrolled ends. The long back held the carving of a lyrical black rose. A blanket had fallen in a heap at the chair's foot. Another blanket was propped upright in the seat as if someone was sitting there. Diana's hair began to rise. She held her pistol out with both hands and approached the stilled rocking chair.

Just as she glimpsed a gray, emaciated figure with coarsened hair, one hand protruding from a tattered jacket, Diana felt, more than heard, the door opening behind her. The floorboards creaked as someone entered the room.

Her breath locked in her lungs, Diana whirled, aimed at the shadowy intruder, and pulled the trigger with all her strength. Nothing happened. The trigger was stuck. The figure at the door, slightly taller than Diana, moved into the lamp's circle of light.

"Melissa?" Diana whispered, still aiming the pistol at the girl's chest.

Unhurriedly, Melissa removed a pair of stereo earbuds, let them dangle around her neck, then switched off her cassette player. They stared at each other silently. Diana saw that the girl was no longer sickly looking. She was wearing a long white dress with blue trimmings. She was barefoot. Her black hair was unpinned, loose and curled about her shoulders, and had become more voluminous and glossy since last week. Her eyes were disturbingly black and dominated her face in a strange way; they seemed to swallow the lamp light. Diana would have stared all night if Melissa had not smiled. Then, Diana began to shake. The movement of Melissa's lips was unreal, chilling, as if a marble statue had come to life and smiled like a human being.

"I think the safety is on, Miss Logan." Melissa's voice was soft and ringing, oddly suited to its environment. "That's why the gun won't shoot."

Diana lowered her pistol. The barrel kept wanting to drift toward Melissa.

"You could have knocked or something." Diana tried to keep her voice as controlled as possible, teacherlike.

Melissa approached warily, until she was standing at the table's edge. "I don't think you could've hurt me much with that thing anyway."

Diana replaced the gun in her pack. "What are you doing here, Melissa?"

"I came by to refill the oil in the lamps. It's my . . . chore. My husband likes to keep them lit, to scare away intruders, I guess. I'll have to tell him they don't work."

Up close, Melissa's skin was silken and lustrous, not a mark or pimple to be seen. She had been energetic and pretty in a catch-all kind of way—cheerleader type with a pert attractiveness. Now, her movements were sensual and knowing, and her body was perfectly molded; every eyeblink and finger becoming vivid and lovely in its own way, yet adding up to a supernatural whole.

Not human.

Melissa was gazing at Diana's face, noticing the paint. "What are *you* doing here, Miss Logan? Like that."

"I came looking for you. I've come to take you home."

Melissa stared with liquid eyes. She wasn't smiling anymore. She pointed to the cavern ceiling. "Out there?"

"Yes, Melissa," Diana said. "Your grandfather, your whole family at Madrecita, have sent me. We're all worried about you. We want you to come back to us."

308   "Really," Melissa said, as if she couldn't believe it.

Maybe I'm going about this all wrong, Diana thought. Being too direct never worked with any child I've known. She commented on Melissa's appearance. "You've lost weight."

Christ, now I sound like Emily!

Melissa became sullenly watchful. "Being dead does that to you."

"You aren't dead, Melissa. Your grandfather explained it to me." That's the way to do it! Diana thought: Remind her of her connections to earth, to those people she might still love.

"I'm not alive, though, Miss Logan. I feel different. Everything whirls around me, and there I am just watching it all. Not a part of it. Always waiting."

"Waiting for what?"

Melissa shifted the barest fraction, as if uneasy. "I don't know," she answered. "I sit in these houses alone, knowing I have to do something. But then, the night starts turning to day . . . and I can feel it, too, Miss Logan—my body aches; not like the flu or my period. Then, Boom!, I'm asleep. And I mean like, you know, *really* asleep." Her eyes sharpened. "But you wouldn't understand that, would you?"

"I'm sorry, Melissa, but I don't." Diana looked to the doorway. "Is Falke here?"

In a blink, Melissa was standing next to her. "How do you know about Falke?"

"Oh, we had a fine chat together, several nights ago."

Melissa was incredulous. "What did he say? Nothing about me."

"He talked a little about you and about your grandfather."

Melissa looked away. "He talked about my grandfather?"

"Yes. Doesn't Falke tell you anything?"

Melissa shrugged. It was such a characteristic habit of hers, something she might have done in class if asked what her weekend had been like, that Diana felt a sharp tug at her heart.

"I guess not. He's not here all the time." Melissa lowered her voice, as if he might be listening. "He goes away sometimes, and I'm left here in this dusty old place."

"It's so quiet. How do you stand it?"

Melissa flicked the earphones hung around her neck, then gestured to the withered body in the rocking chair. "And you learn to become like Kuenstler. Mummified."

Diana felt her skin prickling.

Melissa looked at her and grinned. "Oh, but don't worry, Miss Logan! I have plenty of time to waste. Falke says that I need this time alone to get used to my new existence. 'The experience of a harmless passage of time,'" Melissa said measuredly, as if reciting from a book.

"That sounds like something Hanna would say," Diana said, remembering Michael's description of the woman.

Melissa's gaze suddenly fastened on Diana, who felt its power as an electrical surge vibrating in her body.

"You know about Hanna?"

Diana nodded, hugging herself. "Only from what Michael . . . your grandfather told me." Should a judgment be made about Hanna? Is Melissa far enough gone that she would resent it? Diana's thoughts made her even dizzier.

Melissa frowned. She shifted the blank papers on the table back and forth. "And you know Falke. Then you know . . . Elizabeth?"

"I've spoken with her, sweetheart."

Melissa glared at Diana, outraged. "How do you know about them? Why are you here? What business is it of yours!"

Diana couldn't answer. She'd been so caught up in her search, in learning from Michael and Emily, that she really had no idea why Melissa might choose to come home with her. What did she have to offer anyone, her own broken life?

Fragile laughter broke into Diana's thoughts. Melissa eyes glittered with tears.

"You see? You see how I felt, Miss Logan?" she stammered. "Before Falke found me? Huh uh, no way do I have any second thoughts about leaving that shitty world behind. What I have here is much better."

Diana grasped at that tiny straw. "This better place, Melissa, is a tomb. Look around you! Really, look at this place. Who built it up to look like this?"

Melissa wiped angrily at her eyes. "Kuenstler." Then she laughed shakily. "He's dead now."

"Is this going to be your new world? Is this all Falke has to offer you?"

"He gives me strength, Miss Logan. And there'll be lots more! Falke's been sick, but now he's well. We're planning to leave this hopeless desert, and thank God for that!"

"Melissa," Diana said tightly, wanting to shake the girl. "This place is creepy. Those cottages out there were not built by a sane man. Or even a happy one! This is an evil place."

"Look, this is my home, no matter who built it. I appreciate your concern, we all do. Now, fuck off!"

Diana tried to keep her hands from slapping Melissa. "What do I tell your grandfather then?"

Puzzled, no longer angry, Melissa came closer. "Tell him, tell them, that I'm happy . . . you can tell my mom, too."

Silence stretched between them like a river with deep, merciless currents. Diana remembered how somber official-dom had knocked on her Aunt Sue's door the bright morning after her parents had been killed in Utah. She remembered the sad pink men, the shape of the black police car against the snow, the deadly shotgun erect between the seats, and how the sun had blistered the sky.

Gently, Diana reached out her hand. "Honey . . ."

Melissa stepped back, her eyes growing into frantic circles.

"Melissa . . . your mother is dead."

Melissa hooked her fingers into whitening claws. "You . . . You're lying!"

"Honey, she was . . ."

"*Shut up!*" Melissa screamed.

Diana unzipped the top half of her coat and unclasped the silver chain that had belonged to Melissa's mother. To wear the necklace had seemed the safest way to carry it. Some of the chain links were still stiff and red from dried blood. The turquoise cross dangled prettily. Diana hesitated, not sure what to expect. She held it out to Melissa.

"This is yours," Diana said. "It belonged to your great-grandmother, Michael told me, before it was given to your mother. Michael wanted you to have it . . . when everything was finished."

"*Mom . . .*" Melissa moaned and snatched the necklace. Ghostly, black clouds erupted from her body. Melissa curled into billowing mist, vanishing completely, as if she and the clouds had slipped into a gash in the atmosphere.

Diana's right hand began to shake so violently that she had to grip it with her left. Nothing was finished yet. And she wasn't going home by herself, either.

311

The eerie dollhouses surrounded Diana, their searing eyes marking her resolute passage among them; a gathering storm of monsters that were making plans to hunt her down and kill her. Diana cocked her pistol, her heart blazing. The cottages glared after her, harmless. She was too close to Melissa to be scared away, and the monsters were only ghosts immobile in the sand. They weren't laughing at her now. Diana flew past all of them, as if she had sprouted wings. Fresh, galvanizing air streamed from somewhere, filling her body, strengthening her muscles; a gift from the Holy Ones, as William had said.

A gift from Wind, her guardian.

Sixty-three

Angry stars wheeled above Michael's head in complicated spirals too intricate to follow, all of them dancing and chanting in a deadly chorus, no longer playful. Crystal knives sliced into his skin. Michael wept at the evilness he breathed out into the pure winter air.

A frightening power flowed through his muscles, but it was not connected to him in any way. He was merely the antenna. His sense organs were swollen and painful. Flexing fingers numbed to the freezing air, Michael used them to block out smoke from fireplaces and poisons from automobiles, which arrowed into his flesh. He had become the unnatural force that witches called up and shaped in their ceremonies.

"I am not human, any more," he said to the watchful land. "I am Eye Killer."

Michael crouched to the snow, groping among hibernating flowers, digging out their roots. His hand plunged into an underground space, clutched a furry body. Viciously, he wrenched the twisting, screeching animal out of the ground and offered it to the night sky, a tiny sacrifice to his new existence. He was unable to remember the animal's name. Michael ripped the animal apart and drank its steaming blood.

Distracted, he lifted his mouth from the carcass. The night was changing. The stars and planets had now settled into their familiar patterns. Rich smells, frequent at this time of early morning, became visible mists. A wind began to rise. Snow flew from weary clouds. Michael heard snowflakes scraping against the landscape, the sound like steel nails scraping porcelain. His heart hammered. Instinct warned him to find shelter before the coming daylight.

No!

Michael stood up, straightened, his mind rebelling against his new nature, which screamed at the back of his brain—Hide from the sun!

There is time left, Michael thought. Just enough.

He wasn't sure how to bring about the change. No one had taught him the proper way. The blond woman in the square of moonlight had said to follow his new senses, to remember a song.

Michael hunched under a storm of fear, unable to remember. A woman spoke.

"First Warrior."

The voice was hushed, but it pierced through his yammering heart like an arrow of sunlight. Michael looked up and saw a tall Navajo woman standing against the dark, cloudy sky. Her black hair wove about her shadowed face as she watched the falling snow. Then she looked at him. Michael felt a scorching pain along his back as he writhed under the woman's sun-brilliant eyes. There was no hate in her voice, only sadness.

"You have given song and love to Eye Killer's woman. You have revealed your name to the enemy. You have touched the dead. You have created wild air. Why have you done all this?"

Michael crouched into the snow, to scare away the heat. "I was angry," he answered.

The woman's voice broke the night. "You are not Eye Killer. Remember those who came before you. The mothers and fathers who suckled and hunted for you and gave you songs, 313 then urged you from the den, with great fear in their hearts, out into the open cold land. Remember your grandfathers and grandmothers who remembered the songs to make you strong. For they are the wise ones, your teachers . . ."

The voice intertwined with the growing wind and vanished.

Michael clutched at the earth beneath the snow and whispered the end of his grandmother's song.

Changing Woman's child, I am;
Changing Woman's grandchild, I am.

Michael stood and looked at the scattered stars. Melting water trickled down his arms and legs. He remembered one of the first stories of the Navajos: How Coyote had come upon First Woman, who was carefully arranging the stars across the night. Impatient, Coyote had swiped the stars from First Woman and blew them randomly into the black sky. There, they swirled crazily for a time before settling down and coming to rest, forming the mixed-up Milky Way. Coyote had created chaos in the universe. To add insult, Coyote plucked some of his hairs, blew on them until they turned red, then hurled the hairs into the sky. Among the stars, red suns had been formed.

Red was the color of war.

Red was the color of blood flowing into the sand.

What is Coyote telling me now?

For a long time, Michael stood gazing over the awakening city. All remnants of his past life were vague ghosts; except for one—she burned across his mind like the sun. Cold air blew against him but did not touch his inner core of warmth. Michael sniffed and snuffled, attracted by purple vapors and scents. He sent his mind out onto the wind; his predator mind scanned the landscape. There was a tiny piece of night left, and it was flowing away rapidly.

Suddenly, he caught a thin scream in a familiar voice, a girl's voice calling from far to the west. He tasted mental tracks he had sensed before, paths he hadn't at first understood. Now the trail was clear to him. Michael spoke.

"I am First-Warrior. I am First-To-Hurl-Anger."

A glassy pain tore through his skeleton as his joints separated and rearranged themselves. His legs drew up and bent themselves into a strange angle. The muscles whipped furiously, forcing him onto the ground on all fours. His fingers, clenching into the snow, shortened and sprouted claws and pads. His ears lengthened into large, furry cups. His body shifted and molded itself into a streamlined, bullet-shaped animal—not a wolf. Coyote. Its tailbone shot out into a bushy tail to give balance while running.

Coyote opened his eyes to his destination: The ancient land of his ancestors and the place of his emergence.

A monster hunted there, its song of evil and murderous intent. It was killing children.

Coyote lifted his muzzle and raised his voice into a raging, thundering howl.

He began his race with the dawn.

Sixty-four

"Melissa!"

Diana walked in agitation through lamp-lit, descending corridors. Days seemed to pass. She imagined the sun outside flinging itself into the sky and down again, illuminating mesas, clouds whizzing by in twisting time, stars blinking in rapid succession. She stumbled in cold darkness until she saw a dangling, wavering string of light. Her groping hand brought her to a partially open door. She pushed it open and stalked through the opening.

Vertigo caught her head in its hands and jerked her toward the edge of a precipice. Instead of flinging her arms about wildly for a handhold, Diana fell back through the doorway and bounced hard on the ground, teeth clicking painfully. She calmed her whirling brain and righted herself, then crawled the few feet to the door, propped herself against it, and stared through the opening.

The vast cavern looked as if it had been shaped from the blow of a gargantuan axe. The walls encircling Diana dropped at steep angles to a zigzagging trough far below. Across from her, the far end of the cavern lay in deep blackness. But it was the ceiling that had sparked her vertigo. A looming oval, it was hung with tiny, scattered lamps; it looked like a dark lake reflecting bright stars. An upside-down lake. Walking in here unsuspecting she had thought the world had suddenly turned over.

A voice boomed against the jagged walls. "Come down and talk with me, Diana Logan."

Diana stood carefully, moved to the edge of the narrow crumbling stairway, and saw Falke standing below among a circle of lamps and tapestries hanging from desolate rock walls. Her dizziness returned. She looked away and saw that the stone next to her had been worked into an image of people feasting in a gallery of gargoyles and flying demons.

Diana closed her eyes. "Where's Melissa?"

"Melissa is ill," Falke said. "She has removed herself to her room."

Diana groped in her fanny pack and aimed her pistol down toward the vampire. "You murdered Melissa's mother."

Her voice was steady and cut cleanly into the cavern. She was proud of it.

Falke smiled distantly. "And here you are, Diana, to exact revenge."

"I'm here to take Melissa home. Back to her family, where she belongs."

"I think that you will be surprised at what Melissa wants." Falke moved to the center of the floor. "Come down. Stand before me, and we can discuss Melissa's future like civilized beings."

"I'm fine right where I am."

The vampire's eyes became dangerous. "I insist."

"No, thanks."

Falke sighed. "You have no need of weapons."

"If it's all the same to you, I'll keep them." An icy spot began to grow on her throat, below her left ear; it throbbed and ached. "Why did you have to kill Melissa's mother?"

"It is a necessity to weed out faltering hearts. Melissa was strong, Diana; is the strongest of them all."

"She's a kid, for Christ's sake! She didn't even know what happened to her mother."

"Do you know?"

"I know."

"Melissa will have time to heal. All the time in the world."

Diana shook her head. "She won't heal. No one will love her or hold her. No one will want to take care of her. And who is she going to take care of? That's important, too."

"We will have many children."

Diana grew chilled. "I'm not arguing anymore. Make her back into what she was. Make her a person again, or I'll take her anyway."

Falke frowned. "All of the old witches you talked to, Diana, the stories you heard, the songs you learned . . . and still you don't understand."

Diana wanted to bellow, roar across the cavern and rip his heart out. But her body was held rigid. Paralyzed. She couldn't move to tie her shoelaces. Falke chuckled.

"You don't come from their world. You don't even truly understand it. Yet, here you are."

Diana cleared her throat; at least she could do that. "I believe them."

"Diana Logan, do you believe in yourself?"

Be honest. Diana felt suddenly weary. "I'm trying."

"You storm my home as a maiden with a child's eyes, painted as one of their warriors, carrying a gun and wooden sticks. I see into your heart, Diana. Your belief is hard to fathom."

Diana straightened. "As long as they help me get Melissa back."

"The weapons you carry are not to be played with. They contain a power that is strange to me. I have lived nine hundred years, and still I do not understand such might." Falke gazed at her, and began to move toward the stairs. "I will not touch them. I do not understand their savage's magic, but I respect it. I believe in it, also, Diana. It comes from a world apart from this one you inhabit. The ancestors of your old savages understood such powers. They understood creatures such as me, though they gave us different names. I believe that you have begun to trust in their songs . . . and that is very good. Together, we will destroy them. To protect our precious Melissa."

317

Black snow blanketed Diana's mind and understanding. Falke scowled as he mounted the bottom step. His voice rang in her ears.

"You are the perfect guardian for my new wife. Belief in this savage's magic brought you to her. This sisterly love you hold for Melissa will last for centuries, longer than I will exist, perhaps."

A cold spike pierced her brain, wedged itself in her mind. Diana screamed and stumbled blindly forward. Falke's head rose out of the stone floor. Cruel shadows swept across his features as he spoke.

"Welcome home, Diana."

"No!" yelled a clear voice.

Diana felt a cold vortex of wind. Small hands gripped her arms, pulled her back from the abyss. Diana whirled and saw two luminous red pools staring out of the dark. No longer human. Vampire eyes.

Melissa's eyes.

"Melissa!" she cried. "Get away. Now!"

"You go, Miss Logan. I can't leave Falke. There's just him in this big, empty place. And he's so alone. He chose me to be his wife. And I've chosen to love him. You can't break that. And Grandpa can't either. My choice!

Diana wanted to carry Melissa away. She reached inside her jacket and began to unwind the prayersticks.

"Falke doesn't love you, Melissa. He's twisting your love, shaping it around himself, making it into a weapon."

Diana thought of Michael and Elizabeth; hunter and prey living out precious moments together before one or the other's death. And fully aware of the consequences. An odd love had existed between them. Diana had felt it the first time she saw Michael leave with Elizabeth; she had seen it in the man's eyes.

Nothing logical. Total intuition.

"Melissa, if Falke truly loved you, he wouldn't have made you into what he is, no matter how much he wanted you with him."

Melissa scurried down several steps, just beyond Diana's reach. "You think I'm too stupid to see through your lies. But I can see the whole web of them! Hanna killed my mother. Falke told me. And I'll kill Hanna for that."

"Spin all the fantasies you want," Diana said. "While you murder everyone who loves you. Including me."

"You liar." Melissa seemed to retreat inside darkening clouds. "I hate you, Miss Logan."

"Stand back, Melissa." Diana removed one prayerstick.

Melissa crouched on the steps, her eyes fiery points. Her voice rumbled like breaking mesas. "To catch my husband, you'll have to kill me first."

A vast shadow detached itself from the ceiling and fell onto Diana. An ironlike fist slammed between her breasts, in the place above her heart. Nauseating heat flooded her insides. Diana dropped to her knees and retched into the dust, feeling as if all her internal organs had exploded.

Melissa screamed.

"Please . . . Melissa," Diana whispered. The girl was weeping somewhere in the darkness; the cavern echoed with the helpless sobs of a newborn baby. Then something entwined itself in Diana's hair and she was yanked viciously off the ground. She heard a sickening, ripping noise as hair was ripped out of her scalp. Blood trickled around her ears. Her feet swung in vacant air.

"Melissa . . ." Diana winced as strong fingers tightened around her throat. ". . . please don't cry."

"Life passes too quickly, teacher." Falke's canine fangs drew closer. "Melissa holds the strength of the greatest of warriors. And she will live forever, even without your protection. Be glad for her."

Diana made use of her fading breaths.

"Go suck an egg, asshole."

Sixty-five

Elizabeth studied the vampire in front of her.

Hanna's face was bloated and her eyes were greedy slits. Her speech was slurry as if she were drunk. "Did you like my paper of pins?"

"Why did you do it, Hanna?"

The vampire walked to the end of the classrom and paused at the far wall. "Why, why, why!" she said, turning to Elizabeth. "All these questions you throw. My head is spinning with 'why'!"

Elizabeth studied the softening colors between them, noted the vampire's relaxed body movements, and thought—Hanna is no longer afraid!

To hide her excitement, Elizabeth shrugged passively. "It's something I learned during the years I was left alone: Wait, and the world will unfold itself to you. Like a rose."

"There is no one left to protect you, Elizabeth. All of them . . . destroyed by me."

Elizabeth remained silent, pushed all distractions from her mind. Hanna smirked.

"They weren't so easily destroyed, I'll grant you." Hanna counted on her fingertips. "They each made a good show for themselves."

"I never asked for anyone's protection," Elizabeth said.

"Sister. I've come up out of the darkness; that timeless hole that Falke locked me in. And now, I have borne vampires— sisters!—to stand by my side. I've drunk up their souls and absorbed them into my body. I am a complete entity; no longer human. Vampire."

Elizabeth recognized the truth of what Hanna was saying. Standing across the room was a creature of unknown proportions. Its female body was only a mask over its true force, its fatal power. Invisible tentacles reached for Elizabeth, groping for her thoughts, her dreams, and her soul.

"I see precious knowledge in your eyes, Elizabeth. And love. I might have killed you for it, too, during that half-dead, jealous state I was in. Up until then, I thought the only way to gain your heart, keep it for myself, was to rape the life from you."

Hanna moved closer. Stray beams of light coruscated along disembodied fangs and knifelike eyelashes, streaking through eyes of blackest midnight. Unstoppable. Elizabeth was frozen, unable to tear her eyes away. Hanna loomed over her.

"In my short portion of life, I had no experience of gentle touch or love. If I closed my eyes even for one second, it would have been a surrender to violent death. Then, I met Falke. And of course! once his male eyes had fastened on me, he charmed me, then he raped me—stripped me of life and love. Like all men." Hanna ruminated, and giggled. "Then Falke spirited me to his sanctuary and introduced me to you, sister . . . his guileless wife."

Soiled air. Soiled air flying near enough to touch; Elizabeth remembered the words her mother had often used to describe Satan's presence, and applied them to the vampire.

Hanna smiled, remembering. "A gentle creature who needed protecting. Your husband seemed to think I was the only one who could do it. Why? Because he didn't trust himself."

"I didn't trust either of you. It took me a while to understand why. I'll never trust you, Hanna."

"We are vampires, and beyond your comprehension . . . or trust."

"That's part of it. That's why it took me so long to understand. But, Hanna, we are both forgetting Christiane."

"I've never understood Falke's obsession."

"You can't—not yet. I understand it only too well."

"I know you do, Elizabeth. Explain it to me. Teach me."

"I see Falke's and Christiane's hands entwined together, their secret tryst of passion, their carriage driving under leafy trees and speckled sunlight. Death was not his queen, Hanna. Christiane was. Passion weakened him; love did too. And it could have strengthened him so much." Elizabeth felt a tentative touch on her arm. "Oh, yes. Things Falke can't see, I see very clearly."

"Don't hate me, sister," Hanna whispered. Elizabeth's hand was encased within fingers of cold steel; there was a warmth in them, but it was distant. "Please, continue."

"You have to stand back, away from memories, if you want to see the intent of the original person. Peer through the leafy trees, Hanna, touch the walls of their mind and listen to what they are telling themselves. Sift through this chaff, and you will glimpse into their world. But you must always remember that it's not a truthful world. All of us lie to ourselves. And to each other. We are only human, after all. Full of tricks."

"What about the present?"

Elizabeth shook her head. "Real thoughts are too quick to follow. And many of them are contradictory. Learn to study passions, for they are slow-moving. And don't just follow them, Hanna; push them to your advantage."

Hanna nodded agreeably. "I can do that."

"But do you really follow what I'm saying? It's very important to me that you understand . . . sister."

"It'll take me time to understand fully."

"Not just time, but experience. However, as you keep saying, we dominate time. He will bend to our wishes."

"Sister, I gave the old man to you. Let me give back what he has stolen from you. Let me . . . suckle you." Hanna's blindness brought her within a hand's reach. "I love you, Elizabeth."

"I know you do, Hanna."

Elizabeth's fingers joined into a white arrowhead. She crouched in a lithe movement and thrust her hand into Hanna's midriff. In the second of Hanna's widening eyes, Elizabeth reached through spoiled organs and cold flesh, grasped a slick pulsating cable, and severed the abdominal aorta with her thumbnail.

Hanna shrieked like the damned in hell. Elizabeth forced her mind to a complete standstill, thought nothing, imagined blackness. She stepped back woodenly and wrenched her hand out of Hanna's body. The vampire sobbed miserably and groped for the stinking liquid that spewed onto the floor like red sleet. Elizabeth staggered backward, holding her mind empty; a trellis without flowers or vines.

Hanna wheeled upright and shouted, "You haven't won yet, sister!"

"I lost everything when you murdered Michael. There's nothing you can do to hurt me now." Elizabeth paused, ". . . and I'm not your sister."

A gale of hatred smashed into Elizabeth's mind; threw her bodily across the room into a skeletal wall. Dust blew outward. Rigid, bloody hands gripped her throat and lifted her high into the air; her tattered dress fluttering, she felt as if she had topped the ascent on a ferris wheel. She was hurled into solid sections of wall. Broken plaster pieces slid to the floor. Ventilation shafts crumpled. Wood frames splintered. Copper tubing and bundles of cable were scraped clean under her bare back. Then she was thrown to the floor. Pointed objects cut into her thighs and arms. A viscous, red rain splattered on her hands and face.

"Now, Elizabeth, I'll show you what it's like to be raped."

Elizabeth glanced up in time to see the sky fall. Razor-edged fingers slashed out of a descending thundercloud. Elizabeth held them off. Hanna's face appeared, swelled, and a blackened skull like a roach's carapace burst out of Hanna's face, spiked and grinning with masses of curved teeth. Hanna stared with eyes that dribbled flame. Rancid flesh fell like gray snowflakes. A reek of putrescent meat blew into Elizabeth as gnarled arms coiled around her, wrapped her arms to her body and tightened. Elizabeth was pressed backward against the shattered floor and a frozen weight crushed her. Metallic eyeteeth swooped at her throat.

"No!" Elizabeth kicked into Hanna's gaping stomach. The vampire shuddered and screamed. Elizabeth wriggled her hands free, then saw rootlike fingers grappling her left leg; before she could do anything, Hanna cracked her shin bone.

Savage fire blazed through broken bone. Elizabeth kicked Hanna's head with her other leg. Hanna was slammed backward onto the floor where she writhed, trying to stand. Through a swooning haze, Elizabeth thought Hanna had become a furious ball of snakes.

Elizabeth gripped hanging electrical wires and pulled herself up, then limped out of the school room without a backward glance, gritting her teeth at crunching bones. The corridor was unlit. No flow of electricity ran through the school building's veins anymore. The old hulk remained dead around her. She tried to ignore the pain in her leg, but with each step she took, a wave of grayness covered her eyes. She approached the stairwell and tried to ascend into the churning air and found she couldn't. She had forgotten how to fly. She had felt such physical pain only once before; her heart remained in fragments.

323

"I should be able to withstand anything," she said to the rising walls. The lobby floor held an ocean of blue dust. Her passage across was marked by a swirling cloud of orange motes. She exited through the leaning doors, and realized only now why she and Hanna had fought alone.

The sun is coming, Elizabeth thought. Hanna had sent her coven away to seek shelter. I should find shelter too. Heal myself, for the final fight.

But Elizabeth's mind was racing on new tracks. Parked on the street below, several chrome and black motorcycles waited under a line of artificial suns, beckoning. And from behind Elizabeth came a piercing, animal-like howl, which vibrated through rotting walls and rolled against her body, urging her forward. Hanna's voice crashed against the paling sky.

"Now my love begins!"

Elizabeth burned her fingers as she clutched Michael's medicine bag and lifted its string over her head. The bag bounced hotly between her breasts; a glowing coal. She hurried into the heat of coming dawn, toward the patient machines.

Sixty-six

Glittering steel and chrome.

Elizabeth sensed movement. She glanced around, expecting to see Hanna. The street was dead, but a wild energy was shifting the atmosphere. She mounted the nearest motorcycle. Her splintered bones grated together. She hissed in agony, became blinded, swayed ponderously, as her mortal pain grounded her to earth.

"I'm getting old," she said firmly, killing her fear.

She kicked the machine into life, ignored a flare of heated colors in her eyes. The machine shivered and roared underneath her. Its headlamp searched out the darkness. Speeding away, she glimpsed a monstrous shadow flying to the remaining motorcycle. An engine shouted behind her. She changed gears swiftly. Her motorcycle bucked like a horse wanting to throw off its rider. Elizabeth gripped her mount tightly, lowered herself over its sleek back. The wind teased down her spine. Winter cold became a whirling funnel cloud as she raced into its heart.

Icy tentacles probed her mind.

Elizabeth coaxed her machine to run faster, and followed a trail of streetlights toward the freeway.

Sixty-seven

Coyote raced across the landscape, a bolt of angry fire that wove past white boulders, leaped across blue snowy washes, zigzagged through orange tamarisk stands, and smashed apart black shadows. Air rippled in his fur. His legs and heart shouted out super-heated, thudding drumbeats. Barrel cactus needles and yucca spikes vibrated in the wind of his passage and chanted Coyote's war song. His sharp nose guided him true and the scent became sharper, more elaborate—the monster's power was dying under the coming dawn.

Good time for ambush.

The reddening, standing rock where Eye Killer dwelt rose into the dawn sky. Asphalt boomed for an instant under Coyote's paws. Shining, metal beetles shrieked and scattered at his passing. Deer fled fearfully to the gray hills. And the eagles marked Coyote's race with approval.

Sixty-eight

"Falke . . . you killed my mother."

Distantly, Diana felt the vampire's fingers slackening around her throat. Her feet touched the ground. She opened her eyes to see Falke staring down past her toward the foot of the stairs.

"Diana was telling the truth." Melissa's voice flew up from the darkness. "You killed my mother—I saw you do it!"

Diana pulled Falke's fingers away from her throat and collapsed onto the ground. She kicked feebly at his legs. But Falke was no longer aware of her. She tried to stand; couldn't summon the strength. She rolled onto her back. Her throat was numb, and the back of her neck, where the spine joined the skull, tingled horribly. She didn't want to think how close she had come to having her head snapped off.

Boots scraped against rock. Diana scuttled back in fear, then stopped, awestruck, as she saw Falke rising toward the ceiling. His yellow-gold hair flared around him and billowed with his descent. Diana pulled herself along the cold stone floor and looked over the stairwell precipice. Down below, Falke settled gently on the main floor. Between Diana and Falke, Melissa sat huddled on the bottom step.

"It is almost dawn, Melissa." Falke said. "Go into your room and sleep."

"Why did you do it?" Melissa wailed.

Diana searched the floor around her and saw the prayerstick lying near the doorway.

Falke spoke gently. "The price of our existence. I saved you the task of doing it yourself."

The girl paused in her weeping. "I don't know what you're talking about."

Diana forced everything from her mind. She imagined herself wading in a slow-moving river, drifting in its currents; the waves soothed her body and limbs, washed her tired brain in a warm bath. Slowly, Diana pulled herself toward the prayerstick.

Falke spoke. "One of us would have forced you to take your mother's life. That is how vampires are, Melissa. We cannot allow ourselves even one distraction."

"She was my mother!"

"Yes. The woman gave birth to you, and I was grateful. Her death was serene."

"You *fucker!*" Melissa screamed.

The vampire sighed. "It will be one night, far in the future, that you will see existence as I do: A long, arduous climb within a starry tunnel. Temper yourself in ice, girl. Keep your life behind you, at the furthest end, and content yourself with that small bit of sunlight."

Even from this distance, Diana could feel Melissa's fury wavering. Her lonely figure shivered under Falke's presence. Diana leaned against a freezing wall and cleared her throat. Her eyes teared at glassy pain.

"Let me take Melissa home," she said hoarsely. "If you truly love her, then do that much for her."

Falke looked up at Diana and smiled thinly. "I will not do that. I have existed, and indeed I have been hunted, for so many centuries of darkness. I am tired. And I am lonely."

"Then God help you." Diana eased herself the last few inches, until she could have reached out and picked up the prayerstick.

"Not yet." Wind touched her face.

Diana waited.

Melissa shrank down to the floor and wept pitifully. Falke kneeled and engulfed her in his arms.

"I will be the hunter now," he said. "And Melissa will walk at my side—as my wife."

Falke opened his arms, releasing Melissa. Her tears had left a bloody smear down each cheek. Melissa grimaced blackly as she began to walk up the stairs toward Diana.

"Go to your sister, Melissa," Falke said. "Make Diana understand how much we need her strength."

Slender, white thorns winked delicately as Melissa looked up and smiled. "Please be my sister, Miss Logan."

Without warning, Diana saw her parents grinning from a canted field of sunflowers, and she pictured the irrelevant stop sign. She began to laugh. Warm tears pattered on her hands as she lifted the prayerstick from the stone floor.

327

Healing water and sunlight, Michael and Emily might have said; and flowers also, Patsy's sister, flower-loving Leslie, would have added. Melissa hesitated in the shadows and grew still. Diana stood firmly. The sun house colors painted on her face grew hotter. She smiled down toward Melissa and began to descend the steps. The air sparked around her. Dust motes swam like exploding stars as Diana whispered, "Close your eyes then, little sister."

The arrow painted on the prayerstick flashed out with a yellow-white brilliance. The black cavern air shivered apart as a shaft of sunbeam appeared in Diana's hands. Sunlight flowed outward in hot, soothing streams, chased away the dark and revealed a small, wan face below her. Melissa screamed and covered her face with her arms. Diana lifted the prayerstick higher into the air. Her jacket strained against its zipper, then blew wide open. The front of her shirt flamed, crisped, and fell away in molten strips. White beams of sunlight rayed out from the painted disc between her breasts and revealed the entire cavern in sharp relief. Melissa fell back, mouth open in a silent scream. Her shadow slid from Falke, and cascading sunlight struck his body. The vampire burst into flame. Orange hands groped across his legs, chest, and head, engulfing him in a hungry fire. A tremendous shout burst against the ceiling.

"Christiane!"

Diana looked to make sure Melissa was safely out of the way, then released the wildly tugging prayerstick. It flew from her hands as a living weapon and arrowed into the center of Falke's chest. His rib cage cracked loudly, like an oak tree trunk snapping in two. The vampire grasped for the prayerstick digging into his body, tried to pull it out. The weapon slid from his hands, edged deeper into his chest, then stopped.

The sunlight died away. Dark fell.

Diana saw the vampire's blackening eyes through weaving flames. Melissa stared at Falke and pressed herself closer to the steps at Diana's feet.

"Help me!" Falke reached for Melissa. "Christiane!"

"Melissa!" Diana shouted. "Get back!"

The girl's eyes passed over her, not seeing. Then, Melissa raced passed Diana, scampered up the stairway, through the doorway, and vanished.

The vampire wound his left hand in a tapestry hanging above him. The lower half of the thickly woven material caught fire as his fingers touched it. Flames washed excitedly across images of mounted, rejoicing knights circling a heap of amputated arms and legs. Falke tore the tapestry down and used the highest, untouched images to beat out the cocoonlike flames covering his body.

"Jesus," Diana whispered.

The fires died. Gray smoke from the charred vampire spiraled up to the ceiling. Falke joined with the rising smoke, followed its arc across the stone ceiling above Diana, and disappeared through the doorway after Melissa.

"No!" Diana lurched into motion, and almost immediately stopped herself. Tiny flames snapped behind her. Diana turned and regarded the swaying tapestries.

Melissa is far away, her mind whispered. Outside. Probably into a zero-degree morning.

Diana shuddered in the descending cold, tugged out the flashlight from her fanny pack, and went to the nearest hanging tapestry; one decorated with a mass of running horses. She used a pocketknife to cut away large strips and patiently rolled the strips into a single thick bundle. Diana cradled the bundle in her arms, mounted the stairs, and chased after Melissa.

Sixty-nine

The highway thudded beneath Elizabeth.

She dipped into memory.

"This machine'll stay under you, Eliza, for as long as you want her. Give into her gently, and feel that wind blowing into you. It'll tell you a lot."

She saw the boy who had given her songs; dark-haired and

alive. John. Tattoo of a heart under his left ear, above the carotid artery, just for her. She had felt alive with him, her heart racing, almost producing its own blood, her mind free of gloomy distractions.

"I want to run away!" she had shouted above the wind.

John turned a fraction, his gaze never leaving the road. "Where do you want to go?"

"I want to see the ocean. Love me on the beach, will you promise?"

"There's nothing in this town for us. I don't know why we stayed so long."

"A home is like that." Elizabeth watched the fading night. "It can catch you like quicksand."

But they hadn't reached the outskirts of town. Elizabeth pressed against John's wide back, felt his knotted stomach muscles under her wrists. He was a human shield against wind, rain, and unfolding night.

"I can't go any further," she whispered into his mind.

"We're almost out, Eliza."

"You go on without me."

"My bike is purring. She really loves you."

Elizabeth listened to his slow, easy heart. "I can't stay with you."

"Are you frightened?"

"Yes."

"Of what?"

"Of the morning sun. He doesn't love me."

"I'm not leaving you."

"I want to see you in the sunlight. That's what I'm afraid of. You can never see me like that."

"Make me like you. We'll die together, as true lovers should."

"No."

"Why?" John asked.

"Why, why, why! Why do you think?"

"I don't know. Tell me."

"If I stayed with you, I'd have the strength to stare down the sun . . . I don't want to die yet."

But now the man of my heart is gone: My true husband. And I'm no longer afraid.

330   Elizabeth let her energy flow to her bike. "Just a little faster,"

she whispered. She listened to the morning wind. Its voice warned of oil spills and the remains of exploded tires; dangerous obstructions she must avoid—for if she fell, the wounded monster would snatch her up in its mouth and eat her, heal itself, before she could kill it.

Her bike shivered as if it might fly apart at the slightest touch. Behind her roared a murderous heart; black tentacles reached forward. Elizabeth looked up to the sky and saw a star disappear, swallowed by the coming sun.

Seventy

The black air lost its coolness. Melissa ran blindly, remembered all the cavern's turnings and narrow places in her desperation.

"Christiane!"

The vampire was coming.

Melissa slammed into a visible wall of heat. She staggered backwards. Her vision rippled. She rubbed her eyes and glimpsed a sinuous landscape covered over, eaten up, by rosy-orange fires. A purple sky glowered. Flames crawled up columns of cloud, licked a swirling red ceiling. A freezing ash like black snow stabbed onto her arms and face. Melissa hesitated, then ran into the inferno.

Her skin began to crackle. Steam hissed off her bare arms and legs. Melissa remembered Falke burning like a torch and began to whimper in fear. Steps thudded behind her. She ran faster, unsure where to go, only knowing she must escape the monster descending on her.

Blistered hands gripped her elbow.

"*Let me go!*" Melissa struggled and ripped at Falke's scorched face and clinging hands. Falke jerked her to him, hit her savagely across the face.

331

"I will never let you go," Falke rasped. "Never again! If I have to nail you to the bedpost, I will do that!"

He began dragging her back toward the labyrinthine caverns. The landscape flowed away from Melissa, glowing with solemn fires. Tortured juniper trees dripped flame onto the shuddering earth. The stink of burnt hair encased her in a fog of misery. Melissa remembered a sun-washed house that her mother had taken her to, a house which had smelled of dust and rain and corn, a house where her grandfather herded his sheep and where he had taught her the Navajo names of all the guardian animals; a beautiful house that had now become pestilent and hellish in her vampire sight.

Melissa wept.

She heard a yipping howl from behind the screen of flaming trees. Before Melissa could turn around, Falke flung her to the ground. She tumbled into the snow; wet ice shocked her awake. Tree branches cracked. With clear eyes, she looked up and saw a gray, furry shape as tall as the dawn-lit junipers emerging from the stubborn shadows. Its paws crunched in the snow. Yellow eyes became red disks as it glared at the vampire standing in front of Melissa.

Melissa recognized the animal.

Ma'ii. Coyote.

"Away, old man!" Falke shouted, and he grabbed Melissa's arm with his peeling hands. "This is my world you are walking in now!"

The coyote lifted its muzzle and barked piercingly. Silvery canines flashed in the dying starlight. The animal's clipped barking sounded like laughter. It tensed suddenly, shoulders bristling, and launched itself at Falke.

The animal landed on Falke's chest, its fangs outstretched, aiming for the throat. Falke stumbled backward, flung the coyote into the glowing ice, then rolled swiftly into a crouch. The coyote wheeled and leaped. Melissa held a scream in and heard tearing cloth, gnashing teeth, the pounding of a fist on heavy hide. The coyote threw Falke down and tore into the vampire's throat. A sheet of blood spilled over Falke's shoulders; he gripped the animal's scruff and peeled off a length of bushy fur. Pink, knotted muscle revealed itself. Blood spewed in a dense shower. Dark droplets dotted the snow. The coyote howled, pushed backward.

"No!" Melissa screamed and scrabbled for a weapon.

Startled, the coyote looked at her. Falke swung his fist down on the animal's skull. Falke roared and cursed the animal, kicked at it, stamped at its legs and head, tried to smash it to bits. The coyote struggled to rise on red-matted legs. Falke tightened his fingers, making them into a spearhead, and slashed at the animal's neck. The gray coyote slumped into the snow, convulsed on its side—not rising, not fighting back.

Falke stood above the animal, shivering. He kneeled to it, took the coyote's throat in his hand. With his other hand, he reached to his chest and slowly drew out something Melissa couldn't see at first. He stabbed the object into the snow, and it remained erect; a blackened stick of wood.

Melissa saw a path of escape, but she remained still, her gaze fastened to the coyote. A terrible heat clamped onto her head, began to crush her skull. The air became a sheet of milky glass. Melissa, ignoring her festering bones and the growing dawn, stood up, walked to the animal's side, kneeled beside Falke, and stared.

The stilled coyote was shrinking. Its paws curled, twisted, grew into human hands. Its legs filled out, became unbent. The barrel chest widened out into a man's shoulders; the skin swallowed an open gash which quickly faded to a red line, then vanished completely. The coyote's snout sniffed inward, its black nose becoming smaller and more human. Silver-tipped fur sagged and blew away in a small whirlwind. Dense black hair spread itself over reddening shoulders.

"Grandpa," Melissa whispered.

Clawed hands grasped Melissa. Falke's face was a shattered, charred mask against graying clouds. Burnt, leaflike skin shook free, exposing the skull underneath. The eyes were red fragments of sapphire. His cheeks hung in rags; ridged muscles glistened, worked, and a hideous grin thrust itself into Melissa's face. Gray smoke rolled out of his mouth. The eyeteeth growing out of his skull remained yellow and carious.

"Christiane is truly dead," Falke whispered. Torn ligaments clicked in his throat. "And the old man will die also. I trusted you completely, Melissa. Now I have paid for it. You have destroyed me."

333

Melissa shook her head. She tried to speak. "Save . . ." was all she could utter.

Save my grandfather, was what she had wanted to ask.

And Melissa saw the only way to save his life. She reached out, touched the prayerstick with her fingertips, grasped it. The hard wood trembled and came alive in her hand like a small, powerful bird. It flew away from her. Melissa sobbed miserably and chased it with her stiff fingers, hurrying to catch up, not realizing until the last second that she was still holding it tightly in her hand. Out of the corner of her eye, Melissa saw the prayerstick streak into Falke's chest and disappear inside him.

Stiltedly, Falke struggled upright, his bleak eyes staring at her. Melissa, aware of what she had done, screamed his name.

A black, distorting fire crept over Falke's face and covered his eyes. Snaking flames danced out of his boiling skin, wove around his body. Bones snapped as his skeleton was crushed.

A wind sighed against Melissa, pushed her back.

Held upright by invisible hands, Falke's limp body began to revolve. His riding boots cut circles in the snow. Then, gently, he was lifted into the dawn sky. Veils of blue, wispy cloud, attracted by the movement, spiraled into his body, cocooning him in a swiftly turning shroud. A white tornado slowly appeared above the shroud and, swallowing it, the tornado shrieked and became incandescent, almost blinding. Melissa covered her ears. But she wouldn't close her eyes.

The whirlwind collapsed, boomed out of existence. Melissa was thrown against a tree, ears ringing. A dark cloud of ash drifted and dissipated. She lay down in the snow. Her throat felt as if nails had been driven through it. She scooped up some snow and sucked at it. She couldn't swallow. Moisture trickled down her chest.

She felt a growing heat on her arms. An orange oval opened up like a vast yawning mouth above the dawn horizon. She shaded her eyes and flattened herself to the ground, knowing full well what happened to vampires caught in the morning sun. Melissa glanced away and saw her grandfather lying in a white bowl. She crawled to him, sliding over patches of hard ice, and touched his warm shoulder. Melissa huddled in his arms and listened to his heartbeat under her ear as she waited

334   for the sun to rise.

Seventy-one

Elizabeth left the city.

Memories like gazelles raced alongside her. John had guided her understanding of artificial suns: Streetlamp bulbs, mercury lights, neon gases. He had taught her about the skeletons and arteries of inhabited buildings and family houses, explained patiently the inner workings of machines, their capabilities and limits. Simple, everyday things innocent of the blood-hunger, endless night, and violent death.

Elizabeth imagined John now as a man with a family, in a house of his own that he took care of, perhaps built himself. If she hadn't lost her life way back when, along the foothills of the Sangre de Cristo Mountains, far from the merciless Arkansas River and far from the place of her birth near Sugartit, Kentucky, she might have met a man like him; she might have borne children with a human husband. Perhaps, she would have even died a real death before Michael had been born.

Elizabeth smiled.

Dreams and fantasy were fleeting. Memories were solid and gave strength. Like love. A power Hanna would never understand.

Elizabeth remembered Michael saying he had been tricked by Coyote, and thought:

Maybe I can show Hanna a trick of my own.

She looked up and saw a brief flare of light. A streak of lightning torching the clouds, the passage from night to dawn. A grinning spider-beast on a black-cowled machine eased up beside her. A piece of bloody cloth fluttered in a mottled, bony hand; a strip of cloth from Michael's dancing shirt.

"I'm through waiting, Elizabeth," Hanna said above the wind.

Elizabeth swerved her bike away and nearly lost control of it. Headlights flared. A car horn blatted, quickly fell away. Hanna shot close behind, thoughts laughing, her invisible fingertips covering Elizabeth like drapes of silken webs.

The wind changed and blew them away. An uplifting pocket of hot breath swirled into Elizabeth's hair. Two more stars vanished.

"Time has left us, Hanna!" she shouted.

Silent, Hanna gazed inward, searching her memory. Elizabeth maneuvered past a station wagon, saw a reflection of purple sky on its curved fender. Glowing semis thundered like rain clouds. Windshields threw shards of reflected light into her eyes. Sunrise was coming too quickly; or not quickly enough.

Hanna's motorcycle screamed closer.

"No escape, Elizabeth," she promised. "We'll die together."

Elizabeth laughed and turned to Hanna. "As true lovers should!"

Hanna's eye sockets dimmed. Her head tilted, as if hearing a new sound.

"How much do you love me, Hanna?" Elizabeth crooned. "Catch me and show me!"

The answering roar of Hanna's motorcycle was all Elizabeth needed for answer. She guided her machine onto the freeway's shoulder to avoid two semis lumbering up a steep hill. She leaned into the bike gracefully and, in a burst of winsome speed, spurted forward into the slowing traffic. Car horns yelled around her. Headlights smudged across her vision. Elizabeth heard the shouts of human thoughts as the moisture on her body began to steam away.

The sky in front of her burst into a glorious pastel of warm colors and soft flame. Cirrus clouds sparked orange fire as Elizabeth rode into the mouth of the sun's furnace. Her sight held long enough to see, far ahead, a silver cylinder that she had hoped to find.

Elizabeth reached down by her foot, took hold of the bike's muffler, and wrenched it off. Blistering-hot metal scorched her hand, exhaust blasted her broken leg. The motorcycle wavered as Elizabeth hid the muffler close to her body. Swift behind her rose the echoing roar of Hanna's machine, coming closer.

Hanna remained silent, as if trying to fit all of Elizabeth's scurrying thoughts into her brain. Elizabeth offered her right hand.

336 "Paper of pins, Hanna," she said.

The spider-beast edged closer, glaring with killing eyes, its masses of fangs glittering in a greedy smile. A white hand reached for her. The massive, silver cylinder loomed.

A gasoline tanker.

Elizabeth judged the flickering wheel spokes of Hanna's bike and tossed the bent muffler into them. The bike cracked, wheeled, whipped itself around Hanna, and popped into the air. Frantic eyes stared, unbelieving, as Hanna and her motorcycle bulleted into the gasoline tanker's curving, silver sides.

"Eliz—"

A clipped name. Sloshing liquid.

Sparks scattered like butterflies, tickling into Elizabeth's hair, as the gasoline tank erupted. The sheer sound of the explosion picked Elizabeth off her motorcycle and flung her into the freeway median. She bounced among bottles and stiff weeds, rolled along rocks and snow until her momentum quit. Elizabeth panted and rose shakily, wiped her face clean of broken glass, slapped the ice from her dress, tested the ground gingerly with her right foot. Another explosion ripped into the atmosphere, urging her toward the coming sun.

Elizabeth limped eastward. Sounds vanished. She lifted Michael's medicine bundle from around her neck and clutched it in both hands. In the sky, the clouds changed into white roses. An ocean wave of heat sucked her breath out of her lungs, carried it away to distant pine trees. The weight of death pulled her down. She staggered helplessly and fell into the wet snow, sobbing for breath. Tan, graceful shapes streamed past her, lifted her in their windy vortex, then vanished. Strengthened, she coaxed her legs a little further. A faraway line of mountains were rimmed in silver flame. Her vision blurred with tears. Her joints ached as if they were sliding against broken glass.

This must be how old age feels, Elizabeth thought.

She began to laugh.

A stillness settled as the land waited. Then, the pure rim of a blue-white circle glared over the horizon. The sky rippled into a white sheet. Liquid fire surrounded Elizabeth, washing her in fierce waves, cauterizing the evil from her soul.

And for a brief moment, she saw a sunflower glowing in a field of daylight.

Seventy-two

Melissa sat up and waited, shivering, in night's remaining shadow. A cold wind stirred her hair. Within a few minutes, a pink light covered her, drowning her in a strange, claustrophobic heat. Not warming or comforting; she felt as if she were being cooked alive. She lifted her head up and saw a yellow circle dissolving into boiling clouds. The morning was quiet. All she heard was the mournful traffic on I-40.

Her shoulder muscles relaxed, then began to ache miserably. Her skeleton shifted inside a heavy sack of skin. She hunched down until her forehead touched one knee. Her hands slid from her lap into the snow, trembling, becoming so heavy she could hardly lift them. The snow abraded her legs like sandpaper. Her feet were numb. The ice was beginning to melt underneath her.

Alone in a desolate sea, Melissa began to weep.

Seventy-three

This hill is familiar, Diana thought.

She had never been here before; yet she had. Her heart beat warmly, remembering the fierce glow it had felt when filled with the wind. Now, only a whisper of a breeze blew against her face. A few yards away, Melissa stood emotionless, blanketed in a strip of tapestry decorated with galloping horses, and she watched while her grandfather gathered up bits of bone and feathery wisps of skin and placed them onto a strip of buckskin. Michael, wrapped in a piece of the same type of tapestry as his granddaughter, gave Melissa a pinch of yellow corn pollen.

"Hurry," Michael said to her, pale.

Melissa took the pollen, kissed it to her lips, and sprinkled it toward the east horizon; all the while looking at Diana. She then blew on her fingertips and trudged up the sides of a steep knoll without speaking. Diana followed after her, swaying with exhaustion, crunching over ice crusts, until she stood next to Melissa. Diana restrained herself from touching the girl. Instead, she studied Melissa, searching for signs of injury or illness.

"I'm worried about Michael," Diana said, not really listening to what she was saying either. "We have to get him back to the city. Get you two to a hospital."

Diana looked at I-40, a walk of a mile or so away, and watched the colorless vehicles traveling along its back. "You have to help me, Melissa," she whispered.

A massive, welling of sadness made Diana close her eyes. There was something not clear to her; a secret, almost, between Melissa and Michael. Diana wanted to understand it. Melissa had returned to life, but with a shattered heart. Diana could see that for herself; she knew the symptoms. And Emily had said that for the Navajo, there was always a price to be paid for being healed. It hadn't always been that way, the old woman had said, promising to explain when Diana returned with Melissa.

Diana wanted to know what Michael had offered.

Melissa stared at Diana, her eyes scraped of life. A young girl shouldn't have that expression so soon, Diana thought. It wasn't right.

"Grandpa wants to talk to you," Melissa said, her voice gravelly, too loud.

Diana gave a weak smile. "Maybe he wants to speak to both of us."

Melissa twitched her head. "I don't want to speak to him. He'll understand if you go alone."

Diana hesitated, then descended the knoll. Michael was standing in a perfect snowy bowl, with a tapestry sack slung over his bare shoulder. He held a juniper stick in his hand and looked almost the same as when Diana had first seen him; except that his hair now lay on his shoulders like a wide, gray blanket. As she approached Michael, and slowed, he smiled at her. Her heart began to keen, even before he spoke the words.

"I must go now, *shi'yazhi*, my little one. Here we must say goodbye."

Diana cleared her throat, opened her mouth to argue, but nothing came out.

Michael came closer. "I can't give you your Navajo warrior name, because this monster might hear it. Emily will give it to you. When you receive your name, keep it close to you. Always know where it is going and where it has traveled. And only give it to those people you love, for your name is your strength."

Diana couldn't answer. Michael continued.

"I'm not through with this Eye Killer. Long ago, the first chanter sang a powerful song of fire, which destroyed it; but didn't break apart its body. That first chanter didn't understand the vampire way. And didn't have a warrior helping him who understood the vampire's chant." Michael patted the sack firmly. "That's why Eye Killer came back . . . grew again. But Emily remembered that first chanter's song, and where it was born. She gave it to you, *shi'yazhi*. You have broken Falke. And you helped me understand him too. Helped all of us. You have brought Melissa back home. I don't know what to say, except—you are a fine, strong woman."

Tears pushed out of Diana's eyes like beads of molten iron. "Michael, you always know what to say." She wiped her face, felt paint crinkle off in her fingers. "What are you going to do then?"

"I must take Falke's remains to a sacred place and bury him there. The Mother will keep him safe, where he can harm no one ever again. You must tell Emily that I have done this."

Diana shook her head. "No, Michael. Give me the remains and I'll take them."

"Take Melissa back to the city and take care of her. She'll need you now, more than she'll ever need anyone. Her mother is dead, and Sarah had no more children. Melissa needs a sister. You know the songs of this hunt. Only you can take Melissa to Emily and help heal her. You must bear the song to its end. And so must I."

"When you're finished, then you'll come back to us."

340   "No."

All her rage expanded in a red cloud, faltered, exhausted itself, withered, and died. Only Melissa remained in her heart. And strength. Both had been there all along, it seemed.

I've got the Navajo name to prove it, Diana thought.

She nodded. "I'll take care of Melissa. We'll be okay."

Michael's voice was gentle. "I'm sorry that I didn't teach you to make a good pot of hunter's coffee."

"I hate coffee, actually. I only drink it when I grade papers." Diana leaned close to Michael. "With the students I have, it helps me from going out and getting totally bombed."

Michael grinned. "*Ayaah'ah!* and I was going to teach you to make strong coffee that doesn't look like it saw a ghost. Why didn't you tell me this before?"

"You didn't ask me."

"Then I'm sorry we didn't go out and get bombed together."

Diana offered her unsteady hand, even though her whole body ached to be held. "Goodbye . . ." Her tears flew from her body in a driven rain. She couldn't even see Michael's hand closing over hers, only felt it. He seemed to hesitate. Diana looked up. His dark eyes reflected the snow around them.

"You have tiny orange rings in the centers of your turquoise eyes, *shi'yazhi.* What does that mean?"

"It doesn't mean anything. They're called Irish eyes."

"They're very pretty."

She saw that Michael's feet were bare. Snow folded against his ankles like sheaves of paper. Diana held onto his hand. "Everyone always leaves me. Why can't you stay?"

"Because I asked the Holy Ones for a final gift. I don't know if they have granted it, but I must hope that they did and pay for it anyway."

Diana released his hand and tugged off her wedding ring. It came off painlessly. Letting go was easier than she had expected. Katy would be happy, at least, and approve.

"Here, Grandfather. Give them this too. Maybe it'll help."

Michael took it, eyes solemn.

"Goodbye, my granddaughter."

Michael drew the tapestry around himself. Little clouds puffed out of his mouth. Diana hugged herself and watched Michael walk away from her across a snowy ocean speckled with golden brush and sandstone boulders. She remained watching long after his tiny form had vanished among the juniper and piñon, motionless, beneath the blue slopes of Mount Taylor.

Small hands took Diana's hands from her face, squeezed them, wrapped them in warmth. Her tears had begun to freeze.

"It's getting cold," Melissa urged softly. "Let's go home, sister."

Epilogue

Michael was bone-weary. His burden dragged at his heart, soul, mind, bending his back down, pushing his face into the snow. Yet he trudged on under a pale sun, cut his palms on rocky hills, waded through snowdrifts. His strength was leaving him.

And the monster's whisperings were growing louder. Eye Killer was laughing.

From time to time, Michael glanced toward the Sandias far to the east. A swirling sheet of snow covered them. His head filled with stones. Soon, he couldn't even lift his eyelids to see his blue feet. He stumbled on in a black night, wishing for the woman under the moon, needing her soft words to carry him just a little further.

He heard water trickling. Michael opened his eyes and saw a gurgling spring at his feet.

Quickly, he told himself.

He sat along the spring's tiny shores, unfolded the dark tapestry. His vision blurred. His eyes wouldn't refocus. He was blind.

"Must sleep," he muttered.

Then he sensed someone standing next to him, felt a touch as soft as moonlight on his shoulder. "It must be done quickly," a woman whispered. Then she was gone.

Michael chuckled. "I can hear you dreaming, Elizabeth Mary."

Gaining strength, he opened his eyes and saw a bright circle in front of him. He scooped fragments of blackened bone and patches of leathery skin with his hands and scattered them into the warm pool. He watched the sad objects tumble in the bubbling water, dissolve, and disappear. The water blackened, changed to red for a time, became clear once again. Michael washed his hands thoroughly, and let them soak. He heard a whirring buzz behind him.

Cicadas?

He turned and saw brilliant sunlight falling through the mouth of the cave. He stood up and looked outside.

All the snow was gone. Dry dust blew against his cheeks. He saw a thin, green river reed hanging beside the cave, which rose up into the bluest sky he had ever seen. A sky clear of mechanical tadpoles. Behind him, the sand and rock hills were empty of digging machines. Even old man I-40 was gone. And the railroad tracks. Michael felt saddened about leaving the old trains behind.

He took hold of the reed and climbed it, watched the mesa's red face slip by him. Drawings of spirals and spiders flew inside the orange rock like birds. He came to the top and stood on a ridge. In front of him lay a wide desert filled with sagebrush, mountain brome, green yucca. Rainbow mists flickered above high clouds. Hawks circled in lazy spirals. Somewhere, a prairie dog barked.

Michael removed the cloth hung around his waist, rolled it into a headband, and tied it around his head; he remembered fully the song his grandmother had given him long ago. His feet followed its rhythm as he began his race. Soon, his song was echoing throughout the yellow hills, calling.

And he was heard.

They appeared over the crests of the hills and mountains; the Old Ones who had vanished long ago. They raised thundering, rolling chants to the clouds, unafraid. They swept around Michael, surrounding him, and he raced them, keeping his beat steady. They recognized his song. Feet and paws caught its rhythm, held it, danced to it. Sunlit hills and valleys flew underneath their stamping feet. A smiling girl with twin ponytails raised his name to the sky.

A tall woman with flowing black hair danced beside him. Her moccasins rang with tiny bells. She called him by his name.

She sang him into sleep.